Secrets of the Sword III

Death Before Dragons, Book 9

by Lindsay Buroker

Copyright © Lindsay Buroker 2021

Illustration by Luisa Preissler

No part of this book may be reproduced, scanned, or distributed in any printed or electronic form without permission. Please do not participate in or encourage piracy of copyrighted materials in violation of the author's rights. Thank you for respecting the hard work of this author.

This is a work of fiction. Names, characters, places, and incidents either are the product of the author's imagination or are used fictitiously, and any resemblance to locales, events, business establishments, or actual persons—living or dead—is entirely coincidental.

DEATH BEFORE DRAGONS

SECRETS OF THE SWORD III

LINDSAY BUROKER

FOREWORD

When I started writing the first novel in the Death Before Dragons series, I had tentative plans to publish five or six adventures and see how it went. I hadn't done much contemporary/urban fantasy, and I wasn't sure how well my regular readers would receive it. I don't usually write in first person, nor do I set many stories on Earth with protagonists who tote around semi-automatic weapons. The only things I brought over from my steampunk and high-fantasy books were the dragons. Though Zav (ahem, Lord Zavryd'nokquetal) is in a league of his own. He's my first sauna-loving, Crocs-wearing dragon. I have a feeling he's the *only* sauna-loving, Crocs-wearing dragon.

I'm glad that so many people have enjoyed Val and Zav's adventures. As I write this foreword, this is the last book I have planned in this series, and I've started on a new project in a new world, but I am tempted to return someday for a spin-off series. We shall see. I hope you enjoy this final installment. Thank you for reading, and thank you to all who have left reviews and shared the series with friends or on social media pages. As I've said before, this is the best "marketing" an author can hope for.

Let me also thank my beta readers—Cindy Wilkinson, Rue Silver, and Sarah Engelke—and my editor Shelley Holloway. Also thank you to Luisa Pressler for the illustrations for this trilogy and Deranged Doctor Design for turning them into covers. Last, but definitely not least, thank you to Vivienne Leheny for narrating the audiobooks.

That's it from me, and thanks again for reading!

CHAPTER 1

"HE ATE A COW FROM the farmer's property in Snohomish that we leased for the wedding," Colonel Willard said, alternately glowering at me, at Zav, and at Mary Watanabe, my stalwart therapist, whose typical unfazed expression remained intact during the diatribe.

Mary *did* shift at her desk to type a couple of notes into her computer. More than once, she'd offered to let me read the file she was keeping on me, but I didn't want to see myself analyzed. I already knew I had issues. That's why I kept coming to Mary's office.

"It was most succulent." Zav lounged in a chair between Willard and me, his ankle propped on his knee, the hem of his silver-trimmed black robe in danger of hiking up far enough to show everyone evidence of his refusal to adopt the human custom of wearing boxers or briefs.

"That cow was someone's *property*," Willard growled, waving toward the rain-spattered window, though it looked out toward Lake Union to the south, and Snohomish was off in the other direction. "Not only that, but it belonged to the farmer who was kind enough to rent us his beautiful grassy field along the river. He said he didn't even mind if a few quirky guests showed up."

Quirky guests, such as my elven half of the family, Zav's dragon family, and all the troll, ogre, orc, and goblin patrons of our coffee shop that Zav had invited to the wedding, promising them a great feast. Who didn't love free food?

"It is a dragon custom," Zav said, "that one should hunt in an area being considered for festivities. If the prey is ample and succulent, that is an auspicious omen."

"A domesticated cow isn't *prey*." Willard was still growling. That was her normal tone whenever she and Zav argued about how the wedding should go.

I'd figured out weeks ago that asking her to help with the planning hadn't been the best idea, but it was too late to rescind that request now. When Willard had a mission, she wouldn't let slings, bullets, or prey-munching dragons deter her from it.

"That cow belonged to the farmer," Willard repeated. "I had to promise him that Thorvald would pay for it."

"I'm used to paying for what Zav eats," I said, glad a recent mission had left my coffers well-lined with gold. Zav was an expensive date, and it looked like he would be an even more expensive husband.

"Even if it's something that wasn't for sale?"

Mary lifted her hands in a placating manner. "I suggest we acknowledge that this incident happened, accept that cultural differences will add a few caltrops into the wedding planning, and find a way to go forward with all parties feeling satisfied." She smiled at Willard, then said, "Lord Zavryd," and looked at Zav, but she made the mistake of glancing down, her eye perhaps drawn by the slightly singed fluorescent yellow Crocs that were his new favorite footwear. She must have caught a glimpse of more than footwear, because she faltered and looked at the ceiling with a discombobulated, "Er." Her elbow bumped a stapler on the desk, knocking it to the floor. She didn't pick it up.

I reached over with two fingers and pushed Zav's foot off his knee and down to the floor. *Your nether regions show when you do that,* I told him telepathically.

He lowered his eyelids halfway and gazed at me through his lashes. *I enjoy it when you touch my knee.*

I know you do, but we're not going to have sex in my therapist's office. I asked you and Willard here in the hope that Mary could offer some advice on settling your disagreements so we can have a wedding that will make everybody happy. We're less than a week away, and there continue to be… incidents.

Your wedding planner is not acknowledging that this is a mixed-species wedding and that accommodations must be made for dragons. Thanks to your idea, I've convinced my family to come to the event, including my mother, the queen. All must be perfect if she is to come to this wild world.

It'll be great. And you're going to import your own animals to hunt, right? And drop them off in some woods a couple hundred miles north of Snohomish and far from the nearest town. Nobody needs to eat the cows of any farmers, right? I raised my eyebrows hopefully. As I now knew well, an entire cow was a lot more expensive than a forty-pack box of ground beef patties from Costco. Especially when the farmer added on an emotional-trauma fee. His eight-year-old daughter had been the one to find the carcass in the field behind her playhouse.

I will import animals, yes. Far more spirited prey than that cow.

I squinted at him, concerned that he hadn't acknowledged the part of the plan where these animals would be dropped off hundreds of miles away. Before I could ask for clarification, Willard cleared her throat.

"Your therapist can't take notes if you're talking to each other telepathically," she said.

Mary had recovered her equanimity and was resting her folded hands patiently on her desk. "As I was saying, it is important for both families—and both the bride and groom—to feel welcome at the wedding and, whenever possible, to have their cultural preferences accommodated for, but it is also important to obey the laws of the area. Consuming another person's livestock is illegal here in Washington. And likely all over the world."

"On my world, no being, not even a dragon, may own living animals," Zav said. "When the Stormforge Clan came to power and assumed the majority of positions on the Ruling Council, we outlawed slavery. We rule over others for the good of the Cosmic Realms and for the good of the intelligent species within it."

"You're an enlightened people," Mary said with a straight face.

The noise Willard made deep in her throat reminded me of her cat hawking up a hairball.

"We are." Zav leaned back and propped his ankle up on the opposite knee. "I have no need to hunt further prey in that area. I have deemed the chosen location acceptable. The nearby river is appealing. If the guests get restless, they may fish." He eyed me. "The farmer does not also own the *fish,* does he?"

Zav's tone made it clear that the whole idea of owning animals was ridiculous to him. At least he seemed willing to go along with our laws.

I hoped the rest of his clan would too. In retrospect, maybe we should have planned for the entire wedding to take place two hundred miles from anywhere. But it would have been difficult to get the priest, caterer, and musicians to show up that far away.

"The fish are free for all." I leaned over, pushed his leg off his knee again, and pointed to the floor at his feet.

"How have you been doing with your meditation during this busy time?" Mary asked me.

"Uh." I didn't want to talk about this, or the fact that I'd needed my asthma medication more frequently lately, not in front of Zav and Willard. Was it strange that the wedding planning was more stressful and prone to make me wheezy than facing bad guys trying to kill me? "Fine."

"You've found some quiet time to work on your breathing and calming your mind?" Mary smiled hopefully and poised her fingers over the keyboard, clearly wanting to add that I was making progress.

I wished I could tell her yes so she could type in that note, but between work, the wedding plans, cooking for Zav, and trying to establish a stronger relationship with my teenage daughter, there hadn't been much time for self-improvement. And I was beginning to think that no amount of learning to calm my body and reduce stress and inflammation levels would get rid of the asthma that had been plaguing me this last year.

"During quiet time," Zav said, lifting his ankle back up to his knee, "Val and I mate vigorously in the nest."

Willard propped her elbow on the armrest and dropped her face into her palm.

"It is excellent exercise," Zav continued, "which is good for one's health. Dragons know this."

"I wouldn't have agreed to come," Willard said, "if I'd known you'd be talking about your sex life."

"Sorry." I lifted a hand. "Zav is enthusiastic about mating."

Mary made the mistake of glancing down—Zav *was* right in front of her desk—then jerked her gaze away again.

Willard reached over and shoved Zav's ankle off his knee.

His eyes flared violet in indignation. "It is not appropriate for a female who is not my mate to presume to touch me."

"Yeah, yeah," Willard said, not intimidated, even though Zav made most enemies quail when his eyes glowed and his aura radiated power and menace. "Just keep your enthusiasm in your pants."

"I do not *wear* pants."

"That's the problem." Willard's phone rang, and she walked to the window, probably glad for an excuse to escape the discussion.

I sighed. Maybe this had been pointless. I should have simply come by myself.

"Is the planning otherwise going well?" Mary pulled a couple of empty folders out of a drawer and propped them along the back edge of her desk, creating a barrier so she could no longer see below Zav's chest from her seat. Well, that was one solution.

"It's... fine." I would be relieved when all of this was over.

I *did* look forward to the day itself, even though I was far from a romantic or someone who'd dreamed of weddings as a girl, but everything leading up to it had been a pain so far. Was I naive to believe that the wedding could go well? Given my eclectic guest roster?

Mary lifted her eyebrows, encouraging a more thorough answer.

"My elven half-sister Freysha mentioned that our father and her kin—*our* kin—are supposed to arrive soon. I'm not sure where they'll stay or how many there will be. I haven't really met any of my kin except for her and my father. Also, I'm a little nervous about introducing—er, *reintroducing*—my father to my mother. He's married to an elven lady now, and Mom is... well, I think she's never entirely gotten over him. She never married, and she doesn't even date. Unless one counts the werewolf across the street that she has coffee with."

Mary didn't bat an eye at the talk of elves and werewolves. After months of these sessions, she'd gotten used to me telling her about my interactions with members of the magical community that few mundane humans knew existed on Earth.

"It is often the case," she said, "that the concerns we have about possible conflicts in the future are worse than the actual conflicts themselves. I know it's difficult, but I urge you to try not to worry about it, especially if there is nothing you can do."

Willard had been talking quietly on the other side of the room, but her voice rose in disbelief. "What do you *mean* we can't use the field?"

"Uh oh." I looked at Zav. "You weren't out there this morning hunting more cows, were you?"

"I was not," he said. "The weather is damp and unappealingly chilly. I visited your mother's hot box."

"Her sauna? Uhm, did you warn her first? Or ask for permission?"

"A dragon does not ask for *permission* from lesser species."

"A dragon should if he wants to use something that belongs to someone else."

"Humans are overly preoccupied by *owning* things."

"I see," Willard said, her tone flat now. "You're sure? There are still several days until the wedding." She paused. "I see. Thank you." She hung up and frowned down at her phone.

"Problem?" I didn't want there to be more problems, but it was inevitable.

Willard sighed as she turned back to us. "Thanks to all the rain this past week, the field we leased has flooded. The farmer is positive it won't dry out sufficiently by Saturday. Even if the water recedes, it'll be muddy." She wrinkled her nose. "I'm not wearing the fabulous bridesmaid dress that your daughter picked out if I'm knee-deep in mud."

"Hm." I wondered if the field was truly flooded beyond help, or if the farmer had decided that the risk to his livestock was too high. "Do we get our deposit back?"

"The deposit went toward the cow that your fiancé ate."

Meaning we wouldn't have the money to put toward another venue. Wonderful.

"Zav can breathe fire," I said. "Maybe he could dry the field out."

He lifted his chin. "It is a simple thing to dry mud."

"*Dry* it?" Willard asked. "Or bake it in the kiln of your fiery dragon breath, leaving the land as cracked and desolate as in the Atacama Desert?"

"Where is the Atacama Desert?" Zav asked me.

"I've never heard of it," I admitted.

Willard frowned at me. "Still not reading books without smut in them, I see."

"My signed Harry Potter and Game of Thrones books are not smutty," I said.

"Are there dragons in them?"

"Yes."

"Then they must be smutty." Willard walked over and pushed Zav's leg to the floor again—he really found that position comfortable. "Your dragon oozes smuttiness."

I didn't know what to say to that. She wasn't wrong.

"I did intentionally choose a form with sex appeal," Zav said, "but I do not believe I am smutty."

"Perhaps you can postpone the wedding?" Mary suggested. "An outdoor wedding in late winter in Seattle isn't typical, but the location you described earlier does sound beautiful."

"We can't," I said, not mentioning that Zav had refused to allow the wedding to be put off until the summer, when one had the best shot of a rain-free event in the Pacific Northwest. "We've got guests coming from all over. Including other planets. My father, the elven king, already rescheduled some highfalutin meeting with diplomats from four worlds in order to be here. Zav's mother, the queen, shifted around hearings at the Dragon Justice Court, and my roommate Dimitri found a temp to work for him at the shop on Saturday."

Was it strange that the quarter-dwarf enchanter and tinkerer Dimitri was the most normal person I'd invited to my wedding? Even Mom, Thad, and Amber weren't exactly average examples of mundane humans.

"Don't worry." Willard straightened her back and firmed her chin, determination in her eyes. "The wedding will go on. I'll find another location. One that's less water adjacent."

My phone buzzed, and Dimitri's number popped up.

"Val," he blurted before I could say *hello*. "Someone blew up the *Sable Dragon*!"

CHAPTER 2

THE ENTIRE COFFEE SHOP HADN'T been blown up—as I'd feared as Zav rushed me over, flying me on his back since it was faster than driving—but it was bad. The wall opposite the coffee kiosk had been blown out, taking portions of the bathroom, a storage room, and cases of Dimitri's yard art and Zoltan's potions with it. Yellow siding, roof shingles, drywall, and wood blanketed the puddle-filled alley where we'd landed, and our toilet was now lodged in the wall of the ice-cream shop next door. Drizzle fell from the gray sky, droplets glistening on the cracked porcelain.

Fortunately, that building hadn't been severely damaged, shrapnel and toilets aside. *Unfortunately*, numerous patrons had been visiting our shop when the explosion occurred. Through the missing wall, I had no trouble seeing trolls, shifters, goblins, and half-blooded humans sitting or lying amid the wreckage inside, tending to each other's wounds. Our barista, Tam, stood behind the kiosk, a bloody dish towel pressed to the side of her head.

Should I call an ambulance? Would the medics be able to find our place through the magical glamour that hid it from mundane humans?

The familiar guilt that this might be my fault crept into my soul. What if this had been done by someone angling for me? Or wanting to hurt those near me?

These people had been coming to our coffee shop, expecting to enjoy themselves without threat from outside attack, and because they were here supporting us, they'd been hurt. Some of them badly.

Zav waited until I'd slid off his back before shifting into human form. Willard had passed on the offer of a ride but promised to drive over.

"Val!" Dimitri charged outside and gripped my arm. "This is insane. Were they after *you*?"

"I don't know." I tried not to bristle at the accusation, but it struck close to home. "Is that my ten percent they targeted?"

I waved at the missing wall, then glanced again at the toilet. It was stuck a good six feet up.

"It's more than ten percent. The place is *decimated*!"

"That would be precisely ten percent, actually."

Dimitri's exasperated look promised he didn't appreciate my precision. "People were injured."

"I know. I see." I reined in my natural tendency toward sarcasm. "Nobody was killed, I hope?"

I didn't see any inert bodies in the wreckage, but I hadn't gone inside yet.

"No, but some people were hurt badly. We're lucky the doctor was here."

"The doctor?"

"The one that your boss hates."

"Oh, Dr. Walker is here? Good."

"He comes in for coffee in the mornings. Or he *did*. His car was parked close and took a bunch of damage in the explosion." Dimitri pointed at the now-mangled red SUV in the parking spot closest to the alley. Normally, someone would have been stoked to find street parking that close, but today... hadn't been a good day to get lucky. "Nobody is going to want to come back if they know our place is the target of bombers."

"Take it easy. We'll get it fixed, and I'll figure out who did it and make sure it doesn't happen again."

It had been a couple of months since anyone in the magical community had tried to kill me—other than enemies and criminals that I was also trying to kill. Maybe I'd gotten complacent. Admittedly, I'd hoped that with the popularity of our coffee shop, the vengeance-prone members of the community might have forgiven me for being an assassin who'd mowed down some of their kin in the past.

"It might *not* have had anything to do with me," I said. "Usually, my enemies can sense magic and tell if I'm in the building or not."

"Well, I don't have any enemies." Dimitri pushed his hands through his short, dark hair, as he looked around while shaking his head in disbelief. Soot smeared the side of his face, and one of his sleeves was torn to the elbow, dozens of small glass cuts in his forearm. "I don't think. I *shouldn't*. I give our customers coffee and art, and I have a gentle artistic soul."

"Your yard art shoots flames at people."

"Gentle flames of mild correction."

"That incinerate people's eyebrows. Did you see who placed the explosive?"

Dimitri shook his head. "No."

"How long ago did it happen?"

"Less than fifteen minutes ago. Oh, man. I need to call the landlord. His insurance will cover this, right? It *has* to. Val, this place was just getting off the ground. We were making real money. I was just getting used to not having to live in my *van* anymore."

"Yeah, a room in a haunted house means you're really moving up in the world." I reached over to Zav, who was standing apart, gazing vacantly toward the sky. That usually meant he was using his power to search the area. "Do you sense anyone around? Someone magical who might have done this?"

"There are more than a dozen trolls, goblins, and shifters within several blocks of this establishment," Zav said. "It is impossible to tell if they are fleeing from the area because they caused trouble or because they fear for their lives."

"Can you read their minds?"

"Not accurately from a distance, and I can only check one mind at a time."

"If you can find who was responsible, I'll make you more Moroccan Harissa lamb tonight." Earlier in the week, we'd discovered that Zav, who loathed all sauces and glazes with even a hint of sweetness, didn't mind unsweetened spice rubs.

"I will check their minds."

"Thank you." I tapped Sindari's charm on the off-chance that a magical silver tiger could pick up the trail of the saboteur, but that was unlikely for the same reason that Zav would struggle. There were too many magical beings here, and dozens if not hundreds of people had been through this alley today. Questioning the patrons might get us further, though they all looked rattled. I didn't spot anyone hunkering in a corner, rubbing his hands gleefully.

You have called me forth to do battle? Sindari asked after he formed in silver mist at my side.

"Possibly. If you find whoever blew up the side of our coffee shop, I'll let you help me beat him or her to a lumpy pulp."

I see. You believe an explosive was placed and that the miscreant skulked away.

"I'm sure skulking was involved, yes."

Dimitri was on the phone with the landlord, but he glanced toward me at that, so I switched to telepathy for my conversation with Sindari.

Is it possible that an explosive was hurled from afar? Sindari asked.

Unfortunately, yes. I envisioned a van full of orcs rolling down the street in front of the shop and realized Sindari wouldn't be able to pick up the trail if the hoodlums had never gotten out. And if they hadn't been on foot, they would now be too far away for Zav to telepathically interrogate. *But let's start with the assumption that whoever did this was on foot and hasn't gone far. Let's rule that out first.*

I will investigate the area. Sindari padded into the alley, sniffing at the debris and refuse.

Thank you.

I was about to go in and see if anybody had witnessed anything when Willard arrived on foot. She must have parked around the block.

"The police haven't arrived yet?" she asked, eyeing the mess.

"Police?" I didn't expect the Seattle PD to help with a problem likely caused by someone in the magical community. "Thanks to the glamour, they don't even notice the shop exists most of the time. It's safer that way. Due to our eccentric clientele."

A green goblin clutching a homemade dice launcher stumbled out, supported by a buddy.

One of them pointed at me. "The Ruin Bringer will find who did this. The sweet mocha waves of honeyed gold must flow again!"

"I think he's talking about the coffee," I told Willard, who was nodding her agreement about the eccentricity of our clientele.

"Yeah, I got that."

I held up a hand to stop the goblins. "Did either of you see who did this?"

They shook their heads, white mops of hair flopping into their eyes. "The entire wall blew out without warning! We're lucky the roof didn't cave in. Human engineering is so shoddy."

His buddy nodded sagely.

"Not enough bottle caps and mattress springs used in the construction," I said.

"*Exactly.*" The chattier goblin reached his hands upward. "But you will prevail, Ruin Bringer, and we will all feast at your wedding. Nefarious evil-doers will not dare attack you or your guests there, not with terrifyingly powerful and menacing dragons nearby."

They looked at Zav and bowed deeply, though he was busy telepathically scouring minds and didn't acknowledge them.

"They had better not attack anyone at my wedding," I muttered, though the words prompted an uneasy feeling in my gut.

With all the important elves and dragons who would be at the ceremony, was it possible that someone *would* attack? I hadn't considered it before, but I still had a lot of enemies out there, and in Zav's excitement, he'd invited half the city—and half the cities on other worlds—so the wedding wasn't a secret. Maybe that had been a mistake.

"They won't, Ruin Bringer. Or your mate will smite them."

"And incinerate them with the powerful plumes of flames that gush from his hot nostrils!"

"You're quite the wordsmith goblin, aren't you?" I asked.

Willard had left to tramp around inside and investigate, but she halted abruptly and looked at something in a corner not in my view.

"I'm practicing." The goblin winked and elbowed me. He probably meant to elbow me in the ribs, but his height made it more of a hip-elbowing. "I believe that Tam, the pourer of divine and sublime ambrosia, finds me attractive. She makes hearts in the foam of my lattes. I plan to woo her with my witty words."

His buddy rolled his eyes. "She makes hearts in everybody's latte foam."

"Not so. Gondo gets garlic cloves."

"That's what the hearts look like when she's in a hurry."

"She's never in a hurry when she makes *my* latte." He touched his chest and beamed a smile back over his shoulder toward Tam.

"Thorvald," Willard barked at me, giving me an excuse to flee the conversation.

I stepped inside through the destroyed wall, not bothering to use the front door. Smoke lingered in the damp, chill air. The heater in the back was still on, thrumming at the effort of warming a building that now lacked an exterior wall.

"I've ruled out those two as suspects." I tilted my thumb over my shoulder toward the goblins, lest Willard think I'd been slacking off. Neither Sindari nor Zav had reported back to me that they'd found anything yet, though Sindari had disappeared around the back of the building, so maybe he was hot on the trail of a suspect.

"The goblins would all fall on their own swords before letting this place be damaged," Willard said.

"I've never seen a goblin with a sword."

"Their own screwdrivers then."

"That's apt."

Willard pointed to the corner she'd been gaping toward earlier. The tall, fit, dark-skinned Dr. Daku Walker, with his thick mane of red-blond hair, stood out in any room and was hard to miss even kneeling amid the wreckage. He was taking care of an older ogre lady, blood running from one of her ears and her clothing torn. Walker had managed to lose half of the Armani shirt that *he* wore. Ripped and singed, it dangled artfully from one shoulder Captain-Kirk style.

"Are you admiring his rippling six-pack abs and pronounced pecs?" I asked.

"No." Willard shot me a scathing look. "Are *you*? Your dragon will object."

"I'm indifferent to the pecs of other men, but I know you like the brawny types. I've told you about his thick tail, right?" I didn't know if Willard had ever seen Walker in his prehistoric marsupial lion form, but I had.

"More often than a prepubescent boy just learning sex jokes."

"Then my work is done."

"I was wondering what he was doing here," Willard said.

"Helping people, it looks like." I headed over, feeling I should also offer to help.

"I'm sure he'll send them an invoice later," Willard muttered, following me.

People kept coming up to Walker to ask questions. He handed out bandages and gauze pads from his medical kit and gave quick advice on how to handle injuries.

"Hey, Doc. You look like hell." I waved at gashes on his shoulder, burns on his chest, and a deep cut dribbling blood from his temple. "Who's treating *your* wounds?"

Walker smiled up at us, though the pain tightening his eyes made it more of a grimace. "I was hoping Colonel Willard would come in and lovingly tend my wounds. Perhaps with a warm, moist sponge."

"Which I, of course, keep in my car," Willard said.

"Every first-aid kit should have one." Walker, who must have pulled his own medical kit out of his vehicle, patted the ogress's now-bandaged arm. "I've cleaned the wound, and the ointment should make that feel better," he told her. "Make sure to keep it covered for a few days, and don't let it get dirty."

"You know I live in a cave, right, Doc?" The ogress's voice was as feminine as boulders grinding together.

"Is it not a hygienic cave?" he asked mildly.

"I try to keep it clean, but it's a wet muddy climate." She grumbled and pushed herself to her feet. At nine feet tall, she loomed over all of us, though I was six feet myself, and Dr. Walker had a few inches on me. "How much do I owe you?"

"Nothing. Happy to help." Walker waved her toward the door, then called for whoever else needed attention to come over.

Willard's eyebrows rose. Did she not believe he would help people for free? Just because he lived in an expensive condo and drove a luxury car? I'd only spent a day with Walker, when we'd visited the gnomish home world on a mission, but it had been enough to learn he was a good fighter and a good guy. Maybe if he was less flippant with Willard—and vice versa—they would *both* realize the other person wasn't bad.

A goblin hurried over and flopped dramatically onto the floor, holding up a hand with a cut on the back. It wasn't that deep or that bloody.

"A most grave injury," Walker said in his Australian drawl, his humor shining through his pain. "I had better clean it, so it doesn't get infected. We wouldn't want any of your limbs to fall off."

The goblin flung his arm over his face and moaned pathetically.

"Are *any* goblins normal?" Willard wondered.

"I think this *is* normal," I said. "For their species."

An older female goblin with a deeper gouge in her arm came over, bracelets made from bicycle chains and bottle caps rattling on her wrists. I'd met her before and groped for her name before it clicked. Work Leader Nogna. She was from the goblin community we'd imported from Idaho and dropped off in the old elven sanctuary beyond Granite Falls. I hadn't seen her at the coffee shop before.

Since Walker was busy with the melodramatic goblin, I dug into his kit for antiseptic and a bandage and waved for Nogna to show me her wound.

There are numerous scents out here, Sindari informed me. He was back in the alley, standing near Zav. *Trolls, ogres, goblins, humans. It's impossible to guess who might have been the culprit, but I have found what may be shrapnel from the explosive device used on the building. Perhaps it is a clue?*

It could be. I'll be there in a minute.

"By all the gods in the realms," blurted a familiar voice from the doorway. Gondo. He gripped the doorjamb as he gaped into the shop, looking around at the missing wall, the damaged display cases, and the upturned tables. "What happened?"

Nogna spoke to him in goblin. Sternly. I could have tapped my translation charm to activate it, but it was usually better when I didn't know what goblins were saying.

Gondo's response came in a protesting tone as he walked over, his head bowed. Maybe he'd been the one to recommend the Sable Dragon to her and she hadn't expected to nearly be blown up.

"May Work Leader Nogna attend your wedding, Ruin Bringer?" Gondo asked.

I blinked. Was *that* what the conversation had been about?

"It's being touted as the event of the year," Gondo continued, "and since her clan has known you and your mate since the water-box incident across the mountains, she believes that she and her kin should hold a place in your heart."

"Oh, they do. And they're welcome to come." Everyone else was…

"Excellent."

"We will make you and your mate a wedding gift for your home," Nogna said.

Uh oh. Was it too late to revoke the invitation?

I forced a smile. "Thanks. Oh, but the wedding isn't going to be where we'd originally planned. There was some flooding. When we find out a new location, I'll let you know." I'd finished wrapping a bandage around her arm and waved that she could go, but she leaned her head toward Gondo, and they conversed in their native tongue in low voices.

"The elven sanctuary that is now the *goblin* sanctuary—" Nogna rested her hand on her chest and bowed, "—is available for the use of your wedding."

"Uh."

"It is dry and magically protected."

That was true. The elves who'd originally created the sanctuary had used their spells to make it difficult to detect; most people had no idea that anything but forest was in that area. Still, I didn't have the fondest memories of the place.

"No offense, Work Leader," I said, "but the last time I was there, a leftover elven guard beast tried to eat Gondo, and a jealous female dragon flambéed all the old elven tree houses, almost toasting me and my half-sister along with them."

"We offer our sanctuary free of charge," Nogna said.

"Is there an open field?" Willard asked.

"Yes."

"A dragon-started forest fire has a tendency to clear areas," I said.

"Is it picturesque?" Willard asked.

"Our sanctuary is very beautiful."

"We'll take it," Willard said.

"Hey." I lifted a hand in protest. "You haven't even been there."

"We didn't get our deposit back on the other field," Willard said. "And we had to pay extra for the cow. If someone offers you a free field, you take it."

"We will also prepare food for the event," Nogna said. "And gifts."

"We have a caterer," Willard said.

"Not who'll be able to find the place through the elven magic that hides it from everyone," I muttered.

Undeterred, Willard said, "They can leave the trays by the side of the highway, and we'll transport them in."

"Weren't you the one who thought my wedding should be right and proper?"

"Yeah, but your dragon has convinced me that isn't a possibility. Having your wedding hidden from the rest of the world by elven magic sounds like an excellent idea. Maybe Zav can put his imported animals for the hunt in there too."

Gondo raised a finger. "Do his animals like to eat goblins?"

"Hopefully not before the dragons eat *them*," I said.

Gondo didn't look reassured.

"Sindari found something. I'm going to check on it." I pointed toward the alley.

"I'll go back to the office and see if any agents have a lead on this," Willard said. "Walker, do you need a ride to the hospital? You look like you're going to pass out from loss of blood."

"Do I?" Walker was working on his next patient and only glanced at her. "I was hoping I looked alluringly sexy."

"Half of your left eyebrow was torched off, and there's dried blood all over your face."

"So… not sexy?"

"Sorry. Ride?"

"I need to finish up with a few more people, but then the answer is yes, though I would prefer it be for a sanger and a coldie than a check-up. With a little food in my belly, I can regenerate my damaged flesh on my own."

I expected Willard to tell him he could get his own food—what the heck was a sanger?—but she huffed and said, "Fine."

As I turned to leave, she thumped me on my arm and made me pause.

"Have you considered that someone might have done this to get at you?" she asked quietly.

"The instant I saw the place, yes."

"I'll also see if any of my agents have heard about people with a grudge against you."

"That's no small list, I'm sure," I said.

"Been irritating the world this week?"

"No more than usual, but you know as well as I how long my list of enemies is." I refrained from pointing out that I'd gained a lot of them by doing work for her and her predecessors. I didn't want to put any blame on her. I'd chosen this life.

"That's another reason the sanctuary is a good idea. It'll be harder for your enemies to find you there."

"You don't think the stack of catering trays lined up alongside the road will lead people in the right direction?"

"I'll take care of that. There won't be any stacks. Keep your eyes open until we figure this out."

"Oh, I will." I headed out without pointing out that anyone who'd seen through the glamours that Zav and Dimitri had put on this place could probably see through the illusions hiding the sanctuary.

CHAPTER 3

I HAVE SEARCHED THE SURFACE THOUGHTS *of as many of the beings leaving the vicinity of your commercial establishment as possible*, Zav said telepathically to me as I returned to the alley.

My senses told me he had shifted to his dragon form and was perched on a nearby rooftop. Since Sindari was visible at the end of the alley, sitting patiently next to a pile of rubble, I picked my way toward him.

It's called the Sable Dragon, I reminded Zav. *It's named after you. You should be honored to call it by name.*

As I have informed you, I am a black dragon, not a sable dragon.

Should I have Dimitri rename it the Black Dragon so there's no doubt in people's minds? I *had* suggested that when Dimitri had first been painting the sign, but he'd resisted. That wasn't *poetical* enough.

If you wish to remove doubt, it could be named The Beverage Dispensing Establishment Marked by the Noble Lord Zavryd'nokquetal, Son of the Dragon Queen Zynesshara.

That's not going to fit on the sign. What did you find in people's minds?

Little of use. Primarily, fear and concern that their new favorite haunt will not be safe to return to in the future. Also fear that the magical community is being targeted by humans who've learned about them and detest them.

That was a motive I hadn't considered. The idea that this hadn't been done by some personal enemy of mine was appealing, but I doubted I should hope for that hypothesis to prove true.

I have not sampled the thoughts of every mind in the area, Zav continued. *Some left my range too quickly, and others near the building are victims and preoccupied by their injuries. They are unlikely suspects.*

Agreed. Thanks for checking. I crouched beside Sindari. "What'd you find?"

He rested his large paw on a piece of blackened metal with ridges that I would have dismissed as junk blown off the building in the explosion. But it did have a faint magical signature. I picked it up and turned it over in my palm.

It smells of the chemicals that your people use to create explosives, Sindari said.

"It looks a bit like a piece from a grenade. Actually, it looks a *lot* like a piece from one of the grenades that Nin sells to me. I wonder if it was one of hers."

The scent is similar, yes. I have smelled many types of explosives on this world, and they are not all the same.

The feeling that I was being watched crept over me. Instead of jumping up and peering about, I pretended to continue studying the grenade while stretching out with my senses. With so many magical beings around, I hadn't been paying much attention to the auras in the area, but I detected a troll at the end of the alley. He was leaning around the back corner of the ice-cream shop to spy on us.

My suspicions rose, and I shifted just enough to see him out of the corner of my eye.

The blue-skinned, white-haired troll was young, maybe not any older than Reb, the ward that our half-troll helper Inga was fostering. This kid had probably come to play with Reb and had nothing to do with the explosion. But he caught me looking, jerked back around the corner, and took off down the cross street. That made me suspicious again.

I stood, tempted to chase him down in case he *had* been responsible or had seen something, but I decided to ask Zav to check his mind instead.

Before I could, my phone vibrated. It was a call, not a text, and it was from Zoltan.

That startled me into answering it. It was the middle of the day. Why would our vampire-alchemist roommate be awake, much less calling me?

"What's up, Zoltan?"

"Dear robber," he said, using the appellation he'd given me early on and refused to change, "this is *completely* unacceptable."

"You heard about the explosion?"

"What explosion? I'm talking about the intruders in the house who want to *kill* me."

I pressed the heel of my palm to my forehead—what *else* could happen today? "What intruders?"

"Elves."

"I assume you're not talking about Freysha."

My half-sister had returned to Earth and was continuing to tutor me in forest magic. She'd also been translating the dwarven texts I'd brought back from Dun Kroth, so I would have a head start on studying my ancient dwarven sword before Lord Chasmmoor arrived to teach me how to draw upon its secret powers.

"Certainly not," Zoltan said. "Freysha is a capable assistant and permitted in my basement. These *legions* of elven intruders are not. They have been inside your house, and now they are attempting to breach my defenses in order to slay me. They *told* me that. I insist that you come and deal with them immediately."

I frowned at the phone, not voicing disbelief but wondering how much of this was hyperbole. Even if elves *had* shown up at the house, Zav's magical defenses should have kept them from getting onto the property.

"Are you coming, Val?" Zoltan surprised me by using my name. "I am certain these are *your* kin, and they are all armed and have threatened me."

I doubted my kin would invade the house or threaten my roommate, but his tone turned uncharacteristically worried, and that worried *me*.

"I am not an evil vampire," Zoltan went on. "I do little lasting harm to anyone, even when I feed. They have no right to terminate my existence."

"Hang on. I'll be right there." I closed my fist around the grenade fragment. I'd research it later. And the troll…

He'd disappeared from my senses. Of course he had.

Zav? I reached out. *Can you give me a fast ride home?*

Yes. I sensed a portal opening at your domicile. It will be good to see who it is.

If Zoltan's description of legions of hostile elves was to be believed, I wasn't sure about that.

CHAPTER 4

"DIMITRI ASKED ME TO ASK you if you would apply your home-renovation skills to the coffee shop." I rested a hand on Zav's scales as he flew me over Fremont toward our neighborhood in Green Lake.

I have much to do at the goblin sanctuary to make it suitable for my dragon kin, Zav replied telepathically. Ugh, he'd already heard about our new venue? Word traveled quickly. *Also, I have not perused any magazines with instructions on how to repair a coffee shop.*

"It should be simple. You know that place where there used to be a wall? We'd like a wall there again. And the portion of the roof that crumbled down? We'd like that back up there too. Dimitri and I can handle buying a new toilet and installing it."

Would not your half-sister who is training in engineering be an ideal person to repair the establishment?

I think engineers just draw up blueprints.

She is very capable.

True. I took that to mean Zav wasn't interested.

Or, more likely, it was exactly as he'd implied. He was stressed about his mom coming to Earth and wanted to make sure everything was perfect. I couldn't blame him for that.

Green Lake came into view, and in the sea of surrounding houses, I spotted our familiar Victorian with the pointed turret roof. We were close enough for my senses to pick up the auras of magical beings.

Zoltan might have exaggerated about the legions, but there were a *lot* of elves on the property. Full-blooded elves.

If I do these repairs, will you rename the establishment? Zav must have sensed the elves by now, too, but he didn't sound concerned.

"I already told you we can't fit the name you suggested on a sign."

The Black Dragon would be superior to the Sable Dragon. In addition to being a type of weasel, your dictionary informs me that sable can refer to smoked sablefish. I have no desire to be associated with such inferior creatures as fish and weasels.

"Do you keep one of our dictionaries in your interdimensional pocket?"

In the magical pocket sewn inside my robe. I refer to it frequently to better understand your people.

"How come you can keep a book inside your robe but not underwear?"

Elves do not wear any clothing under their robes.

"You're a dragon. And when you shapeshift, you're a human. Humans wear underwear."

It's an elven *robe.* Zav flapped his wings, taking us down for a landing. *Underwear is not worn under it.*

I imagined running through the rows of seats at my wedding, having to push the ankles off the knees of any robe-wearing elf inclined to sit Zav-style.

As we flew over the trees between the neighbor's yard and ours, numerous elves came into view. They weren't in the house, as Zoltan had suggested, but they *were* on the property. How had they gotten past the defenses?

Nearly three dozen elegant male and female faces lifted toward us as Zav descended, tucking his wings so that he didn't hit the house or the trees when he landed. Most of those elves, all with their long blond or silver hair tied back in braids or tails, wore brown or beige tunics and dark brown or green pants, but a couple of white-haired males at the edge of the group had mage robes similar to Zav's. Almost every elf was armed with a bow, sword, or staff, and the weapons radiated power.

Freysha was among them, standing at the top of the steps that led down to Zoltan's basement. Her hands were lifted, as if she was trying to hold the visitors back.

Visitors or intruders? They *did* look like they were trying to get past her to storm Zoltan's lair.

Fortunately, none of them raised their weapons toward Zav or me. Not that many people—or elves—would dare point their bows at a dragon.

I picked out Eireth's aura a couple of seconds before he stepped out of the conservatory attached to the back of the house. Two stern young males strode out after him, carrying swords and looking like they wanted to grab his shoulders to pull him back inside. The king's royal bodyguards?

Another two warriors leaped out after Eireth, hustling to walk in front of him and glaring defiantly at me, at Zav, and at Zoltan's door. Or maybe at the magical cannon resting on the cracked cement pad in front of Zoltan's door. It was full-sized, not a replica, and its barrel pointed up the stairs at the intruders.

When did we get a magical cannon? I asked Zav as I slid to the ground.

It is new, but I have sensed it on the premises previously. In the vampire's closet. Zav turned, talons clacking on the patio, to face Eireth, but his wing clipped a ceramic pot holding one of Dimitri's blueberry bushes and almost knocked it over. The backyard was a tight fit for a dragon, and after growling in irritation, Zav shifted into his human form.

If he keeps a cannon in his closet, where do his suits and bow ties go?

We have not discussed this.

"Good afternoon, Daughter." Eireth stepped past his guards to face me, pressed his hands together in front of his chest, and bowed. "And honorable dragon, Lord Zavryd'nokquetal." He also bowed to Zav. "We have arrived for the wedding."

"That's good, but it's not until Saturday." I realized they had a different calendar, not to mention different year, month, and day lengths on their world, and that *Saturday* wouldn't mean anything. "It's still a few days away."

"It is elven tradition to spend time with one's son or daughter before the wedding ceremony since he or she often leaves to live in another part of the world afterward. You are in an entirely different world." Eireth smiled wistfully, as if he truly regretted that.

I wouldn't mind a chance to get to know him better, but, uh, what about all of these other elves? Who *were* they?

"I would have invited you to visit us in our home—" Eireth lifted a hand to acknowledge Freysha and said nothing of his wife, "—but I assumed you have a few chores to complete before the day of joining."

Chores, right. My to-do list included: tell all the guests about the new location of the wedding, go to the final dress fitting, find out who bombed the coffee shop, and, oh, figure out what to do with all the elves in my yard. Were they planning to *stay* here? The old Victorian house was big, and we had three guest rooms not being used, but that wouldn't accommodate three *dozen* elves. Especially given that a king probably expected his own room, if not his own entire floor of a house.

"That's true. Ah..." How did I broach this?

"I regret to inform you," Eireth continued on when I paused, "that your home has been invaded by a vampire. I ordered my people to eradicate it, but Freysha says it... lives here." He arched his eyebrows in disbelief, and I remembered someone mentioning that the undead weren't permitted on elven worlds.

"Yes." Freysha still had her hands up, palms outward toward the newcomers, many of whom kept fingering their weapons and eyeing the basement door. "I've tried to explain—"

My phone vibrated.

"Hello, Zoltan," I answered.

"The *legions* are still present! I sense you up there. And your fanged and hulking mate."

Zav touched one of his perfectly normal-looking canine teeth and arched his own eyebrows.

"Can you not do anything?" Zoltan demanded. "Tell them that my cannon is alchemically enhanced and that it will automatically annihilate any who attempt to force their way into my abode."

"I'll let them know."

"And make them go away!"

"Working on it." I hung up on him and smiled at Eireth.

"We are not welcome in your home?" He tilted his head.

"Of course you're welcome. Just not in the basement. And, er, I don't have room for all of your groupies."

"Groupies?"

"Your entourage." I smiled at the stern warriors who were standing so they could keep an eye on Zav, me, and the entrance to Zoltan's lair. Considering we weren't anywhere near the basement door, it was an impressive feat.

"Ah, my bodyguards, yes, and the rest of these elves are your cousins." Eireth spread his hand toward them. "Lord Zavryd'nokquetal invited them to the wedding. He invited our entire *city*."

Zav stepped forward and slung his arm around my shoulders. "I was most pleased to announce that Val and I would be mated in the human way—and the elven way—as well as the dragon way."

I leaned into his side and patted him on the chest, though I couldn't wipe the daunted expression from my face. There were a couple of guest beds, an air mattress, the couch in the living room, and then there was Dimitri's Gamersac. Would an elf sleep in a glorified beanbag chair?

Sorry, Freysha spoke into my mind, even as I looked at Zav. *I did not think so many of our relatives would come.*

Do they actually care about our wedding, or is it a particularly boring week in Elfdom? I thought back to her.

They are intrigued to have an excuse to visit one of the wild worlds and are curious about the half-elven warrior who bested the infamous assassin Varlesh Sarrlevi. There are rumors about your showdown with him and how you utterly demolished him.

Who the hell started those rumors? Only Nin, Sindari, and Amber had been there to witness the battle, and I was positive they hadn't been texting elves in another world.

The fae queen came to our court recently to negotiate a trade agreement and also proclaim her interest in being visited by virile elven males. While there, she denigrated Sarrlevi, saying you pulverized him and that it would be foolish for anyone to hire him in the future. She said this in front of many witnesses. If Sarrlevi hears about it, he may not be pleased with you.

Me? I'm not the one who was bashing him. Why would the queen do that?

She did not give a reason. It was odd because she rarely leaves her realm to visit the courts of other worlds. It is possible the interest in trade was a pretext. It seemed she had developed a grudge against Sarrlevi and simply wished to besmirch his reputation.

Uh, why? Isn't it a bad idea to piss off assassins?

Freysha shrugged. *One would think so.*

I leaned into Zav more, needing the support. Was it possible that Sarrlevi had hurled that explosive?

No, I couldn't see it. He'd been an annoying dumbass about stalking and inconveniencing me, but he'd been an honorable opponent when we were actually fighting. It was hard to imagine him intentionally hurting other people to get at me.

My phone buzzed again.

"Yeah, yeah," I said, before Zoltan could complain further. "I'm taking care of it." I hung up on him and focused on Eireth again.

"You're very welcome to stay, so long as nobody attacks Zoltan—he's an annoying vampire, but he's a talented alchemist, so we've decided to keep him around. Did your people bring tents, by chance? It's chilly this time of year, but we do have a patio heater."

I looked around at the silent elves, imagining them ignoring the patio heater in favor of building campfires in my backyard.

"Tents?" Eireth asked. "Ah, yes, like our yurts. If there is no room in your home, some can return to our world and retrieve temporary domiciles."

He spoke to the gathering in elvish, which resulted in a lot of muttering and frowns. Again, I decided not to activate my charm. I didn't need to know if they were complaining about camping out in January or not being allowed to eradicate Zoltan.

Freysha said something to them in elvish. It sounded placating. Maybe it was an offer to share her room.

I was not aware of this elven custom, Zav said, speaking telepathically, though Eireth was conferring with his bodyguards and one of the older robed elves, so he probably wouldn't have heard us speaking. *Will some of the elves stay in our room? I know you are inhibited about mating in front of others.*

Yes, I am. And, no, they won't. I thought of how keen elven hearing was and of Freysha's previous remarks about how she sometimes went downstairs so she wouldn't overhear our lovemaking. That made me blush, and it was horrifying imagining my father listening to me having sex. I barely knew the guy, but it was still horrifying. *We're going to be chaste until the wedding.*

Zav's eyebrows drew together. *Chaste?*

Isn't that word in your pocket dictionary?

It is, but I am puzzled by your use. Do you perhaps invoke the third definition? Without unnecessary ornamentation; simple or restrained.

No, and that wouldn't apply to either of us anyway. I looked down at his holey yellow footwear and patted his chest again. *We'll have wild raucous sex as soon as our houseguests leave.*

I do not approve of this plan.

It's less than a week until the wedding.

They may stay longer, Zav pointed out.

They won't. Would they? What if the custom was that they spend a week before and *after* the wedding? Or a month after the wedding?

Elves lived for centuries. Maybe they thought nothing of spending a *year* visiting their relatives.

"Uhm, King Eireth." I turned back to him, lifting a finger.

He'd finished his confab. "Yes?"

"How long will you, uh, grant me the joy of your company and of getting to know my relatives?"

"We were discussing that. I am most pleased to stay in your domicile—or outside of it—but some of our people are not comfortable with the idea of a vampire residing nearby. They believe his undead aura permeates the area and the taint may have ill effects on those nearby."

"Well, I guess that explains that rash I had last month."

Eireth blinked quizzically. *It is nothing more than superstition*, he said telepathically, *but as their leader, I must be diplomatic and listen to their concerns.*

"How do your people feel about the auras at the Staybridge Suites? I can pay for—wait." I snapped my fingers as inspiration struck. "You said you're willing to stay here? Just some of the people—like, say, half to two-thirds—don't want vampire taint oozing all over them?"

"That is not precisely what I said... but that is roughly correct."

"Perfect. I have an idea." The Staybridge would be expensive, and it was probably rude to foist one's myriad elven cousins off on a hotel. A hotel that wasn't used to pointy-eared customers with weapons. This was a *better* idea. Assuming she agreed.

I was poking through my contacts on my phone when Zoltan called again. I tried to hang up on him, but my thumb was over the call button, and I accidentally brushed it. Damn technology.

"It's two p.m. Don't you need a *nap*?" I demanded.

"Really, dear robber. Could *you* nap if there were hordes of inimical enemies at your door? I am most concerned that their auras remain on the property."

"Well, get over it. Some of them are staying until the wedding. These are my kin."

"Preposterous!"

"Maybe you can house-swap with Jimmy for the week," I said, naming the vampire who'd lived in the basement when we first moved in. "Or *stay* with him for the week. The elves don't like your undead aura."

"I do not find their *live* auras appealing. I will speak to Jimmy." He hung up.

"I miss the days when I lived alone." My next call was to my mother.

I know that is not true, Zav spoke into my mind, his voice a calming influence.

I needed calm. My chest was tight, the stresses of the day adding up and making my fingers twitch toward the inhaler in my pocket. Just what I wanted. To have an asthmatic fit in front of a bunch of strangers. Strangers I was apparently related to.

"Good afternoon, Val," Mom answered, sounding calm herself.

That might change after I made my request. "Hey, Mom."

Eireth's eyebrows drifted upward again. Was that intrigue on his face? He must have known he would run into Mom if he came to my wedding, but I had no idea how he felt about that. I knew Mom was nervous and worried about what he would think when he saw her more than forty years older than she'd been when they'd been lovers. He was also forty-odd years older, of course, but no doubt looked the same.

"You rarely call," Mom said. Warily?

She couldn't *already* know that I wanted something, could she? Parents had weirdly accurate sixth senses about that stuff.

"I'm not sure that's true, but since I know about your interest in all things elven, and that you've always found their people intriguing, I have a treat for you."

Eireth's eyebrows seemed stuck in the upward position, though I wasn't sure the expression conveyed intrigue anymore.

"Are you setting me up for something?" Mom asked.

"Yes." Better to pull off the bandage quickly, right? "I have an overabundance of houseguests that have arrived early for the wedding, and some of them are protesting sleeping in the vicinity of a vampire, and I was wondering if they could stay at your house."

"It's a cabin, it's small, and there isn't a guest room."

"There's a sauna and a pottery shed."

"Are these guests you dislike?"

"Not necessarily, but they're going to get yurts and don't mind staying outside. They also happen to be elven. At least some of them are my cousins. Or half-cousins. However that works."

Mom was silent so long that I checked to make sure I hadn't lost the connection. She *did* have a sketchy cell signal out there in rural Duvall.

"Will he be coming?" she asked quietly.

"No." Maybe I should have backed away to a private corner of the yard before making this call. Not that I could have escaped elven hearing without taking a walk to the lake. "He's okay with vampire germs."

"Okay." Did she sound relieved?

I knew she wanted to see him but was also anxious about seeing him. Understandable.

"Thanks. I'll send them your way." Just one problem. Elves weren't dragons and couldn't fly. From what Zav had explained of portals, they would have to return to their world in order to open a portal to another place on Earth. That seemed like overkill just to get out to Duvall. "Or I'll show up in Dimitri's van with the back packed with elves."

"That should be amusing."

Amusing, right. Hopefully, I wouldn't get pulled over and asked if the two dozen elves were all wearing seatbelts. From what I'd seen, only one of Dimitri's seats even *had* working seatbelts.

Mom said a curt *goodbye* and hung up, maybe to prepare the pottery shed for guests.

"Mom's property has a lot more room," I explained, since Eireth and his bodyguards were all watching me. "And she lives in the trees."

"She adopted our ways?" Eireth asked.

"*Under* the trees," I clarified. "In a cabin. It's homey. Your people will like it."

"She has a hot box that is most appealing in this dreary, chill climate," Zav stated.

"It's a sauna, not a hot box." Not that the elves would know the difference. "And, yes, I'm sure she will make it available to guests."

"I will inform the others." Eireth inclined his head and turned to address his people.

I slumped against Zav, again glad for his calming presence. "Any chance you can give all the elves that hate vampire cooties a ride over to my mom's? You can visit her sauna while you're there. Though make sure you put a sign or something on the door if you're going to get naked inside."

"I would be most pleased to enjoy the dry heat, but it is time for me to leave to pick up your other houseguest."

"There's another one? It's not a dragon, is it?" For a horrified moment, I imagined Zondia showing up in her human form with a sleeping bag slung over her shoulder. Or *Xilneth*.

"It is Lord Chasmmoor, the dwarven master smith and enchanter who will instruct you on the ways of your sword. *Thrallendakh yen Hyrek de Horak*." He said the long name firmly. He must have noticed that I hadn't switched over from calling it Chopper yet.

I would. After ten years, the name was habit, but I wanted to honor the sword, especially since it seemed quasi sentient. *Hyrek* meant Storm. I could manage to call it that.

"You're going to pick up Chasmmoor from the dwarven home world today? He's ready? I wouldn't mind waiting a week to start my training, after all the wedding craziness is over." I eyed the elves. They were arguing, their voices raised. Maybe they'd been monitoring the conversation and had heard about the pottery shed.

Zav gazed blandly at me. "Do you not believe it would be wise to further your understanding of the blade *before* our wedding?"

"Do you think I'll need to?"

Maybe he'd also been thinking that the explosion at the coffee shop was a sign that someone new was after me.

"Given how many dragons from different clans will be coming—" Zav sniffed, and I knew he was thinking of Xilneth, "—it's possible the event will have tumultuous moments."

"As in moments when innocent people might be mowed over by dragons on the hunt?"

"I trust your guests will be wise enough to take cover when the situation demands it."

Was he joking? I couldn't tell. And here I'd been worried about an irate bomber.

CHAPTER 5

BY THE TIME I GOT half of the elves settled into rooms—or set up in yurts—at my house and the other half driven over to Mom's cabin, it was long past dark and too late to visit Nin at her food truck. I could have swung by her house with the grenade fragment, but she might need her tools in the truck to examine it, and I didn't want to force her to go back to work. Besides, Zav might be back any time with Lord Chasmmoor. Since the dwarf was coming all the way to Earth to help *me*, it would be rude not to be home to greet him.

My phone buzzed as I was driving back to Green Lake in Dimitri's van. It was now empty of elves, though a faint forest scent reminiscent of cedar lingered, overriding the marijuana odor that usually lurked inside. When I'd visited Veleshna Var, I hadn't noticed that the elves there smelled like the forest, but their city had been in the *middle* of a forest, so the whole place had smelled of sap and pine needles and the like. Maybe they made a cologne of the stuff to sprinkle on themselves when they left home.

"Hey, Willard," I answered the phone. "Did you find out anything about our explosion?"

"Nothing concrete, no. If there's a mob of angry magical beings after you, they haven't announced it to any of my informants."

"Not even Gondo?"

"*Gondo* is too busy helping Work Leader Nogna plan your wedding present."

"Should I be afraid?" I remembered the unique wood-fired hot tub on wheels they'd made for us on our last visit. Would they try to top that?

"Do you really have to ask that?"

"I guess not."

"Anyway, I haven't seen much of him for a few days," Willard said. "I have other agents out in the city, but they don't catch everything. Sometimes, it's not until after the fact that I hear from them. Like if someone succeeded in killing you, they would learn about it. There would be much bragging by whoever was responsible."

"Gee, thanks."

"Just telling it how it is. I'll let you know if I hear anything. Keep your head up."

"Always."

I parked the van in front of the house, sliding into a wide spot right in front of the walkway. Since Zav had installed the dragon topiaries, with their glowing eyes and tendency to shoot flames at passersby, it had been much easier to find a parking spot out front.

The auras of elves and a vampire filled the house, Zoltan hunkered in the basement, the magical cannon still blocking his door. No dragons. Zav hadn't returned yet.

As I walked to the porch, it occurred to me that I'd given away all of the guest bedrooms, including the couch and Gamersac, and hadn't reserved a spot for Lord Chasmmoor.

"Crap." I bit my lip and stared at the front door, our dragon door knocker gazing blandly back at me.

Would I have to give him *my* room? All I knew about Chasmmoor was that he was a smith, enchanter, and buddy to his king. In other words, someone who probably expected a room of his own. If he was taking time out of his life to train me on how to use Chopper—Storm— the least I could do was give him room and board. Ideally, board that wasn't a sleeping bag in the hallway.

The scent of something strange cooking wafted to me. I couldn't identify the smell, but it reminded me of grilled eggplant. Maybe the neighbors were grilling outside. Or maybe the elves were experimenting in my kitchen.

I pushed open the door, hoping my guests weren't doing anything that would break the expensive commercial appliances I'd gotten to better service Zav and his bottomless stomach. I almost crashed into Dimitri's back.

With all the other more noticeable magical beings around, I hadn't picked out his faint quarter-dwarven aura. He stood with his back toward the door, his chin in his hand as he gazed around the living room and dining room with a concerned expression. Elven voices floated from the kitchen, and the scent of cooking was stronger inside. That ruled out the neighbors.

A strong floral odor also filled the air in here, the scent familiar. It smelled like the conservatory outside where Freysha was growing all manner of native and non-native plants.

"What's going on?" I asked.

Instead of answering, Dimitri stepped aside, giving me a view of our living room, now with flowering vines growing up the walls, over the back of the couch, and across the television screen. There weren't any pots. The plants had sprouted from flat brown ovals someone had placed on the floor, faint magic emanating from them. The leaves on a few of the vines rustled, even though the windows weren't open, and there was no breeze. Scenes from *Little Shop of Horrors* popped into my mind.

"Our guests redecorated, huh?" I asked.

"You didn't mention that we were getting houseguests this week."

"I didn't know until recently."

"How recently?"

I checked the time on my phone. "Three hours ago."

"You know there are yurts and more elves in the backyard?" Dimitri must have gotten home recently.

In my attempt to get everything organized—everyone properly placed—I hadn't thought to call him and warn him about this. Maybe Zoltan hadn't either. He must have used up all of his minutes that afternoon calling me repeatedly.

"Yeah. If it helps, there are even more yurts at my mother's place. She took half of the elves. Hopefully, they don't pester the werewolf across the street from her. I'm pretty sure that Liam and my mother are having mature adult relations now."

"Is it just me, or is your life getting stranger with every passing month?"

I lifted my brows. "Is it really stranger this month than last? Is there some kind of scientific tool for measuring this?"

A female elf walked into view holding a bottle of Hoisin sauce. "This smells wonderful. May we use it to baste the *aruthnila*?"

"Go for it," I said.

"Excellent. We are making enough to feed everyone. We hope you will dine with us."

"I will. Thanks." Once she'd returned to the kitchen, I murmured, "What's *aruthnila*?" to Dimitri.

Since he'd been here longer than I, maybe he knew.

"From what I saw, something like giant portabellas. They're in the meat smoker."

"I hope there's still something available for me to warm up for Zav. Portabellas won't cut it for a dragon. I wonder if dwarves like mushrooms."

"I prefer pizza."

"I assume that's your human three-quarters talking. How is everything at the shop? What did the landlord say? Do you need help with anything?"

"Yeah, repairs."

"The landlord's insurance won't cover it?" Surely, bombings by nameless miscreants fell under the Act of God clause. It wasn't as if a dragon had been involved.

Dimitri pushed a hand through his hair. "I don't know. Maybe. But the landlord is out of town, and it sounded like… Well, I read between the lines that he might let the building go into foreclosure if the insurance won't cover it fully and it turns out to be too expensive to rebuild. I'm going to get some brick, lumber, and drywall, and do my best to fix it myself."

"I'll help as soon as the wedding is over and my life is less complicated."

The twist to his lips suggested my life would *never* be less complicated. That was possibly true.

"Can't you just give me some money for the supplies?" Dimitri asked.

"You'd rather have my cash than my help?"

"I've seen you wield a hammer. If your elven blood didn't give you magical regenerative powers, you wouldn't have any fingernails left."

"Ha ha. Cash it is." Since the odds were good this would turn out to have been my fault, in however roundabout a way, I wouldn't begrudge paying for the repairs.

The magic from a portal forming nearby plucked at my senses. Zav flew out of it, and I sensed the aura of a full-blooded dwarf with him. A successful taxi pickup.

"I don't know for sure," Dimitri said, going back to my question about the dwarven palate, "but if we had a dwarf houseguest, I'd get him a pepperoni supreme."

"Funny you should mention that." I rested a hand on Dimitri's shoulder and smiled. "Would you mind sharing your room with a guest for a couple of weeks?"

I didn't know how long it would take for Chasmmoor to show me the ropes with my sword, but I assumed he wasn't planning on staying on Earth for years. Dwarves reputedly had advanced civilizations. That had to mean day jobs with only a certain number of vacation days allowed a year.

"Yes, I'd mind," Dimitri said. "It's bad enough that there are elves roaming all over the house. I won't be able to go to the bathroom without putting clothes on."

I stared at him. "Are you saying you usually wander naked to the bathroom?"

"In the middle of the night? Yes. You and Freysha are on the second floor and hardly ever visit my bathroom."

"That'll be even more true going forward," I muttered.

"No roommates. There's no room for an air mattress on the floor, and I'm not cuddling up with whatever weirdo you've got coming."

"He's a dwarf." I sensed Zav and Chasmmoor walking from the street toward the porch. "A smith and an enchanter. I thought you might like to learn from him while he's here."

"I'd be happy to learn from him, but not from a bed adjacent to mine." Dimitri looked toward the door, his eyes widening with interest. "There *is* a dwarf coming."

"Yup. You sure you don't want to offer him space in your room? We could fit an air mattress in there if we squeezed."

"I'm sure." Did he sound slightly less firm this time? "But he can sleep in my van."

"He's a lord and good friends with the dwarven king. He might expect more posh accommodations."

"How much poshness can he need? You were going to stick him in my room on an air mattress."

"I was envisioning *you* on the air mattress."

"It hasn't escaped my notice that you haven't volunteered yourself for an air mattress. Isn't one of those elves a king?"

"Yes, and my father. I suppose you're right and that I should offer him my room. I've slept on a lot worse than air mattresses. I'm just not sure what Zav's opinion would be on that."

"Don't dragons sleep in caves on rocks?"

"They can, though I understand they prefer nests in eyries. The more fearless and able the dragon, the more likely he or she is to sleep in the open. Those who are less certain of their status—and worry that some other dragon might come by and kick their ass—opt for caves. They're more protected, you see."

Zav had given me that explanation when I'd been puzzled by his sneering insult that Xilneth had probably spent his whole life sleeping in caves. Zav had been even more miffed with Xilneth than usual since Xilneth had claimed that Zav's sister Zondia had a thing for him.

"What status does air mattress convey?" Dimitri asked.

"Spineless minion, probably."

"So naturally you want me to sleep on one."

Hm, telling him that might have been a misstep. "You're not a dragon. It's not the same."

"Uh huh."

I sensed Zav and Chasmmoor outside, but for some reason, they'd paused on the walkway. I opened the door to invite them in, and damp chilly air brushed my cheeks.

Zav was pointing and gesticulating at his prize topiaries, their eyes glowing in warning as wisps of smoke wafted from their arboreal nostrils. Hopefully, Zav was adjusting them so they wouldn't torch our dwarven guest, and not just showing them off. Somehow, the elves had gotten past the topiaries—and *all* of Zav and Dimitri's defenses around the property—without activating them. Presumably, the robed guys that had come with Eireth were uber mages who had been sent, along with the armed bodyguards, to help keep him safe. Maybe they would extend their protection to me if the elven assassin showed up to mangle me and prove that the fae queen's words had been lies. Or maybe they would watch the show.

That thought made me grimace, as the scenario seemed plausible. Even worse, what if Sarrlevi showed up at the *wedding* to mangle me? In front of not only all of the important elves but all of the important *dragons* that would be there? Oh, man, if Zav's uptight mother saw me getting my face ground into the dirt by an elf, she might revise her opinion of me and revoke her approval of Zav claiming me as his mate.

As these visions blossomed in my mind like a fungal rot, my chest tightened and a faint wheeze came from my air pipe. Damn it, I had no proof that any of that would happen. I had to stop stressing out about stupid stuff.

"Mom was right," I muttered. "We should have eloped to Vegas."

Dimitri didn't seem to hear me. He was gazing—no, *gaping*—out the door at our guest.

I poked him in the shoulder.

"Do you see his armor?" he whispered.

"Yeah. It's nice and shiny."

The golden plate armor was more impressive than what Chasmmoor had been wearing for our first meeting. It radiated powerful magic that seemed equal to that of my sword. Was it some ancient relic he'd inherited? Or an example of his own work?

Our four-and-a-half-foot-tall visitor also carried a giant—giant by dwarf standards—battle-axe in a harness across his back. A short sword and a dagger hung in scabbards on his wide belt, and other points of magic in his pockets and on his wrists promised a variety of charms. In all, it was more gear than he'd worn to the lich's lair. I wondered what stories his people had heard about the dangers of Earth.

Dimitri turned his gape to me. "Do you sense how *powerful* it is? And how intricately woven the numerous enchantments on it are? It looks like it can defend not only against weapons but against hot and cold attacks, and probably a dozen other things I'm too sense-dull to interpret. I bet you could throw a fireball at him, and it wouldn't even singe his beard!"

"We can't try that because I haven't yet found an elf willing to teach me how to hurl fireballs. All of Freysha's magic involves green growing things."

Dimitri didn't hear me. He was back to gaping at Chasmmoor. Or Chasmmoor's *armor*. Which was apparently ten times more magnificent than the axe and other stuff.

Zav and Chasmmoor headed toward us, and my nerves kicked in, adding to the discomfort already derailing my lungs. This guy was here to teach me how to use my sword. That should have filled me with delight, but all I could think about was that he might be horribly disappointed when he found out how meager my magic skills were and that the rumors about my greatness as a warrior had been exaggerated. What if he decided I wasn't worthy to carry one of his people's ancient dragon blades, after all? And what if he decided to take it back to his world?

"Greetings, my mate." After they climbed to the porch, Zav spread his arms and hugged me before stepping back. "I have brought your tutor."

"Thank you." I managed to keep the wheezy rasp out of my voice, though I would have to sneak off and use my inhaler. I hoped the asthma flare-ups would die down again after the wedding. When Zav had remodeled the house, getting rid of all the mold in the walls, I'd started feeling better and relying on my medicine less, but lately...

"Your armor is *magnificent*." Dimitri reached out a hand, as if he might fondle the breastplate, but he managed to restrain himself.

I thought Chasmmoor might issue a cocky, "Yes," but he wasn't a dragon.

"I am pleased that someone on this wild world admires the craft and enchantments in the piece." Chasmmoor bowed as much as he could in all that gear. He was speaking in his own language, but the words seemed to come out in English, or they somehow translated themselves by the time they reached our ears. One of his trinkets, no doubt.

"This is Dimitri, my roommate and business partner," I introduced. "He does some enchanting himself."

Dimitri shook his head vigorously at me, looking horrified. What, he didn't want Chasmmoor to know he'd created some of the yard art? Maybe the powerful dwarf was causing him to have doubts about his abilities too.

"Dimitri," I said, "this is Lord Chasmmoor of Dun Kroth."

"Dun Kroth, which is now free of a vile dragon lich, something my people are grateful about." Chasmmoor held up a finger, then removed his axe and a backpack. He dug into the latter and pulled out two boxes, one made from wood with iron bands—it looked perfectly normal—and one made from stone with hideous leering monsters on all sides—*not* normal. A gargoyle on the top leered at us, its eyes glowing a faint red. "The king has given me a couple of traditional dwarven wedding presents to give to you and your mate." He nodded at Zav, then at me.

I hoped that gargoyle box wasn't one of the presents. If I put that on a shelf or the fireplace mantel, it would scare the crap out of anyone passing through the living room in the middle of the night. As if I wasn't already going to be unsettled wandering around the first floor after dark, knowing that Dimitri might be on one of his naked trips to the bathroom.

Zav beamed a smug smile at me, unfazed by the gargoyle box, as Chasmmoor dug into his pack for something else.

SECRETS OF THE SWORD III

You already know what the gifts are and approve of them? I asked him telepathically.

I do not know what is in his pack—its contents are protected by magic that keeps me from seeing or sensing inside—but I know what traditional dwarven wedding presents are.

It's something to do with food, isn't it? I couldn't imagine Zav looking so pleased over jewelry or a luck tchotchke for the mantel.

His smile broadened.

After setting the boxes on the porch railing, Chasmmoor found the third thing he'd been looking for. He slowly drew out a handle followed by a wide rectangular blade, a blade far too large to have fit in that pack.

Dimitri whistled in appreciation. "Even his *bag* is powerfully enchanted."

"He's the Mary Poppins of the dwarf world," I said.

Dimitri pointed at the pack. "Is that hard to learn? To enchant bags to have more space inside? Val, can you imagine how much we could sell those for at the shop? Every woman would want a purse that can hold ten times as many things as physically seems possible."

"You're going to get into making purses? Is that manly enough for you?"

"Well… I could decorate them with cogs and bolts to make them more my style."

"Those'll fly off the shelves."

Chasmmoor presented the weapon to me. Only then did I realize it wasn't a weapon—not in the traditional sense—but a giant magic meat cleaver.

"In the kitchen, this will make short work of even the toughest of haunches," he said.

"Oh, that's very thoughtful. I do hate an ornery haunch." I held out my hands to accept the weapon. "Thank you."

The cleaver had the heft of a forty-five-pound power bar at the gym, so it was good that I used both hands. It would have been embarrassing to drop his gift—and have it crash through the wood boards of the porch to the ground below.

"It's sturdy." I smiled.

"Yes." Chasmmoor's dark eyes twinkled. "I trust that as a half-elf, you inherited some of their strength."

"Naturally. It'll be no problem tackling haunches with it." Maybe I would invite the weight-lifting Willard over to help prepare meals.

"Indeed. Now for the second gift." Chasmmoor offered me the plain wooden box. Phew. He hadn't mentioned a third gift, so that gargoyle thing had to be something he'd only taken out so he could get to the others.

I accepted it, pleased that it had a normal weight. "Should I open it?"

"Yes," Zav said immediately.

Chasmmoor only spread his palm, as if to say that was up to me.

I opened the lid to reveal numerous small glass bottles filled with powders of various colors and granularity. They had labels, and I shifted the box toward the porch light so I could read them. Then promptly felt silly because they were written in dwarven.

"I will translate." Chasmmoor stepped in and pointed at the first label. "This is stone ash salt. The next is volcano chili dust. Then savory musk blend and ore of oregano."

"*Ore* of oregano?" And savory *musk* blend? Why did I have a feeling these labels were getting muddled in translation?

"They're dwarven cooking spices," Zav explained. "There is some dwarven humor in some of the names, but they will taste fabulous on the meat that goes in the smoker."

Chasmmoor nodded. "These spices were grown and mined from all over our world, the blends put together by the same master culinary artist who handles the meals for the king and his court. Even though elven palates are somewhat questionable, I trust you will enjoy them. Your mate will also enjoy them. Dragons are known to appreciate a finely seasoned haunch."

"I have no doubt." I closed the lid and lifted the box. "Thank you. I look forward to experimenting." With very minute amounts until I was certain that there was no actual ore in the ore of oregano.

"Excellent. I must return to my world in one week to resume my duties for the king, so once I put away my gear, we will ideally start training within the hour."

Within the hour? It was after ten. But if we only had a week…

I nodded. "I'm ready. And Dimitri can show you to—" I started to point to the van, but Dimitri swatted my arm down.

"The guest room in the back," he blurted. "We've reserved it for you. Hopefully, you won't mind all the elves in the house."

"Not at all. With the wedding forthcoming, I assumed the Ruin Bringer's relatives would arrive en masse. That is the elven way."

Zav nodded. How come everybody knew that and hadn't told me?

"Come with me." Dimitri picked up Chasmmoor's pack and waved for him to follow him into the house.

You're willing to have him snoring in an air mattress beside you now that you've seen his armor? I sent telepathically to Dimitri.

He can have my room. I'll sleep in the van. Put in a good word for me, will you? I'll wash the windows for the whole house if you can get him to teach me a few things.

Inside and outside?

Yes.

Deal.

"One moment." Before following, Chasmmoor grabbed the hideous box from the railing, hopefully intending to stuff it back in his bag. But he held it out to me.

"Uh, no, I couldn't possibly accept any more gifts." I hefted the spice box. "This is already too much. Your generosity is wonderful."

Zav snorted.

Chasmmoor's fluffy red eyebrow twitched. "This is for your training."

"Training? I thought you'd mostly be teaching me command words to activate Storm's magic."

"I will train you on how to activate the magic and use it in the best way against foes. This requires foes. We will start calling them forth tonight. Although…" Chasmmoor frowned around at the house and the yard, or maybe the neighborhood as a whole. "Your domiciles are very close together here, and there are so many bystanders in your house. I trust the elves can defend themselves, but the destruction to your dwelling could be inconvenient."

Foes? Destruction?

"Yeah, we've already had our business destroyed today," I said. "I'd rather not see the house go up in smoke too."

"Perhaps there is an open area that we could use? Devoid of people?"

I eyed the glowing red eyes on the box, hoping it couldn't unleash a mob of predators capable of razing the city and eating citizens. "The park at the lake shouldn't have many people in it at night."

Maybe we could use the dog park where I'd battled a dragon months before. Just in case a chain-link fence would work to keep confined whatever Chasmmoor wanted to throw at me.

"Very well. I need a short time to prepare myself for the training, and then we can begin. I trust you have been studying the magical terms denoted on the scrolls you took images of?"

"Of course." I'd *looked* at them, at least. It had been a busy few weeks.

"Good. You will need to have them memorized." Chasmmoor handed the gargoyle box to Zav, then followed Dimitri into the house.

"You will perform excellently at the training, my mate." Zav wrapped an arm around my waist.

"I hope so." Was it my imagination, or did the eyes on the gargoyle box flare brighter? "Dwarves are long-lived. When one says he needs a *short time* to prepare himself, does that by chance mean hours?"

How long did I have to cram for this test?

"He will likely brush up on his summoning spells, since he is an enchanter by trade, not a mage. He must be able to control the creatures he orders forth from the box. But it should not take long."

"Ah. Can you put our gifts in the kitchen?" I pointed to the massive cleaver that I'd set down to accept the spices. "I need to have a quick chat with Freysha."

"Certainly." Zav stepped inside with the items but paused to sniff, then crinkle his nose at the smells wafting from the kitchen. "I will speak to the elves about what is appropriate to cook in the home of a dragon."

As he headed to the kitchen, I thought about pointing out that he didn't own or pay rent on this home, so it wasn't *his,* but I was more concerned about how quickly I could memorize that list of gibberish Freysha had translated for me.

CHAPTER 6

I PACED FREYSHA'S ROOM, INASMUCH AS I could with three elven sleeping bags—they looked more like green cocoons on the floor—and mumbled the foreign words on the list, trying to commit them to memory. They weren't as long and impossible to pronounce as dragon names, but there were more than twenty of them.

Freysha had translated them for me, and I remembered all of the *English* terms, but that wouldn't do anything. I'd already tried saying, "Defensive barrier," to my sword instead of *darayknar zerek*, but Chopper—*Storm*—had ignored that. Of course, saying the actual dwarven words hadn't done anything either, despite Freysha's assurance that my pronunciation was acceptable. With the more complex magics, she said, it would take learning a mental component in addition to simply speaking the words. Presumably, Chasmmoor would teach me that aspect.

"You will do fine." Freysha sat at her desk in front of a laptop displaying a railroad trestle she was designing for a class, but she kept glancing at me.

Maybe I was pacing too loudly. "Did you know he would bring a box that summons monsters?"

"I know little about dwarven weapons and how one is instructed to use them. I'm more familiar with their mining engineering and how they use keystones and arches in clever ways to hold up a great deal of weight."

"Yeah, I hear keystones are fascinating to elves."

She gave me a lopsided smile. "No. The only engineering that is *supposed* to be fascinating to elves is that done with magic and nature.

Even though you cannot build a railroad trestle out of living trees. My people do not transport as much freight over large distances as yours do, but it *is* done, particularly when establishing a new colony. They use only magic and the *evinya* birds to carry things. It is not practical."

I supposed she would be offended if I told her my fantasy-novel-reading self would find an elven world covered with train tracks to be extremely odd.

"My people do not welcome change," Freysha added, "particularly change that might come from the influence of other worlds. Father has humored my desire to learn goblin engineering—and now human engineering—but I know he would not give his approval if I wanted to return home and *build* something using my new knowledge. Even if I blended your technology with elven traditions to create new infrastructure that would be pleasing to all."

"That's your goal?"

"Yes. But if I want to build, even in such a blended way, I will have to leave our world. Mother has already said that, and even though Father wasn't as firm about it, I know he feels the same way. He is a traditionalist. All elves are. They see me as... an oddity." She sighed and looked toward the open door.

The sounds of elven voices drifted up, Zav's stern voice occasionally punctuating their chatter, as he no doubt told them that they had to make room in the smoker for a couple of racks of ribs. He was speaking in elven, so I couldn't be certain, but I knew him well enough to believe I was right.

I lowered the page of dwarven terms. "Is that why you're up here alone instead of down there with all of our cousins?"

Cousins that I couldn't even name. Freysha and Eireth had done introductions before we'd taken half of them off to Mom's cabin, but it had all been a blur.

"No," Freysha said quickly. Too quickly? "I just... have this homework assignment. It's due soon." She lowered her eyes, and her pale cheeks grew pink.

"Are you *lying* to me, Freysha?"

"I *do* have a homework assignment that must be completed by... a week from next Friday."

"Are you almost done?"

She hesitated. "Yes. I'm going over it to make sure it meets all of the professor's requirements."

I felt some weird older-sister urge to go down there and *make* our cousins play with her, but it probably wasn't that bad. When I'd been to the elven city, Freysha had led me through it and hadn't seemed ostracized in any way. Of course, I hadn't actually seen her hanging out with her peers. And her room *had* been a project-filled place where she clearly spent a lot of time. Was it possible that my sweet elven sister preferred hanging out with goblins because they accepted her quirks?

"Well… if you need any help with anything, let me know." Not that I knew how I could help her. As I'd told Amber not that long ago, it wasn't as if *I'd* ever fit in either.

"With the engineering project?"

"Oh, sure. You know how much I love protractors and compasses and…" That was the limit of engineering tools I knew about. "Things."

Freysha smiled. "A secret you've kept to yourself."

"My depths are vast and unplumbed." I frowned. Had I gotten that saying right? Probably not. "I just meant that I'd be happy to stand side by side with you and inform our elven relatives that you're a cool person that they shouldn't snub."

"I appreciate that, but given their feelings on half-bloods… it is unlikely they would allow your assessment of me to influence them."

"They're still calling me a mongrel, huh?"

"Not when Father can hear."

I snorted. "So just all the other times?"

"They will not insult you to your face." Freysha smiled. "They are somewhat afraid of you, now that you've bested an infamous assassin in battle."

"Oh, wonderful."

Shaking my head, I went back to memorizing the terms, but it was only a few minutes before a knock came at the door. Zav and Chasmmoor stood in the hallway, and Zav strode in carrying a plate. I assumed the dwarf had been the one to knock, since dragons were incapable of knocking or using doorbells. They went where they wished when they wished.

"It is time," Chasmmoor said, still wearing his armor and carrying his weapons, though he'd left his pack in Dimitri's room. "Lord

Zavryd'nokquetal informs me that it is winter in this part of your world. This is good. It will be dark many hours, and we will have plenty of time to train tonight. And in the nights that follow."

Meaning I wouldn't get to sleep at all for the next week? Unless I cat-napped during the day? Fun.

"That's good." My nerves returned full-force as I glimpsed the gargoyle box tucked under Zav's arm, though his steaming plate of food distracted me. The steak was normal enough for him, but the giant sauce-covered mushroom cap was out of place in one of his all-carnivore meals. And... "Is that a salad?"

"Elf fare." Zav sniffed. "They insisted on putting these items of low caloric value on the plate. You will consume the meat first. It will give you strength tonight. I made it myself." He handed the plate to me.

"You made me dinner?" I touched my chest as I accepted the plate. "With a plate and utensils and everything? Does this mean you think I might die tonight, and want to do something nice for me before I go?"

"I do not make food because *you* have the ring that enhances culinary skills. Also, you have not been enthusiastic when I have offered you delicacies in the past." Zav tilted his head. "I assumed you found my food preparation methods unappealing."

In the past, his offerings had been raw liver freshly plucked from a moose, a whole chicken—feathers still on—charred black from his direct-fire method of cooking, and some dubious animal he'd caught and similarly flambéed for me on Dun Kroth. It was possible I hadn't made enough appreciative noises as I'd eaten these dragon *delicacies*.

"I just like a few more seasonings on my meat. And for the inside to be as cooked as the outside. But this steak looks good."

"Excellent. I rubbed it in stone ash salt and ore of oregano before broiling it."

Chasmmoor cleared his throat. "Our time is not unlimited."

"Right." Without sitting down, I cut a few pieces of steak, tried some of the elven mushroom, and gave a thumbs-up to show I was ready. As the three of us headed downstairs, I spoke telepathically to Zav. *Are you coming along? I'm concerned that we might be unleashing horrible monsters that will escape into Seattle.*

I believe the horrible monsters will attack you. *Chasmmoor will instruct them thus.*

I guess that's okay.

SECRETS OF THE SWORD III

I will come along to ensure that you are not slain.
That's thoughtful of you.
I wish you to be alive for our wedding.
I wish that too.

Chapter 7

THE CITY HAD LAID FRESH sawdust and repaired the fence and the sign since the last time I'd been to the dog park. The trees that had suffered under Shaygorthian's flames had been trimmed so that little evidence of torched branches remained. I trusted the hole that Ti had dug to temporarily bury his chest of gold had also been filled in, with fresh grass planted over it. My tax dollars at work.

Chasmmoor seemed bemused by the twin gates I led him through to enter the dog park. Zav sneered at droppings smashed into the sawdust, and levitated himself over the fence to stand on a bench inside. I supposed if I were wearing shoes with decorative holes in them, I would be concerned about droppings too.

"This is an arena?" Chasmmoor waved at the flat area with benches at the bottom and wide timber-and-packed-dirt steps that led up a hill to the top.

"Yup. All kinds of ferocious wrestling and running goes on in here."

Thanks to the late hour, the chill, and a drizzle that had started up, there was nobody in sight. Now and then, a car drove past over on Green Lake Way, its headlights piercing the mist, but nobody turned toward the dog park.

Chasmmoor touched the stout wood of the covered sign, where posters of lost dogs were attached next to a bin of found dog leashes. "There may be damage."

"Let's go up there then." I headed toward the top of the hill, tapping my feline-shaped charm on the way.

Sindari materialized, looked around, then strode to catch up with me. *I remember this place. We battled a dragon.*

I think it's gargoyles tonight. Or some other odious monster. I couldn't have named the other beasts carved into the sides of Chasmmoor's box.

Truly? Leave it to Sindari to sound excited.

"You will not need a Del'nothian tiger companion," Chasmmoor said, following me up the hill.

Zav stayed on the bench, though he gave me a supportive nod when I looked back. That probably meant he believed I could handle this and wouldn't interfere unless my death was imminent.

"The foes you will face will be for you alone," Chasmmoor added, "to train and strengthen your bond with the blade while allowing you to practice the commands that summon its power."

"Sindari can cheer me on then." I stopped on top of the hill, making note of trees to hide behind if necessary. "Or comment critically on my failings."

I am adept at that, Sindari noted.

I've noticed.

Did you also notice that it is raining?

That's just a drizzle. You won't melt.

My fur mats when it gets damp.

I'll blow-dry you later.

Since you will need both feet for battle, I will not threaten to gnaw one off.

That's mature of you.

And regal.

Clearly. I took a deep breath and drew Chopper. No, *Storm*. I had to get used to calling it by its real name now that I knew it. *Thrallendakh yen Hyrek de Horak:* Lightning Harnessed from the Most Ferocious Storm. At least I'd managed to memorize that. The command terms on the list were fuzzy in my memory after the first five.

I glanced at my left palm—I'd taken a pen and written the hardest to remember and pronounce there earlier, but there wasn't enough light to see the ink scrawls. Dang, I should have foreseen that. Maybe we could move this to the tennis courts. Those had lights, didn't they?

But Chasmmoor had knelt a few steps away, his hand on the lid of the gargoyle box, and looked like he would open it any second. After he was done staring intently at it. Communing with the monsters inside?

Chasmmoor looked toward me. "Which commands are you already familiar with?"

"I've used *krundark, keyk*, and *eravekt*." Heat, cold, and illumination.

"With this first foe, you will practice *darayknar zerek*, the command to create a defensive barrier around the sword and its wielder."

"Oh, good." I knew that one.

"Are you prepared?" Chasmmoor looked critically at me—or maybe my lack of a fighting stance.

"We're starting now? No warmup first? What if I get a Charley horse?"

"You will say the words," Chasmmoor said, not cracking a smile, "and also focus on the sword and envision it protecting you. Do not strike the being that I summon. Simply defend against its attacks. Repetition will imprint the skill in your mind."

That went against my instincts, but this was training, not a real battle. I nodded firmly. "Got it."

Nervous and hoping not to embarrass myself, I shook out my arms, bent my knees, and readied Storm.

We can do this, buddy, I thought, then started repeating the command words over and over in my mind. Practicing.

Chasmmoor lifted the lid.

Hazy crimson light flowed out of the box, turning the green boughs of the nearby evergreens blood red. A smoky figure appeared in the haze, dark and blocky like a genie on steroids. It solidified into a two-legged golem-like creature that floated in the light above the box.

It grew and grew until it towered more than twenty feet above me. When it landed, the ground trembled, proving it was no illusion. It carried a giant club that it hefted over its blocky head as it stomped toward me.

The instincts I'd worried about reared up, and I sprang away as the huge club swung down toward me. As I evaded it, the blunt weapon slammed into the ground. Dirt flew, splatting against my cheeks as the hill and the trees shook. Pine needles rained down. The golem spun to face me again, knocking a thick branch off a tree as it raised its club again.

"Defend yourself," Chasmmoor said sternly. "Do not dodge."

As the golem swung its club again, I said the dwarven words flawlessly and envisioned a magical barrier forming around me, willing Storm to use its power to form it. The club whistled toward me. Was the barrier there? I couldn't sense it.

I said the words again, now doubting my pronunciation, then sprang to the side. If the command had failed, and I let the club hit me, it would shatter every bone in my body.

Storm flared blue. That was typical, but when that blue flare swelled and created a bubble all around me, that was new. The golem's club slammed into the ground—two feet outside of the range of the bubble. Dirt flew again. This time, it didn't hit me in the cheek. The barrier deflected it.

I was proud of the accomplishment, but Chasmmoor frowned.

"I said not to dodge," he said. "You will allow it to strike your defenses. Many times. You will learn what the barrier can take and how much you can enhance it by blending your inherent magic with that of the blade."

"Okay."

The golem, not pausing during this instruction, had already lifted its club again. As the tree-trunk-like weapon whistled toward my head, my instincts urged me to duck under it, then dart in and attack, but I made my feet root to the ground as I whispered the words repeatedly and focused on keeping that barrier up. It was easier now that there was a visible representation of the magic, but I still closed my eyes at the last moment as the club smashed down.

It struck the barrier three feet above my head. I winced, anticipating pain, since I'd been hurt back on Dun Kroth when the undead creatures had bashed at my personal defenses, but I didn't feel anything this time. Not the faintest bit of jarring pain.

The golem stumbled back. Storm blazed like a blue lightsaber.

Again, I had to wrestle against my natural desire to go on the offensive. The golem recovered, roared—I hoped the people in the houses on the other side of Aurora would assume that was traffic noise—and swung again.

The club bounced off the barrier. More roars rolled through the park as the golem swung again and again, attacking my barrier like a kid having a temper tantrum with a piñata that refused to break and spit out goodies.

After fifty or sixty blows, Storm's light faded slightly, and a strange weariness crept into my muscles. Using the magic had to be taking something out of me as well as the sword.

Even though I was standing still and not physically exerting myself, a familiar and irritating tightness came to my lungs. Damn it, I'd used my inhaler only an hour ago. I shouldn't need it again.

I repeated, *"Darayknar zerek,"* and willed my own energy to add strength to Storm's.

Chasmmoor had said something about that, hadn't he? I glanced over at him, wondering how many blows I had to take before passing the test. This golem was like a machine rather than a living being; if it was winded at all, I couldn't tell. Its roars certainly hadn't diminished.

"Shuuuut up!" came a yell from across two streets and somewhere near the lake.

That distracted me, and the barrier wavered. The golem lunged in, its club passing through the blue light, and I dropped and rolled away a split second before it would have brained me.

Swearing, I leaped up before it could turn to track me, and ran in and stabbed one of its fat legs. This needed to end.

But the golem's leg might as well have been made from solid steel. Storm barely bit in, and the wound didn't bleed.

Chasmmoor said something, and power surged from the box. The golem paused with its club up, clearly wanting to attack me, but magic and crimson light flowed out and wrapped around it.

I scrambled backward and, afraid I'd get in trouble for detouring from the script, whispered the command again. Energy seeped from my body, but Storm flared brighter, and the blue barrier re-formed around me.

The golem did not attack again. The hazy crimson light bathed it, and its shape de-solidified, turning to smoke that flowed back into the box. Chasmmoor closed the lid, and the only remaining light came from Storm.

A handy power to master, Zav spoke into my mind. *If you can command the sword to protect you from enemies, that will free you to use your own magic for other things.*

He'd gone from standing on the bench to sitting on it, and he looked like he was munching something. Maybe he'd brought a few steaks along.

Like wrapping my mate's enemies in entangling roots? It was one of the few spells I'd gotten good at.

That is always permissible.

"Rest for a moment," Chasmmoor said.

Gladly.

"If I must." Even though my mushy muscles urged me to collapse on the ground, I casually walked over to a bench and sat down like a lady.

That was odd to watch, Sindari said from a nearby spot, *and not nearly as interesting as a battle.*

I'm sorry my training is boring you.

You didn't need both feet to raise a barrier.

So you're regretting that you didn't gnaw one off?

Perhaps not. You did almost *need it. When it looked like you would fail to raise your defenses in time, I tried to spring in to bite that creature in the rump. The dwarf pinned me with his magic and forbade me to enter the arena.* Sindari's silver tail swished along the needle-strewn ground, a sign of his irritation. *Normally, I would not expect a mere enchanter to have the power to stop me, but he has a great deal of magic.*

Good to know they didn't send a second-rate dwarf to help me.

Do not vex him.

I'll try, but tamping down my vexation tendencies is difficult.

I've noticed.

Chasmmoor looked over, and I smiled as brightly as I could. "That was fun. Are we done for the night?"

"As you know, there is a substantial list of commands for that blade. The more you master, the more capable you will be in battle. For the sake of that great and ancient weapon, I will attempt to ensure you master *all* of the commands that were contained in the scrolls."

"But not all tonight, right?"

"We will practice four or five tonight, so we can work on perfecting them during subsequent nights."

Does that mean my performance tonight wasn't acceptable? I asked Sindari and wiped dirt from my cheeks.

I wouldn't call it perfect.

You guys are a tough crowd. I looked at Zav.

He waved a steak at me.

Chapter 8

It was almost four a.m. by the time Chasmmoor was done with me and Zav and I returned to the house. I stripped off my weapons and clothes, too tired to shower or even turn on a light, and flopped into bed.

Even though the first exercise hadn't involved actual battle, a number of the ones after that had, as Chasmmoor used that box of horror to summon everything from ogres to wolves to giant spiders to a flippered and finned beast that should have been in an aquarium. They'd all been designed to give me practice using the different powers that Storm offered. Among other things, I'd learned how to knock an enemy back with a blast of wind, magically increase my foot and hand speed, and command the sword to take control of my limbs to guide them in defense against opponents too challenging for me.

Some of those abilities I'd inadvertently called upon before, even without knowing the command words, but it was good to know that I could reliably activate them. Just as long as I didn't have to activate anything else tonight. Every muscle in my body ached. After the hours of torture that Chasmmoor had put me through, I peevishly wished Dimitri had made him sleep in the van. Friend of the dwarven king or not.

"You do not desire to mate?" Zav removed his robe and draped it neatly over a chair, then used a trickle of magic to pick my clothes off the floor, fold them, and rest them on the same chair. My tidy dragon.

Later, I would feel guilty for being too lazy to do that myself, but in addition to being fatigued, my whole body hurt. How many battles against how many monsters had I fought? Seven? Eight?

"Too tired," I mumbled, the side of my face mashed into a pillow. "Too sore. Aren't you tired?"

"I did not exert myself tonight."

"No, but you were awake and paying attention the whole time. I saw that. Thank you for coming."

"Even though I know Lord Chasmmoor is an accomplished enchanter and capable warrior, I believed there was a possibility that a monster would escape his control and might represent a true threat."

"So you were watching over me to keep me from being hurt?"

"Yes."

"I appreciate that. You're a good dragon. A good *fiancé*."

"I know this."

I snorted and smiled as Zav settled into bed beside me, nudging the blankets into lumps around the edge to form the sides of a nest. The first night we'd slept together and he'd done that, I'd woken up with nothing but a sheet to keep me from freezing. Since then, I'd purchased more blankets, including one made out of bamboo fiber—even though it felt like a normal blanket, it had amused me to think it might be a better *nesting* material than wool or cotton. I also kept a couple of backup blankets folded and stacked under the bed.

"You are sore from your battles?" Zav rested a gentle hand on my back.

"Yeah. I'll be hobbling in the morning, I'm sure." Everything from head to toe ached. Normally, my body healed quickly enough that I recovered from soreness from exercise by the next morning, but since dawn was only a few hours away, that might not be the case this time.

"Muscle exhaustion is not the same as a regular wound, but I will attempt to heal you."

"I would like that. Don't suppose I could talk you into a massage too." I closed my eyes, wanting to sink into oblivion, but I was still wound up and doubted I would fall asleep right away.

"A massage is… the manipulation of tissues, as by rubbing, kneading, or tapping, with the hand or an instrument for relaxation or therapeutic purposes," Zav said, as if reading from his pocket dictionary.

"Yeah, I guess we haven't covered that yet. Maybe your healing magic is safer." I doubted he would hurt me, but who knew how someone without any personal experience with a massage would interpret *manipulation of tissues*? "I'll massage you one night when I have more energy and show you the ropes."

"As with the feather?"

I laughed into the pillow, remembering how *that* encounter had gone. "It's slightly less erotic."

"Less? That is disappointing." Zav leaned over to his bedside table, turned on the light, and opened the drawer. "I have prepared the area for the next time we use feathers for foreplay."

"Oh?" I didn't know whether to be wary or intrigued… or if I wanted to open my eyes or not. What if the goblins had given him some weird sex toy made from bottle caps and duct tape?

Zav drew the largest feather I'd ever seen out of his drawer. Green with a blue sheen, it had been half-folded so it would fit. The faintest hint of magic clung to it, so minimal that I hadn't noticed it emanating from the bedside table before.

"Is that a roc feather?" I asked.

"Yes. I do not know if the magic will enhance its titillating effects, but it is sturdier than the feather we used last time."

"If you hadn't been thrashing around and enjoying yourself so much, you wouldn't have broken it."

He lowered his lashes for his bedroom-eyes look. "I *like* to enjoy myself."

I giggled, then felt silly because grown women weren't supposed to giggle, but he smiled, pleased by my response. Maybe I could muster some energy for sex after all…

But he returned the feather to the drawer—it took a few tries to get it to fit again—then turned off his light and rested his hand on my back. Warm tingles of magic spread from his fingers, and I closed my eyes, happy to let him soothe my aching muscles with his magic. It was as good as a massage, though now that I thought of it, we would have to experiment with tissue manipulation another time.

"Do you think I did okay tonight?" I asked quietly.

Chasmmoor hadn't been an enthusiastic coach. There'd been no encouraging shouts of *You can do it* or *You got this* as he unleashed his monsters on me. Not that I was a ten-year-old playing after-school volleyball and needed that, but I kept worrying that if he found my skills lacking—or he found *me* lacking—he would change his mind about the sword and take it back to his world. After all I'd been through with Storm, the idea of losing it now was heartbreaking. And I wouldn't even be able to fight to get it back. The dwarves were, after all, the rightful owners.

"I do not know precisely what Lord Chasmmoor wished to see, but I thought you performed adequately."

"I strive for adequacy," I muttered, though I wasn't truly insulted. Zav tended to state things as he saw them—I'd done all right tonight, but I hadn't been as brilliant and intuitive as I would have wished at grasping the new magics. That was fine. It would mean more when he gave me warm praise.

"None of the monsters slew you. Neither I nor Sindari nor Chasmmoor had to step in to assist you." He sounded pleased at that and patted my shoulder.

Already my muscles ached less. The warmth of dragon magic made even Zoltan's tinctures seem piddly in comparison.

"I'm relieved I wasn't slain." I was more concerned that I'd needed to use my inhaler several times during the night's training.

Feeling embarrassed, I'd gone off behind the trees so Chasmmoor wouldn't witness my weakness. After the third time, I'd resolved to make an appointment with my doctor, which should have set my mind at ease, but I worried that I might be advancing to some higher level of disease. Would I have to go live on the elven world with Freysha, where the air was cleaner? It would be hard to continue teaching Amber sword work if I wasn't on Earth.

"I will not allow you to be slain." Zav rested on his stomach beside me, the magic fading as he laid his arm across my back and closed his eyes. His aura lingered, familiar and always there, its power enrobing me. "Not when I've selected the appropriate prey to bring to Earth and have promised all the attending dragons that the hunt will be magnificent."

"Are you saying that my death would inconvenience your plans for Saturday?"

"It would be *extremely* inconvenient."

"Guess I'll try to stay alive then."

"Do."

He leaned over and kissed me, and I shifted to snuggle closer, relieved that my muscles didn't scream a protest.

Tomorrow, I will investigate the sanctuary, Zav said, switching to telepathy. *Last time, I did not scout it thoroughly and determine if its boundaries were sufficiently expansive for a hunt.*

Oh, there's room there for hunting. That female dragon who was after you had plenty of room to try to flambé Freysha and me.

Velilah'nav. He sniffed. *Were she still alive, she would not be invited to the wedding.*

Good.

Do you wish to come to the sanctuary with me?

I have a training session with Amber in the morning, and I need to figure out who threw the grenade at our shop. You can scope it out without me. Just make sure there's a nice scenic field somewhere.

I will ensure the sanctuary is appropriate for all aspects of our wedding. If it is not, the goblins will assist me in making it so.

Don't be bossy and push anyone around, please.

It is their honor to serve a dragon.

Uh huh. Offer to pay them to serve you.

The customs of this world are so strange.

Yeah. I kissed him and closed my eyes.

Zav fell asleep first. Despite my fatigue, I lay awake, worrying about everything and wondering if it was too late to call off the wedding. I wanted to marry Zav, but the fear that something awful would happen Saturday and that people would be hurt—or worse—wouldn't leave me.

I was finally on the verge of nodding off when some instinct urged me to use my senses to check outside the house for people—magical beings—who shouldn't be there. Someone was, someone with the notable aura of a full-blooded elf.

One of my guests out on a walk? In the dark?

The aura was familiar, but my breath caught when I realized *why* it was familiar. Not because it belonged to one of my houseguests, but because it was another elf that I'd encountered before. The assassin Varlesh Sarrlevi.

I checked three times, hoping I was wrong, but I wasn't. He was across the street, near the bushes where he'd stood once before to spy on the house.

I licked my lips. Zav had his arms wrapped around me, so there was no way Sarrlevi would try anything. Not *now*. But why was he here? Was it possible I'd been wrong and he *had* attacked the coffee shop to get back at me? Maybe he'd put his honor aside out of rage and bitterness from the stories the fae queen had been telling.

Damn it, I'd sent her a bunch of chocolate—*good* chocolate—per our agreement. Why was she out there stirring up trouble?

After debating whether to wake up Zav, I eased out of his arms. I put on a robe, padded to the window, and parted the curtains. I would check on Sarrlevi first.

The lights around Green Lake gleamed yellow in the distance, and a closer streetlamp shed illumination on the intersection. If not for my senses, I wouldn't have been able to pick out the cloaked figure blending into the bushes between two of the neighboring houses. From his spot, Sarrlevi had a clear view of our front yard... and my turret bedroom on the front of the house.

His dark hood was up, no hint of his short blond hair visible, so I couldn't tell if he was looking at me, but he didn't react to me parting the curtains. With his elven night vision, he could have seen them stir if he'd been looking this way.

A car drove past, tires splashing through puddles and drawing my eye. When I looked back, Sarrlevi was gone. He'd disappeared from my senses too.

"Well, isn't this a wonderful new development?" I murmured.

CHAPTER 9

I WOKE UP TO OBNOXIOUS BUZZING from my bedside table. My phone. A loud tapping accompanied it, a woodpecker or some other bird attacking the home's wood trim.

Gray daylight filtered in through the curtains, but I didn't realize how late it was until I picked up my phone to check the time and see who was calling. Zav had gotten up earlier, and my senses put him down in the kitchen with a bunch of elves, though not the whole pack. Eireth and his bodyguards were gone. Exploring the neighborhood? Hopefully, they would keep caps over their ears and attempt to blend in.

"Amber?" I croaked to answer the phone and noticed that a stream of texts had come in from her while I'd been sleeping. She'd been asking what time we were meeting for our sword practice. Even though I wasn't as sore as I'd expected, my beleaguered body clenched at the idea of doing more with a sword.

"No, it's the gnome under her bed that uses her phone," came a typical sarcastic response.

"No kidding. Do gnomes have to pay rent?"

"Ha ha. Why didn't you answer my texts? You sound like crap. Were you out drinking last night?"

"I wish my night had been that sedate. I had to battle monsters that a dwarf conjured out of a box to help me harness the magical powers of my ancient dragon-slaying blade."

"You know I'd really prefer it if you just said you'd been drinking."

"Sorry. As you've pointed out *many* times, I'm not normal."

I sat up and swung my legs over the side of the bed. My head pounded, making me wonder if I *had* been drinking and had blacked out and forgotten about it. No, the hangover was from focusing so hard and trying to use my magic to enhance Storm's powers. And the pecking at the house wasn't helping.

"I know," Amber said, "but I keep hoping for growth and change."

I lumbered over to the window, opened it, stuck my head out, and caught a northern flicker hanging from the siding under the eaves of my turret. The big bird had a spotted chest, a black bib, and a long black beak that was succeeding in pecking a hole in the trim.

"Knock it off, or my fiancé will roast and eat you," I told him.

The flicker tilted his head in consideration but didn't seem to find me that threatening.

"I also have a sword capable of beheading werewolves, trolls, ogres, and pesty birds." I made stabbing motions out the window with my arm.

That alarmed him enough to fly off to a nearby tree and call me unkind things in bird language.

"It's a vain hope, I'll admit," Amber grumbled.

"Huh?" I closed the window.

"I've got a study group this afternoon. Can we get our practice out of the way soon?"

"Yeah." I still needed to get down to Nin's to give her that grenade fragment to check, but I could squeeze Amber in first. Too bad her house was in the opposite direction. Unless... "Any chance you want to come down here to practice?"

I sensed Eireth and his bodyguards coming back into my range. They were a good half mile away, wandering through the neighborhood.

"I guess I can."

"You can meet your grandfather." I'd wanted a chance to introduce them. This would be perfect. They could get any drama and awkwardness out of the way before the wedding.

"Uh." Amber didn't sound tickled by my plan.

"It'll be fun. Or at least an interesting and educational cultural experience."

"Will you pay me?"

"Pay you to meet your relatives?"

"To be cordial and nice," Amber said. "Dad pays me to be nice to *his* parents."

"He *pays* you? If I call him, will he corroborate that?"

"Yeah. But technically, he pays by taking me to Red Robin to get a mud pie afterward. He says I'd have to file taxes if he paid me actual money. I think that's just an excuse for him to be cheap though."

I snorted. Thad was enough of a stickler for bookkeeping that he probably *would* file taxes for Amber if she made any money.

"I'll give you… How do you feel about *lytasha*?"

"What the hell is that?"

"An elven delicacy." Or so I'd been told. There was a pan of it on the kitchen counter. It smelled like a lavender satchel had been mauled by a pine cone before being mixed into the batter, which hadn't enticed me to try it.

"Ew, I only take cash or mud pies, Val."

"Fine, I'll owe you a mud pie." If I had to take her to Red Robin, it would be an excuse for mother-daughter bonding time. Assuming she didn't make me sit at another table and just send the bill in my direction.

"Deal. I'll be there in an hour."

***

My muscles had warmed up by the time I was trading practice lunges and parries with Amber in the backyard, but despite taking far more than the recommended maximum dose of ibuprofen, my head was still throbbing. The idea of a week's worth of nights spent with Chasmmoor torturing my body and mind filled me with angst, and I imagined myself hobbling down the aisle at my wedding, unable to keep up with Zav.

Amber stepped back and lifted a hand for a break. The sky was gray, with a chilly breeze rattling bare branches in the trees, but sweat gleamed on our foreheads.

"I can't concentrate when there are creepy people watching us." Amber tilted her head toward the conservatory attached to the back of the house, where four elves were inside with Freysha as she pointed out native Earth species she was growing and what medicinal qualities she'd discovered in the plants.

"They're not watching us," I said, though I'd also caught the elves peering through the clear glass walls from time to time. We were making a lot of noise with our practice swords, so it wasn't surprising. "They're playing with Freysha's plants."

"The blond one keeps staring at me."

"They're all blond."

"The *really* blond one." Amber scowled over her shoulder toward the conservatory.

"That's one of King Eireth's bodyguards. He's probably determining if you're a threat." I'd had a telepathic conversation with Eireth when Amber had been on the way to the house and asked him to come meet her, but to wait until we were done with our session. I'd told him I hadn't wanted her to be too distracted to train, but mostly, I was hoping to wear her out so she would be too tired to be lippy. Wishful thinking there.

"Not as long as someone gives me a mud pie." Amber shook one of her arms and rubbed her shoulder. "I think I tweaked something. Can we call it a day? I've got a swim meet next weekend."

I thought about suggesting footwork drills that wouldn't bother her shoulder, but we'd been at it for an hour. Since I was nervous about the introduction between grandfather and granddaughter, I wasn't in a hurry to end our practice, but it would be better to get awkwardness out of the way sooner rather than later.

Maybe I would get lucky, and it *wouldn't* be awkward. Fat chance given how *my* first meeting with Eireth had gone. At least Zav wasn't here to talk about mating habits. He was still at the goblin sanctuary ensuring it would be suitable for our wedding needs. More specifically, suitable for the needs of dozens of dragons who seemed to be coming for the entertainment value more than any interest in seeing Zav and me wed.

Before he'd left, I'd thought about telling him about seeing Sarrlevi, but I'd started to doubt if the elf had truly been there. It was possible I'd dozed off and only dreamed of getting out of bed and spotting him. Maybe.

"Sure. I can get you a tincture to help your shoulder heal faster if you want." I glanced toward the steps leading to the basement. Zoltan's magical cannon was still guarding the door, so slipping in to raid his shelves wouldn't be wise, but I had some of his alchemical formulas in the upstairs bathroom.

"A tincture?" Amber curled her lip. "Like Bengay?"

"Bengay with magic. It's more effective. Wait here, and I'll grab it." I waved her to one of the garden benches.

Dimitri and I hadn't yet gone shopping for a patio table and chairs, in part because it was winter, and in part because I worried that Zav would be tempted to resume his habit of landing on such chairs and demolishing them.

I grabbed the tincture from the bathroom and was on my way back downstairs when the doorbell rang. My senses told me it was Inga, our part-time half-troll employee and Reb's foster mother. She'd never come to our house before. Since she wasn't my biggest fan, I doubted she had come to see me, but Dimitri was working on repairs at the shop, so I opened the door for her.

"Ruin Bringer." Inga's broad shoulders hunched, and her fingers curled into fists. A cloud of irritation hovered around her, and I thought she'd come to beat the snot out of me for some reason.

"It's Val, and how can I help you?" I kept my voice cordial but wondered if I should have brought Storm to the door with me.

"Reb's missing."

"Oh? Did he say anything before disappearing?"

"No."

"Do you think he was kidnapped? Or did he run away?"

It was hard to imagine anyone wanting to kidnap the surly boy. But Reb butted heads often with Inga—and anyone who wanted to exude authority over him and help him grow into a responsible troll adult—so I could envision him taking off after an argument.

"I don't know." Inga shook one of her fists in agitation as if she was looking for something to punch.

I thought about moving Freysha's flower pots to the other side of the porch.

"He's been gone since yesterday," Inga added. "He didn't take any of his things."

"What things does he have?"

The kid was an orphan and had been wearing rags when Inga had taken him in a few months earlier.

She lifted her chin. "I am a good surrogate mother. I've purchased him the necessities. Learning supplies, a punching bag, clean clothes, and LEGO Mos Eisley Cantina and LEGO Minecraft The Zombie Cave."

"Those *are* the necessities."

"I am also saving to buy him an Xbox. Children are very expensive. I am doing the best I can."

I lifted a hand. "I know, and I didn't mean to imply you aren't a good mother. I'm glad you took him in, and he'll be grateful too one day. The trolls were treating him poorly."

"*Yes*," she said with fervor in her eyes. "But he does not remember, or he doesn't care that they are bullies. He sometimes wants to go be with the males that run in gangs and make trouble. He misses his father. I do not know how to replace his father."

"You can't. You can just help him grow and be safe."

"He *was* safe." Rare anguish flashed in her eyes. "I think someone took him. He would not have run away without his belongings."

Not without the LEGOs anyway. I'd seen him carrying those around before. "Did it happen before or after the bombing of our coffee shop?" I thought of the troll boy I'd spotted in the alley after the explosion. "Maybe it's tied together."

"I'm not sure. I was working at my fence-enchanting job in Woodinville, and he did not have a shift at the Coffee Dragon." Another person who called it that instead of the Sable Dragon. Maybe Dimitri should order a new sign when he put in his order for drywall and repair materials. "The neighbor, Sasha, looks in on him when I am gone. There are no daycare options for troll children, and my boss doesn't let me bring Reb to work."

She sounded defensive, as if I would blame her for not being there twenty-four-seven to keep an eye on him. As if I could judge other people's parenting skills when I'd been absent for so much of Amber's childhood. Besides, trolls were a special situation, and Reb was independent and had been on the streets, taking care of himself for weeks before Inga had taken him in.

"Sasha said he was there at breakfast and gone at lunchtime when she checked in."

I closed my eyes, trying to remember what time the bombing had taken place. Early afternoon. The timing was a little suspicious, but I had a hard time believing Reb could have had anything to do with the incident. We paid him to work there a few hours a week, he got free milkshakes, and he enjoyed hanging out with the goblins. But that troll boy lurking in the vicinity niggled at my mind and made me want to believe Reb's disappearance and the bombing were related.

"That isn't that unusual," Inga continued. "But he *always* comes back for dinner. I am a good cook." Her eyes narrowed. "Even without a special ring."

I blinked. Was Zav telling *other* people about that? I'd heard him promise Chasmmoor that I could make him ribs and that they were good, but I hadn't guessed he was bragging about my meat-smoking skills to everyone.

"Good to know," I said.

"I searched the neighborhood for Reb. I thought he might have been playing with friends and stayed over..." Inga frowned, clearly suggesting that wasn't allowed. "But when he wasn't back this morning, I knew to worry. I searched *everywhere* and asked a few friends with troll blood if they'd heard anything. They hadn't."

"Have you checked with any of the local troll gangs?"

Her lips thinned. "I do not know where they're hanging out right now. They don't keep me updated. They don't have any interest in half-trolls, especially since my mother died."

Had her mother been the troll in the family? I wondered how that hookup had happened and if her father was still alive. Inga rarely shared details about herself, so I had no idea.

She gazed past me, maybe sensing the elves in the house. "Your... elven kin accept you?"

"Not really, but my father came for the wedding, and he brought some of my half-cousins along. I gather they wanted a chance to see Earth."

"Still... they are willing to be in your presence." A hint of wistfulness softened her craggy face. "I am envious of even this level of acceptance." Her forehead creased as she focused on someone walking down the stairs behind me.

I glanced back in time to see one of the male elves wandering barefoot into the dining room wearing... *hell*, was that my Hobbit nightshirt? Had he been raiding my *closet*?

No, I realized. I'd left it and some other clothes folded on top of the dryer the day before. I rubbed my temple, worried about what else I would see on one of my cousins. There had been underwear in that stack of laundry. Sexy underwear that Zav liked.

"Don't be too envious," I muttered.

Inga shook her head. "This is not important now. I must find Reb. I have been looking since before dawn, and I would not come for help if I were not desperate." Her grimace implied that she would rather gnaw off some of her limbs than ask the *Ruin Bringer* for help.

"I'll help. I've got some research to do today, but it may tie in. I'll let you know if I find anything, and if I don't, I'll help you search the streets for him."

"Good. May the beasts leave your cave unbothered."

That was a troll saying, and probably as close as I would get to a *thanks*.

Inga bowed and stalked away, still looking like she wanted to punch something. She eyed one of the dragon topiaries when she passed it, but its eyes flared orange, and smoke wafted from its nostrils. If she'd been thinking about lashing out, she reined in the urge and instead kicked a branch that the wind had blown onto the sidewalk.

I fished in my pocket for the grenade fragment and texted Nin to see if she was at the shop and I could come by. While waiting for a response, I remembered Amber's shoulder and the tincture and headed to the backyard. Only to lurch to a stop before I reached the door. Eireth had returned to the property, and I sensed him outside with Amber.

My walk turned to a jog—no, more of a sprint—as I hurried out to make sure she wasn't offending him or getting me ostracized from the elven home world.

Eireth stood on the patio with his hands clasped behind his back, his face stoic and hard to read as two of his bodyguards lurked a few feet behind him. Amber stood in front of him showing him the magical short sword Willard had lent her.

"Hey, guys." I smiled and waved to hide my nerves. "How's it going?"

Amber shrugged. "I'm trying to get the scoop on why you're not a princess and why *I'm* not a princess." She squinted at Eireth, who'd no doubt given her a political answer that hadn't used the words *mongrel* or *tainted human blood*.

"Freysha has that job. Morning, Eireth. How was your outing?"

The guards scowled at each other. Maybe I wasn't supposed to use his name, *his majestic elfness* being the preferred address from mongrel children.

Eireth inclined his head toward me. "Not without incident, but we managed to avoid having to draw our weapons."

That wasn't the answer I'd hoped for.

"Apparently," Amber said, "they tried to get a froyo at Menchie's and didn't know you have to pay. And the guy at the register didn't know that elven royalty is supposed to eat free."

"I had forgotten that currency is required to acquire food here," Eireth said. "We were forced to hunt at the park, which also caused a ruckus. Human passersby yelled at us and said shooting squirrels and ducks there is forbidden." He tilted his head. "Is that true? There were a great many very plump water fowl. It seemed that the flock needed culling. I did not know if we were truly disobeying the law, or if they were treating us unfairly because of our foreign dress—and foreign ears."

"No hunting in the city parks. It is a rule." I dug into my pocket for some money. "Sorry, Eireth. I should have foreseen those problems. And should have given you a rundown of the customs here." I doubted he'd spent much time in the city when he'd visited Earth before. Even today, the old elven sanctuary was remote; it must have been really far removed from suburban sprawl back in the seventies, before the population of the county had tripled. "I've been distracted and haven't been a good host."

"That is forgivable. I understand your place of work was attacked."

"Among other things, yes. I don't technically do much work there since I'm only a ten-percent owner and busy hunting down criminals for Willard. Mostly, I just show up to loom menacingly when needed. And I give Dimitri money to fix things." I made a mental note to stop at the bank and replenish my cash supply on the way to Nin's.

Eireth accepted the twenties that I pressed into his hand, though he appeared bemused by them. The bodyguards stepped in close, and I tensed. What, did they think I was handing him poisoned money that would slowly kill him?

They extended their palms, and it took me a moment to realize what they wanted. Snorting, I gave each of them a twenty. I might have given them more, but the elves in the conservatory filed out and got in line, also holding out their palms.

Who knew elves were so interested in frozen yogurt? Didn't they know it was winter?

More of my guests that had been in the house also appeared, making me suspect a telepathic message about me acting as a broken ATM spitting twenties was going around. One of the hands that stuck out belonged to Amber.

"Nice try," I said, catching myself before I put money in it. "You're getting a mud pie. Assuming you've been personable."

"I've been *super* personable. I haven't made fun of anyone, even if someone who wants to combine carrot-cake-oreo-cookie froyo with a meal of squirrels and ducks is extremely deserving of mockery. You should give me a couple hundred for so nobly refraining."

Eireth smiled slightly. That was promising. He was so reserved that it was hard to tell what he was thinking, but at least he didn't seem offended by his ten minutes with Amber.

"Uh huh." A text came in from Nin, saying that she was at the food truck and mentioning that Thad was visiting. Good. I could drop off Amber with him instead of driving her back home. "Want to get some beef and rice, Amber?"

She rolled her eyes. "Dad brings that home *all* the time. I get that they're dating, but it's not necessary to have that same meal four times a week."

"Nin likes to give friends food. It's her way of sharing her love."

"Can't she come up with some other menu items?"

"Squirrel, perhaps?"

"Never mind. Suea rong-hai is fine."

"I thought it might be."

CHAPTER 10

"Hm," Nin said for the third time as she examined the grenade fragment under a magnifying glass. An unused grenade rested on the counter next to it for comparison.

Thad and Amber were outside, noshing on beef and rice at one of the benches. Despite her complaining earlier, Amber had accepted a package of food without a word. Maybe she'd been hungry enough after our training not to be picky. Or maybe the discussion we'd had in the Jeep on the way down had stirred her appetite, a musing of whether Menchie's should add squirrel as a topping for their elven visitors.

"You can sense the magic in the fragment, right?" I stood behind Nin in the tiny shop on the back end of her food truck, the inner door ajar, so we could hear her assistant cooking and taking orders. The lunch rush was on, and Nin had warned me she might have to leave to help. "*Familiar* magic."

"If you are implying that this might have been one of *my* grenades..." Nin squinted closer at the fragment. "You may be correct."

"Huh."

After a few more seconds, Nin sighed and put down the fragment and magnifying glass. "This was used to blow out the wall in our shop? I am deeply distressed. Dimitri informed me that many people were hurt. I am relieved that nobody was killed."

"Me too." I refrained from making a joke about how deaths were bad for business.

Nin's expression was too grim as she surveyed her little workshop, tools hanging on pegboards and boxes under the counter overflowing with parts.

"As a manufacturer of magical weapons, I am, of course, aware that what I create can be used to kill, and I sometimes have doubts that I am doing the right thing in employing my grandfather's knowledge this way."

"As someone who buys and uses your weapons and ammunition to do *good* against criminals preying on innocent people, I'm glad you do it."

She smiled, but it was fleeting. "I do try to sell to customers that I believe are unlikely to use the weapons for criminal activities, but it is sometimes difficult to tell. As you know, this side business is under-the-table. Many of my customers are from the magical community and do not officially exist, so it is impossible to do background checks on them."

"Do you keep any records about who buys what?" I thought I'd seen her scribble down notes about my orders before.

"Yes. I do thorough bookkeeping for accounting purposes." Nin knelt and rummaged in a low metal drawer.

"Can you tell me who's been buying your grenades lately?"

"Besides you?"

"Yeah. I'd know if I'd blown up my own coffee shop. Even if I only own ten percent, I'm partial to it."

Nin drew out a ledger, opened it, and ran her finger down rows with people's names—or at least descriptions of anonymous buyers—and what they'd purchased and for how much.

"When I first opened my food-truck business in this country, I saw the potential immediately, but I also saw that it would take many years to reach my goals. I *still* have not earned quite enough to purchase a house and move my family from Thailand. I am very close, but the cost of a house keeps going up, so sometimes, it feels as if… what is the American phrase?"

"Someone's moving the goalposts?"

"That is football, yes?"

"Yeah. Or maybe you feel like Charlie Brown with Lucy yanking out the football as he goes to kick it."

The crinkle to her forehead suggested that Charlie Brown comics hadn't been a big part of her childhood. "Moving the goalposts, yes. I was always very patient and willing to work hard for many years to achieve my dreams, but I also realized that my grandfather's teachings could be useful, and when I learned that there were few weapons being made in this area that could handle dangerous magical beings... it seemed that I could be useful *while* growing my income and establishing myself in this country. The weapons-making business has been *much* more profitable than my food truck, but perhaps it was a mistake to allow myself to seek profits in such an industry."

Her finger had paused on a name in the book, but she had stopped reading the page. Her eyes had a distant look as she gazed toward a pegboard.

"I knew the weapons could be used to harm people," she continued, "but I did not envision them threatening friends or non-magical beings. I believed the magical community would most likely fight amongst themselves. Not that I wished to encourage that, but since they would be doing it anyway..." She sighed and shook her head. "I am making excuses, justifying the business that I chose to get into. Perhaps it is time for me to retire from this work, Val."

"Uh, except for making stuff for *me*, right?" I kept my tone light, hoping to pull her out of her funk. This wasn't her fault.

"I am certain I could continue to supply you."

"Good. Anything in the notebook?"

"Recently, I have only sold grenades to your employer—"

"Willard?"

"Yes. And also to yourself..."

I nodded. I'd ordered a backpack full before going to the fae realm.

"And to a couple of officers in the Seattle Police Department who were planning a raid on a werewolf pack running drugs up from Mexico—that is what they told me. Those are the only recent sales of grenades. Perhaps the miscreant got a magical grenade from someone else."

"But you said that's from one of *your* grenades." I pointed to the fragment.

She winced, as if she didn't wish to be reminded. "Yes."

"Have you sold to any trolls lately?"

"Not grenades and not weapons that I can recall. You suspect a troll?"

I told her about the boy I'd seen and that Reb was missing. "But if it *was* a troll—or trolls," I mused, "why would they target our coffee shop? Their people come in too. There were trolls drinking there when the explosion happened."

"Is it possible that there are specific trolls who wish to harm you? Or any businesses that you have a concern in?"

It was my turn to wince. "That people are targeting me has crossed my mind several times. Trust me."

A light knock sounded on the inner door, and Nin's assistant leaned in. "Excuse me, but do we have any more of the secret sauce?"

"Yes. In the cabinet by the RiceMaster." Nin smiled—her first genuine smile—as she said RiceMaster, still appreciative of her gift from Thad.

I decided not to point out that if they got married and she moved in with Thad, there would be plenty of room there for her extended family. He had six bedrooms *and* an office, not to mention the mother-in-law apartment over the garage. I smirked at the idea of how vehemently Amber would protest that many strangers invading her house. She hadn't even wanted Thad to have a girlfriend sleep over now and then.

Since Nin and Thad didn't seem to be that far along on their dating adventures, I wouldn't suggest it, unless I needed a reason to torture Amber later. It wasn't wrong to torture one's teenage daughter, was it? It seemed fair.

The assistant paused as she was ducking out and pointed at the grenade. "Are those okay? There were a bunch on the floor when I returned with groceries yesterday morning."

"On the floor?" Nin blinked.

"Yes. Right before that, I saw someone big trying to get the door open, but he ran away when someone jogged past with a dog. He wore a parka, so I didn't see his face, and it didn't look like he'd gotten in—the door was still locked. But then those were lying on the floor, so I wasn't sure."

"That sounds suspicious," I said.

The assistant spread her hands. "None of our food or money was missing, so it didn't seem worth calling the police about. I put those away, then got busy with food prep and forgot about it. Sorry, I should have remembered to tell you."

Nin pulled out a box that held the grenades and removed them one at a time, lining them up on the floor.

"I hope none were damaged." The assistant chewed on her lip and repeated, "I should have told you."

Busy counting, Nin did not answer. I waited patiently, having no idea how many she usually kept in stock.

She finished her count, frowned, and counted again, pointing a finger to each grenade. Then she pulled out another box with only three in the bottom and shook her head vigorously, her blue ponytail flopping.

"This is outrageous." Nin lurched to her feet. "There are fifteen missing."

I'd been afraid of that.

"But the door and window were still locked." The assistant pointed to the open window where someone was waiting for her order.

"Do not worry about it," Nin said. "We will figure it out. Please attend to the customers."

"Maybe what she saw was someone scoping things out," I said. "The guy could have come back later—or even used telekinesis to float the grenades out later in the day when nobody was looking."

"How it was done does not matter. I have been robbed, and my grenades have been used against our establishment." Nin shook her head grimly.

I didn't point out that only *one* had been used and fourteen more were missing. She already knew.

I stepped outside for more room, ducked behind the truck for privacy, and summoned Sindari. While he formed in silver mist, I walked around the truck, eyeing the exterior and underneath it in case the burglar had left behind any clues that might identify him. Or her. If the culprit had been wearing a parka with the hood up, the assistant couldn't have known for sure.

Nothing so condemning as a lost ID or a tuft of white troll hair stuck in a hinge presented itself.

Do you need assistance with something? Sindari's telepathic tone was dry.

Probably because I was on my knees peering between the truck's tires.

For you to track someone if possible. At some point yesterday, someone stole fifteen of Nin's grenades. One of the grenades may have been used on our shop, so I'd like to find whoever took them. Especially if the thief planned to put the rest of those grenades to use trying to get at me or those I cared about.

Would the defenses Zav and Dimitri had put up around our house keep a magical explosive from getting through? I thought so, but Mom's cabin had fewer defenses, only a couple of Dimitri's enchanted yard-art statues. Thad's house didn't have any magical defense at all. Then there was the wedding... and all the *guests* who would be at the wedding. What if someone attacked then and ended up killing someone? Like Eireth? What kind of horrific consequences would there be if the elven king were killed on Earth? At *my* wedding?

"Shit. We've got to find this guy, Sindari."

Can you be more specific about what kind of guy I am searching for? There are many, many scents in this area. Sindari walked from the back of the truck to the front, sniffing the air.

It might have been a troll. I wished I *had* found a lock of hair. He would have a much easier time tracking someone if he had the specific scent.

Ah. One moment.

A woman's shriek came from the front of the truck. "A tiger!"

"It's huge!" a man yelled.

"Get the police!" That came amid the sound of stampeding feet.

"Get the *dog* catcher!" someone else yelled from farther away.

I swore, lurched to my feet, and rushed around the truck. Why hadn't I thought to tell Sindari to employ his magical stealth?

Nin's assistant leaned out the window holding a packet of beef and rice and watched with downturned lips as the customers raced out of the square. Only Amber and Thad remained, wearing jackets and scarves as they sat at the bench, Thad watching the scene with his mouth dangling open, Amber barely reacting.

"Sorry, Nin," I said as she appeared in the window next to her assistant.

Sindari sat under the awning, his tail wrapped around his feet to avoid puddles. *Dog catcher? Really.*

"You should probably use your camouflaging magic any time I bring you out in the city," I told him.

To avoid being insulted? Yes, I see that is the case. I have found the scent of a troll.

"Already? Good."

I warn you that it is faint, the scent more than a day old.

"Can you track it?"

I can attempt to do so. If we are fortunate, he did not go far.

I grimaced, deeming that unlikely. If he'd been the one to throw the grenade at our coffee shop in Fremont, he'd crossed a lot of miles. But maybe he had a hideout in this area.

"Val?" Nin could only hear half of the conversation.

I waved at Sindari. "We've got the trail of a troll. We'll see if we can hunt him down."

"Thank you. I will be most distressed if my grenades are used to further harm our friends."

Or my father. Or my mother or Thad or Amber.

CHAPTER 11

A CHILLY RAIN PICKED UP AS I trailed Sindari along the sidewalks of Seattle with the Space Needle looming nearby. Sindari gave me a few flat looks over his shoulder. *Why is it never glorious and sunny when you call me forth to this land?*

It's sunny in the summer. Sometimes. This is winter.

There is supposed to be snow in the winter, not rain.

Snow is better than rain?

It is less damp. Sindari paused and shook water droplets from his coat, accidentally—or maybe not so accidentally—splattering my cheeks.

I wiped my face. *I would think a regal tiger such as yourself could dry himself with the power of his magic.*

My magic is for hunting down and ruthlessly slaying enemies. Also, my tundra homeland is not as wet as this. He waited for a gap between cars and sprang across a busy street.

Noting a police SUV parked farther down the block, I waited at the intersection for the crosswalk sign to ding. *Such a strange way to track enemies.*

A rumble floated down from the nearby monorail, one of the small trains trundling past on its way from the Space Needle to Westlake Mall. The signal changed, and I jogged to catch up with Sindari. He was trotting in the direction of the elevated tracks.

My phone buzzed with a call from Willard.

"Hey, Will. What's up?"

"*Will?* Not only do you not address me by my appropriate rank, but now you're shortening my name?"

"You're planning my wedding. I figured we were besties by now."

"None of my *besties* call me Will."

"That's probably because they know your first name."

She grunted. "Few do. I've had my agents gathering gossip and trying to figure out who might have been behind the attack on the coffee shop."

"Any leads?"

"Nothing concrete, but you'll be pleased to know that most of the magical community in the city feels affronted."

"On my behalf?"

"On the behalf of your business. The Coffee Dragon—that's what they're calling it, by the way—is considered *the* place for their kind to gather now."

"I know. I'm going to tell Dimitri to change the name on the sign."

"There are people threatening to beat up the evil-doers who blew out the wall if they can find them. I heard a rumor that some ogres are thinking of volunteering to stand watch around the clock to ensure the building won't be attacked again."

"Dimitri will be touched. I have a bit of a lead. Trolls may have been responsible." I told her about the boy I'd seen, the grenade fragment, and the grenade theft. "Sindari and I are tracking a troll through Seattle now."

A bus roared past, spraying a wave from a puddle. Some of it hit Sindari, and he sprang aside like a cat that had gotten its tail caught under a rocking chair. He roared in irritation at the retreating bus.

Sorry, buddy. I hurried to Sindari's side and patted his wet back. *I'll find you a towel later. Or I'll have Zav breathe on you.*

Breathe fire?

I'm sure fire dries fur quickly.

Fire incinerates fur.

One would think he could modulate his flames from an incineration setting to a blow-dry setting.

I doubt it, but it might be amusing to hear you suggest that to him.

"Val?" Willard asked, and I realized I'd missed something.

"Sorry. A bus drove by and soaked Sindari. He's peeved."

"I would be too. I had some troll information come by my desk earlier in the week, so I pulled it out. There's a new underground club in Seattle that's popped up to replace Rupert's. It's called the Bloody Blade and is dedicated to booze and brawling. I don't have a location yet."

"It doesn't come up on Google Maps, huh?"

"The closest my searches gave me is the Blade and Timber."

"That's the axe-throwing place, right?"

"The human-run axe-throwing place, yes. I believe blood is discouraged there."

"It wouldn't interest trolls then," I said.

"I'll see if I can get you an address in case you want to visit and pummel trolls until they spill the beans."

"You know my style well."

"It's not subtle. I'll text you as soon as I have it. You'll want to get this resolved before your wedding."

"Especially with the elven king and the dragon queen coming, I know."

"Especially with *me* coming," Willard said. "I'll be wearing that knockout bridesmaid dress, remember. I don't want it covered with mud and blood and soot from explosives."

"I'll make your dress's safety my priority."

Someone driving a minivan honked at Sindari. He was on the sidewalk, so he wasn't impeding traffic, but some people liked to gamble with their lives. He paused and leveled a cool stare at the driver, as if he were contemplating springing onto the van, clawing the roof open, and chewing on the occupants.

It could be a fan, I told him telepathically after saying goodbye to Willard. *Sometimes, people honk when they like something.*

Fans would not make such a loud and offensive noise. Del'nothian tigers have sublime auditory senses. I can hear a vole munching on a tuber from a mile away.

Next time I need eavesdropping done, I'll call you.

You have a need to eavesdrop on tuber-munching voles?

If they're plotting odious crimes while they munch, yes.

Sindari led us under the monorail tracks to one of the cement pillars supporting them. His ears flattened as another train rumbled past above, heading in the opposite direction.

Tracking in your city is loathsome, Sindari informed me.

Because it's hard to follow a trail or because it's noisy and buses spray you with muddy water?

The latter. I can follow a trail anywhere. Though even sublime olfactory senses can be dulled by muddy water coating one's nostrils.

You're a trooper.

Sindari paced around the pillar, his mud-sprayed nostrils to the ground. I refrained from asking if he'd lost the trail. Since he was already cranky from being wet, I didn't want to offend him.

Sindari sat and gazed upward. *I believe the troll climbed this pillar, then jumped onto one of the trains. In which case, I would not be able to track him farther.*

The monorail only went two places, and I thought about suggesting we check them, but it was starting to rain harder. The odds of following a trail would diminish with every passing minute. Besides, the Seattle Center and Westlake Mall were both crowded, and the troll could have gone in any one of dozens of directions from either spot. Reluctantly, I accepted that we wouldn't find him.

"Let's hope Willard gets us the address to the Bloody Blade. And that it's not so full of drunken trolls that we would be foolish to question people." I would try bribes before pummeling, but either would be dangerous if the trolls decided it would be an opportune time to take down the *Ruin Bringer*. The idea of fighting a couple of trolls didn't scare me. Fighting fifty was a little more daunting.

A text came in from Amber. *Don't forget your last dress fitting is tomorrow.*

I grimaced. Something else to squeeze in.

Don't let your dragon lord come, Amber added. *You know it's bad luck for the groom to see the dress before the wedding. And it's gross when he ogles you in your underwear.*

Couples are supposed to ogle each other. It's romantic.

Candles are romantic. Underwear ogling is gross. Don't miss the appointment, or you'll have to walk down the aisle in your Rambo clothes. Talk about tragic.

Given the way the week was going, I could think of more tragic things that could happen at the wedding, but I didn't want to worry her. *I'll be there. Thanks for caring.*

Don't forget my mud pie.

SECRETS OF THE SWORD III

***

The dress fitting wasn't onerous this time, and as I eyed myself in the mirror, the off-the-shoulder flowing satin dress emphasizing my height and my curves, I decided it looked pretty good. *I* looked pretty good. Zav was a lucky dragon.

But what were the odds that I could keep the hem mud- and grass-stain free for our outdoor wedding? By some luck, the forecast for the weekend was sunny, if nippy, but whatever field the goblins had in mind in their sanctuary wouldn't be mowed and manicured. I imagined wetlands, ponds, and frogs ribbiting in the background—until one of my guests ate them.

"I'm almost done," the seamstress murmured around pins between her lips.

My mate, Zav spoke into my mind, *are you certain you don't wish me to join you in the female garment shop? Per your request, I have been flying over the city, searching for troll enclaves, but I would much rather assist you on this fine sunny day.*

Willard hadn't gotten back to me yet with an address for the Bloody Blade, so I'd asked Zav to have a look around downtown that morning. He ought to be able to sense trolls wandering the streets.

You're in a good mood today, I replied. *Did you visit my mom's sauna before breakfast again?*

Much to my mother's horror, Zav had become a regular visitor at her cabin. Specifically, at the sauna *outside* of her cabin. He'd finally found a place in the Seattle area where the temperature was appealing and acceptable to a dragon.

The night before, Mom had left me a voice mail—a *long* voice mail—with the website, phone number, and address of the company she'd purchased her unit from, along with detailed descriptions of the various models available. She hadn't specifically stated that I should get my own sauna, so Zav would stop showing up naked in hers, but it had been implied.

Yes, I did, he said. *Your mother wakes early for a human.*

I take it that means you ran into her. I hoped nudity hadn't been involved, but that was a vain hope.

No physical contact was made. As soon as I entered, she departed hastily. I do not know why. Lesser beings should be honored by the presence of a dragon. I have marked her hot box as a favor to her.

Uh, you marked it? Magically?

Yes. To ensure that other dragons will not attempt to claim it for themselves. My mark should also keep the riffraff away.

There's not a lot of riffraff in my mom's rural neighborhood.

I once encountered the local werewolf in the hot box.

Liam? They're dating, remember? He probably has permission to use her sauna. Has your troll hunt turned up any trolls?

I detected a group of trolls roaming the caved-in passages under the city, but they must have sensed me, for they disappeared shortly after.

Passages? The old tunnels the dark elves were using? I hoped none of *them* were back in town. It was hard to imagine dark elves doing something as innocuous as bombing a building—they would rather sacrifice children, after all.

Yes. It appears that some of the tunnels have been cleared. They retain some of the camouflaging magic that made it difficult for me to detect entrances and how many beings resided in them previously. I also located a larger group of trolls in an underground portion of a brick building.

Oh? Rupert's had been like that, a bar in a basement with only alley access to get in. *What was the address?*

Address?

What part of town was it located in? I supposed dragons didn't fly down and look at cross streets.

Zav shared a six-block-by-six-block aerial map of downtown Seattle with me. *The building with the black roof.*

That was about a mile from Nin's truck and only a couple of blocks from the monorail. Nice. I think that might be the Bloody Blade.

Do you wish me to investigate it? Wait. I am receiving another telepathic communication.

No call-waiting, huh?

He didn't respond to that, but at least he didn't play hold music in my head while I waited.

Your employer has invaded the goblin sanctuary with large, noisy mechanical equipment, Zav informed me. *The goblin work leader is perturbed.*

Willard is up there? How did she find it?

And what large mechanical equipment did she have? I couldn't imagine her chainsawing down trees, not even to make my wedding perfect.

A soldier is with her.

Hm, maybe she had dragged Corporal Clarke with his quarter-fae blood up there to help her find it.

The work leader says the machine is called a lawn mower. Your employer is riding it through the field designated for our wedding ceremony.

Ah. Yes, waist-high grass wouldn't be ideal for us. *The goblins object to having their lawn mown? Tell them that humans have to pay for that.*

The soldier is wielding something called a weed whacker.

Yeah, that sounds right.

This is not a problem? The work leader does not like the noise or the maiming of the grass.

Is there any chance you can fly up there and try to smooth things over with her? Dragons are known for their diplomatic skills, after all.

I would go with him, but now that Zav had given me a likely location for this troll hangout, I hoped to deal with that problem. The days remaining until the wedding were ticking down.

Not all dragons are diplomatic, but the queen has trained me well, so I am suited for such missions. Yes, I can do this.

Thank you, Zav.

You do not need assistance dealing with the troll problem?

I think Sindari and I can handle a visit to a troll bar. We're just going to ask some questions and spend some bribe money, not start a fight. I hoped.

I sensed dozens of trolls inside.

We can handle it. Maybe I'll swing by the house and get Freysha to help. You know how skilled she is at entangling people with roots. I wanted to check on my elven houseguests too. As my father had explained, they enjoyed the outdoors, even in dreary weather, and did not like being cooped up inside. That was fine, but so far, they'd caused a stir in the neighborhood. Nin had been the one to inform me that *the socials* were lit up with pictures of pointed-eared visitors around Green Lake.

You are not unskilled with that magic yourself now. Zav beamed pride into my mind.

I wished I could beam a kiss into his. It was nice having someone proud of me. My mom had made a sarcastic comment about my abilities when I'd showed off the entangling root spell on one of her porch posts.

It was possible she was peeved because *she* didn't have elven magic. It was a shame that she couldn't learn it. She knew so much more about the culture than I did.

Thank you, Zav.

I am departing now, Zav informed me. *I shall also check in on the progress of the wedding gift that the goblins are making for us.*

What kind of gift is it? And are you supposed to spy on them when they make it?

I have already seen the framework. They wished to measure me to ensure the dimensions are suitable for a dragon and his mate.

It's not another hot tub, is it? I'd started shopping online for hot tubs in my not-so-copious spare time, but I hadn't made a purchase yet. How did I tell a bunch of goblins that I would prefer a store model that had been built in a factory rather than something made from used barn wood and rusted car doors?

They do know of our fondness for water boxes, but I also told them about your mother's hot box.

You mean her sauna. We don't need them to build a hot box, trust me.

They are requesting that you reserve a place of fifteen feet by twenty feet on the patio.

Three hundred square feet? That's huge.

A gift for a dragon should not be small or forgettable.

No chance of that. Goblins don't do forgettable. I pressed the heel of my palm against my forehead as the seamstress hummed and worked, oblivious to my long telepathic conversation.

Indeed not. And they know that it is wise to please dragons and their mates with only their best.

And their biggest.

Yes.

Maybe the goblins would be so irked with the lawn mowing that they would decide not to give us a gift. A girl could hope.

My phone buzzed, and the seamstress gave me a don't-even-think-about-moving look of warning. I'd put it—and my gun and sword—on a table, so nothing would be in the way of the fitting, and I thought about ignoring it, but Willard's name flashed up.

"That's my boss. Can you hand it to me, please?" I smiled as warmly as I could.

The seamstress scowled as she handed me the phone. "This is the important part. Please refrain from moving as much as you can."

"Got it." As soon as I answered, the buzz of lawn machinery filled my ear. "Hey, Willard. I hear you're busy."

"Not too busy to give you an address," she said without explaining the lawn care going on. And was that a goblin cursing in her native tongue in the background?

"The goblins knew it?" I asked.

"How'd you know I was out here?"

"Word gets around. Zav is coming to smooth things over with Work Leader Nogna."

"I've already smoothed things over. They know we can't have a wedding in grass that's taller than their heads. Captain Brisco got the address and texted it to me. I'll send it over. Be careful, and take backup. He said the place is busy and full of a lot of disaffected teenage trolls with weapons."

"I'm taking Freysha as backup." Assuming she was home.

"Good thinking. Bring the big guns. Nothing is as intimidating as an elf holding a fern."

"Ha ha, you know she's got magic. And I've always got Sindari. Our winter weather is making him cranky, so he'll be extra good for intimidation."

"Just take care of it before the wedding. I can only do so much." Willard hung up, but not before the lawn mower roared to life again.

She was doing a lot more than I ever would have asked. Maybe I should pay her. Would that be weird? Paying a friend for wedding planning? At the least, I should get her a gift. Maybe she would like a fifteen-foot-by-twenty-foot goblin surprise.

Her text came in with an address, one that matched up with the telepathic map that Zav had sent me.

"This looks good." I patted my hip and slid a hand down the fabric. Amber had done a good job making suggestions to the designer. It was sleek and beautiful without any frills or lace that would have made me look goofy. There wasn't a slit so I could reach my gun, but I'd been overruled on that. Zav had promised he would be at my side to flambé anyone who menaced us. "Is it about done? I need to go kick some troll ass."

Alas, Amber wasn't there to tell me how strange I was.

"Yes." The furrow to the seamstress's brow suggested she had a similar opinion of me, but she was too polite to share it aloud. "You'll be a radiant bride on your wedding day, in a gorgeous dress."

Proud of her handiwork, was she?

"Thanks. I don't get to be radiant that often."

"Weddings are special. Let me help you take it off, so you can… what did you say you needed to do?" There was that furrow to her brow again. Maybe she thought she'd heard me wrong. Or she *hoped* she'd heard me wrong.

"Drop off a check for the caterer and meet some new friends." New *troll* friends.

"Ah, yes. That's lovely."

CHAPTER 12

I SENSED NEITHER FREYSHA NOR EIRETH when I pulled into what had become my dedicated parking spot in front of the house. If I'd known that flame-shooting dragon topiaries could keep our curb free of competing cars, I would have had Zav install them on moving day.

A few other elves were tinkering in the conservatory, and I thought about asking them where Freysha and Eireth had gone, but my stomach growled, reminding me that I hadn't eaten since breakfast. Maybe they would return while I was making a sandwich.

My fancy black-pepper turkey was still in the refrigerator, but someone had discovered what *had* been a nearly full pickle jar and demolished the contents. Briny fermented vegetables were either an elven delicacy or one of them was pregnant. I pulled out a new jar to finish off my creation, or what I *thought* was a new jar. Judging by the small number of pickles floating in the liquid inside, this jar had also been sampled. Later, I would explain to my guests which food items needed to go into the refrigerator after opening.

Despite it not being a new jar, the lid was affixed so tightly that even the strength boost I got from the elven half of my blood wasn't sufficient. Someone with *full* elven strength must have assumed the lid should be replaced as tightly as possible.

I located the jar-opening tool only to discover that a goblin—or perhaps Freysha—had made adjustments to it, confusing adjustments involving rubber bands and cogs that rendered it, as far as my simple mind could tell, inoperable. Sighing, I went for my old standby. My sword.

I set the pickle jar on the floor and leaned Storm's tip into the top, intending to annihilate the annoying lid and transfer the contents to a reusable container, but I paused. Maybe there was a way to do this without destroying the jar. In the past, I'd tried my lock-picking charm on pickle jars, but it had proven ineffective.

"Is there a magical word for lid removal?" I wondered, mentally combing through the dwarven terms from Freysha's list.

The night before, I'd practiced six of the terms with Chasmmoor and more of his summoned monsters. In addition to the term that created a defensive barrier—he wanted to make sure I had that one down flawlessly—there had been one that weakened an opponent's magic defenses, one that created shadows to hide in, and one that camouflaged its wielder. There was also a command that drew energy from one's opponent and channeled it into Storm's wielder. The idea seemed a little creepy—vampiric, even—but I could see it being handy. Not necessarily against pickle jars.

Since none of the terms were quite right, I focused on the jar again and willed Storm to unfasten the seal. It didn't work.

"How about the strength-sucking spell?" I mused, then spoke the command word, willing the sword to steal the strength of the seal and give it to me.

At first, nothing happened, but then a tingle of magic flowed into my arms.

"What are you doing?" a male voice asked from the door. Chasmmoor had woken up for the day.

I felt silly since I was standing with the pickle jar on the floor between my feet and Storm's tip pressed to the lid. "Practicing calling upon the sword's powers."

I set Storm aside and picked up the jar. Already, the tingle of magic—of strength?—that had flowed into my arms was fading, but the spell truly had weakened the lid's hold on the jar. With a quick twist, I opened it. Huh.

"Against a worthy opponent, I see."

"I didn't have your box of horrors for easy access to terrifying monsters."

"Had I known you wished to continue your lessons during the day, I could have lent it to you." His eyes were twinkling. Amused, was he?

SECRETS OF THE SWORD III

"No need. We have a no-monsters-in-the-house policy." I grabbed a pickle and finished making my sandwich. "Do you want one?"

"This is a typical human food?"

"A sandwich? Yeah. Have you seen Freysha and King Eireth, by chance?"

"They left together a while ago saying they were going to the lake."

"That ought to be okay."

I made him a sandwich, then reached out with my senses to see if I could detect them in the park. With so many people between here and the lake, it took me a couple of minutes, and Chasmmoor wandered off sniffing his sandwich.

Eventually, I picked up their auras on the far side of Green Lake. They seemed to be on the trail that circled the water, so nothing alarming there. Except... they were moving quickly for walkers. They weren't *running* from someone, were they?

If Willard were zooming along that quickly, I would assume she was training for a triathlon, but I hadn't noticed Freysha running laps around the house in the time she'd been here. With concern hollowing a pit in my stomach, I ran back out to the Jeep and drove to the parking lot closest to Eireth and Freysha.

There weren't any police cars or flashing lights that would suggest trouble in the park, just the usual people braving the chilly winter air to do their workouts on the lake trail. That didn't mean that a troll or something worse couldn't be chasing Freysha and Eireth. They were the only elves I sensed. Where were my father's bodyguards?

After parking, I grabbed my weapons and hustled to the trail to intercept them—or help them if they needed it. With Storm in hand, I was about to summon Sindari when Freysha and Eireth appeared over a hill. They zoomed down the paved path on the side reserved for those using wheels.

I blinked and lowered my sword. Freysha and Eireth were on inline skates. Their blond locks flowed out behind them as they skated toward me with the practiced ease of pros—or natural athletes.

Freysha waved, and they slowed down. I rubbed my face, the visions of elves being chased by monsters fading from my mind.

Eireth wobbled a bit as he leaned his heel back to brake, the first indication that this was his first time on skates. After a couple of arm flails, he recovered and grinned at me.

"A delightful sport," he said.

"We used the money you gave Father to rent these wheeled boots," Freysha said.

"We also purchased frozen yogurt." Eireth was still grinning. Maybe he'd forgotten how much fun Earth was.

I wondered if he ever regretted leaving Mom to go back to his world.

"They are appealing, but they are also rather simple, engineering-wise, and they are ineffective when traveling across gravel and grass." Freysha rubbed at a green stain on her sleeve. Maybe there had been a few mishaps before their elven agility kicked in. "I believe Gondo and I could build more robust wheels and perhaps adjust the bearings. Do you think the cycle shop owner would mind improvements?"

"On skates you rented for the day? I think tinkering with rentals is frowned upon." I waved for them to step off the trail since a trio of bicyclists was speeding down the hill, two guys and a kid using training wheels, but Eireth was experimenting with skating backward and didn't notice.

"Look out, Eireth," I said as the bikers approached.

Freysha saw the imminent collision and lunged for him, but she wasn't that accustomed to the skates and ended up pitching forward before recovering her balance. I sprinted after Eireth, but he'd already caught the hang of skating backward and was picking up speed. His face was down, tense in concentration, and he didn't notice the bicyclists until the last second. With walkers on the other side of the path, they couldn't go around him. Eireth jumped to the side—an impressive feat while on wheels—but the bicyclists also careened off the path in that direction.

They avoided hitting him, but one rolled out of control over the grass and crashed into the tree. The kid with the training wheels never left the pavement, and he ended up being fine. The adults on the other hand...

"One way, you dumbass!" the man who'd avoided crashing but was also over in the grass now shouted.

The one who'd crashed sprang up and raised his fists. "That could have been my kid, you idiot."

He charged forward, as if he meant to demonstrate his irritation with a punch to Eireth's nose. I started to raise Storm but couldn't hack an innocent biker to pieces, so I sheathed it, instead stepping in to block the punch if needed. But Freysha acted first. Roots grew up from the grass and wrapped around the ankles of the bicyclists. The one who'd crashed pitched into the grass again, landing hard on his knees. He was having a bad day, and his buddy went to help him.

"Sorry," I called to them. "My family is visiting from another country. They don't have skates in, uh, Lothlórien."

"Keep them off the pavement until they learn what they're doing. And what the hell is on my legs?"

"Freysha," I whispered, making a cutting motion across my throat. "Nix the magic."

She frowned in disapproval at the belligerent bicyclists, but she obeyed, and the roots disappeared back into the earth. The men's young charge was sailing off on his training wheels, so they had to hurry after him and refrained from making any more threatening moves at Eireth.

"Would you two like to come help me question some trolls? Willard said I should take backup." Which was true, but I mostly wanted to keep any more international incidents from happening between the United States and Lothlórien.

"You need our assistance?" Freysha pointed at Eireth a little dubiously.

Maybe kings weren't supposed to be taken into brawls as backup.

"Roots might come in handy. Uh, Eireth... where are your bodyguards?"

He blew out a wistful breath and looked over his shoulder as four familiar elves in armor and carrying weapons appeared, running over the hill and down the path on foot.

"We outdistanced them." Freysha looked sheepish.

"Accidentally?" I eyed Eireth.

"No," he admitted. "They can be stifling at times."

Joggers sprang out of the elves' way as they charged down the path. I rubbed my face again. Hopefully, nobody would end up in jail.

"We would be delighted to assist you with the trolls," Eireth said, "so long as you don't mind... backup for your backup." He pointed to his bodyguards as they charged up, surrounding him and looking menacingly at nearby passersby, who were looking at *them* like they were weirdos who'd taken a wrong turn on the way to the Renaissance Faire.

"The more the merrier," I murmured.

CHAPTER 13

THE BLOODY BLADE APPEARED TO be in the basement of an office building downtown. I parked the Jeep, Eireth in the front and Freysha jammed in the back with two bodyguards—it had taken a ten-minute negotiation for Eireth to convince the other two to go back to the house.

"Let's see if there's basement access from the alley." I couldn't imagine tall, blue-skinned, surly trolls riding in the same elevator as the business-suit-wearing, briefcase-carrying employees of the building. "I'm hoping there won't be that many trolls at this time of day."

It was about two in the afternoon, far too early for drunken orgies in bars, right?

"I sense approximately thirty trolls in the below-ground level of that building," Eireth said.

Thirty was more than I'd hoped for, but if I threw enough money around, maybe they would be amenable to talking and wouldn't make trouble.

Val. Freysha hadn't gotten out of her seat yet and gazed at me with concern. *It would be extremely bad if something happened to Father while he is here. Not only because he's our father, and we care about him, but because the elven people might interpret it as an act of war if he were harmed on this world. Mother was not pleased about his decision to attend the wedding and kept telling him to tell you to come marry your dragon on Veleshna Var, like a civilized couple.*

You mean if a troll punches him, the elves could decide to make war on Earth? I looked at Eireth and then at his bodyguards in the rear-view mirror.

They were peering out the windows at the eclectic Seattle pedestrians and didn't seem to think it strange that we hadn't gotten out yet.

It might take more than a punch, but a serious injury would be viewed with... hostility.

"All right, guys," I said. "Here's the plan. Freysha, Sindari, and I are going to go have a chat with the trolls. What I need from you three is to let us know if any *more* trolls rush this way and look like they're going to try to trap us inside."

"You wish us to sit outside and do nothing but watch out the windows?" Eireth did not sound approving, and he frowned at Freysha, maybe guessing what she'd told me.

"Also to keep my Jeep from being stolen. This is a sketchy part of town." I pointed to bearded men in black trench coats and hats striding past. "See the gangs?"

Never mind that I was fairly certain those were Hasidic Jews.

"They lack magical blood or powerful artifacts," Eireth said.

"But they could have carjacking tools under their coats." I patted his arm. "This won't take long."

"We will wait here," one of the bodyguards said, giving Freysha an approving nod.

Freysha nodded back. Eireth sighed. Why did I have a feeling that brief bit of rebellion when he'd skated out of sight of his bodyguards had been the highlight of his month?

Freysha and I walked past the lobby entrance of the building, its twenty stories gleaming with huge tinted-glass windows, and headed past a parking garage and around to the back. Now that we were closer, I could also pick out the auras of trolls in the basement.

"Our father is feeling hemmed in now that our people have heightened security and want him under guard at all times," Freysha said.

"I gathered. Because of the poisoning magic that almost took him down?"

"Yes. It is also believed that some trouble may come from the fae queen's visit and her insistence on denigrating the assassin Varlesh Sarrlevi."

I halted. "I think I may have seen him last night. I'm not positive it wasn't a dream... but I'm not positive it was."

"You saw him?"

"At the house."

"I did not sense him, nor did any of our kin mention anything."

"I think everyone was asleep. Even Zav was asleep."

"If it is true, his presence here does not bode well."

"Back in the fae realm, Zav made Sarrlevi promise that he wouldn't take revenge on me or attack me again. I thought... he seemed to be into honor. I thought he would keep his word."

"He is reputed to be honest and not without honor—though our people find assassinating others to be deplorable and many would say his profession alone means he has no honor—but it is possible he could obey his promise while finding... what is your word for it? A loophole."

"Like by attacking people at my wedding or attacking our coffee shop while not hurting me? You think he's that pissed?"

"I do not know. Did you speak with him?"

"No, he disappeared as soon as I spotted him skulking in the bushes. He's gotten through the defenses around the house before, but he never attacked when Zav was present. And I assume the house is even more intimidating now with so many elven heavies around."

Freysha tilted her head. "Heavies? My people are generally slender and light."

"Never mind." I waved to an alley ahead. "Let's deal with one problem at a time."

"I may be able to place a ward that extends beyond the perimeter of the house and that would wake me with a mental ping if Sarrlevi returns another night."

"Good plan."

In the alley, we found a fire-escape ladder next to a row of dumpsters. It did not look like the secret entrance to a pub for magical beings. It led up to escape windows. If there were any doors on this side of the building, I didn't see them.

I thought about summoning Sindari to put his superior tiger nose to work, but Freysha held up a finger and led the way deeper into the alley. She stopped in front of a cement wall with sheets of a soggy newspaper stuck to the ground in front of it.

"I sense magic," she told me.

I joined her and pointed to a large dirty footprint on one of the newspapers. It either belonged to a troll or a human with sasquatch ancestry. Now that I was right in front of it, I also sensed a hint of magic to the wall. Freysha slid her long fingers along the cement, probing thoughtfully.

"Let's see if my lock-picking charm can open it." I rested a hand on the wall. "It failed me on the jar, but it was *designed* to unlock enchanted doorways."

"Jar?"

"Yeah. Do me a favor and have a chat with whichever of your people channels Hercules to seal jars. Pickles don't escape in the dark of night. They don't need to be so forcefully restrained."

"Ah, the *pickle* jar. My people have been enjoying that food."

"I noticed."

"They're crunchy and appealing with a delicious zing."

"Uh huh. I'll add them to the list of items I buy from Costco."

"Will you take me with you to purchase a jar? I would like to bring some home to my mother."

"Sure. Nothing shows the universe Earth's best like a hundred and twenty-eight ounces of kosher dills." I gripped my charm with my free hand and willed it to open the door.

The cement wall wavered as an illusion dissolved, revealing a timber-frame opening to a short tunnel that led to a chain-link gate and an elevator. It looked like the entrance to a mine shaft, not a bar.

"Why do I have a feeling this place isn't built to code?" I asked, heading inside. The only light filtered in from the alley.

The gate handle didn't budge until I used my charm again. It creaked open, and Freysha and I stepped onto a square of plywood—the floor of the elevator—that bowed under our weight. The sides were made from chain link with another square of plywood for the ceiling.

"Seems sturdy." If I hadn't sensed the troll auras less than twenty feet below, I would have worried that this would take us down to the depths of hell. As it was, it concerned me that it might not be easy to escape from the pub if this was the only way in or out.

A metal box with open wiring held four glowing buttons with unfamiliar symbols on them. Freysha pushed one, and the elevator lurched alarmingly before descending downward.

"You can read trollish?" I asked.

"No, but I can read goblin." She waved at the symbols. "The trolls must have employed goblin workers to construct this place. It's likely the original building didn't have a basement."

"So they dug this out? Someone made a pretty big investment in this place." I drew Storm as the elevator slowed to a stop. There wasn't any light, and I couldn't hear any drunk trolls chitchatting yet, but my senses told me we were level with them now.

"The goblins may have been enslaved and forced to work," Freysha said quietly. "That is common."

"Maybe we should have asked Gondo if he knew anything about this place."

"I believe he is busy assisting Work Leader Nogna with the wedding gift."

I might have asked how much Freysha knew about that—and how worried I should be about it—but clanks sounded, like a portcullis being cranked up.

Orange light appeared as something closer to a wooden garage door than a portcullis rolled upward. Now, the sounds of mugs clinking and trolls chatting reached us. A thud rang out—an axe being hurled at a target? Or maybe a troll head being smashed into a wall.

The noises faded as Freysha and I walked out of the elevator. A short brick-walled tunnel led us into the pub we'd been promised, the same orangish lantern light brightening the space. Maybe it was hard to get electrical service in a secret basement.

The trolls occupied tables or mingled around a boxing arena and axe-throwing lanes. A couple of ogres were also present, but this didn't have the same variety of magical beings as Rupert's had once hosted.

A broad-shouldered troll with a stoop was pouring green sludge from a keg at the bar, but he paused to eye me and say something in his native tongue. I activated my translation charm and thought about calling Sindari, but maybe the troll would surprise me and answer my questions without violence.

"...knew it was only a matter of time before the Ruin Bringer showed up," he was saying, though he looked straight at me instead of any of his patrons. "Knew she'd be worried about a little *competition*."

"This would be our chance to take care of her," one of the axe throwers said, fondling his metal blade. "She came to our territory with nothing but an elf for backup."

It will be difficult for us to create the ensnaring roots here, Freysha told me telepathically, waving to the cement floor. Right, no nature present to draw upon here. *But I have other methods that I can call upon.*

Yeah. Me too. I patted Fezzik's handle.

I walked up to the bartender, doing my best to ignore the mossy scent wafting from the mugs of sludge. Even more unappealing scents came from what looked like a kitchen behind the bar, with a swinging door standing ajar.

"I'm looking for some information." I laid a twenty-dollar bill on the bar. "I heard you're a smart guy and know a lot about the goings on in the magical community."

Actually, I hadn't heard anything and didn't know his name. But buttering up potential informants never hurt.

"I *am* a smart guy, which is why I know better than to chat with the Ruin Bringer."

"Come on, now. Nobody calls me that anymore." Not since Sunday, anyway. "I'm a partial owner in a legitimate service that caffeinates the magical community at an affordable price. We should make an alliance since you're in the business too. Alcoholizing rather than caffeinating, but similar ideas, right? Maybe we could go in together to buy ads for our businesses on the social-media platforms."

I smiled, doubting the troll would be interested, but hypothetically, it could be a legitimate offer. Assuming this establishment hadn't had anything to do with the bombing of *my* establishment. Just last week, Nin had suggested we start an online advertising campaign. She had one running for her food truck. The problem, from what I gathered, was targeting the *right* kind of people. I wasn't convinced that trolls, orcs, and goblins surfed the web that often. Gondo frequently lamented that goblins couldn't afford smart phones.

"Not interested," he said. "We can get customers without *your* help."

"Okay. But can you at least tell me who might have visited the Crying Tiger food truck yesterday and walked away with more than beef and rice?"

"No. Even if I knew, I wouldn't rat him out to you."

"I didn't say it was a male."

"Female trolls don't raid enemy strongholds."

"Does a food truck qualify as a stronghold?"

"If it's the food truck of a weapons maker with guns and grenades in the back, yes."

"I see you're familiar with Nin's place."

Trolls are creeping closer to us. Freysha stood a couple of feet behind me, keeping an eye on the patrons. *Perhaps you should summon Sindari. A fight seems likely.*

I will, but this guy is pretty chatty for someone who isn't interested in talking to me. I'm hoping something useful will slip out. There's some magic in this place. Are you able to tell if any of Nin's grenades are in here? My senses weren't refined enough to pick them out if they were here, not among all the magical beings and weapons. *Besides the two clipped to my belt under my duster.*

I'll check. Give me a moment.

"Are you a customer, perhaps?" I added. Questions were more likely to get answers than comments.

"We used to buy from the panther-shifter brothers," the bartender growled. "Now they're dead. *She's* still alive."

Ah, he was a buddy of someone I had killed. The odds of me getting out of here without a fight had gotten poorer. I'd already scoped out the place and decided which corner I would spring into with Freysha and how we would put our backs to the wall.

"She has more powerful friends than they did," I said. "And she makes better weapons. You should shift your allegiances and pick up a couple of semi-automatics for your pub here. Don't troll clients get rowdy?"

Get ready, I warned Freysha, casually reaching up to brush my chin—and Sindari's charm.

"*Very* rowdy. If you leave in the next ten seconds, I *might* be able to keep them from killing you."

The offer to let us leave surprised me, and I paused instead of summoning Sindari. If I didn't *have* to fight, it would be wiser to avoid it. I doubted all of these guys would jump in, but more than a few could be problematic, even with the new powers I'd unlocked in my sword.

"So long as you leave before Ogdar returns," the bartender added. "Years ago, you killed his brother. He has not forgotten."

What did it say about me that *I* had? I'd lost track of how many trolls I'd hunted down for Willard and other clients, but they'd all been criminals, and if this Ogdar was a criminal, I would take care of him too.

"*He* is the one who warned us," the bartender said.

"About what?"

"That you seek to win the loyalty of our people by selling them addictive drinks, but that you will betray them all in the end. Nobody should trust the Ruin Bringer."

"Uh huh. You're sure you aren't interested in telling me who stole Nin's stuff?" I glanced at Freysha, wondering if she'd finished scanning the area for grenades.

Her face was tight with concentration. *They are here. In the back. And someone familiar to you is also here.*

Who?

"Nobody here wants her *stuff*." The bartender pushed the twenty back toward me. "Be gone. And know that if you weren't letting a dragon screw you, you'd already be dead."

A blue-skinned face appeared in the gap of the kitchen door, a *familiar* face. Reb. One of his eyes was blackened, and a cheek was bruised and swollen.

The youth who works at your coffee shop, Freysha replied, nodding slightly toward him.

The bartender caught the nod and glowered over his shoulder. "Get back to work," he snarled.

Reb sprang out of view, and the door swung shut.

"You're hiring away my employees?" I kept my voice as indifferent as I could, though I wanted to clobber whoever had clobbered Reb. "That doesn't bode well for our future alliance."

Reb, I spoke telepathically to him. Now that I knew he was there, it was easy to pick out his aura among the other trolls working in the kitchen. *Did you run away and come here intentionally, or are you a prisoner?*

Uh, he replied uncertainly.

"The boy injured my nephew. Now he works for us as punishment." The bartender squinted at me. "There's no damn alliance. Get out of here *now*, Ruin Bringer. It's your last chance."

Prisoner, Reb added. *Will you rescue me?*

Yes. Stay in there.

I groped for a way forward that wouldn't involve battling fifty trolls. This searching-for-information mission had just grown much more complicated.

CHAPTER 14

THE BARTENDER REACHED FOR SOMETHING under the bar. I grabbed Freysha, pulling her close, and whispered, "*Darayknar zerek*," as I drew Storm.

The bartender whipped up a sawn-off shotgun with a faint magical signature, but two trolls behind us fired first. Freysha flinched, but I'd already activated Storm's barrier. After all the times I'd had my bullets bounce off when I shot at enemies with magical defenses, it was keenly satisfying to hear a *bzzzt* as theirs ricocheted off mine and hit walls. One gave a troll a buzz cut. Perfect.

An angry patron roared and flung himself at my barrier. He *also* bounced off.

Unfortunately, I couldn't attack anyone as long as my sword was creating an impenetrable wall, but I would rather grab Reb and run away anyway. How I would do that without lowering the barrier, I didn't know, but I would figure that out on the fly.

"We're taking a walk," I whispered to Freysha and eased toward the end of the bar, so we could get back to the kitchen.

The barrier wobbled and almost dropped. Shit. I paused, whispered the command again, and focused on reinforcing it. I hadn't yet practiced moving while keeping it up.

The bartender fired at me. He was so close that I ducked reflexively, not completely trusting my barrier. The sound from the shotgun boomed in my ear, but Storm protected me. A dozen pellets ricocheted off, thudding into the door and the wall behind the bar. The bartender ducked down, but not before taking a pellet to the shoulder.

"Get Ogdar!" he roared. "Or another shaman!"

Uh oh. A shaman might be able to tear down my barrier.

"Hurry," Freysha urged. Her hands were up, but she hadn't yet cast a spell. Maybe she couldn't do that through my barrier.

"Working on it." Keeping her close, I surged around the end of the bar and tried to rush to the kitchen. But the barrier caught on the wall and a cupboard. I needed to shrink it somehow.

I huffed with impatience. Why hadn't Chasmmoor had me practice these things?

"*Kay zruk!*" came a shout from the far side of the room.

A buzz filled my mind, Storm flared an indignant blue, and my barrier disappeared. Ogdar.

Ducking lower than the bar top, I tugged Freysha down with me and pushed her toward the kitchen door. We could make a stand in there, and I could—I hoped—reestablish the barrier.

Guns fired, and bullets hammered the wall above our heads. Others thudded into the front of the bar, wood splintering and flying.

The bartender, who was also hiding below the bar top, lunged in to grab my sword arm. I yanked it back before he reached me and managed to spin and launch a side kick without rising from my squat. My heel slammed into his stomach, and he toppled backward, striking shelves full of glasses. They clattered and crashed to the floor all around him.

Freysha lunged for the kitchen door. It swung inward, only to strike someone and halt. She dove through the gap and disappeared inside.

The bartender snarled and lunged for me again as more trolls shot in my direction. Green light flashed, and a thunderous boom hammered my ear drums. What the hell was *that*? A magical shockwave rattled me to the core and kept me from reacting for precious seconds.

This time, the bartender succeeded in grabbing my sword arm. He tried to tug Storm out of my grip, but I recovered enough to thrust the heel of my palm at his nose. Cartilage crunched, and he reeled back, hitting his head on the shelves again. His grip loosened, and I twisted my wrist, pulling my arm free.

When I dove for the kitchen door, nothing impeded it this time. Shouts and grunts of pain came from inside as Freysha engaged the chefs.

As I scrambled into the room, I tapped Sindari's charm and summoned him, annoyed that I'd hesitated before. I should have walked in with him.

Freysha stood with her back to a wall between a fridge and a stove, her hands lifted, her eyelids closed to slits. Nobody in the kitchen had firearms, but a hulking troll chef strode toward her with a cleaver even larger than the one Chasmmoor had given me.

I stepped out of the doorway, drew Fezzik, and fired at the weapon. The bullet struck the handle of the cleaver, and it flew out of the chef's hand.

"Thank you," Freysha said calmly as magic swelled around her.

Fuzzy green balls grew out of the cement walls and the appliances and flew across the room. I expected them to pelt the three trolls in the kitchen with us—where had Reb gone?—and distract them, but they did more than that. As if made from Velcro, the balls stuck to the trolls' clothing and skin and did something to irritate them, for they roared and tried to claw the projectiles away.

"Get her!" someone outside of the kitchen yelled.

"*You* get her!" the bartender snarled back.

By now, Sindari had formed. He crouched and sprang for the trolls in the kitchen.

The door swung open, revealing two armed trolls trying to charge in. I kicked the door shut, and it slammed into them. That only bought me a second. One of them roared, grabbed the door, and ripped it off the hinges.

"Not my pub, you idiot!" the bartender yelled.

I whispered Storm's command term again, focused on re-forming the barrier, and leaned in to block the doorway with it. The troll that had ripped the door off the hinges tried to rush in, but Storm's barrier appeared in time. He struck the invisible field and stumbled back.

More preparation before a battle is always nice, Sindari noted.

Behind me, one of the chefs screamed as Sindari sank his fangs into his thick calf. More trolls cursed and swatted at the air as Freysha's green balls attached to them, tiny hooks biting into clothing and flesh.

You sound like you're doing okay, I replied.

I am doing magnificently, as befitting an apex predator.

Of course. "Where'd Reb go?" I called aloud over my shoulder.

On the other side of the bar, a dozen trolls lined up with guns that they pointed in my direction. Behind them, the one that had to be the shaman raised his hands. Hatred burned in his dark eyes as he focused on me. Yup, I had no trouble believing I'd killed his brother. I braced myself and created a mental shield of fern fronds around my mind, hoping to deflect what would doubtless be another attempt to strip me of my barrier.

The angry buzz zapped my mind again, but this time, the barrier didn't slip. Storm flared with what seemed like triumphant power, and the urge to charge out and start lopping off heads came over me.

"Easy, Mr. Bloodthirsty," I muttered. "We're just trying to get the kid, not start a war."

Weapons fired, bullets slamming into Storm's barrier.

Maybe it was my imagination, but the sword seemed to send indignation into my mind.

"Yeah, yeah, they aren't following the script. I know."

As two trolls charged forward, attempting to break my barrier by poking it with daggers, I searched for Reb with my senses. He'd hidden in... the walk-in freezer?

Come out, I told him. *We've got to get out of here. I'll protect you.*

Something struck my barrier, not a bullet this time. A gray cylinder bounced off it and back over the bar into the group of gun-wielding trolls. It clattered to the floor and spewed dark gray smoke into the middle of them.

They cursed and scattered. Even from several feet away, I caught a whiff of an overpowering sewer scent. It seared my nostrils like mustard gas. The trolls were every bit as affected as I, and someone cursed vehemently at whoever had thrown the canister.

I stumbled back from the doorway, wishing Storm's defenses would keep the awful odor out. Sindari roared what sounded like a protest rather than a battle cry, and I was sure his nostrils had also taken a hit.

"You can come out," Freysha said, opening the walk-in freezer door.

The troll chefs were all down, two on their sides, clawing at balls stuck to their eyelids, and one on his back under Sindari. With his massive weight, he pinned his foe.

Reb stepped out, only to be swept up to the ceiling. He squawked in alarm, dropping something that clattered to the floor. The damn shaman.

Freysha gaped, then jumped for him, but Reb zipped away from her, his white hair skimming the ceiling. I prepared to lower the sword's barrier so I could leap and grab him, but something gray whizzed through the doorway at foot level. Too late, I realized that I'd lunged back far enough that my barrier didn't fully block the doorway anymore.

The cylinder clattered across the floor, spewing smoke and that awful odor into the kitchen. I lunged and smashed Storm down on it, vainly hoping that would keep it from spitting out its entire load. The blade sliced through, but that only let more smoke escape. Worse, Reb was sucked out of the kitchen while I was distracted.

I spun, intending to raise Storm's barrier again and rush after him, but one of the trolls shoved the door back into the jamb. Snorting, I lifted my leg to kick it—and him—backward. But the shaman had another trick up his sleeve. A surge of magic swelled around the door, and when the sole of my boot connected with it, it was as if I'd kicked a cement wall.

Cursing, I stumbled back. Dark gray smoke filled the kitchen and scoured my nostrils and air pipe. I raised Storm, intending to hack at the door with the magical blade, but my lungs spasmed, and I broke into a round of coughs. They wrenched my body so badly that I couldn't keep from dropping to my knees.

Belatedly, I thought to grab the charm Zoltan had once made to repel toxic air and activate it. But he'd made it to deal with a specific substance, and it didn't help with whatever this awful stuff was. The smoke grew too dense to see much through it, and my lungs tightened like a fist. Tears streamed from my eyes, and snot ran from my nose.

Freysha rushed to the door and hurled a magical spell at it. I sensed her using her power, even as I was busy covering my face and trying not to inhale more of the smoke.

But whatever magic the shaman had used kept the door in place. Freysha also bent over coughing. We were trapped.

CHAPTER 15

MY LUNGS TIGHTENED FURTHER AS the smoke filled the kitchen. I checked to make sure the three trolls locked in here with us weren't a threat—they were as bad off as I was, coughing and still trying to get rid of Freysha's green balls—then pulled out my inhaler. Who knew if the medicine would help with this miasma, but I'd die from an asthma attack as easily as the magic. The only consolation was that even more coughs came from the other side of the door. The trolls had dosed themselves as badly as they had us. My senses told me some were fleeing. I wished that helped us more.

After breathing from my inhaler—and taking in even more tainted air—I stumbled to the oven, hoping there was a range hood with ventilation that I could turn on. There wasn't. It figured.

I coughed again, barely able to see in the haze.

That smoke is intolerable, Sindari spoke into my mind.

I'll try to stop it, Freysha said telepathically. She was also on her knees with tears streaming from her eyes.

I grabbed the mangled canister—it was still spewing smoke—and stuffed it in the oven, then closed the door. That might keep more from flowing into the room, but it wouldn't help with the stuff already inside.

I drew Storm, intending to bash down the door—its magic *had* to be greater than the shaman's. Grimly, I advanced on it as coughs continued to plague me. I'd stopped wheezing, so at least my medicine had helped, but that might only be temporary.

"Good idea," Freysha rasped.

I hefted Storm and willed its magic to cut through the troll's magic as I took a swing. The sword connected with a solid thunk that bashed through the wood, though the door itself remained as secure in the jamb as if it had been bolted. I swung again. If I had to destroy it piece by piece, I would.

A breeze swirled through the room. Freysha had her hands up again as she concentrated on using her magic. How would *wind* help if there was no place to blow the smoke to?

My senses told me that half of the trolls in the main room were stampeding for the elevator and half were running down a hall next to the kitchen. Toward another exit? That group had Reb. Maybe there was still a chance that if we got out, we could rescue him. Inga would pummel me if she found out I'd been in the same room with him and let him be swept away.

As I hacked away pieces of the door, the smoke *finally* began to clear. Freysha's wind did more than swirl it around the room. It was funneling the smoke into the walk-in freezer and somehow keeping it in there. A dark gray cloud filled the space, engulfing the slabs of meat hanging from the ceiling.

Enough of the door gave way that I could kick out the rest. My foot buzzed unpleasantly as it struck the remains of the shaman's spell. I didn't care. I kicked a piece so hard that it hit the floor on the far side of the pub and skidded all the way to the elevator.

The barroom was almost as smoky as the kitchen had been, but I could make out the last of the trolls in the elevator as it disappeared up the shaft. I sprang over the bar. Maybe I could still catch the other group.

Sindari rushed out to join me and then passed me, turning down the hall in the back. In the kitchen, the freezer door thudded shut, the smoke in there trapped. Unfortunately, that didn't help with the smoke out here.

I dashed tears out of my eyes and fought down another round of coughs as I ran down the cement hall after Sindari. Only a couple of trolls remained at the end, both bent over and coughing.

They whirled to face me. My throat spasmed like a dying jellyfish, and I barely managed to heft Storm and rasp the command words again. The shield surrounded me a split second before one of the trolls hurled a throwing knife at me. As it pinged off my defenses, the other troll flung himself into a dark circular opening in the cement wall. Some escape tunnel?

Sindari sprang and buried the remaining troll in a frenzy of claws and snapping teeth, blocking my view of the tunnel.

Thanks, but don't kill him, I told him. I'd never truly thought the owner of this establishment would want an alliance with me, but the last thing I wanted was some weird feud where we repeatedly sabotaged each other's businesses.

I am only maiming him, Sindari replied calmly as his fangs sank in and the troll screamed.

So humane.

The troll, though bleeding from fresh bites, managed to heave Sindari back. He lifted his arm to throw another knife, the blade meant for my ally this time. I lowered my defenses so I could spring past Sindari, then swung Storm, willing the blade to help me deflect the knife.

Metal clanked as my sword knocked it into the wall. Sindari roared and crouched to spring, but the troll was already scrambling into the tunnel. We charged after him, but he pulled a hatch shut with a resounding clang.

Sindari reached it first but could only stop in front of it. It looked as sturdy and secure as a submarine hatch.

I am in need of thumbs, he said.

I have those. I squeezed past him.

Behind us, Freysha stumbled into the hallway, her shirt up and pressed to her mouth and nose. What was visible of her face was green. She was as sensitive to bad air as I was, if not more so, and looked like she might throw up at any second.

"You okay?" I asked, my voice as raspy as a nail file.

"I will be—" She coughed and finished telepathically. *As soon as we get out of here.*

"This place has lousy ventilation." I grabbed the door hatch.

I tried to tug it open slowly, afraid the two trolls would be waiting, guns poised to fire at us. My senses told me nothing was on the other side, but magic had fooled me before.

The hatch didn't budge. I swore.

They are climbing, getting farther away. Sindari nosed the hatch. *More than a dozen of them. And they have the boy.*

I know. I grabbed my lock-picking charm to use on the hatch, though I feared we'd lost too much time. The group with Reb must have gone first. His aura was up at street level now, maybe already outside the building.

Sindari shook his head and sneezed several times. *The battle is not the only thing you should have prepared me for.*
Sorry. I didn't know about the smoke grenades.

My lock-picking charm worked on the hatch, but by the time I swung it open, revealing a dark circular tunnel heading back to ladder rungs that led upward, it was too late. The trolls were gone.

I slumped against the wall. A tantalizing hint of fresh air wafted in from the dark passage.

Val? Freysha gripped my shoulder, her fingers desperate, her eyes hungry as she looked at the escape route. *I must have fresh air.*

I nodded and waved for her to use the tunnel. *Go ahead. I'm going to check for clues.*

Reb had dropped something when the shaman's levitation spell had hefted him into the air. Maybe it would lead us to the trolls' home or wherever they'd run off to hide.

Be careful. The air is dangerous. Freysha crawled into the tunnel and hurried away, like an underwater swimmer desperate to reach the surface for air.

"Wasn't planning to dawdle," I muttered and hurried back to the kitchen.

You can go, too, Sindari. I don't think any of the trolls left down here are a threat.

Actually, the trolls we'd left in the kitchen weren't there any longer. They must have hurried up via the elevator while we'd been checking that hatch. Too bad. I might have grabbed one to question.

Val? Eireth's voice spoke into my mind.

Yes? I stepped back into the kitchen—the least smoky place left down there, since Freysha had trapped some of the smoke.

We have apprehended a criminal.

One of the trolls? The elves must have seen some of them running past. Good. *Hold him there for me, will you? I want to see if there are any clues here, and then I'll be right up. Freysha should already be on the way.*

Certainly.

Maybe Eireth had caught the bartender, and I would get to question him again, more thoroughly and without his buddies around.

I hunted for whatever Reb had dropped, wishing *he* was still down here. Even though I hadn't expected him to be here, and hadn't made plans to rescue anyone, I felt awful for letting the trolls get away with him. The idea of explaining this mess-up to Inga made me wince.

I found the toy he'd dropped—a LEGO speeder bike. I recognized it. Reb had been carrying it around since before he lost his father. Even though Inga had gotten him new LEGO kits, he'd always kept this one.

Out here, Val. Sindari hadn't left and was poking around in the main room. *Clues.*

After tucking the toy carefully into my pocket, I joined him next to a disgusting lavatory that rivaled the smoke bomb for its stench. There were a couple of rooms with curtained-off sleeping areas. Maybe the owner lived here. Had Reb also been stuck staying here? The sleeping areas were little more than thin mattresses with scratchy wool blankets.

One area also had a desk and a few more possessions. I spotted a familiar brown wrapper with a sticker for Nin's food truck on it. Had this room belonged to the troll who'd stolen the grenades? Unfortunately, I didn't see any sign of *them,* but one of the drawers held something else that was familiar, and my stomach dropped. It was one of my wedding invitations.

"That's not at all creepy," I muttered, opening it.

The address and date were circled. Even though Zav had invited half the magical beings in the world—and in a couple of other worlds—I'd never seen these trolls at the coffee shop, and I was positive this was a stolen invitation. These guys were going to target my wedding. With Nin's grenades, a pissed-off shaman, and who knew what else?

My nostrils twitched, still raw from the smoke bomb. Since we'd done the last-minute change from the farmer's field to the goblin sanctuary for the wedding, the address on the invitation wasn't accurate, but with as many people as were coming, it seemed likely that the trolls would figure out the new location.

"Unless I can stop them first." I stuffed the invitation in my pocket. "And I will."

I headed back to collect Sindari and Freysha. It was time to see who Eireth had caught.

CHAPTER 16

EVEN THOUGH THE DOWNTOWN AIR was full of traffic fumes, I sucked it in cheerfully when I spilled out of the troll escape tunnel and into the alley again. There was another hatch, this entrance also hidden from passersby with magic.

Freysha was waiting for me outside, gripping her knees as she hunched over. Her face wasn't quite as green now, but she still looked like hell.

"Sorry for leaving you, Val," she said.

"It's fine. Your—our—father said he caught someone."

She nodded, and we strode back toward our parking spot. My fingers clenched into a fist as I envisioned questioning the troll who'd beaten Reb. In my vision, my fist was sinking into his stomach with each question.

Eireth and his two bodyguards were standing outside of the Jeep, with a police car now parked in front of it, the lights flashing. Had someone reported all the trolls streaming into the streets?

I jogged up, hoping to speak to Eireth's prisoner before the police decided to arrest him. But where *was* the prisoner? None of the elves were holding on to anyone. They stood facing two uniformed officers getting out of their car.

Only when I drew close did I see a teenage boy tied to the hood of my Jeep by magical green vines.

"Uh." I didn't know what to say. The boy was human, not troll, and upon reviewing my brief telepathic conversation with Eireth, I realized he'd never said he caught a troll. "This is your prisoner?"

Eireth turned toward me while his bodyguards stepped forward to keep the police from reaching him. The police who were probably wondering why these weirdos with pointed ears had someone tied to the hood of their Jeep. The hood of *my* Jeep.

"He attempted to steal your conveyance," Eireth said, using the same word for car as Zav did. One day, I would show them all the main types of vehicles in the world and the names for them. "As requested, we kept that from happening."

"All I did was lean on it," the kid, who couldn't have been more than sixteen, complained.

"You placed your hand on it," Eireth said.

"I like Jeeps! I was trying to see if it had any cool mods. Let me go. This can't be legal." He twisted his head, his eyes lighting up as he spotted the police. "Help! These guys are kidnapping me."

"What's going on here?" a sergeant I'd crossed paths with before asked.

"We have apprehended a conveyance thief," Eireth said.

"I'm not a thief!" the boy cried.

I stepped around the elves and waved to the familiar sergeant. "We just have a little misunderstanding, Sergeant Dominguez. I've got family visiting from out of town, and they're easily confused by our customs." *Freysha*, I added telepathically to her, *can you undo those vines, please?*

The sergeant eyed the elves' ears, braided hair, and green and brown Aragorn-inspired clothing. "How *far* out of town?"

"Lothlórien." I wondered how long it would take for someone to get the reference.

Dominguez frowned. "Is that in Norway?"

"On the border, yeah."

The vines unraveled, and the kid rolled off the hood and sprinted away.

"Did anyone see any hordes of trolls fleeing the area?" I asked, though my hopes were dwindling.

The policemen stared blankly at me.

Eireth frowned. "A few minutes ago, I thought I detected the trolls coming up from their basement, but they disappeared from my senses, and then I was distracted by what I believed was a conveyance thief."

His bodyguards nodded agreement. If only I hadn't made that joke about car thieves.

"Just don't apprehend anyone else, all right?" the sergeant said, eyeing Eireth.

"They'll be good," I promised, hoping he would go away.

My phone buzzed.

"Willard," I said, "please tell me you know where the trolls who hang out at the Bloody Blade go when they're not there."

"I don't. Did you drive out everyone there?" There wasn't any lawn machinery operating in the background. Had she finished tidying up the wilderness sanctuary?

"Temporarily. Reb was there, and I'm pretty sure one of the trolls that lives there was the one who raided Nin's food truck and stole her grenades."

"Ah, you haven't been keeping me fully updated."

"You were busy mowing things." I gave her a summary.

"If they live there and own the place, they'll be back. Possibly with large pit bulls trained to chew on half-elves who breach the premises."

"Yeah, but will it be this week?" Before *Saturday*?

"I don't know. I'll have an agent keep an eye on the place. You say they had one of your wedding invitations?"

"Tucked in a desk drawer, yes. I'm hoping someone is a fan of dragon–half-elf marriages, but I doubt it. We didn't find the grenades, but the wrapper from Nin's makes me think one of them was responsible for taking them."

"Maybe trolls simply love her food."

Another call came in. "That's my mom. Did you have something else for me?"

"I just wanted to talk to you about something."

"What?"

Willard hesitated. "It can wait."

I frowned at the phone. It wasn't like her to be evasive. "You sure? Everything okay with the wedding plans? Aside from the possibility that the troll Unabomber will show up?"

"Everything's fine on *my* end. You better make sure that troll doesn't show up."

"I'm planning on it."

"Good. Talk to your mom. I don't need anything."

I was still frowning at the phone when she hung up. Why had Willard called if she didn't *need* anything?

"Hey, Mom," I answered. "How's life running the Four Seasons for Elves?"

"You owe me for this," she replied.

"Is it not going well?" I eyed the hood of my Jeep, freshly scuffed from the kid's shoes. "What could possibly go wrong when hosting visitors from another world?"

"While I was at the grocery store, they declared war on Liam. When I got back, he was across the street, pinned in his house by elves with bows pointed at the doors and windows, telling him they would perforate him with arrows if he did anything to the mother of their half-cousin. They were in the process of setting traps to ensure he couldn't come out. He wanted to fight them, but he refrained because I'd told him they were your kin. They're lucky, or he would have kicked their asses."

There was something odd about hearing my seventy-year-old mother say things like *kicked their asses*. She had been spending time with Amber. Maybe that was rubbing off. Admittedly, I spoke of ass-kicking on occasion too. Mom might have gotten it from me.

Eireth, Freysha, and the bodyguards were looking at me. I waved for them to get in the Jeep. I needed to let Inga know that Reb was alive, if not exactly okay, and it sounded like I might need to go over to Mom's cabin. Did all brides have so many problems to solve scant days before their weddings?

"Have you seen Liam fight?" Mom's tone turned a touch reverent. Nothing like a badass guy with rippling muscles to melt the heart of a lady. Of course, if he'd been furry at the time, the muscles might have been obscured by his pelt. Maybe *it* had rippled. "For a painter with a gentle soul, he's a *very* capable warrior."

"I have no doubt. But why are they fighting? Something must have happened. Some misunderstanding?" I could understand why the elves would assume Zoltan was an enemy, since he was a vampire and they didn't allow the undead on their world, but shifters had an entire planet of their own and were well-known in the Cosmic Realms. They probably had diplomats that went back and forth to Veleshna Var, asking for permission to hunt in the elven forests.

"Nothing happened." Mom's tone had shifted from reverence to exasperation. "Nothing worth fighting over. It wasn't a misunderstanding. They're just being stupid and possessive, and *Val*."

Yup, very exasperated. Even without details, I felt guilty. I'd wanted to alleviate the burden of so many houseguests at my home, but I'd truly believed Mom would enjoy getting to know some elves again. Maybe I'd *wanted* to believe that so I could get them out of my hair.

"Sorry, Mom. Do you want to come help?"

"*Yes.* Liam still can't leave his house."

"Right. I've got to swing by the shop, but I'll be there as soon as I can."

"By all means. Get some coffee on the way. The war on my street can wait."

"Is it really that bad?"

"*Yes.*"

I bit my lip. Even if I drove straight there, traffic would ensure it would take at least an hour. "I'll send help."

"Not your nudist dragon."

"If you really have a problem, he's the best one to stop it."

"Fine. Send him. I'll put an out-of-order sign on the sauna."

I rolled my eyes. This *couldn't* be as bad as she was saying, not if she was worried about backyard nudity. "You do that, Mom."

Zav? I projected my thoughts in the direction of the goblin sanctuary, assuming he was still there and hoping it wasn't too far away for him to hear me. My telepathy couldn't usually cross that many miles, but he was attuned to me. *I need a favor.*

Greetings, my mate, he replied promptly. *What favor? I am installing the eyrie launches for the great races.*

I imagined huge wooden platforms at the tops of trees. *Can you take a break and help my mother? Her elven houseguests are fighting with her werewolf neighbor, and she needs someone to mediate things and get them off his property. And to remove any traps they've laid.*

Ah! I am always prepared to help your mother.

Because she's my kin and means a lot to me or because she has that sauna?

Both those things, yes. Zav beamed pleasure into my mind along with an image of him sprawled naked on the bench with his heels kicked up on a heating element. *Afterward, you can join me in the soothing dry warmth of the hot box, and we can enjoy this peaceful week together.*

I think you're having a different week than I am. Also, Mom said the sauna is out of order. Was I lying to my mate? It wasn't *technically* a lie, was it? Mom wouldn't put a sign on it if there wasn't an issue…

Out of order?

In need of some repair to be operable again.

Ah, I will bring a team of goblin engineers to fix it. Your mother will be most appreciative.

Uh.

I am an excellent mate, Val. Our years together after our wedding will be glorious.

I'm certain that's true.

I'd hung up the phone, but I eyed it again, wondering if I should warn Mom about the team of goblin engineers. No. Sometimes, it was better *not* to have advance warning about bad news. If she knew they were coming, she would only worry.

Shaking my head, I climbed into the driver's seat. I had better not dawdle at the shop, but I would grab some coffee to take to my mother. Given the day she was having, gifts were appropriate. Maybe I had better stop by the liquor store too. Potent gifts with a high alcohol concentration would be even *more* appropriate.

CHAPTER 17

WHEN I ARRIVED AT THE coffee shop with my Jeep still full of elves, I found Dimitri in the alley with his tools. He worked next to freshly purchased stacks of lumber and drywall protected from the drizzle by tarps. Inga was with him, hammering nails with more power than the task required. She was probably still frustrated and worried about Reb being missing.

Much to our patrons' pleasure, the coffee kiosk hadn't been damaged in the explosion, and Tam was filling orders, though urging people to take their beverages to go. A long line stretched out the front door and around the far corner of the building.

No fewer than four goblins were cavorting about on the roof, one pointing and barking orders, the others making measurements as they pulled off damaged shingles and tossed them to the sidewalk. A few people in line glanced upward warily as they struck down nearby.

Were the shingles supposed to come *off*? I'd assumed the repairs would involve building materials being put back *on*.

"Oh dear," Freysha murmured. "Dimitri told me about the explosion, but I didn't realize the whole wall had been taken out."

"You should have seen it when the toilet was sticking out of the neighboring building."

That damage had been repaired—I assumed Dimitri had prioritized that, perhaps assisted by some grumping from the ice-cream shop owner.

"You guys don't need to come in," I told my elven passengers as I parked in front of the mystic's shop. "This will just take a minute. Then we'll head out to my mother's house."

On the ride over, Eireth had grown pensive when I'd told him we would go visit her. I knew he wanted to see her, but maybe he was as nervous about the reunion as she was. Did he fear that she would be old and bent and wielding a walker? Did elves *have* walkers?

"I will come with you." Freysha got out as soon as we stopped. "I saw Yog carrying blueprints. I want to ensure he isn't planning anything impractical for your establishment."

Erg, how had I missed seeing that? That must have been one of the goblins on the roof. Did replacing a wall and a little roofing require *blueprints*?

"Good idea." I grabbed my weapons, and we strode to the shop. "Thanks."

"Perhaps I should assist with the repairs," Freysha said, keeping pace.

I almost pointed out that Zav had suggested that, but I didn't want her to feel obligated. "Your engineering skills would be useful, but you don't need to do manual labor for us. It's not like we pay you. You don't even drink the coffee."

"I find the brews bitter to my taste buds. But I enjoy being helpful and doing work. You are not available that many hours a day for your lessons, and my studies do not require all of my waking hours. I like to be useful."

"Maybe you can usefully see what those goblins on the roof are doing." I waved toward them, meaning that she could yell up and have a conversation with them.

But she nodded and shimmied up a drainpipe at the corner. Dimitri spotted her and gaped.

"Elves are good climbers," I said, joining him.

"I see that."

Inga pulled a piece of lumber off a pile. I groped for a way to tell her that I'd seen Reb, without prompting her to run off alone to the Bloody Blade to pick a fight with fifty trolls. As I could attest, that rarely went well. I doubted the trolls would return to their haunt right away anyway. Now that they knew *I* knew where it was, they would be wary about opening up for business. For all they knew, I might return with Zav to obliterate them. A thought that probably shouldn't fill me with the wistful desire to do exactly that.

"Will you ask her to talk to the goblins?" Dimitri asked. "I have some concerns about the second-story addition."

"I already asked her to— Did you say *second-story addition?*"

"Yeah."

"Was that *your* idea?"

"No. The goblins have been talking about adding more seating and a dedicated gaming area for weeks."

"The *goblins* don't own this building."

"They are our best customers."

"Dimitri, *we* don't even own the building. We have a lease."

"I know. But things have been going pretty well. I'm thinking of making an offer on it. Nin said real estate is never a bad investment."

"Don't you think you should wait to renovate until after the landlord accepts your offer and all the documents have been signed to make it yours?"

"Yes." He shrugged. "It wasn't my idea."

"You have to be firm with goblins, Dimitri."

Freysha's voice floated down to us, far more stern than usual. Since she was speaking in goblin, I didn't know what she said, but I hoped she was being firm.

"I know, but I don't like to disappoint people."

Speaking of that, Inga was coming over…

I patted Dimitri on the shoulder and walked up to meet her. Behind me, Freysha hopped down, now holding a long tube of paper that might have been the blueprints she'd mentioned. I hoped she was taking them to the dumpster, but she walked inside as she pulled a pencil and a short ruler out of her overalls pocket. I made a note to explain to her the part about how we didn't yet own the building and couldn't make additions.

"Ruin Bringer," Inga rumbled. Her eyes were bloodshot, and she didn't look like she'd slept much. "Have you any news on Reb?"

"Actually, yes." I summed up my adventure at the Bloody Blade, watching her expression change from weariness to surprise to anger. By the time I finished, her fists were clenched, and she was glowering off toward downtown Seattle.

"I will go there and retrieve him. He is my adopted boy. They have no right to take him."

I rested a hand on her shoulder, lest she plow past me and go right then. The only weapon she had was the hammer she'd been wielding against the nails.

"I agree with you, and I'm going to get some help and find him. They cleared out of their pub, so there won't be anyone there now, but my boss has someone watching the place. She'll let me know if the trolls come back or if anyone spots Reb."

"I will search on my own, and I will find him. It is my duty as his foster mother."

"I can't stop you if you want to search." Maybe she had connections and would have an easier time finding the trolls than Willard or I would. "But don't confront them alone, okay? I'll help. And so will Zav." Assuming he was done making peace between Liam and the elves, and I could entice him to give up eyrie building for a few hours.

"If I cannot get him by myself, I will ask for your help," Inga said reluctantly, though her obstinate eyes promised she would rather handle this without my help. "But I have some money saved up. I will attempt to pay them if necessary."

"Or you could stay here and help Dimitri and let the professional combatants handle it." I smiled and patted Fezzik.

She only scowled. "If there is a battle, Reb could be hurt."

"I won't let that happen."

Still scowling, she stalked back to the lumber pile for more wood. I kneaded the back of my neck, wishing that had gone better. And hoping she wouldn't get herself kidnapped right alongside Reb.

"This is a *much* better design," Freysha's voice floated to me.

She'd already made revisions to the blueprint and now stood in the alley, the large paper unrolled as she showed the sketches to Dimitri. "The goblins hadn't even added a staircase," she told him, shaking her head with disapproval.

"How were people going to get up and down?" Dimitri sounded dazed as he looked at the blueprints.

I thought about going over to take a look, but I had enough things dazing me this week.

"A fireman's pole." Freysha clucked her tongue. "Completely impractical. We may even want to consider an elevator if you wish to extend service to the upstairs lounge and game room."

"Do we need permits to do all of this?" Dimitri looked at me.

I spread my arms. Thanks to the various illusions and glamours masking our place from human passersby, we wouldn't have to worry about building inspectors unless they had magical blood. It would be alarming to the neighborhood if we ever moved out of the building and removed the camouflaging magic. Until the toilet had embedded in his wall, the ice-cream shop owner had probably forgotten that there was a building here.

"I will handle this," Freysha said. "In my engineering class, I am learning about such things and how to file the appropriate paperwork."

I noticed Eireth watching from the street—he must have gotten bored sitting in the Jeep—and joined him and his ever-present bodyguards. They were glaring down the sidewalk in each direction, possibly searching for more hoodlums to strap to the nearest car hood.

"Ready to go visit my mother?" I asked, joining him. "I think Freysha may be busy here for the rest of the day."

A thunk came from the roof, shingles rained down on the people in line, and Freysha barked a bunch of orders in goblin up to our green-skinned workers. Hopefully, they included suggestions not to pelt people waiting to buy our coffee.

"Yes." Eireth regarded Freysha with a curious expression. "It is strange to see my shy, quiet daughter ordering around a team of workers."

"She's in her element. She just redesigned some blueprints in two minutes. That takes most architects hours, if not days." Even if I hadn't looked at the plans, I trusted that Freysha's work was good. The goblins wouldn't be willing to follow her lead otherwise.

"Perhaps I should have been more supportive in her... unusual interests. It is difficult to know with children which passions are passing fancies and which will turn into lifelong hobbies."

"Or even careers," I suggested.

His lips twisted. "Yes."

"You don't approve?"

Even though Freysha had implied that our elven cousins didn't understand her and didn't support her engineering interest, I'd assumed Eireth was generally supportive. He gave off that vibe. After all, he'd been willing to marry Zav and me the first time we'd met, before he'd known if I was anything other than an odious assassin without scruples.

Eireth sighed. "I wish her to do what makes her happy, but as my only full-blooded child, at least so far, it would be nice if she had an interest in politics and leading our people. Elven rule isn't predetermined based on bloodlines, but if you are the child of a ruler, you are often well-known by the council and court, and you have presumably had a chance to shine on diplomatic missions, so you are usually in consideration."

"Do you *want* your kid to rule after you? No offense, but I've seen you running—*skating*—away from your bodyguards. That implies that you find it stifling and aren't that enamored with the gig."

"My interest in experimenting with the wheeled footwear in your world implies all that?" He glanced back at the two guards, though like the Buckingham Palace guards, their faces rarely showed any expression. All they needed were the fuzzy bearskin caps, and they would be shoo-ins for the job.

"Experimenting with it at top speed while your bodyguards are struggling to catch you does, yes."

One of the guards made eye contact with the other and nodded.

"I don't dislike the work," Eireth said, "and I have been able to keep the peace between the various factions, for the most part. One should do what one is talented at and trained for and what can help the world, even if it can occasionally be stifling. If Freysha does not want to urge her flying mount to follow mine, that does not bother me. What is more disturbing is the thought of her leaving our world for long periods of time in order to pursue this interest. I've already missed her in the months that she has been visiting you here."

"At least she's happy to go home to visit, and the portal travel makes that swift and painless, right? Don't you think that people should also do what they're talented at and trained to do in order to help *other* worlds?"

"I suppose."

"Or maybe you could try to change *your* world so she could do her work there. It sounds like she thinks she could improve elven architecture and make it safer and less reliant on magic."

"I see she's discussed this with you," Eireth said dryly.

"Yeah. We're sisters. Sisters discuss things. I'd prefer it if she would discuss how to hurl fireballs with me, but that seems outside her wheelhouse."

Eireth ignored my pyromaniac tendencies and said, "Our people are long-lived and have long memories. They are not particularly interested in drastic changes to things that have always worked sufficiently."

"So innovation isn't allowed?"

"It is difficult to sway the elders. Everything must be weighed and balanced, and they are more willing to listen to people who have, over the centuries, proven themselves practical and reasonable."

"Practical centenarians. Exactly the types of people known for innovation."

"*Reasonable* young people will be listened to and considered."

"We have a quote here on Earth. Reasonable people adapt themselves to the world. Unreasonable people attempt to adapt the world to themselves. All progress, therefore, depends on unreasonable people."

"Hm."

I doubted I could change his mind, so I let it drop. If he wanted Freysha to stay at home, he would have to start fighting to make their home a place where she could do her work. If he wasn't willing to do that, or couldn't do that, he would have to accept that she would go where her talents were welcome. They would figure it out. I actually thought Freysha might fit in on the goblin home world just fine and would enjoy it there. What would Eireth—and his stuffy wife—think if Freysha married a goblin?

Since Eireth appeared thoughtful about—or consternated by—our conversation, I resisted the urge to smirk wildly.

"All right," I said. "Mom's waiting for us. I haven't gotten an update from Zav, but she may need more than a dragon to help smooth things over with the elves and her neighbor."

Eireth frowned with concern. "There is a problem at her home? With my people?"

"A misunderstanding. But it may be helpful if you tell them not to attack any vampires, werewolves, or other denizens of Earth while they're here." I realized I hadn't filled him in on that. I also realized that taking him over there might mean introducing him to Liam, the neighbor that my mom was definitely not dating, even though they had coffee together regularly. And possibly sex.

Since Eireth had married someone else decades ago, he shouldn't have a problem with her not-dating somebody, right?

"We should go immediately." Eireth waved to his bodyguards and strode toward the Jeep.

Hoping the day couldn't get any worse, I made myself walk briskly after him.

CHAPTER 18

I BREATHED OUT A SIGH OF relief when I sensed Zav's aura. We'd driven through the town of Duvall and were speeding down the back roads toward Mom's cabin. After leaving Freysha to lead the work team at the shop, only Eireth and his two bodyguards remained with me.

Everything okay? I telepathed Zav.

I am preventing hostilities from occurring until the king is able to facilitate a stand-down or truce between the warring parties, he replied. *I sense that he is with you.*

Uh, yeah.

Excellent. I am more than capable of keeping elves from attacking werewolves, but their tiff is preventing me from relaxing in the hot box. I have not been able to discern the reason for the hostilities, but the arguing I have overheard makes it seem insignificant. All parties should simply agree to ignore each other.

Maybe Eireth should invite them all into the sauna for a peace accord.

After I am done using it, that would be acceptable. The goblins have not been able to determine the reason for the out-of-order sign. They are testing the hot box now.

How are they testing it?

By operating it from the inside and monitoring the temperature and settings with their tools. I believe they are also making improvements, as I hear hammering and drilling. Your mother will be pleased.

Poor Mom. I drove faster.

As I turned onto her street, my phone vibrated.

"I'll be right there, Mom," I answered.

"There are naked green *goblins* in my sauna!" She didn't shriek often and was a relatively calm woman by nature, but that qualified as a shriek. "And they're hammering something. I can't even get in there to pull them out. They locked the door. Val, there isn't even a lock *on* it!"

"Maybe that's one of their improvements."

"Valmeyjar Thorvald, this is completely unacceptable!"

"That is Sigrid?" Eireth was looking at the phone. It wasn't on speaker-mode, but that hardly mattered. It wouldn't take enhanced elven ears to hear her angry words.

"Yeah," I said. "She's having a bad week. It's my fault."

Mom had fallen silent. Had she heard Eireth?

"I see your cabin, Mom," I said. "Almost there."

I hung up.

Technically, what I saw was her mailbox and driveway and, through the trees, a great black dragon perched on the roof of Liam's house. Well, that was one way to keep elves from encroaching.

You're looking fearsome and majestic up there, Zav, I told him.

Yes. That is my natural state.

Instead of swinging into the driveway, I parked alongside the street in front of the chain-link fence that bordered Liam's yard. Though Zav's aura and the auras of almost two dozen elves in my mom's front yard cluttered up my senses, I did manage to pick out the werewolf aura. Liam was inside his house. Hopefully not *trapped* inside his house, but Mom *had* mentioned something about traps.

"Will you see if you can get them to put down their weapons and ask them why they're attacking my mom's neighbors?" I pointed Eireth toward his people. "I'm going to check on Liam."

Mom wasn't out in the yard with the elves, nor did I see her trying to force open the door to her sauna, though I'd half-expected to find her with a screwdriver, removing the hinges. Since she didn't have magical blood, I couldn't sense her, but I did hear Rocket barking from inside the cabin.

"Yes, certainly." Eireth stepped out of the Jeep, his bodyguards following him, and immediately started speaking in elvish to one of his people.

Though I usually butted out of private conversations in other languages, I rubbed my translation charm so I could get the gist as I let myself through Liam's gate. A gate that was dented and half-hanging off one of the metal hinges. I sensed little spots of magic around the front yard and on the gravel driveway. Damn, the elves truly *had* laid traps. To force Liam to stay inside his house? *Why?*

"...the werewolf was attacking her, Your Majesty," one of the elves reported, the words floating across the street to me.

"He had her pressed against the fence and was *smothering* her," another reported.

"Uh oh." Why did I have a feeling that smothering had been a lovers' embrace? I stepped carefully around a circular spot emanating magic. Whatever the traps did, I didn't want to find out firsthand.

"We rushed out to put an end to the inappropriate behavior. The werewolf grew belligerent and refused to leave the premises. We knew you would wish the human mother of your daughter to be unharmed, so we *forced* him to leave."

I sighed and met Zav's violet eyes. He'd gone from sitting upright on the roof to lying across it, his tail dangling down into the backyard. If it was possible for a dragon to have a long-suffering expression, he did. I regretted taking him away from the wedding preparations, since I got the impression that he was enjoying preparing everything to be appropriate for his people. At the least, he felt the need to put a lot of effort into it. He probably wanted his mother to approve of everything and worried that Xilneth and his clan would screw things up.

Thanks for coming, I told him. *Have I mentioned lately that I love you?*

It had taken me a while to get comfortable saying that. It always seemed like an admission of vulnerability, and we all knew how bad I was at sharing vulnerabilities.

Last week, as you writhed in passion due to my expert ministrations, you informed me thus.

Well, good. It's true. And you were writhing, too, don't forget.

Naturally. I also have feelings of human passion for you. That was his way of saying he loved me. *And you are most excellent at pleasing me in the nest.*

I'm glad. I glanced back at the elves, noticed them all watching me, and hoped none of them could listen in on our telepathic conversation.

We should discuss final plans for the wedding ceremony later, Zav said, *and determine where the dragons will stay when they come to this world. It is likely that my family will arrive the day before the wedding to ensure they will not be tardy. The queen may come early to make sure the Starsinger Clan will not ruin anything. Our plan to get her to come to the event worked; she believes her powerful presence is needed to keep them in line and that mischief and embarrassment to our clan is otherwise a possibility.* His violet eyes closed to slits. *But it had better not be a possibility.*

The Starsinger Clan is the least of my worries right now.

There are other worries?

A few things. I'll fill you in later when we sit down to talk. Even though I hoped I would be able to handle the troll-grenade situation before the big day, I had better let him know about the threat.

We will talk in the hot box. Zav sat up enough to spread and shake his wings. Droplets of water from the on-again-off-again rain flew in all directions. *It is damp and chilly out here. My scales may molder.*

Your magic doesn't keep that from happening?

Even dragon magic has its limits. He sounded amused, so I took that for a joke.

Maybe we should take our honeymoon in Hawaii. We hadn't discussed the honeymoon yet. Given that there were so many potentials for disaster with the wedding, I'd thought it best to make sure we were successfully joined in holy matrimony before booking a hotel.

Hawaii is an island, yes?

A tropical island, yeah.

Thus warm.

Thus.

I approve of this idea. Is there sufficient meat there?

Yes. It's a large island. They do luaus with pigs wrapped in banana leaves that slow-cook for hours in a pit. Super succulent.

This is of interest to me.

I thought it might be. In Hawaii, you can also surf, snorkel with fish, walk on the beach, and hike up volcanoes.

Tell me more about the pit pigs.

I snorted. *Later.*

"No more elves!" came a snarl from inside the house as I approached the front porch.

"It's Val." I lifted my arms to show him my empty hands. "I came to apologize and, uh, de-escalate the situation."

"The dragon already did that. He also bent my stovepipe."

"You should see what he did to our chimney."

I repaired that, Zav said primly into my mind.

Mind if I volunteer you to repair Liam's bent stovepipe?

It will be a simple matter.

I took that for a yes. "Zav says he'll fix it. Uhm, can I come in?"

More magical traps oozed menace from the porch floorboards and the doorjamb. The magic didn't feel elven, so they were probably Liam's own addition. That made me think of the cannon still poised in front of Zoltan's door. Given that elves were usually painted as a serene and pleasant race in fantasy books, it was amazing how many people my kin were upsetting. Or maybe not. If they were related to *me*, it probably made sense. I couldn't blame my mom for all my belligerent genes.

"You're alone, right?" Liam asked warily.

"Yes. You should be able to sense that."

"Earlier, four of the elves camouflaged themselves to my senses and tried to get to the back door."

"Why did they want to get in your house?"

"They had lumber. They may only have wanted to bar the way and force me to stay in. They're treating me as if I'm some child molester. All I was doing was... never mind."

"Kissing my mom?" I asked quietly. "Vigorously enough to be mistaken for something more aggressive?"

"*She* instigated it. And she *likes* vigor."

Details I did not want to know.

"It's not my fault that Rocket took that moment to overreact to my presence," Liam added. "And that the elves overreacted even more than the dog, which I wouldn't have thought possible."

A shadow fell over me, and I jumped. Zav's head had come down, extending on his long neck so that he could peer over the edge of the roof at me.

Are you eavesdropping? I asked.

This conversation is of no interest to me. I thought you might need assistance in obliterating those puny traps.

I'm being diplomatic and waiting to see if Liam deactivates them for me.

I thought you might be vexing him. Undiplomatically.

Nope.

He sounds irked and defensive.

Because of the elves, not me.

Hm. Was that a skeptical expression? Dragon faces were so hard to read.

I squinted at Zav and tried to shoo his head out of sight, especially since I sensed Liam on the other side of the door. He was probably peering out the peephole at us.

"My father came to talk to his people," I said. "There shouldn't be any more hostilities."

Liam opened the door. He wore one of the plaid flannel shirts that were his mainstay, though this one was more rumpled than usual for him, and his hair was tousled. Even his silver beard, usually tidy and combed, was tousled today. Dealing with a pack of hostile elves had to be harrowing.

"Your father? The elven king?" His lip curled.

Uh oh. What had Mom told Liam about Eireth? She hadn't waxed nostalgic about her lover from more than forty years ago, had she? Given how private she was, that was hard to imagine, but she *did* have that portrait of Eireth above her fireplace. Had Liam seen that and asked who it was? And then possibly felt like their burgeoning relationship might be doomed because Mom still had feelings for her old elven lover?

"Yeah," I said casually. "That's him."

"He doesn't look that impressive."

"Not everybody can have a werewolf for a father," I said dryly.

Liam's gaze shifted back to me. "I apologize. I did not mean to insult you or your lineage. I just thought... He's bigger in the picture."

He *had* seen the portrait. I'd have to suggest to Mom that she take down pictures of former lovers when she was dating a new guy. At least it was in the living room instead of over her bed. That would be a buzzkill for a night of romance with a new boyfriend.

"His face certainly is. It *is* a headshot."

Liam grunted. "Will the elven *king* have his people remove their traps from *my* property?"

"Zav could probably do that."

Liam's gaze shifted over my shoulder. Zav hadn't shooed. His head still hung over the eaves as he alternately watched us and the elves in Mom's driveway.

I can easily disable the traps, Zav informed me.

We'd appreciate that.

Buzzes of magic plucked at my senses as bursts of flame appeared in the driveway and the yard. Smoke wafted upward. Who would have thought that magical traps had components that could be lit on fire?

Voices in Mom's yard grew louder, and several elves pointed over at the traps. Maybe they thought Liam had done that. I pointed up at Zav.

Eireth, still speaking to his people, lifted his arms and uttered soothing words.

"Thank you," Liam said gruffly. "How much longer will *they* be staying?"

"Only until the wedding on Saturday." I hoped.

"And how long will *they* be staying?" Liam tilted his chin toward the outdoor sauna. The goblins weren't visible, but bangs and thumps emanated from the small structure.

"Only a couple of hours, I think." Especially since there was nothing to repair. What were they *doing* in there? Installing cup holders?

"Good. Do let your mother know that I would be happy to see her again, Rocket's disapproval notwithstanding, but perhaps we should wait to have coffee until after her houseguests are gone."

If all they had been doing was having coffee, the houseguests wouldn't have cared.

"I'll tell her." I glanced at her property again. She'd opened the door to look out and had spotted Eireth. He'd also spotted her. "I better go make sure this… goes well."

As well and as unawkwardly as it could.

Liam followed me to the street, and I realized there was absolutely no chance of this meeting not being awkward. Maybe I should have left him trapped in his house.

CHAPTER 19

"HEY, GUYS." I WAVED INANELY as I walked up to the gaggle of elves in the driveway. The gaggle of elves and *Mom*.

She'd come outside and walked up to face Eireth. Her face was as reserved and difficult to read as I'd ever seen it. Eireth smiled at her, but it looked like a pleasant and diplomatic smile, and I sensed a tense uncertainty from him.

The elves watched like it was opening day at the movies. Mom glanced at them, and I wished there was a way to make them disappear so she and Eireth could have a private moment. A fresh round of bangs came from inside the sauna.

Maybe I should suggest that they go inside the cabin? But then what would Liam think? He stood a few feet behind me, watching the reunion a lot more warily than the elves. I hoped Mom had told him that Eircth was married now. Just in case the fact that they now appeared forty years apart in age didn't suggest a hookup was unlikely.

"Good afternoon, Sigrid." Eireth bowed to her. "I'm pleased to see that you're well."

"Thanks." Mom surprised me by emulating the bow-curtsey that Freysha always did. An elven custom she must have learned when she'd spent the summer visiting with his people. "I see that you're... the same."

"But not pleased to see that?" He smiled again, that strain underlying it.

"Amazed, I suppose. I know your people are long-lived, but I thought being a king would have turned your hair white. That happens to our presidents, and they only serve four-year terms."

I blinked. Why was she bringing up *presidents*? Was this what passed for nervous babbling from Mom?

"I'm happy for you that you seem well," she added quietly, then glanced at the elves again. "I..."

"Maybe you guys should have a chat in the cabin," I suggested. "I can show the elves my sword and what I'm learning about it. Or we can help the goblins with their improvements."

The look Mom shot me hinted more of *butt-out* or *beat-it* than *thanks-for-trying-to-help*.

Liam cleared his throat and walked around me to stand closer to Mom. He didn't do anything as obnoxious as putting a possessive arm around her, but he did make sure to plant himself in Eireth's view.

"I'm Liam. I live over there. Are your people done taking pot shots at me and trying to chain me inside my own house?"

Eireth's eyes narrowed. "My people say that you assaulted Sigrid."

Mom shook her head, but the men were glaring at each other now and didn't notice.

"I did no such thing. We're friends."

Mom must have left the door ajar, because Rocket took that moment to shove it the rest of the way open and run into the yard. He rushed up to Mom's side, raised his hackles, and growled at Liam.

Liam sighed and looked skyward.

"Friends?" Eireth asked skeptically.

"*Friends*," Mom said firmly.

"Rocket gets uppity around predators," I explained, trying to be helpful. The elves looked like they were ten seconds away from pulling bags of popcorn out of interdimensional pantries and noshing while the show continued.

Mom shot me another look that suggested I should shut up and stay out of it. But I was the reason they were face-to-face now. It seemed like I should do something to smooth over any discomfort, especially if discomfort might lead to another fight. A few of the elves had gone from passively observing the reunion to glaring at Liam again.

"Liam," Mom said in her take-charge, no-nonsense tone, "go home, please. I'll call you when things settle down here."

He opened his mouth, as if to object, but after a pause, he only said, "Am I still invited to the wedding?"

"Yes," Mom said as several of the elves said, "*No*."

"*Yes*," I said. "If Mom comes with the elves, you can come as Gondo's date."

Liam's eyebrows rose. "Was that the over-caffeinated goblin I met at the coffee shop?"

"One of them, I'm certain. He's fun at parties."

Actually, *center-of-attention* was the term Dimitri had used when describing the goblins at the bachelor party he'd thrown the month before for Zav. A party Zav had only stuck around for because Dimitri had bribed him with pepperoni sticks.

The sauna door creaked open, and a puff of steam came out. Or was that smoke? Two goblins coughed, batted at the hazy air, and rushed into the woods without looking at our gathering.

"Bathroom break?" I wondered.

They came back soon, half-carrying and half-dragging a large branch. They tried to take it directly into the sauna. When that didn't work, two more goblins hopped out with axes and saws, and they trimmed the branch to suitable dimensions.

"I..." Mom said, "am not certain whether to put a stop to that or wait to see what they build. I've heard goblin engineering is creative."

"Yeah," I said, "it creatively voids the warranty on all of your products. I'll check on them. You two go have your chat. Catch up. Get in a good mood before the wedding, so we don't add more tension to what's already going to be a varied and possibly testy collection of guests."

"Nobody's tense, Val," Mom said tensely.

"Uh huh. Hey, Rocket. Why don't you go with them? I think a ham might have fallen out of the fridge while you've been outside."

That earned me Dirty Look Number Three from Mom—and a more interested look from Rocket as his head tilted and his ears cocked—but she did invite Eireth, and Eireth alone, inside. He said something to his people, patting the air with a conciliatory hand, and trailed her into the cabin.

Liam glowered after them. Rocket growled at him before trotting in with Mom to look for that ham.

"Help me check on the sauna, will you, Liam?" I nodded in that direction, wanting to have a few words with him—out of earshot of the elven herd—before returning to hunting trolls. I *hoped* he was mature enough not to start trouble or sulk like a jealous lover, but maybe I could assuage any tendencies toward immaturity he might be feeling. Not that I'd proven apt at soothing ruffled feathers today.

He followed me without objecting, though he kept glancing over his shoulder at the elves. Probably worried they would shoot arrows into his back as soon as Eireth was out of sight.

You are entering the sauna? Zav asked me from his rooftop perch.

Just for a minute to talk to Liam. I approached the door, wondering exactly how many goblins were inside. The bangs and clanks had shifted to the whir of a drill. It shouldn't have surprised me that goblins kept battery-operated power drills in their pockets.

You will speak with me next? Zav didn't make it a command, as he once would have. My haughty dragon had gotten more polite of late.

Yeah. I'd rather speak with you instead of Liam. Trust me.

Excellent. I am a superior conversationalist.

Yes, you are. Did you fix that stovepipe?

I will. I am scratching an itchy belly scale on it currently.

It's important that dragons not be itchy.

It is. It is possible that I must shed a few scales. I will attend to this before the wedding so that I'm not unkempt.

I appreciate your dedication toward kemptness. I would appreciate it even more if he spent most of the wedding in his human form, especially our walk down the aisle, but I supposed he planned to hunt with his kin. And race against them. *I had no idea dragons were like geckos.*

Dragons are not *like geckos. We feast on superior prey, so we do not need to eat our own sloughed scales to retain mineral content. That is a disgusting habit.*

No argument here. I knocked on the sauna door before opening it, just in case the goblins were naked and wanted to cover themselves with towels. Or tool belts.

"Are you sure you want to go in there?" Maybe Liam had dealt with goblins often enough that he had similar concerns.

"It'll give us a private place to talk. And if they're defiling my mother's sauna, I should put a stop to that. It's slightly possible, however inadvertently, that it's my fault that they're here."

"The hot box is not ready for the big reveal," a reedy voice called out.

"Tough." I opened the door, dry heat wafting out, and jerked a thumb over my shoulder. "Take a break."

Six goblins trundled out, the last one stopping to ask, "A coffee break?"

He looked hopefully toward the cabin and sniffed the air, though I didn't smell any coffee brewing. It was only a couple of hours until dark.

"No. Why don't you go chat up those elves? Tell them how much their cities would be improved by the addition of goblin engineering." I wondered if Eireth could be talked into telling his people he planned to hire goblin engineers. That would horrify them enough that they might find Freysha and her architectural plans a delightful alternative.

"Oh, fantastic. A brilliant topic." The goblins trotted toward the elves, who were now milling and muttering to themselves, no doubt wondering what they were supposed to do now that the show was over.

"If you're going to sell them on that, you might not want to let them see this place." Liam stepped into the sauna and waved at leaves and twigs all over the floor. And the benches. And smoking on the heating element.

"You don't think the elves will be impressed with the additions?"

I brushed the burning debris off the coals and nodded at branches now affixed to the walls. They appeared to be... magazine racks? And there were the cup holders I'd guessed at. Somewhere, the goblins had found some metal and plastic and molded them into a little table they'd built at the end of one bench. Nuts and bolts had been drilled into the wall by the door. Robe and towel hooks?

"They're... not horrible, I suppose." Liam prodded a bolt, looked at grease on his finger, and wiped it on his pants. "If you like that mechanic-shop decorating trend."

"Who doesn't? You're definitely still invited to the wedding, by the way. And I'm sure Mom will want you to be her date. This is just her first time seeing Eireth in over forty years, so it's a little... weird. It's not like they're going to get together or anything. He's married, and she's..." I stopped myself from saying *too old to interest an elf in the prime of his life* since Liam was about the same age, and I didn't even know if that was true. After all, I was pretty sure Mom could have *Gondo* as a date if she wanted. She was, after all, as much of a coffee snob as he was. Besides, I would like to believe that age wouldn't be a deal-killer in a relationship with someone from a long-lived species, given that I was about to *marry* someone from a long-lived species. "She's in an intriguing new relationship with a neighbor," I finished.

"She called me intriguing?"

"No, she doesn't say anything about you. She's very private about... everything. I'm assuming intrigue."

"Thank you. I'm not truly worried. Well, not *that* worried, but it was hard not to feel threatened when the guy in her portrait showed up with an army of elves."

I *knew* that portrait had been a contention point. I made a note to ask Mom to put it someplace that intriguing male guests wouldn't be subjected to it when they visited.

"Technically, the army of elves preceded him," Liam said. "I haven't known what to think of them. And then with the incident this morning…"

"Did they *really* misinterpret a passionate embrace for a fight?"

Liam stuck his hands in his pockets and prodded a twig with his boot. "We started out arguing, so maybe that led to them thinking… Oh, I don't know. Honestly, I'd forgotten they were all back there in their yurts and could listen. Sigrid was saying that we couldn't spend so much time together because Rocket found it stressful, and I got grumpy. It's not my fault the dog doesn't like werewolves. I've done my best to be friendly to him. And it's not right that she be lonely for the rest of her life because her dog doesn't like men. I mean he doesn't like *me*." Liam sounded more exasperated than grumpy. Maybe both. "He likes *everyone*. I don't understand why he can't get past me smelling like a wolf."

"Maybe you could start bringing over steaks every time you come."

Liam snorted, though his eyes grew a touch speculative. I couldn't believe he hadn't tried that yet. Of all people, he ought to know that the stomach was the way to a predator's heart. Also a dog's heart.

"I do have a freezer full of elk I caught this fall."

"And you've kept this information from Rocket? No wonder he's irked with you."

"I'll give it a shot," Liam said. "If the elves will let me close to the yard again."

"I'm sure Rocket would settle for elk steaks lobbed over the fence."

"I want him to know they're coming from *me*. Not those pointy-eared aliens he has no trouble snuggling up to." Ah, another bone of contention. Rocket liked the elves but not Liam. No wonder he'd been grumpy. "Val, I want you to know we weren't fighting. Just arguing. They completely misinterpreted it. Sometimes when we argue, emotions get heated, and lead to— er." He shrugged.

"Vigor? Amore?"

"Yeah."

A text came in from Willard. *My agent spotted Inga in the alley going into the Bloody Blade. She found it empty and soon left, but I thought you'd want to know. I also just saw a troll near my apartment. I've got my gun ready in case they come after me. It was probably a coincidence, but I have a lot left to do before the wedding, so I'd appreciate it if your troll problem didn't spill over into my preparations.*

I held up a finger to Liam and texted her back. *I'll come over with Sindari, and we'll look around to make sure nobody is planning anything untoward toward you or your apartment.*

I can take care of myself. If those trolls try anything untoward, I'll shoot the snot out of them. And then I'll sic Maggie on them.

Her meow alone could scare them away.

I like a cat with attitude.

Shocking.

I rubbed my face, frustrated that I had someone else to worry about. Maybe Zav would help me hunt down all the trolls in Seattle and lock them in a nice vault until after the wedding.

"Everything okay?" Liam asked.

"It will be." I lowered my hand. "Eireth won't let the elves bug you again, and after my wedding, they'll all return to their world."

"Any chance you'll offend them terribly and they'll leave tonight?"

"There's always a chance of that."

Liam smiled. "I'll wait at home until Sigrid calls."

"A good idea."

We stepped outside to find Zav in his human form, his robe draped over one arm, his body naked save for his yellow footwear.

Liam almost pitched over sideways. Averting his eyes, he said, "I guess it's not *you* who is most likely to offend the elves, Val."

The robe was covering only Zav's arm and elbow, none of his naughty bits.

"Nope," I said agreeably.

The elves had all disappeared. Maybe a naked dragon was enough to make them hide in their yurts. If that was true, I should have sent Zav in like this from the start.

"Can you put your robe on and hop in the Jeep, please?" I asked Zav. "We need to take care of some trolls."

"You agreed that we would speak now."

"And we will. The Jeep is as good a place to speak as the sauna." I waved toward my vehicle as a chilly breeze kicked up, raising gooseflesh on Zav's bare skin.

"It is not." He gazed longingly into the sauna, leaning toward the hot air wafting out.

"Yeah, you're right. But I'll buy you some chicken strips on the way. You can warm your bare legs by the flames of the breading and sauce that you incinerate."

Liam blinked a few times. "And here I thought my relationship with Sigrid might be considered odd."

"Nope. You'll be the normal couple at my wedding. Trust me."

Zav strode toward the Jeep, his naked butt on full display.

"Oh, I do," Liam said.

CHAPTER 20

WE HAD TO DRIVE BACK to Woodinville before finding a drive-through supplier of fine chicken strips. I waited until Zav had incinerated the breading off and consumed his eight servings before asking what was on his mind. Surprisingly, he hadn't brought it up yet.

After I'd made sure Mom and Eireth weren't staring at the floor awkwardly and not talking to each other, I'd left Eireth and his bodyguards with the rest of the elf pack, trusting they could find their way back to my house if they didn't want to spend the night.

"Everything going okay at the goblin sanctuary?" I glanced at him, though it was getting dark, and I couldn't see much of his face.

"They are suitably pleased to serve a dragon."

Did that answer my question? "So they're letting you install the... What was it? Eyries?"

"Yes, and I have deposited *ornax* and *yorak* into the forests around the sanctuary. It would not be proper to hunt them until they have acclimated to this new world."

"Are those predators or herbivores?"

"One of each. Predators are more challenging prey, but herbivores are much tastier prey. Dragons enjoy both a challenge and a succulent feast."

"No doubt." Maybe it was a good thing that we'd planned the wedding for late winter. There shouldn't be many hikers in the national forest at this time of year. Fewer chances of innocent people being maimed by alien predators. "What did you want to talk about?"

Zav had donned his robe, but he had the heater on high and kept glancing longingly in the side mirror, as if the sauna might be floating along after us. Or as if he was thinking of *causing* the sauna to float along after us. I would have to order him one for a wedding present. I'd looked up the prices after Mom had supplied the information. Like hot tubs, they were not inexpensive, but one couldn't have a cold dragon wandering around the house. A cold dragon was a grumpy dragon. Just as a wet Del'nothian tiger was a grumpy tiger. Apparently, I should have relocated to Phoenix if I wanted magical allies from other worlds.

"I am concerned," Zav said slowly, "that the queen will not find the preparations sufficient or the event worthy of her time. I am also concerned that the Starsinger Clan will make a farce of our festival. Further, it is possible that I erred in inviting so many beings that are largely unknown to us. I wished the entire world—many worlds—to know we are to be mated permanently and in all the ways that matter, but these relative strangers may cause trouble." He looked intently over at me. "They may not be suitably reverent to my mother—to the queen presiding over the Dragon Ruling Council and Justice Court and making policy for the entire Cosmic Realms. If she deems their offenses criminal, she will take them back for punishment and rehabilitation."

"I don't think many people will dare be irreverent with a dozen dragons present."

"Three dozen," Zav said.

"That many people, er, dragons from your clan are coming?" I'd never even seen that many dragons at once. Every time I'd been around more than a few, they'd been fighting, and I'd barely survived the situation. What if a war broke out at my wedding?

"Yes. My brothers, sister, and I have numerous cousins. Just as you do."

Right, my cousins that snubbed Freysha and whom I couldn't even name. Three days ago, I hadn't known they existed. "Maybe we should have both kept the guest list smaller, but it would be rude to start uninviting people."

"Yes. It is unwise to be rude to dragons."

"I've heard that. Do you want me to pat you on the back and try to assuage your concerns about the dragons and the wedding, or do you want me to share my own concerns?"

Zav gazed thoughtfully at me. "You are worried that the troll who bombed your establishment will attack you or others at the wedding?"

"Among other things, yeah." I summed up my week for him.

"Trolls are insignificant to dragons. Even with their explosives, they will not be able to harm dragons."

I thought about pointing out that there would be a lot of non-dragon guests who weren't nearly as well armored, but he might not be concerned about them. Better to stick with what might worry him. "What if they bomb the eyries and perches you've built for the races?"

"That would be problematic. The queen would most certainly capture them for rehabilitation and punishment then."

"I suppose I shouldn't feel hopeful about that happening."

"I would prefer if there were no explosions," Zav said. "Nothing that would lead the queen to believe I was incapable of creating an event suitable for even the most eminent dragons."

"It sounds like it's important to you that she think highly of you."

"It is important that she not believe I am *lacking* in any way." Zav lifted his chin. "I have proven myself to be a powerful and competent warrior *many* times, but it took me many months to round up all of the criminals on the list she gave me. It should have been a simple matter, as she informed me numerous times."

I decided not to point out that his mom was kind of a dick. "It can be hard for kids to live up to the expectations of parents."

"Yes. But I will do so this weekend. The event will go smoothly, and the dragons will be entertained and fed as they witness our union."

"I'm glad. Entertained dragons are superior to crabby dragons."

"Always. While you speak to your wedding planner, I will search for suspicious trolls and the missing troll boy."

"You don't have to do that. If you need to go back to working on the sanctuary, I understand. I can handle my troll concerns."

"I will *assist* you with your concerns. A mate should do this. Just as you assist me with mine."

"Have I done that? All I did was buy you chicken strips. Admittedly, an order suitable for *eight* people." I'd hidden my own order under the seat, though that probably wasn't necessary. Zav didn't usually swipe my food, not on purpose. He even saved chicken strips for me, but he tended to prepare them to *his* tastes. Much to his amazement, I liked breading on my strips. And dipping sauces.

"You have listened to me speak on this matter, and you have not judged me for not being perfect in the eyes of the queen."

I patted his leg. "Is anyone perfect in her eyes?"

"She believed my eldest brother could do no wrong."

"The one who was…" I hated to remind him of his past with the elven assassin. "The one who's dead now?"

"Yes. He was a good brother and a good son to the queen. I am striving to be the same."

It was strange to think of the huge, powerful, and fearsome Zav as a little brother trying to live up to an example set by a big brother. Somehow, I'd imagined Zav coming out of his egg fully formed and fully badass, but maybe he'd once been a goofy, snaggletoothed baby dragon who got picked on by the older dragons. The urge to see Young Zav made me grin. Too bad dragons didn't take photos of their young and keep baby blankets and other souvenirs of childhood.

Zav was still looking in my direction, so I stifled the grin.

"I'm sure your mother believes you're a good son too." I *hoped* that was true. "There aren't many dragons better than you. Now that I've met several of your kind, I'm positive I'm right. There's no way I'd marry any of those other snooty dragons."

"Your confidence in my magnificence pleases me." He purred the words, putting bedroom thoughts into my mind even without using telepathy.

"I'm not sure *magnificence* is the word I used, but you're pretty special." I patted his leg again, letting my hand stay there and feeling the heat of his thigh through his robe, the outline of his muscles… It was too bad we were almost to Willard's. It would be rude to pull into her parking lot and have a quickie with my fiancé, especially when she might have trouble lurking nearby. Though it was unlikely any trolls would approach if Zav was outside of her building.

"You are also special." Zav laid his hand on mine, and a little zing of his magic flowed up my arm. "I would not have chosen an inferior mate."

"Glad to hear it."

"If any trolls *dare* interfere with our wedding, I will bite their heads off." Zav shared an image of himself, flying in his dragon form and chasing after trolls running through the forest with grenades. The focus was more on him and the interplay of his muscles under his gleaming black scales than the trolls. Maybe he was trying to emphasize his magnificence. I found his human-form muscles sexier, but I could appreciate the dragon aesthetic.

"Is that allowed? I imagine punishment and rehabilitation is difficult when the subject is headless."

"It is not allowed, but they do not know that."

One-handed, I turned the wheel into the apartment's parking lot. Zav hadn't yet relinquished my other hand. His thumb traced my tendons as he continued to gaze at me, his aura growing more noticeable as he touched me. Even though I'd grown more accustomed to being inside the influence of his power, when he started thinking randy thoughts, I always felt his energy—magical and electric as it brushed my nerves—more keenly.

"I will capture the ones who have been pestering you and find the boy," he said. "Then, when all of your concerns have been assuaged, we will mate."

"We won't mate until then?" After parking, I unbuckled my seatbelt and faced him. "What if that takes days?"

"It will take an hour. Locating a lost youth is not a difficult task for a dragon."

"You're still a cocky dragon, I see."

"I am aware of my own abilities." He smiled cockily and leaned in—or maybe I leaned into *him*—and kissed me.

I kissed him back, sliding my hands through his short soft hair and wondering if we could truly wrap up everything in an hour and be back home in bed. The thought was appealing. As was knowing that I had someone who wanted to solve all my problems and concerns for me… while letting his hands slip under my duster and stroke me through my shirt. Maybe he was thinking of preliminary mating in the Jeep too.

The lights were on in Willard's apartment, but the blinds were closed and none of the windows were open. I doubted she knew we were here. She hadn't sounded that worried on the phone, and I didn't sense a troll in the vicinity, so there was no reason to hurry up.

Zav broke the kiss and drew back with a sigh. He left his hands on my sides—one had slipped under my shirt, fingers leaving trails of pleasure where they touched my skin—but he lifted his gaze toward the night sky.

"Problem?" I murmured.

Then I sensed it. A pair of dragons flew within range of my senses. Zav's sister, Zondia, and was she with Xilneth? I hadn't expected those two to fly around together, despite Xilneth's statement that Zondia found his wingspan and musculature appealing.

"My sister and that Starsinger oaf have been sent ahead of the rest of the clans to inspect the area and ensure it's suitable for the queen and for the Starsinger matriarch." With palpable reluctance, Zav lowered his hands. "I must delay hunting for the trolls so that I can show them the sanctuary, but I hope to finish quickly and address your concern tonight."

"So we have to wait two hours for sex instead of one?"

"Unfortunately, that is likely." Zav kissed me again, then opened the door, got out, and changed into his dragon form before launching himself into the air.

CHAPTER 21

TRAFFIC RUMBLED PAST ON A nearby arterial as I headed across the parking lot to Willard's door. Streetlamps left yellow reflections in puddles large enough that they could have inspired goblin engineers to build bridges.

Willard hadn't texted an update since mentioning the troll, and I still didn't sense anyone magical around, aside from Zav flying off to meet the other dragons. The lack of dead bodies, broken windows, and battle sounds led me to believe that all was well, at least for the moment. Maybe it had been a coincidence that a troll had wandered past when Willard had been looking out her window.

As I knocked, I wondered if she would chew me out for presuming to come by uninvited. Even though I saw Willard all the time, and she was planning my wedding, she wasn't one to fraternize with employees or, as far as I'd seen, invite people to her home for movies or gaming nights. The handful of times I'd been by, she'd either needed help moving or for me to feed her cat while she was out of town.

The door opened, revealing Willard in sweatpants, weightlifting gloves, and a T-shirt with a ragged neckline and hem and a huge black barbell on the front.

"Either you're working out," I said, "or your pajamas are even more dreadful than I imagined."

"Big talk from someone who wears a dragon nightie."

"It's a *Hobbit* nightshirt, and who told you about it?" I didn't think Gondo had seen me in it, and Dimitri and Freysha wouldn't gossip.

"Your fashion-conscious fiancé mentioned it while complaining that it featured a dragon but not *him*. It's rude of you to sleep with other dragons on, Thorvald."

"Thanks for the tip. Can I come in? I need an opinion on something."

The screech of a perennially moody cat tumbled out of the apartment.

"Maggie is always willing to give her opinion." Willard stepped aside and waved for me to come in.

"I remember that." Once I stepped into the living room, another screech—nobody in their right mind would call that a *meow*—helped me spot the gray-furred, blue-eyed Maggie perched atop a bookcase and surveying her domain.

"You didn't need to come by. I can handle a troll." Willard waved at a modified sniper rifle leaning against the wall by the door. It tickled my senses with its magic, and I recognized Nin's work.

"Or any miscreants peeping through your window from up to twelve hundred meters away."

I didn't mention that I'd wanted to check on Willard for more reasons than the troll. From her earlier phone call, I'd gotten the gist that something was bugging her, but she would bristle if I admitted that. I would have to be subtle with my prying.

"I only throw dumbbells at miscreants," she said.

"The fifty?" I waved at the rack. It looked like something out of a gym, not a home-fitness store, and was still devoid of any girlie teal, pink, and purple weights of fewer than ten pounds.

"Depends on how annoying the miscreant is. I might only use a twenty-five against a peeper."

"Any news on the Bloody Blade?"

"Nothing new. I already told you that my agent saw your employee—Inga, isn't it?—go inside. He was suspicious of her, at first, but she only stayed down there for a few minutes and then left. She had the same pissed-off expression coming out as she had going in, so he didn't think she'd found anything enlightening."

"I just talked to Zav." I pointed my thumb toward the parking lot. "He's going to look for Reb and the trolls after he shows the wedding area to Zondia and Xilneth."

"*Talking?*" Willard's eyebrow twitched. "Is that what you were doing in the parking lot out there for twenty minutes?"

And here I'd thought her curtains had been closed...

"Yes, it is. Zav is an excellent conversationalist."

"I bet."

"Don't make me throw a dumbbell at you for peeping."

"Looking out the window into my own parking lot isn't peeping. Besides, I'm expecting someone."

"Oh? I'd ask if it's Walker coming to take you out for dinner, but you're not exactly dressed for a hot date." I pointed at her dumbbell T-shirt.

She frowned at me. "We're not dating. You know I can't stand his ostentatious displays of wealth."

"I thought you might have changed your mind about him after you saw him selflessly healing people in our shop while blood streamed from his own wounds."

"And while the sun glinted off his F.P. Journe."

I blinked. His what? "I'm going to assume that's not a nickname for his willy."

"If light glints off his *willy*, he's got a real problem."

"You know him better than I do."

"As he informed me in the car, F.P. Journe is a boutique watchmaker with a shop in New York. He only makes nine hundred watches a year. Walker has one from a collection where only ten were made. They're worth a fortune."

"He told you all that, huh?" I scratched my jaw. I thought Walker had figured out that the way to Willard's heart wasn't by flashing his wealth. "You know he's trying to impress you because he's interested, right?"

She ignored my question and said, "Watch-collecting is his passion. He says they're investments." She rolled her eyes, grabbed a couple of dumbbells, and sat on the weight bench. It rested in the living room in the spot where normal people would put an ottoman. Or where Dimitri would put his Gamersac. "If I needed a guy, which I don't, I'd want one who's passionate about eating healthy food, maintaining his fitness, and working to make the world a better place."

"If he's dropping piles of money for F.P.-thingies, he's making that watchmaker's world a better place."

"Uh huh. He *is* coming by, but I'm expecting an invoice. He analyzed bloodwork for me yesterday and gave one of my sergeants, who had an altercation with a werewolf, some stitches."

"So he's making the world a better place by healing people."

Willard grunted, sank back on the bench, and started doing flies. "And charging a fortune."

"Watches don't buy themselves."

"He could charge a lot less, help people without much money, and live more modestly."

"Are you sure he charges that much? Maybe he's a whiz in the stock market. Or the watch market."

Surprisingly, she didn't answer. She just kept lifting weights. Maybe she *hadn't* looked into his rates and was only making assumptions. I had no idea what he might charge for the reconstructive plastic surgery he did, but since there wasn't a health-insurance industry for the magical community—and they were his primary customers—I wouldn't be surprised if he had to charge under-market rates instead of over-market.

After finishing her set, Willard sat up. "You said Zav is going to help with the trolls?"

"He's going to try again to find them for me, yes. He looked for them earlier and said they were hiding out in the old dark-elf tunnels and that they're still protected by some lingering magic that makes it hard for him to detect people down there."

"You guys *are* going to catch these thugs in time, right? I'm putting a lot of time into this wedding. I'd like to see things go right."

"I know you are. And in case I didn't say it, I appreciate it."

"Good."

"You're a gracious employer."

"You're a pain-in-the-ass subordinate."

"I'm glad we've had this bonding moment."

Maggie meowed, slightly less loudly this time, though it still sounded more like a baby crying than a cat.

"Maggie is glad too," I added.

"That's how you interpreted that, huh?"

"I do have a translation charm."

"That works on cats?"

"I actually haven't tried it on a cat. Or on Rocket. But Rocket is pretty easy to interpret. Play, play, play, food. I think that's mostly what he says."

"He's a golden retriever, isn't he?"

"Yes."

"That sounds right then." Willard stood up.

I thought she was going to kick me out, especially if she was expecting Walker, but she surprised me by asking if I wanted a drink.

"Do I look like I need one?" I asked.

Maybe she wanted someone else here when Walker came by, so he wouldn't hit on her.

"I was thinking more like mineral water than alcohol, but probably. You must be having a stressful week if you're here hanging out at my place." Willard squinted at me. "Are you avoiding your house full of strange elves?"

"I came because I was worried a troll might be mauling you, but is there anything you *don't* know about what's going on in my house?"

"I have a lot of ears on the street. And like I said, I can handle a troll." Willard disappeared into the kitchen.

It wasn't *a* troll that I was worried about. They liked to congregate in packs of fifty.

She returned with Perrier in a can, as well as a dubious brown liquid in a glass bottle.

I thought that was something for her, but she set both beside me. "There you go. Water, and that kombucha is up to point-five percent alcohol if you need a buzz."

"That's quite a kick. Four or five gallons, and I'll be passed out in that little bed over there."

"That's Maggie's cat bed. She *will* object." Willard grabbed her dumbbells and leaned back on the bench for another set.

"Not going to drink with me?"

"Not now."

"You training for something?"

"No."

She glowered up at the ceiling as she passed twenty reps, her arms quivering under the effort.

Once again, I had that inkling that something wasn't right.

"Everything okay?" I asked.

"Fine."

"Would you tell me if it wasn't?"

"No."

"Would Maggie?" I tapped my translation charm.

"You're hilarious."

"The trolls today thought so. I'm surprised they didn't invite me back to their pub for a standup routine."

Willard clunked the weights to the floor and sat up. She grabbed a couple of hand-grip strengtheners and squeezed them while she "rested." She also eyed me, and I had the sense that she wanted to ask me something. Or maybe confide in me about something?

I raised my eyebrows in innocent inquiry and tried to look approachable, not like someone who would make a smartass remark.

"Are you okay with how the wedding planning is going?" Willard finally asked, setting down the equipment.

That wasn't the question I'd expected. I thought maybe she'd wanted to admit that even though Walker was a pain-in-the-ass with his expensive watches and cars, she was secretly attracted to his rugged handsomeness and ability to shape-shift into a badass prehistoric lion. Had she ever seen him do that? I wasn't sure.

"It's a little more involved than I'd originally envisioned, and bad guys may be planning to bomb it, but otherwise, sure. You and Zav have been doing the heavy lifting. I haven't had to do much." I bowed toward her.

Her lips twisted in an expression that was hard to read. "It's occurred to me that I've taken over and am doing things my way."

"Only recently?" I smiled, but her expression only turned more sour. "It's okay. Zav is doing things his way too."

"Zav is half of the couple. He's *supposed* to get his way. At least half of his way."

I shrugged, not sure what she wanted. "It's fine. I wasn't that married to the idea of a DJ, though I do worry that we may not be able to hear your harpist over the screeching and roaring of dragons on the hunt."

"I'm hoping their hunt is out in the woods, not in the five-acre field that I mowed and cleared. I told the goblins they would thank me later if they ever decide to raise livestock. I'm not sure they agreed, but we couldn't set up pavilions and buffet tables in a tangle of thistle, blackberry brambles, and tansy ragwort."

"You *are* doing more work than I expected. I feel like I should be paying you."

"If you want to throw your purse around, you can pay Walker's invoice when he comes by. I'm just…" She turned a palm upward but didn't continue on.

"Extremely thorough and someone who insists on going above and beyond?"

Even though I had only known her for a few years, I trusted that was true in her personal life as well as her military career. One didn't make full-bird colonel by forty, especially a woman, without being pretty dang impressive.

"Those things are true, but I have to confess... I've been doing my damnedest to make sure you have a respectable wedding, but I've also been trying to put together the wedding *I* never got to have. And, judging by how things have been going lately, that I'll never get to have."

I'd figured that out weeks ago, but I kept the thought to myself. "You're not *that* old, Willard. You can still get married."

I sensed Walker driving up and parking but resisted the urge to point him out as an option again. If she wasn't interested, she wasn't interested. Nagging wouldn't make her fall in love with him.

"The pickings have gotten slim," Willard said, "and I don't get asked out as much anymore."

I didn't know what to say to that. This had gotten deeper than I expected, and I wasn't the best at being nurturing and comforting. Especially to someone who was my boss.

"Maybe your wardrobe is scaring guys away." Opting for levity seemed safer than offering her a consoling hug. She still had those dumbbells nearby, after all.

"Are you standing there in your duster and combat boots and commenting on my wardrobe?"

"Don't forget my pistol—" I tapped Fezzik's handle, "—and sword." The latter she wouldn't be able to see, but she knew I usually had Storm with me.

"All extremely sexy."

"To the right kind of guy."

"You don't think I can attract the right kind of guy in gym clothes?" Willard asked.

Walker knocked on the door.

Even though I'd decided not to bring him up as a potential partner again, I couldn't resist saying, "Here's your chance to try."

Since I was closer to the door, I leaned over and opened it while ignoring the scowl Willard sent my way.

"Hey, Doc." I waved him in. "Willard has been prettying herself up for you."

"I'm going to kick your ass, Thorvald," Willard growled as Walker stepped in with the sort of insulated bag that food-delivery people carried in their cars. It didn't look like he was bringing an invoice after all, not unless it was important that it stay toasty warm.

Walker looked over at her and bowed. "A fit sheila is a beautiful sheila," he drawled.

Willard kept scowling and glanced at his wrist. There was a nice-looking watch on it with a blue face and a blue leather band. I had no idea if it was the F.P.-something one she'd mentioned, but now that she'd brought up watches, I realized I'd seen him wearing them often. But not on the gnomish home world. Maybe, since he'd known he might end up in battle, he'd left behind his investments.

Willard abandoned her workout to stand and join us. "Food delivery?" She waved at the insulated box. "Is that how you're making your car payments?"

"Not this month. This is for you."

"I was expecting an invoice for your visit to the office yesterday," Willard said.

"That's on the house since you gave me a ride home the other day. You'll be pleased to know that my insurance is covering my auto repairs."

Since I had finally, thanks to Ti's generous payment of gold, been able to pay off the loan on the Jeep that Zav had destroyed when we first met, I refrained from feeling bitter about someone else having their expenses covered for damage caused by magical mayhem.

Walker held out the box to Willard. "I made you dinner. Poached salmon with truffles and shrimp in cream sauce, along with a roasted vegetable medley."

"You *made* all that?" She appeared more skeptical than grateful.

"It smells amazing," I said. *Someone* should be grateful. Maybe Willard would share.

"I did. I've taught myself to cook as a way to impress ladies."

"I thought your red toaster was supposed to do that."

"My what?"

I was about to smack my palm to my face and wonder how Willard could lament the lack of a guy to marry one minute and then insult one taking a chance on her in the next. But I sensed a magical being outside, and that distracted me. It was a troll.

"Never mind." Willard accepted the box. "Thanks for this. I haven't eaten yet."

"You're welcome."

"You're sure you're not going to charge me for your services? Thorvald offered to pay."

Walker looked at me, but I was busy scanning the area for more trolls. One should be easy enough to handle, but if a pack of them had shown up...

No. It was just the one. Zav had long since flown out of my range, and this single troll was the only magical being around. His aura was familiar. Was he one of the trolls from the Bloody Blade?

Maybe he'd come with a few grenades and planned to bomb Willard's apartment building.

I let my hand drop to my pistol. That wasn't going to happen. I reached for the door, planning to go out and have a chat with him, but as he came closer, I realized who he was. The troll shaman that had made a lot of trouble for me.

"We've got a problem," I said.

Walker turned toward the door. "I sense him. Troll."

"Troll shaman. A strong one." That Ogdar again. "You guys stay here." I tapped Sindari's charm to summon him. "Enjoy your meal. I'll take care of him. And then I'll question him."

If I was careful, maybe I could resolve the threat to my wedding tonight. If I wasn't, the shaman might hand my ass to me, pulverized like hamburger.

CHAPTER 22

I SENSE A TROLL, SINDARI TOLD me as soon as he formed. *The shaman from the basement pub.*

Yup. We're going to knock him on his butt and question him. Reb is still missing, and so are all those grenades.

As I slipped outside, I wasn't surprised when Willard and Walker came out after me. She had her rifle. Walker had taken off his jacket and pushed up his sleeves. Maybe he was contemplating getting furry.

My senses told me the shaman was positioned out of sight on the street leading to Willard's parking lot. It was a quiet side street with a lot of cars parked along both sides. A battle could do a lot of damage to property, but we were in the heart of the city, so I didn't know where else I could try to lead him that would be better. At least, between the rain and the darkness, there weren't many potential witnesses around.

"Stay here," I whispered. "I'm going to camouflage so he won't sense me coming."

"If he gets close, I'm taking a shot," Willard whispered back.

"Just be careful about bullets bouncing off." I activated my stealth charm, and Sindari and I trotted across the parking lot.

We slowed as we neared the sidewalk. A tall brick building hid most of the street from view, but my senses told me the shaman wasn't far away. He hadn't gotten any closer though. Had he stopped to call for backup? To prepare a spell?

Sindari and I split apart, so we could approach him from opposite sides of the street. With Sindari's magical stealth, he should also be able to get close without being sensed.

Once we reached the sidewalk, Ogdar the shaman came into view. He wore a trench coat and stood in the shadows, but enough illumination came from a streetlamp that I could make out his blue skin and tangle of long white hair. He stood with his head back, as if stargazing, but I sensed him gathering magic around him.

I drew Storm and almost rushed him, hoping to mow him down before he knew I was there, but I jerked to a halt. He gripped something in front of his stomach with both hands, something with a strong magical aura that I recognized.

What the hell? It was Chasmmoor's gargoyle box, the box that had launched more than a dozen kinds of terrible monsters at me the past few nights. How had *this* guy gotten it? And was Chasmmoor still alive? Was my *house* still standing?

That box... Sindari had crossed the street and crept closer to the shaman but also paused.

I know. Get it before he opens the lid.

I ran toward him, not making a sound, but somehow Ogdar sensed me coming. Or maybe he was just ready to attack. He opened the lid on the box, and familiar crimson light flowed out.

I jerked Fezzik out and fired at him, hoping I could knock him on his butt, grab the box, and close it before monsters soared free. But the shaman's magic wrapped around him in an invisible shield, and my bullets bounced off, pinging against the brick building.

This was a job for Storm.

I charged in, but Sindari reached him first. Ogdar flinched, seeing a great silver tiger spring at him, but then sneered.

Realizing Sindari would bounce off like the bullets had, I whispered a command I'd only practiced once, "*Horanik*," and willed my blade to force a hole in our enemy's barrier.

Sindari glided through the opening, startling the shaman. As he flung up an arm to protect his neck, he dropped the box.

The crimson light fluctuated as Sindari smashed into the troll, knocking him into the brick wall, but the lid remained far enough ajar that it didn't go out. Trusting my ally had Ogdar distracted, I lunged for the box, hoping to grab it and slice Storm through it.

But my knuckles bashed against another invisible field. Damn it. This one seemed to come from the box itself.

SECRETS OF THE SWORD III

Power surged from the shaman as he roared, and Sindari flew across the street. The first monster flowed out of the box, not slowed down by the barrier that had blocked me.

The creature was not one I'd encountered in my previous battles, and I knew no dwarven command that would help my sword defeat it. I backed up a few steps as it grew larger, bluish-purple skin reminding me of a sea creature. It had tentacles rather than arms, and several of them waved in the air, preparing to smash down on us.

Something else stirred in the crimson light cast by the box. My heart sank. *More* monsters might come out of it without Chasmmoor here to modulate and control the artifact.

Distract them for a second, I ordered Sindari as I willed my blade to burrow a hole in the magical defense around the box.

All of them? Sindari had recovered but was on the far side of the street from Ogdar, with the tentacled creature blocking his way.

If you can...

"*Horanik,*" I whispered again, focusing on the barrier protecting the box. Its magic faltered, and I hefted Storm, seeing my chance.

But Ogdar was free to focus on me. Another swell of magic was the only warning I got. My airway constricted as an invisible force wrapped around my throat. The shaman's eyes narrowed as he glared at me.

I wanted to brain him, but his defenses were up again. Besides, the box was more of a threat. A second creature was solidifying in the street as Sindari slashed and bit at the tentacled monster, keeping it busy. Who knew how many could come out of that thing?

The barrier around it seemed to be down, so I lunged in with Storm. As soon as I destroyed the box, I would take on Ogdar—and stop him from Force-choking me, the unoriginal Vader-wannabe.

This time, the barrier didn't stop me, but before Storm hit the artifact, an angry crimson lightning bolt lashed out and struck me in the chest. Pain blasted me, and I flew backward, too stunned to keep from landing on my back. I barely kept Storm from flying out of my hand.

That hadn't been the troll. The box was *protecting* itself.

My heart beat erratically in my chest, and I wheezed, not from my asthma—not yet—but from the power still wrapped around my throat. Ogdar snarled from behind his barrier, and the force around my throat tightened. I couldn't get any air in at all.

Gritting my teeth and willing my heart to recover from however many thousands of amps of electricity that had been, I rolled to my feet. I didn't have the air to voice commands, but Storm was glowing a fierce blue and ready for battle. Without words, I willed all of my energy into the blade, commanding it to force down the troll's protection.

It dropped, and he knew it. In a heartbeat, his face switched from triumphant and superior to startled and scared.

I'd been knocked too far away to reach him with my sword, so I drew Fezzik again. He saw the threat and switched from trying to choke me to hurling a typhoon at me. It tore at my clothing and whipped my braid around my head. My own hair struck me in the eyes.

The annoyance didn't keep me from firing three times. But the wind was so erratic and powerful that it moved my arm and affected my aim. Two of the bullets whizzed uselessly past him. One slammed into his shoulder. The wind disappeared as he stumbled backward, yowling in pain. *Good.*

Two more shots fired. They weren't mine.

Willard stood behind the battle, her sniper rifle up. Her shots slammed into the troll's torso, and he dropped to his knees.

Walker had transformed into his marsupial lion form, reddish-blond and stout, with a thick tail, powerful muscles, and great claws. He roared and charged at the second monster, a huge fanged spider that was taller than any of us, and left the first to Sindari. A *third* creature was shambling out of the box.

"Deal with those, Thorvald," Willard barked, advancing on the troll. "I'll take care of this guy."

"I want to question him. Keep him alive." I ran toward the box, knowing we'd all be screwed if I couldn't keep more monsters from coming out.

Maybe I didn't need to destroy it, just close the lid. That was all Chasmmoor did at the end of our sessions. But if I couldn't get close enough to touch it, I couldn't close anything.

The third monster, a towering giant with a club, stomped in the way. It was the creature I'd fought my first night in the park. Chasmmoor wasn't here to tell me to raise a shield to protect against its club, but I barked the order, and Storm obeyed.

I ran around the giant, just missing Willard as she stalked toward the shaman, keeping him in her sights. My towering foe hammered at me with its club. Storm's shield kept it from getting close, but it jumped to block my path again. Did the monsters know to protect the box?

A feline yelp came from Sindari as he skidded across the pavement, blood matting his silver fur.

Fewer arms, Val, he told me as he shook off the pain and sprang back to his feet. *I prefer opponents with fewer arms.*

Those are tentacles.

They are vile and taste loathsome. He spat a piece of the monster's flesh to the street.

You have to deep-fry tentacles. I ran at the giant, hoping my barrier would ram into its leg and force it back.

The barrier stayed up, as strong and sturdy around me as a steel ball, but the giant was as sturdy as steel too. My barrier struck it, and *I* was the one forced back.

Since I couldn't go through it, I tried to go around again. With my half-elven agility, I ought to be faster than a giant.

And I was, but it didn't have to move far to protect the box. Like a goalie defending against the offense, it kept thwarting my attempts to reach my target. Meanwhile, another monster started forming in the crimson glow flowing from the box's interior.

Frustrated, I dropped my shield so I could attack the giant. Person to person.

Too bad I couldn't reach its heart. Instead, I charged in and stabbed its thigh.

My blade sank in, and it yelled, more like a human than an animal. Disconcerting, but that didn't keep me from cutting it again. If I could get its tree-trunk legs out of the way...

It yelled in fury and hefted its club over its head. The heavy wood whistled through the air toward me. I sprang to the side as it struck down hard enough to make the pavement tremble.

Willard swore, not at my predicament, but at her enemy. Ogdar leaped up, leaving a pool of blood behind, and hurled a throwing knife at her. She saw his arm pump and dodged in time.

With the giant swinging at me again, I couldn't rush over to help her. I ducked under a blow meant to smash my skull and ran past my towering enemy, slashing into its calf as I went. Thinking I could hamstring it, I jumped up before it could turn and stabbed hard, sinking Storm deep into muscle.

The giant wobbled and stumbled away from me. That was my chance to get to the box.

After the lightning bolt, I didn't dare take a swing at it. I crouched and carefully reached for it, hoping it wouldn't react to having its lid politely closed. Or *slammed* closed. The fourth creature had formed, another great spider—my head didn't even reach its belly.

Fortunately, the spider didn't come for me. Sindari and Walker were harrying the other two monsters, and the eight-legged monster opted to scurry toward them.

"The spiders shoot venom!" I warned, having encountered them before.

The giant, though bleeding from a half-dozen cuts Storm had given it, stomped toward me with its club raised again.

Once more, I ordered Storm to form a shield around me. My chest tightened, and I growled in frustration and wished I'd used my inhaler before jumping into battle with the shaman. Someday, I would learn to acknowledge my cursed frailty. Maybe.

At least the box was inside the barrier with me. Ignoring my wheezing lungs, I reached for it as slowly as I could make myself, treating it like a wild animal I wanted to pet. A surge of power came from it—a warning. The crimson glow brightened, and I feared another monster would spring out, this time trapped inside my barrier with me.

The giant hammered at the shield, the club striking the invisible barrier a few feet above my head.

"Keep me safe, Storm," I whispered, making sure some of my focus went toward maintaining that barrier. The sword always seemed linked to me, and I didn't know if it would do what I wished if I wasn't paying attention.

Ignoring the box's warning, I reached for the lid, trying to flip it shut quickly. But a sharp burst of power knocked me sideways. The shield moved with me, protecting me as the giant tried to take advantage and pounce.

Frustrated, I rose to a crouch and glared at the box. Earlier, I'd been thinking about telekinesis. That shaman had used it to heft Reb. How hard could it be to close a lid with one's mind?

Though I didn't know any command words for that power, I focused on the box and tried to think of how Freysha would do it. By imagining some plant helping her complete the task. I'd tried this before with fern fronds, but maybe a branch would be better. Or my roots. Could they grow out of cement? Probably not, but I tried anyway, willing them to form in the soil underneath the pavement.

As I concentrated, screeches and roars echoed from the buildings to either side of the streets. Blood spattered the pavement. Sindari's? Walker's? Both? Gunshots fired.

Willard stood with her foot on the shaman's chest and him flat on his back. This time, she was firing at the monsters trying to annihilate Sindari and Walker. One of the spiders was down, but the other remained, joining forces with the tentacled creature to attack the felines.

A couple of people had gathered at the intersection and were gaping in this direction. Sirens wailed in the distance. Concentrating was *not* easy, and I was about to give up when a snap sounded over the din. Cracks formed in the pavement under the box, then widened into a gap. Green tendrils squirmed through. Barely daring to breathe, lest I lose my focus, I willed them to grow up to the lid and push it shut.

Willard swore as she ran out of ammunition. Walker, his powerful lion muscles rippling, sprang up and raked his long claws across the spider's furry brown side. His fangs sank in, and he tore a chunk of flesh out and flung it into the street.

"Gross, Walker," Willard grumbled, digging in her pocket for more ammunition.

My roots reached the lid and nudged it upward.

The spider reared up like a horse, four of its legs rising off the ground. Its body quivered and quaked, and it managed to shake Walker free. It dropped down, skittered back, and instead of going back after him, it tried to run at Willard. It ran into my barrier, bounced sideways, and scurried around it.

Worried it would get to her before the others could help and she could reload, I almost abandoned my task, but the tendrils grew another inch and flipped the lid shut. The red light disappeared.

"*Finally.*" I was tempted to try bashing the cursed box with Storm again, but all I'd done was stop more monsters from coming out. It was still a powerful magical artifact and could knock me on my butt again.

Besides, we had the remaining monsters to worry about. If Chasmmoor had been here, he could have ordered them all back into the box, but I didn't know how to do that, and closing the lid had left them stranded in our world.

Willard, her foot still pinning Ogdar, refused to retreat from the spider. She'd gotten enough ammo into her rifle to fire again, and she plowed two bullets into one of its eyes. It kept going at her.

Walker leaped and caught it, fangs sinking into its backside as he ripped furiously into its flesh with his claws.

I dropped Storm's barrier and sprang at the spider's side, adding my own blade to the battle. It stopped advancing toward Willard and whirled toward us. Its fanged mouth opened in a gesture that I recognized.

"*Arunnat mak*," I ordered, the command that let Storm take over and guide my arms.

A fluorescent green wad of spider venom flew toward me. Storm took over in time to whip my arms up, batting the goo aside as I dodged. Some of the viscous stuff remained on my blade, but Storm flared a brighter blue, and the air filled with a burning stench as it sizzled off.

The spider's focus shifted to Walker, probably because he'd gone into berserker mode and was tearing huge pieces out of the thing. I drew Fezzik again, turning to take care of the giant, now that my attention wasn't divided. A good thing because it had realized my barrier was down. It stomped toward me, raising that club again.

Willard joined me in shooting at it, and bullets pierced its eyes and slammed into its throat and chest. I prepared myself to raise my barrier again, but the giant faltered under the barrage. It tottered, its club dropping from its fingers and thumping down like a great oak falling. The giant pitched over and hit with even more of a thud.

I shifted my aim toward Sindari's foe, but the tentacled creature was down on the ground. Much like Willard, Sindari stood atop it, keeping it pinned. He slashed his claws at any tentacle that dared rise up. Finally, it shuddered and lay still. Bloody but not defeated, Sindari roared his triumph.

"No chance of this not getting reported," Willard muttered as the echoes of the roar died down. She glanced at the growing crowds to either end of the street, sighed, and pulled out her phone. "It's going to be a joy to explain this away."

Under her foot, Ogdar groaned. Blood pooled in several spots underneath him, but he was still alive. Whether or not he was fully conscious, I didn't know. It might be a challenge to question him. Maybe Walker could give him some bandages after he finished mutilating the spider.

Maybe he could give *me* something. I was breathing far harder than I should have been after a fight where I'd mostly been using my magic and my sword's magic.

"I think it's dead, Doc," I said, digging into my pocket for my inhaler and eyeing the unmoving lump of macerated flesh that had dared stomp toward Willard.

Willard eyed *Walker*. Hopefully, he wasn't alarming her with his feline ferocity. Probably not. It took a lot to make Willard bat an eye.

Her expression was as calm and authoritative as ever as she contacted whoever worked the nightshift in her office and ordered him to dispatch several vans for a morgue run. Several *large* vans.

I inhaled some of my medicine, hating the bitter tang at the back of my throat but crossing my fingers that it would help. Lately, it hadn't helped as much as it used to. This week, it had been particularly bad. Staying up nights to train for hours at a time hadn't helped lower my stress levels. Eventually, Mary would give me up as a lost cause.

After making sure all of our enemies on the ground were dead, I gingerly approached the gargoyle box again. It remained dark, with the lid closed, but it still emanated plenty of magic. My roots, with my attention shifted, had slithered back into the ground, though the pavement remained cracked. Given what we'd dealt with, I wouldn't feel guilty about the small bit of destruction.

The box hummed a warning when I touched it, but it didn't zap me. After a few more experimental prods, I lifted it up. Its magic vibrated against my senses, but it let me hold it. It had let the *troll* hold it, so it couldn't be that picky. I held it up to the streetlamp, though I already knew from the monsters it had spat out that it was Chasmmoor's training box.

"So… what happened to Chasmmoor?"

CHAPTER 23

I DIALED DIMITRI'S NUMBER WHILE WILLARD finished lining up the corpse removal. Walker remained in his shifted lion form, and when a couple of curious bystanders tried to creep up the street to take photos, he roared at them. They ran off screaming about mutant animals escaped from a lab. It wasn't clear if they meant the eight-legged and eight-tentacled dead monsters or Walker.

I like him. Sindari sat next to me, licking his wounds and refraining from roaring at people. He'd received numerous deep gouges, so maybe he was too sore for that, or maybe he thought Walker had it under control.

I know. You've bonded in battle before.

Yes. He fights similarly to a Del'nothian tiger.

Therefore making him superior?

Isn't it obvious?

I think so. I'm still trying to get Willard to realize it.

Willard watched Walker as she made a second call to warn one of her agents of troll activity in the area, but it was hard to tell if her eyes were full of admiration for his fighting prowess or if she was about to cuss him out for scaring civilians.

"Hey, Val," Dimitri answered right before it would have gone to voice mail. He sounded tired. "What's up?"

"Are you at the house?"

"No. I'm still working on the shop and making sure the goblins don't add a pool to Freysha's blueprints."

"Where on the property would you put a pool?" It was a *small* lot, and the house-turned-commercial-building took up most of it.

"Exactly my argument. They're trying to turn the Sable Dragon into a rec center for goblins."

"We can talk about that later. Have you been by the house today? Heard anything about Chasmmoor?"

"No."

"He may be missing. Or worse. His gargoyle box showed up in North Seattle in a troll shaman's hands." A troll shaman I was going to question as soon as he was conscious. Still pinned under Willard's foot, he hadn't moved for a while.

"Uh, that's not good."

"I thought not."

"Zoltan should be home."

"My favorite person to chat up on the phone."

"I'll head that way soon."

"Thanks." I hung up and called Zoltan. This was important enough that I couldn't worry about his tendencies to insult me.

If Zav had been nearby, I would have asked him for a swift ride home. In case he was close enough to hear it, I sent a telepathic call of, *Zav, I need help,* out to the greater Seattle area.

Zoltan answered. "Yes, dear robber who is related to far more elves than I ever wanted to see in my life and are here primarily to vex me."

"Is that my name now?"

"Unwieldy, isn't it?"

"It is. Is Chasmmoor there? I need to know if someone stole one of his artifacts."

"I do not sense him in the house. He was here earlier, but I believe he left. Perhaps for a walk."

Why did my guests go on so many walks? Did everybody crave froyo?

"A walk where?" I asked, though it didn't sound like Zoltan knew.

"Despite our growing friendship, he did not inform me what his recreational intentions were."

"How long has he been gone?"

"Two hours, perhaps."

"That's a long walk."

Long enough for Ogdar to have grabbed the box and come down here to attack us. No, to attack *Willard*. The shaman probably hadn't known I would be here.

Why did he want her dead? I added that to my list of questions and pointed at him and raised my eyebrows. Willard had finished her calls and was looking my way.

"Dwarves have short legs," Zoltan said. "It takes them longer to walk places."

Willard slung her rifle over her shoulder, grabbed the troll by the shirt, and hefted him into a sitting position. He yelped, his bullet-pierced shoulder and torso doubtless hurting. After he'd nearly gotten us killed, I had no sympathy for him.

"Can you go look for Chasmmoor?" I asked Zoltan.

Are you in danger? Zav asked, his telepathic voice distant in my mind. *I am some miles north of the sanctuary with Zondia'qareshi. We've just battled a yorak that sprang from the trees to attack us, but I will return swiftly.*

Chasmmoor's box is here—it was stolen by a troll—and nobody knows where he is, I replied, deciding not to ask for details on why they were hunting their imported animals before the wedding hunt. Maybe the animals hadn't *wanted* to be imported and were objecting to it.

The guest of a dragon has been stolen from? Zav asked indignantly.

Maybe worse. I grimaced. What would happen if a dwarf who was a personal friend to the dwarven king died while visiting Earth?

I will return promptly.

Thanks.

Walker prowled back to us and shifted into his human form. For the moment, the bystanders had disappeared.

"Your prisoner is awake, Thorvald," Willard said. "Come ask your questions."

Ogdar rasped something in his own language. I activated my translation charm in time to hear, "...will die before telling my brother's slayer anything."

"You can talk to my boss if you want." I pointed at Willard. "Why were you here trying to sic monsters on her apartment? And where did you get that box? If you did anything to the dwarf who owns it, I'll shoot you again."

Ogdar glared at me and set his jaw.

"I don't suppose you have some truth serum?" I asked Walker.

He was looking at the mutilated body of the spider. A little sheepishly?

He cleared his throat, pushed his rolled-up sleeves down, and adjusted the cuffs. "As far as I know, such a thing doesn't exist. But my medical kit is in my car if anyone is injured."

"We need him to talk, not bask in your healing magic." I waved at the troll.

"I was thinking more of you and Colonel Willard." Walker's gaze fell on Sindari. "And your comrade, if he needs healing."

"Let's deal with this guy first." Willard pointed her rifle at the troll's eyes. "Why did you attack us?"

"Death to the Ruin Bringer," he snarled in his language.

"Did you know she was here? You showed up earlier when she wasn't around."

"You are her ally." This time, he spoke in English with a heavy guttural accent. "You will die. All her allies will die, and her offensive drug den will be no more."

"Do you have a drug den I don't know about, Thorvald?" Willard asked.

"He probably means the coffee shop. From what I've gathered, these trolls have been grumpy that their kind are coming to us for drinks instead of the Bloody Blade. And this guy, Ogdar, has been trying to warn his people that I've got some hidden agenda. Why are you spreading that rumor, Oggie? You have to know it's not true, right?"

When the shaman didn't answer, Willard waved her rifle pointedly. She wouldn't kill him in cold blood, but he wouldn't know that.

"The Ruin Bringer would not serve our people out of the goodness of her heart." He spat. "But they won't listen to me. It is not safe for them, not like Rupert's was. Not like the Bloody Blade is. That human-stinking, goblin-infested coffee place is not safe for *any* magical beings." Ogdar curled his lip and spat again.

Did he truly believe I meant to do in all trolls? With poisoned coffee or some such? Was that the reason one of them had taken a potshot at our shop and his posse was planning something nefarious for my wedding?

"Ask him where he got the box, please," I said. "And if he knows where Reb and all of his troll buddies are holed up. I just want the grenades back. I'm not going to *kill* anyone."

That earned me another glare from Ogdar but not a response. Willard repeated the questions, but he clammed up again.

I sensed Zav approaching, let out a breath of relief, and looked toward the sky. He could mind-scour this guy.

Walker and Willard also glanced up. We were only distracted for a second, but Ogdar took advantage. With a blast of magic that I'd assumed he was too injured to conjure, he hurled us away from him. Power knocked me into Sindari and to the ground. Walker hit the brick wall.

Willard fired as she was thrown back, but the shaman anticipated that and ducked. The bullet only grazed his scalp.

As Walker and I lunged back toward him, Ogdar sprang up and used magic to pin Willard in place long enough to grab her, swing her around, and pull her to his chest. He wrapped an arm around her throat, and Walker and I froze.

Fear surged through me. If, after all that, we lost Willard to this bastard...

Walker growled like the prehistoric lion he'd been minutes before and crouched, pure murder in his eyes.

"Call off your dragon and let me go," Ogdar snarled, his arm tightening around Willard's neck, "—or I'll—"

She stomped on his instep, and he lost his concentration, his magic vanishing. Willard rammed her elbow backward into his gut. When he grunted and pitched over, she shoved her hip into him, grabbed his arm, and threw him over her shoulder.

The shaman should have hit the ground, but Walker roared, grabbed him out of the air, and hurled him against the wall. His head struck first and hard, bone crunching.

Zav landed in the street behind me. *Do you need assistance?*

Willard rubbed her neck but didn't appear badly injured. Walker had his fists up, in case the troll fought back, but the shaman's aura faded as he slumped to the ground. Uh oh. That might have been the blow that did him in.

I was going to ask you to mind-scour that guy to see where the other trolls are and what he did to Chasmmoor, but...

The aura faded completely. Ogdar was dead.

Never mind, I finished.

Walker lowered his fists, his shoulders slumping. He could also sense auras and must have realized he'd killed the guy.

"Sorry," he murmured. "That is not... I chose to be a healer, not a barbarian, but when he threatened..." He swallowed and glanced at Willard, as if he feared her judgment, or her lashing out, at him. Strange that he would fear that from anyone after his display of badassery. "Of course, I should have known you could take care of yourself."

"Nobody can take care of themselves against shamans." Willard rubbed her throat. Her voice lowered and her, "Thanks for your help," sounded somewhat grudging.

Walker must have thought so, too, because disappointment flashed in his eyes. He nodded acknowledgment, perhaps to hide his feelings.

"When Willard says thanks, it means she's *extremely* appreciative," I told Walker, translating for Willard, since I knew she was exactly like me in this. "She isn't capable of effusiveness, and if her gratitude seemed grudging, it's more that she's irked that she needed help than that you gave it."

Willard glared at me. I smiled brightly at her. Walker lifted his eyebrows. Hopefully? Wanting to believe?

Come on, Willard, I thought at her, though I doubted I had the power to send my telepathic words into the mind of a mundane human. *Throw the guy a bone.*

"She's more or less right." Willard shrugged, then stepped forward and kissed Walker.

It was on the cheek, but he was so stunned that he wouldn't have known what to do with lip contact. He touched his cheek and stared at her before recovering and offering a gruff, "Good."

"He says that was amazing, Willard, and he hopes you'll do it again after you two have consumed that salmon meal together, a meal that's probably still warm since he thoughtfully packed it in an insulated bag. In case of dinner delays."

"Now you're just being a pest," Willard told me.

Walker nodded.

"You'll thank me at the wedding. Yours, not mine."

"Hilarious," Willard said, deadpan.

Walker looked a little wistful.

I do not believe they appreciate your matchmaking attempts, Sindari observed.

They'll thank me later. You'll see.

We must go search for my dwarven guest. Zav had transformed into his human form, but only so he could pick up the gargoyle box and frown fiercely at it. He made it disappear into an interdimensional pocket, then shifted back into a dragon. *You will come with me, Val?*

Yes. Sindari, do you want to go for a ride?

On his back? You know I find that stressful. His magic makes it impossible for me to dig in with my claws, and I have no faith that I won't fall off.

Yeah, I've noticed how your claws like to dig into the backs of my seats in the Jeep.

Your driving is almost as nerve-wracking as Lord Zavryd's flying.

I am offended, Zav butted in.

Me too, I thought to both of them.

My flying is sublime. When I soar through the air, lesser winged creatures gaze at my majestic flight with awe and envy.

I've mostly seen them squawk in alarm and flee, I said.

They are envious and awe-filled as they flee.

I'm sure.

I rested a hand on Sindari's back. *You don't have to come along, but Zav won't let you fall. I used to worry about that, too, but I've never even had a close call. Though if you ever succeed at digging your claws between his scales, he might be less inclined to keep you aboard.*

I shall dismiss myself to heal. When you reach your destination, call me forth again if you wish. He disappeared into silver mist that soon faded.

Before I'd taken more than a couple of steps toward Zav, my phone rang. Mom.

"Just a second, Zav." I held up a finger and answered it, hoping Mom had good news and hadn't called to complain about Eireth, elven hostilities with Liam, or goblins adding magazine racks to her sauna. "Everything okay, Mom?" I answered as two of Willard's unmarked corpse-removal vans pulled into the street.

She waved them toward the mutilated corpses.

"Yes," Mom said. "Eireth and I had a long talk, and he updated me on his life. I told him about you and Amber."

"He's met me and Amber."

Admittedly, his chat with Amber had been brief.

"He didn't know what either of you were like as chubby toddlers with dirt smeared all over your faces."

"And he knows now?"

"I got out the family photos."

"Thanks, Mom. I was only ninety-nine percent positive that my wedding would be awkward. You've taken away that last one percent."

"I wasn't going to bring the photos *to* the wedding. Though I suppose I could. Have the decorations for your wedding cake been finalized yet?"

"Is there a reason you're torturing me?"

"Your dragon left a goblin engineering team in my sauna."

"They improved it. Didn't you see the magazine rack?" I almost swore as my feet left the ground. Zav was levitating me onto his back. It looked like we weren't taking the Jeep.

"All I could see were the naked goblins when I went inside to see why the noise had stopped. They were making use of my sauna after their arduous day of work. And they *weren't* using towels."

"That *is* a crime. I have to go, Mom. Zav and I need to check on a friend. And then try to find another friend's son. Half the people I know are missing this week."

"Do you need Rocket's tracking skills?"

I started to say no but paused. Zav and I should be able to find Chasmmoor, but I'd already looked for and lost Reb. Maybe Mom and Rocket *could* help. For that matter, Sindari could try tracking him again. But it might be too late to pick up any trace of him. Unless…

I dug in my pocket and pulled out the LEGO speeder bike I'd been carrying around all day. "Do you think Rocket could track someone by smelling a toy? In downtown? If it's been a day?" If he couldn't, I could try later with Sindari, once we found Chasmmoor.

"I could," came Walker's firm voice from the ground.

"Is your nose as good as a golden retriever's?" I asked from Zav's back.

"Better." He lifted his chin, but not without glancing at Willard to see if she was listening. Was he still trying to impress her?

Willard was knee-deep in spider ichor as she helped her agent manhandle a corpse into the van.

Zav's muscles bunched impatiently, and I could tell he felt responsible for Chasmmoor and didn't want to delay looking for him.

"Will you look for the troll boy, Reb?" I tossed the toy to Walker and explained the Bloody Blade's location. "You don't have to confront any trolls that are with him. Just find out where he is."

"I can do that."

"I've got a solution, Mom," I said into the phone. "Thanks."

"I also don't mind confronting trolls," Walker said after I hung up. "I am not only a healer but a consummate warrior."

"Walker," Willard said. "Use your consummate self to throw that dismembered tentacle in here, will you?"

"Certainly. And then I'll track down the troll boy."

"Fantastic."

"Thanks, Walker." I waved as Zav sprang into the air. "If you find him, Willard will kiss you again."

"Really?" he asked.

"*No.*" Willard hoisted a dismembered tentacle into the van by herself.

"*Yes*," I called as we gained altitude. "Maybe even on the lips!"

I cannot sense Chasmmoor, Zav told me, not commenting on the Walker exchange. *I should be able to. I can sense the elves in your house and also the vampire.*

We'll find him. I felt guilty that I'd been trading jibes with Willard and Walker when my dwarf mentor was in danger.

If he was slain while he was on this world, it will be my fault. The grimness came across in Zav's telepathic tone.

I didn't want to think about the possibility that the trolls might have killed him to take that garish box. *He's alive. We'll find him.*

I hoped I was right.

CHAPTER 24

HAVE YOU FOUND OUR DWARF? Dimitri texted me.
Not yet. I shivered as Zav flew over Green Lake and the surrounding houses, the damp night air tugging at my clothes and my sweat-chilled body.

I wanted a steaming bath, not only to warm myself up but to wipe off the ichor and blood from the battle. But we hadn't found Chasmmoor yet. We'd checked the house and hadn't sensed anything out of the ordinary. No trolls lurking in the shadows, no elven assassins peering out from the bushes, and nothing to suggest a problem with any of our other houseguests.

I hope he's okay, Dimitri texted. *Let me know if you want me to help search. Maybe I could make something.*

Dwarf-finding yard art?

Well, dwarf-finding something. Like a divining rod. I think I could do that. His gear is all here. I could use something of his to make an enchantment that would home in on him specifically.

That made me envision Dimitri walking around the neighborhood with a forked stick.

I'm currently riding a scaled divining rod. I rested a hand on Zav's back, his muscles rippling as he beat his wings.

That sounds uncomfortable.

If he can't find a dwarf, I doubt anyone can. But maybe you could interview the elves and see if they saw or heard anything.

Will do. We need to find him. He's a cool dwarf. And he said that he would show me a few things if he had time after he finishes with you and before he needs to leave.

I'll try not to be too needy and take up all of his vacation days.

Good.

Zav banked as we reached the streetlights and traffic headlights of Aurora, flapping his wings and heading back toward the lake. *I sense the usual shifters and mongrels that live in the area, but I haven't detected a full-blooded dwarf. Unless he has traveled out of the area, I fear he may be dead. The dead give off no aura.*

Wouldn't you at least detect his magical armor if he were dead?

Those who slew him may have taken it. In fact, it is likely they would have. It was very well-crafted and offered great magical protection.

I didn't like that Zav was already talking about Chasmmoor in the past tense. We couldn't give up just because he wasn't in the neighborhood. Maybe he'd had an itch to engage in some friendly axe throwing while drinking beer and had gone to the place on Capitol Hill.

We will fly over your downtown and attempt to detect it or him there.

Good idea. The trolls may also have taken him prisoner. Why kill him and risk a hundred angry dwarves coming to take revenge on them?

As we flew toward the south end of the lake, the dog park where we'd been doing my nocturnal training came into view, the hill a dark spot between the lights of the nearby streets. What if he'd gone there to set something up for the training we'd been scheduled to have tonight?

Wait. I patted Zav's scales again and pointed at the hill. *Let's check down there.*

I do not detect him or his armor.

What if he's got camouflaging magic? I waved to my own charm, though Zav couldn't see me while I was on his back. *He had all kinds of magical doodads, not only the armor.*

I smell the blood of a troll.

I blinked. That wasn't the response I'd expected. *Let's investigate.*

Zav was already descending toward the dog park. He landed in the empty parking lot outside of the fenced area. At one end, beyond the influence of the streetlamps, corpses littered the ground. It was too dark to make out details or tell who they were, but if Zav had smelled troll blood…

I slid off his back and drew Storm. There might be other trolls around who were alive and camouflaged.

SECRETS OF THE SWORD III

"*Eravekt*," I whispered, and Storm flared a brighter blue. My lungs tightened slightly. What the hell? I'd taken my medicine, and I wasn't even *doing* anything now.

Shaking my head, I crept closer to the bodies, hoping Chasmmoor's wasn't among those on the ground. I had no trouble envisioning him engaged in an epic battle with a pack of trolls, eventually succumbing to their superior numbers, and having the gargoyle box ripped free from his dying hands.

Zav shifted into human form and caught up, his aura crackling protectively over me. Maybe he expected more trouble too.

Storm's blue light played over the blue-skinned corpses, troll after troll lying dead on the ground. Several of their skulls were split open, making me think of Chasmmoor's big battle-axe.

"I don't see any short, stout corpses," I murmured.

The trolls had died roughly in a circle, as if they'd had Chasmmoor surrounded. Zav walked around the area, then picked his way through the bodies. He knelt in the empty circle and touched a dark stain on the ground. Blood.

"This is Chasmmoor's blood."

"So he was injured but then got away?"

"His body may have been removed after he died."

"Or he may have survived the fight and stumbled away after defeating his enemies." I stubbornly held on to the belief that he wasn't dead.

Zav gazed over at me. "The trolls got the box, and at least one of them survived to attack you. His armor is also missing."

"I know." I rubbed Sindari's charm, hoping his injuries weren't so bad that he would struggle to return to Earth again so soon. "Hey, buddy," I said when he formed. "Can you sniff around and try to find Chasmmoor's trail?"

I couldn't give up on the idea that he might be camouflaged, though if he had been, the trolls wouldn't have found him in the first place. I sighed.

I will search. Sindari padded around the circle of death as Zav had, then sniffed the blood in the center. His nostrils quivered as he tested the air. Finally, he padded off into the trees, veering away from the parking lot and up the hill.

I followed him hopefully. He paused in a few spots to sniff the ground, then continued on, winding through the trees, his path crooked. Maybe the trail he was *following* was crooked.

"Did he walk away?" I asked.

He stumbled and limped away. Trolls followed him. I do not sense him now. Sindari paused between two trees and sniffed around more thoroughly.

Had he lost the trail? Unless a dragon had swept down and picked up Chasmmoor, it was hard to imagine it disappearing here.

At this point, the trolls turned back. Sindari pointed his nose toward the parking lot, but he kept circling the area. *Chasmmoor's trail disappeared.*

Oh. I almost smacked my head in realization. *Can he make portals? Maybe he's back on his own world.*

Zav was the one to respond. *As far as I know, he cannot. He waited for me to return and transport him to Earth. He is a powerful magic user, but his studies are in enchanting. Making portals is another science, and those who do not travel frequently to other worlds rarely learn it.*

Damn.

Sindari had moved off and stood below a tree. Had he given up?

No, he lifted his paw in the air and let it dangle there. He looked expectantly over at me.

Find something? I asked.

He is here. Camouflaged.

"Hah, I knew it." Not truly, but I'd hoped. I ran over with Zav striding behind me.

It wasn't until I was three feet from Sindari that I could see Chasmmoor crumpled on the ground at the base of the tree. I could also see the blood seeping into the fir needles underneath him and cut marks all over his face and hands. Dents marred his armor, though it had held up far better than his exposed flesh. Too bad he hadn't had a helmet. Blood matted the side of his head.

His eyes were closed, and for a second, I thought he was dead. But now that I was close, I could sense his aura through the magic of whatever camouflaging artifact was hiding him.

"Zav? We could use a healer."

"Yes." Zav knelt at the dwarf's side. He rested a hand on Chasmmoor's breastplate and closed his eyes.

Good work, Sindari. Thanks.

Certainly.

Maybe later, after we've healed Chasmmoor and figured out what happened, you can compete with Walker to track down Reb.

That would not be a competition. I am a far superior tracker to any shifter. They are only part-time predators.

With Zav's healing magic flowing into him, it didn't take Chasmmoor long to stir.

"Thank the Great Forge," he mumbled looking up at us. "You are not trolls."

"No. They're all over there." I pointed toward the corpses. "What happened?"

Chasmmoor tried to sit up but winced and flopped back down.

"Hold." Zav's eyes were closed and his chin bent to his chest as he continued to work on his patient.

"Good idea," Chasmmoor muttered. "I do not know where they came from or why they sprang at me, Thorvald. Thus far, I have not encountered enemies on this world, and I was not expecting it."

"Sorry I didn't warn you that we do have trouble from time to time." I grimaced, certain this had happened because of me. "*I* have enemies, unfortunately."

"Most assassins do."

I thought of Sarrlevi, still wondering if he was tied in to all this somehow. "Yeah. Was your gargoyle box all they wanted? Zav has it, by the way. We recovered it from the shaman."

"Good." Chasmmoor sneered. "The shaman was the only reason I was wounded so. Had I merely been battling troll warriors, I would have prevailed."

I didn't point out that he'd been battling a *lot* of troll warriors. Nobody around me was humble and acknowledged that others could out-fight them, so I shouldn't expect it from a dwarf.

"But his magic was strong," Chasmmoor continued, "and it was with his help that the others were able to sneak up on me. I was coming to prepare the training area for a special battle I had planned to test you with tonight."

"I already got a special battle. I'll tell you about it later."

His bushy red eyebrows rose. "Did the shaman use the artifact on you?"

"Yes. Do give me the command to close that lid without getting zapped later, will you?"

"I can show you, yes. That artifact seemed to be what they wanted from me. They must have been in the area for some reason and sensed me walking to this arena with it."

Some reason. Like scoping out my house and contemplating a way to get their stolen grenades through the defenses? I clenched a fist.

Zav knelt back, but he frowned. "What is that?"

He pointed to Chasmmoor's cheek. At first, I only saw the dried blood on his skin, but when I leaned closer, Storm's blue light brightened his craggy face and revealed more. Splotches and crooked lines of gray-green were stuck to his forehead and one side of his face.

"Dirt?" I asked, though I doubted it. It reminded me of the mold in blue cheese.

"No," Zav said. "Did the trolls throw a spore-net at you?"

A what net?

"They threw *everything* at me." Chasmmoor sighed and scraped a fingernail over a splotch on his cheek. "There was a net, yes. I was too busy fighting and freeing myself from it to examine it closely. It did hurt when it touched me." He grimaced and moved his finger. "And these spots are still sore, though I thank you for healing my other wounds." He touched his head gingerly, then more firmly, and nodded. "Will the splotches go away? I would not wish to look anything other than my best for a historic dragon–half-elf wedding."

"Our wedding is historic?" I asked.

"Unprecedented, at least. I haven't heard of others. A handful of elves have been mated to dragons over the years, and married in the elven way, but half-elves are uncommon."

"That's me. Uncommon and unprecedented."

"A spore-net causes a skin irritation," Zav said, not commenting on how special we were. "It is mostly thrown to distract magic users by causing pain and interfering with their focus. I have seen its effects before and know that those splotches will grow into a more substantial infection if they aren't treated."

"Yes, we call it troll rot." Chasmmoor sighed again. "Any chance you can heal it?"

"Such things are beyond my healing abilities, but my sister may be able to help."

"Zoltan might have a tincture for it." I would rather deal with Zoltan than Zondia. Besides, he was less than a mile away at the house.

"That is the vampire who lives in the basement?" Chasmmoor tilted his head. "I have sensed him but not gone down to investigate. A magical cannon on his threshold convinced me that he may object to guests."

"He objects to guests who want to kill him. If you bring him money and tell him what a brilliant alchemist he is, he'll let you in." I offered Chasmmoor a hand in case he was ready to get up, though I almost pulled it back at the sight of more troll rot on his fingers. Hopefully, that wasn't truly mold, especially a mold I was allergic to.

"He's an alchemist? Are you sure?"

"Quite sure."

"Huh. I was hoping to look at his anvil."

"I'm not sure he shows that to other guys."

Chasmmoor's forehead crinkled.

"Never mind. The anvil bolted to the floor in the basement was left by the last vampire who lived in the house. *He* was a smith. He lives in Woodinville now, enjoying country life over city life. Shall we go?"

"Yes." Chasmmoor accepted my hand.

I hoisted him up and was going to suggest walking, since it wasn't that far to the house, but Zav shifted into dragon form and elevated us onto his back. *All* of us. Sindari flailed and growled a protest as his feet left the ground.

Sorry. I should have dismissed you, I said as we settled onto Zav's back. Correction: Chasmmoor and I settled. Sindari stretched out his legs—and his claws—like a cat balanced on top of a La-Z-Boy rocker with a vigorous owner seated below.

I should have dismissed myself. Sindari hissed as Zav sprang into the air, wingbeats stirring the boughs of the evergreens.

I hadn't known tigers *could* hiss. *Don't perforate his scales.*

They're harder than granite.

It's a short ride to the house. If you survive it, I'll ask Dimitri to pet you.

Dimitri does not need to be asked to pet me. He has good hands, and he knows what to do with them.

I snorted. *He should take you to bars as his wingman. You can say things like that to his dates.*

I have no wish to be a wingman. Sindari glanced at Zav's beating wings, perhaps imagining riding on *them. But should he need someone to praise him, I can do this.*

Zav was heading for our backyard, but he spotted something a few houses away and landed early. As he came down, he inadvertently smashed the Christmas reindeer and sleigh that the neighbor should have taken down weeks ago. Or maybe it wasn't inadvertent, given his checkered past when it came to deck-chair destruction.

"That was a surprisingly ungraceful landing for a dragon," Chasmmoor murmured.

"I think deck chairs and lawn ornaments tickle his belly scales when they crunch underneath him," I murmured back.

Sindari had already sprung down.

"You're saying he meant to do that?" Chasmmoor peered over Zav's side at the smashed reindeer.

"I have hunches."

A dragon lands where a dragon wishes, Zav informed us blandly.

The neighbor's car wasn't parked out front, so hopefully he hadn't seen or heard the destruction. I would stuff an envelope of cash in his mailbox in the morning. A small envelope. The reindeer were—*had been*—plastic, so they couldn't have been that expensive.

There are more dead trolls here. Zav levitated us off his back and was back in his human form by the time our feet hit the ground. He walked toward a couple of bare-branched cherry trees in a side yard. Two more troll corpses were on the ground under them.

"Did your battle start early?" I asked.

Chasmmoor shook his head. "I wasn't attacked until I reached the arena."

The arena being the dog park almost a mile away. Okay, so who had killed these trolls?

"I did sense magical beings out here," Chasmmoor said, "as I was walking past. They might have been trolls. At the time, I didn't consider trolls enemies and didn't think anything of their presence."

Zav crouched to examine the bodies. Sindari trotted over and sniffed around.

"Their throats were cut," Zav said, "precisely and accurately. A single slash to each."

I smell... something familiar, Sindari said.

A niggling feeling started up, mingling with dread in my gut. It occurred to me that we were only two houses down from where I'd spotted Sarrlevi, not once but twice. Once this very week.

Had he been spying on the house—*again*—when the trolls had shown up? But if so, presuming he'd come to stalk me, why would he have attacked the trolls? Had they sensed him skulking, guessed he was one of my houseguests, and decided to attack? A warmup before the battle against poor Chasmmoor?

"The assassin Sarrlevi was here," Zav said coolly as Sindari reported the same thing telepathically.

"Did he leave a coin?" I doubted the trolls had been targets he'd been hired to kill.

"No coin. But he slew these two with his magical blades. I recognize their signature."

And I recognize his scent, Sindari added.

Zav straightened and faced us. "I did *not* invite Varlesh Sarrlevi to the wedding."

"I'd assumed not," I said, though it wouldn't have shocked me if he had. He'd invited everyone else. Maybe I should have checked.

Zav's eyes flared with violet light. "If he has broken our covenant and is here to assassinate or *bother* you in any way, I will wring his neck. Better yet, I will feed him to the *yorak* I've imported so they won't molest the local wildlife."

Ugh, was that happening? I would have to make sure that Zav got rid of any leftover animals that the dragons didn't hunt down. If he'd imported them, he could export them back to where they'd come from.

"I forgot to mention that he was here the other night looking at the house," I admitted. It wasn't so much that I'd forgotten as that I'd decided not to tell Zav, since I hadn't been a hundred percent certain I hadn't imagined it all.

His eyes flared brighter. "Then there can be no mistake. He was here, not once but *twice* to spy on you. What does he want?"

"He didn't mention it. He disappeared when I looked at him." I waved toward our bedroom window, which was visible from here.

"I will go look for him. I know the signature of his twin blades, and I may be able to sense them from a distance." Zav held my gaze. "You must stay inside under the protection of the house until the wedding."

"You know I can't do that. I've got to find Reb, stop the troll plot, and pick up my wedding dress." I didn't point out that Sarrlevi had gotten through our house's magical defenses last time, so hiding inside wouldn't keep me safe. "I've dealt with him before, so I can handle him again."

I hoped. The last time, I'd been assisted by the fact that my magic had been a lot easier to call upon in the fae realm. But I'd learned more about Storm since then, so maybe I truly could best him. Or at least keep him from besting *me*.

"You *did* handle him." Some of Zav's ire faded, and he beamed approval at me. "*And* you vexed him."

"Apparently the fae queen has vexed him too."

"I thought he was honorable, for an elf and an assassin," Zav said. "I believed he would keep his word. When I find him, I will question him before wringing his neck."

"That's noble of you."

"Yes. I will search for him now. You will be careful, my mate." Zav stepped forward and kissed me.

I kissed him back, pleased he had faith in me and that he was done ordering me to do things. Except for his order to be careful. That seemed a prudent command to follow.

Once again, Zav transformed into a dragon and sprang into the sky.

"He did not order *us* to be careful," Chasmmoor observed.

I am simply relieved he did not levitate me onto his back again. Sindari shuddered.

"Come on, Chasmmoor." I waved for them to follow me to the house. "Let's get you un-moldy."

He scratched a spot on his jaw and winced. "I'm amenable to that."

CHAPTER 25

THIS IS *MAGNIFICENT*." CHASMMOOR RAN his hand lovingly over the anvil bolted to the floor in the basement, a hand half covered in that awful troll rot.

Zoltan had already taken a sample and was examining it under his microscope. "At the cellular level, this reminds me of ringworm," he murmured, not paying attention to the anvil stroking. "My spilanthes formula may be able to treat it. It has strong antifungal properties and can be effective even against magically enhanced strains."

"That's good," I offered from the side, where I stood with Sindari and Dimitri, who'd trailed us downstairs, curious about where our dwarf had been.

"The anvil is of dwarven origins." Chasmmoor didn't seem to hear Zoltan at all. "From the Exodus Ore Mine area if I am not mistaken. How ever did it come to be on this wild world? Was it stolen?" He kept any accusation out of his tone, but he did look over at me, the owner of a dwarven sword that had also mysteriously come to be on this *wild world.*

"I have no idea. I assume that Jimmy the vampire acquired it from a flea market."

"No." Zoltan shook his head without looking up from the microscope. "He said it was in the house when he moved here. That was *why* he moved here."

"Yeah, I hear blacksmithing anvils in real estate listings make houses fly off the market."

"Fascinating. You could make great weapons and all manner of tools with the power of such an anvil seeping into your work." Chasmmoor shifted his attention to Dimitri, who was dutifully rubbing Sindari's ears. "I trust you have been using it?"

Dimitri shook his head. "I mostly use my hands, a few simple tools, and welding equipment for my work. Also, this whole basement has been claimed by Zoltan, and I didn't want to presume..."

"*Zoltan* uses it to rest his Petri dishes on," I said. "I'm sure you could take it and bring him a table."

"Yes, it *must* be used. It is a crime to leave it here gathering dust." Chasmmoor rubbed the surface, again lovingly.

"I'm not sure I'd know *how* to use it," Dimitri admitted. "I've never had a magical tool of my own."

"Perhaps, if there is time," Chasmmoor said, "I can instruct you on its use."

"Really?" Dimitri's gloomy expression vanished. If he'd had pointed ears, they would have perked to the ceiling.

"Assuming I survive this troll rot and am not slowly eaten away from the outside in."

"Not to worry." Zoltan whistled as he strode to a cabinet full of crocks, jars, vials, and other strange containers I couldn't name. "I've applied my spilanthes formula to the sample, and it is dying heartily."

"Nothing like hearty dying to perk up a scientist," I said.

"A *vampire* scientist, yes." Zoltan grabbed one of the crocks, removed the lid, and something that smelled like slug slime marinating in tea-tree oil filled the basement.

"You may want to add some ventilation if you're going to work down here," I murmured to Dimitri.

His nose was also wrinkled. "Yes."

Neat and tidy as always, Zoltan used a sponge to extract the viscous mucous-colored goo and rub it on the back of Chasmmoor's hand. "Give it a moment. Should it prove effective, I will ask you to strip your clothing so that I can apply it thoroughly. If any of your skin is untreated, the rot will spread again."

"I believe I'll step out before the dwarven nudity starts." I took a step toward the door, trusting someone would let me know if the gunk didn't work and we needed to try something else.

But Zoltan stopped me with an upraised hand. "Not so fast, dear robber."

"Let me guess. You're going to invoice me for this."

"Naturally, but that's not why I stopped you. I know where to deliver my invoices, after all."

"Under my bedroom door when Zav isn't home?"

"Yes. I would not presume to deliver a bill when a huffy dragon is present." Zoltan handed the crock to Chasmmoor and went to another cabinet. This one was full of computer peripherals and special red lights for his recording. He extracted a digital camera and an expandable tripod and brought them over to me. "I require that you record the wedding, for those of us who cannot go to outdoor events under the brazen sun."

I didn't know how brazen the sun would be in January, but I accepted the equipment. "You actually care about our wedding and want to see it?"

"Certainly. You and Lord Zavryd are my roommates, and you have allowed me to stay in your abode free of charge, even though he could have driven me out at any point. Or *incinerated* me out. I have developed feelings for you and wish to see your relationship succeed."

Sweet, if true, but I was a little skeptical. Zoltan didn't even call me by name.

"A minute ago, you called Zav huffy," I pointed out.

"Many people are huffy. That does not preclude the possibility of others having feelings for them."

"You're not going to record this for your YouTube channel, are you?" I couldn't imagine how a wedding would fit in with his alchemy theme, but it was also hard for me to believe his feelings drove him to want to see Zav and me walk down the aisle and kiss.

Zoltan smiled faintly. "It *is* possible that when I shared a recipe for the formula I'm working on for your wedding gift that my young, easily smitten, female followers requested a video of the wedding."

"You're making us a gift?" I already had enough to worry about from the *goblin* gifts. "Does it explode?"

"It has some interesting properties that you'll appreciate."

"Is it one of your eye-wrinkle creams?"

"Thanks to your elven blood, you are without eye wrinkles. Those dark bags under your eyes are another story. Don't you and your dragon sleep at all in between your sexual encounters?"

"The sexual encounters aren't what have been keeping me up nights." I didn't glare at Chasmmoor, since he was here to help train me, but I did give him a significant look.

"The living have such strange practices. But on the subject of the video, one of my followers said she *loves* weddings and would watch hours of footage. Another said she would watch it fifty times if a live dragon were recorded. I trust you know what that means."

"More ad revenue?"

"Precisely. Have Freysha help you with the lighting. I've taught her the ways."

"It's working." Chasmmoor showed us the back of his hand, the area glistening with goo now free of troll rot.

"Excellent." Zoltan returned to grab his crock. "Now you will strip."

"And I'm leaving," I said. "Sindari, you coming?"

Sindari was leaning against Dimitri's side, his seven hundred pounds almost enough to topple Dimitri, and getting his neck scratched.

Perhaps later.

"Right." As I passed through the light lock, skirted the cannon, and climbed the steps, my phone buzzed. "Hey, Willard. What's the news?"

"That it's difficult to fit a giant into a corpse-removal van."

"You're supposed to tie them to the *top* of the van. Didn't you see *Harry and the Hendersons*?"

"That was a sasquatch, not a giant."

"Same principle."

"In other more relevant news, Walker has tracked down your wayward boy."

"Oh, good. Is he all right? Do we need to battle another legion of trolls to break him out of a safe house?" I thought of Zav's warning that the trolls were skulking in the old dark-elf tunnels.

"He's by himself in a cardboard box under the monorail."

"Not a very impressive safe house."

"No. Walker says he can grab him, but since the kid doesn't know him, he asked if you wanted to go in first. He's also concerned it might be a trap and thought it would be wise to call in backup. I can't help unfortunately. I'm still back by my apartment, cleaning up this mess and handling questions from the police. A lot of bystanders reported the battle, and someone's social-media video post of the giant-prehistoric-lion-slays-giant-spider incident now has tens of thousands of views. Have I mentioned lately how much I love this new era of citizen journalism?"

"I don't think you've ever mentioned that."

"Good. I'm sending you the cross streets closest to the kid's box. You know you left your Jeep in my parking lot, right?"

"Yeah, taking a dragon is faster."

"A nice option."

"Except at the moment when he's busy looking for an assassin."

"Someone *else* is after you?"

"I hope not. I'll get an Uber and be there soon."

"Be careful."

What did it say about my life that everybody felt compelled to say that to me?

CHAPTER 26

"YOU SURE YOU DIDN'T WANT to get out at the Seattle Center?" my driver asked dubiously as I directed him past the Space Needle and toward the intersection Willard had given me.

"I'm sure."

"There's a new show at the Laser Dome. Grunge and heavy metal, an homage to Seattle's music roots."

"I'll be sure to check it out later." I imagined taking Zav inside to lie on the floor in the dark, stare up at the laser patterns, and listen to music booming so loudly that it vibrated our bodies. Given the lack of food at the event, he wouldn't be a fan.

"I'll take you if you're interested." My driver gave me a flirtatious smile. He was in his fifties and had the yellow teeth of a smoker.

"You'd have to take my fiancé too. He eats a lot, so he's an expensive date."

"Hm, is he pretty? I'm open to a threesome."

That had escalated quickly. "Yeah, if you can get past his choice in robes and footwear, but he's not that adventurous in the nest. I'll get out here." The car hadn't fully stopped when I opened the door and hopped out.

"Maybe later," the driver called out the window after me.

"Riding dragons is *much* more appealing than riding with strangers," I muttered.

My senses picked up Walker a couple of blocks away, so I trotted in that direction. As I drew closer, I also sensed Reb. He *did* seem to be under the monorail by himself. Huh. Was this the trap Willard suspected, or had he run away from his troll tormentors? And if the latter, why hadn't he gone back to Inga?

Walker stood half a block away from Reb's location and was talking to a police officer. I got close enough to hear him explain that he was a respected and prominent surgeon in the community and was most certainly not *skulking*.

His usually clean and tidy clothing *was* disheveled after the fight, and his eye was swelling and turning black and blue. I hadn't realized he'd been hurt, but it wasn't surprising that he'd been stoic about it instead of confessing an injury—a *weakness*—in front of Willard. I dearly hoped they got a chance to enjoy that dinner together later.

"Is there a problem?" I asked as I walked up, though I barely glanced at the policeman. I couldn't yet see Reb's box in the shadows of the massive pillars that supported the monorail, but I sensed that he was on the move—away from us.

He might not have recognized or reacted to Walker in the area, but he must have sensed *me* approaching. But why run? Earlier, he'd asked me to rescue him.

"Just walking my beat," the policeman said. "There's been some vandalism in the area, so I'm talking to anyone I pass who's loitering."

"As I said, I'm here waiting for a friend." Walker extended a hand toward me.

"Yup. We're friends. But I've got to go." I waved and walked past.

Reb was moving away quickly—I glimpsed him running up ahead. Only the desire not to be suspicious and prompt the policeman to call for squads of patrol cars kept me from sprinting after him.

I *did* walk briskly. And summoned Sindari again.

Reb ran behind a pillar and didn't come out again. He shouldn't have any magical trinkets to help him hide.

Val, Sindari groaned into my mind. *I appreciate your frequent desire for my company, but I can't stay away from my realm much longer tonight.*

I just need a hand capturing Reb. I should be able to get him, but if you could let me know if any trolls or other threats are in the area, I would appreciate it.

Reb started moving again. Hoping I was far enough from the policeman not to rouse suspicion, I broke into a run.

But he wasn't running this time. He was *climbing*.

"Oh, hell," I grumbled. "Not again."

Was that the rumble of a train coming? What, had Reb been watching that troll I'd followed to the rails earlier for tips?

"Reb!" I called, not caring about the policeman any longer. "It's me, Val." He had to know that, but maybe he'd gone temporarily insane. "I have your LEGO speeder!"

He paused, halfway up the pillar, and peered around it at me. I almost laughed, then realized I'd lied. Walker had it. What if he made me show it to him?

But he ducked back out of sight and returned to climbing.

"Why are you *running*?" I called. *Sindari, can you try to find a way up there to head him off? I think the train is coming from the mall.*

I don't know where that is.

That way. I pointed vaguely as I ran. *And it'll be heading to the Space Needle, so you need to find a way up that way.* I waved back behind us.

With such precise directions, it's shocking you haven't pursued a cartography career.

Hilarious. Just get up on the rails, please.

Sindari bounded back the way we'd come.

Reb had reached the top and swung up onto the rails. I sprang for the pillar, hoping that if he could climb it, I could climb it.

The smooth cement wasn't ideal, but my half-elven fingers found dents and cracks in the decades-old structure. I crept up the side.

One of the trains rumbled toward Reb. It wasn't like some huge freight train roaring along at eighty miles per hour, but being hit by the thing wouldn't feel good.

"Look out!" I called up to him. "Climb back down."

He didn't. Once I got this kid back to Inga, we were going to have a serious chat about obeying one's elders.

The train rumbled closer. He ran down the tracks away from it. As I reached the top, the train reached me, wind batting at my face and hair. Would Reb jump off the tracks to avoid it? I couldn't see him, but I still sensed him. He'd paused. He was going to try to jump on it, the same as the other troll had. What a suicidal race of people.

Reb scooted to the side opposite from me and, with more agility than I would have guessed he had, leaped onto the side of the train car. I held my breath, afraid he would be knocked off and fall all the way to the ground. But he caught a good grip and skimmed up to the roof.

As the end of the train drew close to me, I swung up, barely avoiding planting my face against it, and sprang. I caught the back corner and pulled myself up. Belatedly, I activated my camouflage charm so Reb wouldn't sense my location. I *should* have done that as soon as I'd gotten out of the car. Now, even if I disappeared from his senses, he would know I was here and probably onboard with him.

As the train continued its inexorable trip, the lights of the Space Needle highlighted against the cloudy night sky ahead, I climbed to the roof. A few passengers sat inside the lit cabin, but they were fiddling with their phones and hadn't noticed the stowaways clinging to the outside.

Reb knelt on the roof at the front of the train, peering in my direction and also down to the ground on either side. Looking for Sindari? My senses told me that he'd found a way onto the tracks and was heading back this way.

I crept out onto the roof toward him. I almost called to Reb to stay there, but he hadn't listened to me yet. Better to grab him, pin him down, and wait for the train to pull into its stop.

Alarmed by something, Reb sprang to his feet. He wobbled and flailed his arms. Shit. I sprinted for the kid.

Reb ran in my direction as Sindari sprang off the tracks and came down on the roof behind him. Reb screamed, though all Sindari did was land—he didn't rush after the kid. Reb slipped on the roof and slid off the side.

"No!" I shouted, diving for him.

My stomach hit hard, but I caught his wrist, locking my fingers around it.

The jerk of his weight falling threatened to pull *me* off the train after him. I skidded several alarming inches with my heart in my throat. Sindari's paw came down heavy and comforting on my back, pinning me in place.

"Help," Reb pleaded as he swayed on the side of the moving train.

Someone inside shouted, no doubt having a view of his blue-skinned belly plastered to the window. I pushed myself to my knees and heaved Reb back onto the roof.

Sindari planted a second paw on him, probably more to make sure he didn't escape again than to keep him from falling.

Thanks, I told him. *And we both appreciate you retracting your claws for that.*

I thought you might. Human flesh is fragile.

Yeah, and my jacket is easily perforated.

Don't you have some armor?

Yes, but I don't always wear it. A mistake.

Indeed.

Reb slumped, his face pressed into the roof of the train.

"Are you ready to go home and have a chat, Reb?" I asked.

"No," came the muffled response.

"Are you going to fight us if we take you there anyway?"

He sighed in defeat. "No."

***

Walker, Reb, and I went to Willard's first so I could retrieve my Jeep and Walker could enjoy his meal with her. Then I drove Reb back to my house. I'd already called Inga to let her know I'd found her wayward—or possibly kidnapped—charge and would meet her there.

So far, Reb hadn't said a word, so I didn't know which adjective applied to him. He gazed sullenly out the window, tonguing a fat lip and nursing a swollen black eye. He'd had the bruised eye earlier, but he might have gotten the puffy lip from smashing face-first into the side of the train. I refused to feel guilty for inadvertently causing that. There'd been no reason for him to run from me.

"What's the deal, Reb?" I had gotten his LEGO toy back from Walker, and I offered it to him as we drove into my neighborhood. "Did those other trolls kidnap you?"

"Sort of," he mumbled.

That was more of an answer than I'd gotten when I'd asked him questions earlier, so I chose to find it encouraging.

"How does one get sort of kidnapped? Did they threaten you if you didn't come with them?"

"Yeah. I guess. It was after the thing."

"The thing?" This was going to be a fun interrogation. "The bombing of the coffee shop?"

"No." Reb looked at me in alarm, his first display of emotion or energy. "I didn't have anything to do with that, I swear. I mean... I didn't."

That sounded like it meant he most positively had.

"Did one of your friends do it?" I asked.

"No." Reb slumped lower in the seat. "I don't have any friends."

As I turned the Jeep onto the street leading to the house, I thought I sensed an elf outside, near the yard where we'd found those two dead trolls. Sarrlevi again? Had he moved into the neighborhood? Set up a tent in somebody's lilac bushes? I started to reach out telepathically to him, but he disappeared from my senses.

"Pain in the ass," I grumbled.

Reb looked at me.

"It's a pain in the ass when you don't have any friends," I said.

"Yeah."

"Who's the kid I saw at the coffee shop after the bombing? If he's not a friend, why was he there?"

"I dunno. I wasn't there."

I pulled the Jeep to the side of the road, amused that the available parking in front of my house had expanded. Not only was my usual spot free, but the curb was open along both streets edging our corner lot and well into the lots to either side.

Zav's topiaries seemed larger than ever, and a glimmer of orange light glowed in the hollows that were their eyes. It was, however, possible that my plethora of exotic houseguests had as much to do with the neighbors staying away as the magical shrubs.

Clangs reached my ears as I turned off the engine. Chasmmoor putting the basement anvil to use? I sensed Dimitri down there, too, though oddly Zoltan had left his abode and was upstairs. Not being harassed by elves, I hoped. They were, as usual, spread across the levels of the house and also out in the conservatory. Both Freysha and Eireth had returned.

"Look, Reb." I faced him, also aware of Inga in the house—she would sense us and stomp outside at any moment. "I think some of those trolls want to sabotage my wedding, if not kill my very politically important guests, not to mention Zav and me. I need you to tell me what you know."

He stared sullenly at the glove compartment with his shoulders hunched to his ears.

It crossed my mind to threaten that Zav would mind-scour him, but that seemed like a lousy thing to do to an employee. "I'll buy you a hundred dollars' worth of LEGOs."

"Two hundred," he said promptly. "Quality LEGOs are expensive."

This kid had been going to the same school of negotiations as Amber.

"Two hundred, plus tax," I agreed. A small price to pay to get to the bottom of this.

Inga opened the front door and stepped onto the porch.

He's fine, I told her telepathically, *but give me a minute, please. I think he's going to tell me what happened at the shop.*

You don't think he'll speak with me present? She had some of the same sullenness of Reb. Maybe they were a good match.

Not if he's ashamed or feels guilty about something. He wouldn't want you to find out about it and think less of him. I had no idea if that was true, but it mollified her, for she crossed her arms and leaned against the door to wait.

"Reb?" I prompted gently.

"It started with the grenade," he said in a low voice.

"The grenade that someone threw at the coffee shop?"

"No, the one I took."

"From Nin?"

When had he been to Nin's truck? Inga didn't live anywhere near it.

"From your bag," he said in an even lower voice.

"Er, when was that?"

"Before you went to the dwarf place. You had your bag on the floor in the coffee shop, and I could sense the grenades in it."

It took me a moment to dredge that memory up—it had been weeks ago. But I slowly remembered. Reb and Inga had been arguing in front of the coffee kiosk, and I'd come up to intervene. He'd tripped over my bag. Had that been a ruse? To cover that he was snagging a grenade? It must have been.

"Why did you want a grenade?" I prompted when he didn't continue on his own.

"To scare the others. The trolls that were picking on me." Reb licked his lips. "I wasn't planning to *kill* them. Just scare them, so they'd know I have big weapons and that they should leave me alone until…" He glanced at me. "Until I'm bigger and stronger and I've learned enough martial arts to pulverize them."

"You're studying martial arts?"

"From video games."

"Ah." I couldn't laugh since, as a kid, I'd tried to teach myself moves by watching *The Karate Kid* over and over. It hadn't been until many years later and many real classes later that I'd refined my spinning roundhouse kick. "Is it working?"

"Not really. I'm not strong enough."

"You don't need to be strong for martial arts, just to learn how to use your whole body to generate power. I'm training my daughter in sword fighting. If you want to come to our practices, you can, and I'll show you some stuff."

"You have a sword. Inga says I can't have a sword until I'm older."

"We can do plenty without swords. Even magical beings fly backward if you plant a side kick in their chest."

"Yeah?" His ears perked as he no doubt imagined himself planting side kicks left and right.

"Yes, but let's have the rest of the story, please. You threw the grenade you took at one of your troll tormentors?"

"At a *bunch* of them. There's a whole gang of kids that have been picking on me because I left the streets to live with a mongrel."

"Mongrels can be okay," I said dryly.

"Yeah. I have my own bed and room and toys, and the roof hardly ever leaks."

Hardly ever? Maybe we needed to throw more work Inga's way.

"It's way better than living on the streets and being hungry all the time because nobody will share with a runt." That sullenness had returned to his voice.

This time, I didn't blame him for it. "I imagine. What happened with the grenade? Did you hurt anyone?" *Kill* anyone?

"They ran away before it exploded and only got a little hurt."

I wondered what qualified as a *little hurt* for a troll and imagined arms flying off.

"And my plan *worked*. They were so scared they peed their pants. I *love* it when a plan comes together."

I blinked. Had he and Inga been watching *A-Team* reruns?

"But some grownups were watching," Reb continued.

"Grownup trolls?"

"Yeah. They caught me and pushed me up against the wall and made me tell them where I got the grenade. I said you, and they didn't want to fight you, but then they hurt me some, and I said I knew where you got them."

I sighed.

"Since I hurt one of their kids, they said I owed it to them to work for them for a year," Reb added. "They didn't give me any choice, and they took me without letting me tell Inga or anyone."

It was encouraging that he'd *wanted* to tell Inga. Though I wished he would have told me. I would have put an end to that indentured servitude before it started.

"They said they'd catch me and hurt me if I ran away. They said it was *embarrassing* for me to live with a half-human mongrel." Reb bit his lip and peered over at me. "Is that embarrassing? I want to be tough, and I want to be a *real troll*." He sounded like he was quoting someone there. "But I like my Nintendo Switch and my LEGOs."

"Who doesn't? And you know mongrels can kick ass too, right? Inga is pretty tough."

"She's okay."

Kids gave such ringing endorsements. Maybe Reb and Amber would make good sparring partners. They could be sullen and sarcastic together while practicing their moves.

"You should stay with her until you're a grownup and know how to take care of yourself," I said. "And play games and eat good food and sleep without getting rained on. You're only a kid. You can prove yourself to the world later if you still feel compelled to. Or you can get a job working on video games instead."

"Really? Like making them?" His brows rose but then fell. "Trolls can't work at human places. They don't think trolls exist, or if they do, they're afraid of us."

"If you're interested in computer stuff when you finish your education, I know someone who can get you a gig." I imagined how delighted Thad would be by that request. "Lots of jobs are remote these days. Nobody even needs to know you're a troll if that's a problem."

"Huh. But I still want to be a killer warrior."

"That's an option. Just come to Amber's practices."

He shrugged noncommittally. "Maybe I will."

"Good. But one more thing." I lifted a hand to keep him from opening the door. "Who threw a grenade at the coffee shop and why?"

He truly might not know that if he hadn't been there, but I had to get a lead on those trolls.

"I didn't see it, but I heard it was Doxgar. And Throk. They work for the owner."

"The Bloody Blade owner?"

"Yeah. They want to get rid of you and the Coffee Dragon on account of what the shaman brothers have been saying."

I didn't correct him on the name. Dimitri might as well change the sign at this point. "Wait, did you say shaman *brothers*? Is there *another* one?"

"There were two shaman brothers that came by the Bloody Blade when I was working in the kitchen. They *really* hate you. They were trying to get everyone riled up to destroy you and the Coffee Dragon."

"Which the owner of the Bloody Blade is probably perfectly willing to do since we're his competition. Wonderful."

Reb nodded. "He said that once your place was gone, everybody would *have* to come to the Bloody Blade to hang out. Then he's going to get rich." Reb wrinkled his nose. "I don't know why *real trolls* need a bunch of human money. They're supposed to be warriors and hunt for their food."

I didn't point out that they could also be working to complete their LEGO collections.

"Any idea where those trolls are hiding out now?" I asked. "Last I heard, they haven't gone back to the Bloody Blade."

"I ran away during the craziness of you attacking their pub, so I don't know where they went for sure, but I heard some of them talk about tunnels under the city."

Those damn dark-elf tunnels that still had magic hiding them. There was only one more day until the wedding. What were the odds that Zav and I could find the trolls in time? Especially when Zav's family kept distracting him, and my family kept distracting *me*?

"Can I go?" Reb asked. "I'm hungry."

"Go ahead. Give Inga a hug."

"Ew, trolls don't hug."

"What do they do to express affection with family?"

His face screwed up, and I expected another *ew*.

"Punch and wrestle with each other mostly."

"Maybe you can just shake her hand."

"Okay." He got out and headed up the walkway. The topiaries' eyes brightened, but they'd been programmed to recognize friends, so no gouts of flame shot out.

As I stepped out of the Jeep, a telepathic whisper touched my mind. *Ruin Bringer.*

I froze. It was Sarrlevi, and he seemed close by again.

Will you come speak with me?

SECRETS OF THE SWORD III

Speak? I grabbed Storm's harness and slung it across my back. *Or do battle?*

Are you in need of sparring practice?

I've had enough practice this week, thanks.

I only wish to speak.

Sure. The need to *speak* was why he'd been spying on my house for days.

"I'm going to regret this," I muttered, but I left the safety of Zav's protections around our property and headed toward the assassin.

CHAPTER 27

WITH A LIGHT DRIZZLE FALLING from the cloudy night sky, I walked toward the dark side yard where I'd seen Sarrlevi spying on me before. It was two yards away from where Zav had found those troll bodies. They had disappeared, though I didn't know who had taken care of them.

"*Darayknar zerek*," I whispered, and Storm formed a protective barrier around me.

I couldn't yet *sense* Sarrlevi, despite his telepathic message, and had a hard time believing he didn't plan to ambush me or something equally nefarious. Even if he'd been honorable when we'd fought, and even if he'd told Zav he would leave me alone... things changed. Things changed *all* the time. And it didn't escape my notice that he'd waited until Zav wasn't around to reach out to me.

"Where are you, Sarrlevi?"

The elf stepped out of the shadows less than ten feet away. I kept myself from jumping in surprise—barely. The wavering blond figure stood outside my barrier, just close enough for me to see him—sort of—through whatever camouflaging magic he had activated.

"I have been waiting for an opportunity to speak with you," Sarrlevi said in English with a pleasant lilting accent. It was as if we were buddies meeting up for a walk and a chat over coffee.

As when I'd seen him before, his outfit looked like a mingling of costume pieces from the Lord of the Rings and Davy Crockett sets, with brown moccasins, green trousers, and a tan fringed tunic made from some animal's hide. His twin longswords rode in scabbards on his back, the hilts sticking up over his shoulders.

"I've been here every night." I pointed my thumb back toward my house.

"You have many guests who might object to my presence. Even though I enjoy a challenging battle, I did not wish to be set upon by King Eireth's bodyguards and kin, who might be backed up by Lord Zavryd'nokquetal and perhaps a vampire."

"Don't forget about Dimitri and the dragon topiaries."

He inclined his head. "Formidable foes. Your house has become a fortress."

"One you didn't have trouble getting into before."

"As I recall, I stepped only onto the lawn. I did not intrude upon your abode."

"Yeah, yeah. What do you want?"

"I had not intended to disturb you at all, but you have not left an offering during the nights that I have been observing the aforementioned lawn."

"Offering?"

What was he talking about?

"To the fae queen."

"Oh." I glanced at the part of the yard that still supported the ring of mushrooms and, for those who knew how to open it, a doorway into the fae realm. "You mean the chocolates?"

How had he found out about that?

"The human-made candies that the queen speaks frequently of, yes." His tone had grown dry, but I wasn't sure how to interpret it.

"You're still hanging out with her? I heard through the elven grapevine that she's irked with you and telling everyone that you're horrible in the sack."

"She is irked with me, but not because of inadequacies during sexual performance. I am capable of satisfying a partner, even when feelings are not involved."

This was not the conversation I'd expected to have with a guy who'd tried to kill me a couple of months earlier. He was stating everything matter-of-factly, not with the haughty pride that a dragon might have, but I still didn't want the information.

"You have seen my prowess in battle," Sarrlevi added, perhaps reading my pause as skepticism.

"That being super similar to sex."

He smiled faintly. "When one sleeps with the fae queen, the similarities are many."

I held up a hand. "Is there a reason you're telling me this? I'm not the one running around gossiping about you and ruining your reputation."

Maybe I shouldn't have brought that up, because his smile disappeared and his eyes grew hard. "No, the fae queen has chosen to do that because I refused to continue having sexual relations with her. I performed to the parameters of our deal and owe her no further bedroom visits."

"I'm glad to know you do your part." I eyed his stern face. It was a *handsome* stern face, I admitted, having no trouble seeing why the fae queen had wanted him. "Do you always sleep with women to get what you want from them?"

"No." His eyes grew even harder, his jaw clenching. It took him a moment to unclench it to add, "The queen is a hedonist and would accept no other offering from me. I was willing to pay her handsomely for her artifact." He lifted his chin. "It was beneath me to trade my services in bed for her assistance. I knew immediately that it had been a mistake, but she'd finagled my word out of me, and I do not go back on my word. I also promised not to kill her at any point in the future."

"Kind of you."

"It was part of our negotiations. At the time, it seemed reasonable. Besides, I am not a wanton murderer. Unless I am forced to defend myself, I only kill those I am hired to kill." His blond brows drew together in a V. "But I am currently having a difficult time finding engaging work. The queen's slights against me should not matter to prospective employers. Even if I *were* inadequate in the bedroom—which I am not, or she would not wish me to return—this would have nothing to do with my ability to assassinate targets."

"I wouldn't think so, no."

Sooner or later, he would tell me why he was sharing all this with me and what he wanted. I couldn't believe he'd come to *me* to rant about his personal and professional woes.

"She foresaw that her gossip would damage my reputation and deliberately chose to issue it."

"Why? She didn't seem pissed with you the last time we all met."

We'd given her quite a show, after all. Complete with munchies.

"As I said, I have refused to return to her bed."

"And you're so amazing that she's pining away without you under the sheets with her?"

"I do not presume that is the reason, but she has construed my rejection as a personal attack. The next time I have relations with a female, I intend for there to be feelings involved."

"I hear that's a good idea."

"The queen is attempting to blackmail me. She said that if I return to her bed and visit regularly, she will tell those in other realms that she was mistaken and that I am indeed a capable lover." Sarrlevi lifted his eyes toward the night sky and huffed out a sigh of frustration, making me feel a little sorry for him, even if he'd tried to kill me before. "I will not bow to this strong-arming, but since, per our previous deal, I cannot *kill* her—" Sarrlevi touched the hilt of one of his swords, his gaze growing a bit wistful, "—and I will not stoop to blackmail or threats myself, I am in a difficult situation."

"It'll probably blow over in a year, and people will forget about it."

"The fae are as long-lived as elves, and they are not known for letting grudges die."

"Meaning she'll keep ragging on you to others?"

"That is a distinct possibility. I asked her if there is something *else* she might accept in lieu of my bedroom service."

How much would I have to pay to get him to stop saying *bedroom service*?

"She said the only other thing she's found nearly as satisfying in recent times was the sweets you brought her."

I couldn't stifle a short chortle. "Only *nearly*? They're damn good."

His chin came up again. Had I offended his stiff elven ass? "*I* am damn good as well."

"Uh huh. So what do you want from me? Directions to the store?"

"Store?"

"The place where I get them."

"I assumed you made them."

Sure, I'd made them in my kitchen, then tucked them into those tidy little boxes with the ingredients and calories listed on the back. "All I make these days is smoked meat."

"That will not do. The only thing she will accept is a large assortment of sweets similar to the ones you provided her. Made by Thorvald, she said, though if you do not make them, then I assume the maker of the ones you gave her will do. She wishes some new flavors in addition to the caramels."

"How large is a *large* assortment?" I allowed Storm to extinguish the magical barrier, realizing I didn't need it.

Sarrlevi held out his arms to form the outline of box in the air. It was larger than a shoebox. I shook my head, daunted by the idea of how much it would cost to fill such a box with those chocolates. They weren't inexpensive.

"I can point you to the store," I said, "but do you have money?"

Sarrlevi reached into a pocket and withdrew a handful of rings, the rings Zav had given him to buy out the contract on me. "Is there a place where I can exchange one or more of these for human currency?"

"You could try a pawn shop." If he'd only wanted a few chocolate bars, I would have offered to get them for him, but I didn't want to spend piles of my cash on food to stuff down the fae queen's gullet. I had a dragon gullet to keep filled. "Do you have a pen and paper?" I pulled out my phone to look up pawn shops and the address for the chocolate factory. If he wanted a big assortment, he might as well go to the source. "I'll give you the addresses."

"My memory is excellent. State the locations of these places, and I will find them."

"Wow, a big brain and a big dick? No wonder she wants you back."

His eyelids lowered. "You are mocking me."

"A little bit, yeah, but I'm not blackmailing you into sleeping with me, so you should be delighted."

"Hm."

"Get your brain ready." I read the addresses to him and gave him directions via my phone's map. "You get all that?"

"Yes."

"Good." I sensed Zav flying in this direction. Time to wrap this up. "Anything else?"

"No. I thank you for your assistance." He bowed to me, then glanced toward the northern sky, the direction Zav was coming from. Coming from *fast*. Maybe Zav had sensed Sarrlevi even through his camouflage and believed I was in trouble. It was also possible he'd sensed that I'd activated Storm's powers. "May your union with Lord Zavryd'nokquetal be successful," Sarrlevi added.

"Thanks."

He bowed again and stepped back, fading further from my sight, but he halted before he disappeared. Magical power wrapped around him. Zav's.

It's fine, Zav, I told him telepathically as he approached at top speed. *He just wanted to talk. I'm not in danger.*

But Zav didn't release Sarrlevi. I sensed the assassin summoning his own power and trying to break away, but Zav landed beside us before he could figure out how to escape. There weren't any lingering Christmas decorations in this yard, but Zav almost took out a tree and a mailbox this time.

Why are you here, assassin? he boomed telepathically as he shifted into his human form. *Do you threaten my mate after you gave your* word *that you would leave her alone?*

Sarrlevi sighed. "No, I do not." The twist to his lips suggested he'd foreseen this and that Zav's misunderstanding was the reason he'd waited until he could speak with me alone. "I came to ask her directions to a seller of human sweets. And also an establishment called a *pawn shop*."

Zav didn't look like he knew what a pawn shop was either. His brow crinkled as he glanced at me for confirmation.

"It's true." I slung an arm around his waist. "Sarrlevi is having problems with the fae queen, and there are only two ways to satisfy her. I'm an expert on one way."

"She enjoys sex." Zav squinted suspiciously at Sarrlevi, as if suspecting he'd come to me to ask for tips in that department.

"The other one," I said as Sarrlevi lifted his gaze to the sky again and shook his head. Dealing with dragons wasn't much easier than dealing with the fae queen.

"She enjoys culinary treats." Enlightenment washed over Zav's face. "The assassin came to ask you for advice on rubbing spices onto meat and smoking it to moist and delicious full-flavored succulence?"

"Something along those lines, yes."

Zav sniffed at the air and looked back toward the house. "I smell such meat cooking now."

"I knew I'd have a busy day, so I put a couple of racks of ribs in the smoker this morning."

"And they are ready now?" Zav wrapped his arm around *my* waist and gazed adoringly into my eyes. "You are a *wonderful* mate."

"Yes, I am." I steered him around and pointed him toward the house before he could think to make further inquiries of Sarrlevi.

Zav allowed himself to be steered. He wore his glazed fantasizing-about-meat expression. Funny how few of the fantasy novels I'd read mentioned that slow-cooking meat was the way to a dragon's heart.

If you get everything worked out with the queen, I told Sarrlevi telepathically, *you're welcome to come to our wedding.*

It was a spontaneous offer, made because I was relieved he'd come for something as innocuous as chocolate and wasn't hunting me down at some bad guy's behest. I doubted he would come but decided it was okay if he did.

Will it be full of dragons? he asked.

Dozens, I understand.

Perhaps I will simply send you a gift.

Dear Lord, not more gifts from weirdos...

That works, I made myself reply. *Good luck with the fae queen.*

Thank you.

Sarrlevi disappeared from my senses, either because we'd walked far enough away for his camouflage to be effective again, or because he'd used Zav's distraction to hightail it out of there and was already halfway to the pawn shop. That was fine with me. I was relieved that at least one of my concerns about unpleasantries popping up at the wedding was unfounded.

Now, if some grenade-toting trolls would show up, willing to trade their explosives for a few peanut butter cups....

CHAPTER 28

I WOKE TO SUNLIGHT BEAMING THROUGH the windows of my bedroom, a welcome change from the past week's drear, though its presence meant that I'd slept too late. Given how soon the wedding was, I had a lot to do. At the top of the list was finding those trolls and making sure they were without grenades when the big day came.

With an alarming jolt, I realized that day was *tomorrow*. I was almost out of time.

I sat up, surprised I hadn't woken earlier, especially since the flicker was at work on my trim again, his pecks reverberating through the house. Maybe that was what had dragged me out of sleep. It had been the first night this week that I hadn't had to stay up training with Chasmmoor—he must have decided I'd trained enough in the street by Willard's apartment—but other things had kept me from turning in early. Mainly, Zav had been in an amorous mood after devouring ninety percent of the ribs I'd made for everyone in the house. Fortunately, the elves had been content with salads and a dubious stew that I hadn't asked many questions about. It was possible that there were fewer squirrels at the park today.

The door opened, and Zav strode in carrying a tray with a dish towel draped over the contents. The flicker halted, and I glimpsed orange feathers under his wings as he flew off. Maybe dragons were bird deterrents.

"Greetings, my mate." Zav set the tray on the dresser. "I have been informed that it is a human custom for the fiancé to deliver breakfast in bed to the fiancée on the day before the wedding."

"I haven't heard of that custom, but breakfast in bed is always a nice thing to do for someone."

"You do not know the custom?" Zav tilted his head. "Your roommate informed me that it is imperative and that we should then spend a leisurely time in bed and in the bath while we consume food."

"Were you pestering Dimitri at the time?"

"He is in the basement, learning enchanting techniques from Lord Chasmmoor."

"I'll assume that's a yes." I swung my legs over the side of the bed. "What's under the towel?"

I envisioned pancakes, hash browns, bacon, and a fluffy omelet. Zav swept aside the towel with a flourish, revealing… leftovers from the night before. Ribs. And here I'd thought he'd eaten them all. There was also a half a grapefruit in a bowl with a spoon.

"I kept myself from consuming all of the ribs last night. I thought we might be hungry in the middle of the night after exerting ourselves thoroughly." He showed me his bedroom eyes. "But as you know, we were too busy to leave the nest for refreshments."

"Yes, I remember." Funny how reminders of such things could still make me blush.

"Your sister the princess saw me preparing this meal and suggested a fruit ball would be appropriate to go with the meat, since elves are not entirely carnivorous."

"We call those grapefruits."

"Yes. It has a tangy and pungent smell." Zav wrinkled his nose. "Perhaps you should eat it first so that its aroma does not taint the ribs."

"I'm amenable to that."

He left the tray on the dresser and brought the bowl and spoon. "All is nearly ready for the wedding and the festivities." He sat beside me on the bed. "You will not be disappointed. My *clan* will also not be disappointed. There will be *excellent* races, good hunting, and much of the foliage has been cleared so there will be few spontaneous fires during the flame-throwing competition."

"Few? That's good."

"Yes."

I took a bite of the tart grapefruit and wished Freysha had dumped a tablespoon of sugar on it, but Zav's willingness to serve me breakfast in bed was pretty cool, so I wouldn't nitpick the meal. "Can you truly call them *spontaneous* fires when they start as a result of gouts of flame shooting out of dragon noses?"

"The flames come up from our throats and roil out of our mouths, not our noses."

"Smoke comes out of your nostrils. I've seen it."

"Nostrils are in close proximity to mouths and throats."

"So nose smoke is inevitable?" I bumped my shoulder against his, wishing I could relax and enjoy the next couple of days without any drama.

"Yes. Do you wish to mate again after replenishing your caloric reserves?"

"I do enjoy that, but I need to find those trolls."

Zav's focus shifted toward the window. Zondia's aura came into my range, and I slumped against Zav.

"Does she want…" I trailed off when a second dragon lit up my senses. Was that the *queen*?

A surge of panic rushed through me. Why had she come early? Had she decided this was all a huge mistake and that she wouldn't allow the wedding? Would Zav listen to her?

"My mother approaches." He sounded pensive—or was it worried?

"I noticed. Does she like fruit balls?"

"She likes meat."

"Shocking."

Zav patted me on the shoulder. "I will go outside and greet her." He looked down at me in my *Hobbit* nightshirt—I'd reclaimed it from the elf who'd rooted through my laundry—and bare legs and feet. "You may wish to don your clothing and weapons and come outside in case she desires to speak with you."

"Weapons are required for that?"

"The more formidable and warrior-like you appear, the better."

"So she won't regret that she withdrew her objections to our being a couple?"

"Correct." He touched my knee. "You may remove your clothing again later. *I* find you appealing even without your warrior attire."

"Especially without it, I should think."

He smiled, though it was a worried smile, and he glanced toward the window. "Yes."

Before leaving, he kissed the top of my head, but he hustled away at top speed. It worried me that *he* was worried. Maybe the queen had already spoken telepathically to him and issued concerns.

"Let's see if I can manage not to embarrass myself..." I took a moment to use the bathroom and scrub myself as clean as I could in a couple of minutes, then put on everything from boots to Nin's magical vest armor to sword and gun. If Zav's mother wanted a warrior, she would get a warrior. And I would attempt to be respectful, reverent, and *adequate* to her—even if I was a little tempted to ask her for cute baby photos—or the dragon equivalent—of Zav that I could show around at the wedding.

As Zondia landed on a nearby rooftop and Zav's mother—Queen Zynesshara, I reminded myself—landed in the front yard, it crossed my mind to hide in the shower stall and pretend I wasn't home. But such thoughts were unbecoming of a warrior. Besides, I would have needed to activate my camouflage charm earlier if I wanted her to believe I wasn't there.

On my way to the front door, I passed a number of elves, all wearing wary expressions. None of them jumped up to go outside to meet the dragon queen. In fact, a few sneaked out the back door. Only two remained in the living room. They were perched together on Dimitri's giant beanbag chair while running each other off the road in *Mario Kart*. That was troubling; if they became addicted to video games, they might never leave.

Val? came Eireth's voice from the kitchen.

I paused with my hand on the front doorknob. *Yes?*

He stepped into the dining room doorway wearing my *Princess Bride* apron. I would have laughed if I hadn't been on the verge of having a panic attack.

Do you need assistance? Eireth glanced toward the living-room window. *I have had discussions with Queen Zynesshara before.*

"Oh?" I switched to spoken words since we were standing ten feet away from each other. "Does she like you more than she likes me?"

"Probably not. I am not a dragon and am, therefore, inferior." Eireth smiled.

"I'm inferior too. Even *more* inferior because of my human blood."

He waved a hand to dismiss that idea. "I am impressed that you and Lord Zavryd'nokquetal convinced her to allow your union." His smile faded, replaced by a worried crease to his brow. Those creases were going around this morning. "You *did* convince her, didn't you?"

"More or less. She objected at first but retracted that objection after I helped the Stormforge dragons free some of their kin. Apparently, if you slay an enemy of the clan, you're allowed to hook up with someone in the family."

He nodded. "Good."

"Maybe she's here to give me something borrowed or blue."

Eireth did his puzzled-elf-head-tilt.

"Never mind." I waved. "I'll let you know if I need help."

He inclined his head. A part of me wanted to ask him to come out with me, but Zav was out there. His support was all I needed. I hoped.

Taking a deep breath, I opened the door and walked down the front steps.

Zondia was quite noticeable in her dragon form on the neighbor's roof—and was that the neighbor's broken weathervane on his front lawn?—so I focused on her first. But it was hard not to also notice the powerful aura of Queen Zynesshara. She had transformed into human form—no, *elven* form—and stood on the walkway facing the house—and Zav. She wore a fancy robe more colorful than Zav's, had her gray-streaked hair up in an elaborate coif, and she carried a staff that radiated magic.

My first thought was that she and her uptight expression reminded me of T'Pau in *Amok Time*, my second was to think Thad would have been proud of me for remembering the name of that Star Trek episode, and my third was to hope she didn't look over at me or beat me with her big staff.

She and Zav were staring at each other, no doubt communicating telepathically and privately. Her gaze soon shifted to me, and she eyed me up and down.

You are learning to use your sword more fully, she stated telepathically. Maybe she didn't realize that her elven form came with lips and vocal cords.

Yes. I replied the same way in case speaking was offensive.

Good. You will continue to fight beside my offspring and be an ally to him in the sky, not only in the nest.

That's my plan.

Her eyes narrowed. Maybe that had been too flippant.

Do you want a tour of the house? I smiled and waved at the front door, though bringing a stuffy dragon inside seemed cruel to the rest of my roommates and houseguests. After all, it might interrupt the video game.

This is where you reside when you spend time with her? Zynesshara's haughty nose came up, and she sniffed derisively at the house. *I assumed you would live with her in a cave or an eyrie.*

This is Val's home and headquarters, Zav replied. *She feeds me here, and we nest in the tower. It is acceptable.*

It is beneath you to dwell in this pile of sticks.

Right, the beautiful and recently renovated Victorian house wasn't nearly as nice as a nest on a rock. I forced my smile to stay in place and kept the thought to myself. If she didn't want to come in, that was no skin off my nose.

I have considered building an ancillary cave on the property, Zav said. *I have learned that it is common for married Earth males to acquire something called a* man cave.

I almost fell over. Had Dimitri put that idea in his head?

You must build a dragon *cave,* Zynesshara said. *And dwell in it. Your mate may bring food to you inside.*

What an honor that would be.

Only the land directly surrounding the house belongs to Val, Zav continued. *It would be difficult to fit a cave on it.*

Thankfully...

Then you must acquire more land. Remove some of the nearby stick piles to make room.

I shall consider this. Hopefully, that was Zav being diplomatic and placating, and my neighbors weren't truly in danger of losing their homes.

Your mating ceremony will not be in this inferior place, will it? Zynesshara looked toward Zondia. *Your sister said you were preparing an area in the wilderness with hunting and races.*

Yes. All is prepared. Perhaps she can take you there today, and you may find an appropriate nesting place on this world for tonight. Do you intend to stay?

I do. I will ensure all is prepared before the rest of the clan arrives. Important details cannot be left to such young dragons.

If Zondia objected to being dismissed as young, she didn't show it. Maybe eye-rolling wasn't allowed around the queen.

And you will take me out there yourself, Zavryd'nokquetal. This is extremely important. I have taken this opportunity to invite Sarlynorth Silverclaw, the patriarch of their clan.

Zav's back stiffened. Hell, so did mine. Why would she invite one of *them*?

We are attempting to return sanity to the Cosmic Realms, Zynesshara continued, *by establishing a treaty between our two clans. It is time to* end our feud instead of causing more dragons to die by plotting against each other. He has agreed to meet me here on this neutral ground.

A cessation of hostilities between our clans would be good, Zav said.

Yeah, but why couldn't they do their neutral-ground treaty-forming on another world? Why here? Why at my *wedding?* My fingers twitched toward the inhaler in my pocket, but I wouldn't show that weakness off in front of Zav's mother.

Yes. It is past time. Zynesshara turned her gaze onto me. *You, mate of my son, will do your best to ensure this festivity goes well and is not an embarrassment to our clan.*

I will if you show me some baby pictures, I replied before I could think better of it. So much for reverence.

Baby what? Her icy gaze pinned me, as if she suspected I was teasing her.

Should I explain or say *never mind? I was just curious what Zav looked like when he was a baby—or maybe you would call it a hatchling? Humans keep mementos of their young and share them with family and friends later in life. Was Zav cute?*

Dragons are not cute. We are fearsome predators, hatched from the egg to slay our enemies.

I guess that answered my question.

Zynesshara shifted back into her huge dragon form, her wings extending wider than the property lines, her tail sticking out into the street and into a neighbor's yard. There went another mailbox. *Come, Zavryd'nokquetal. You will show me the ceremony grounds.*

Zav looked at me, not commenting on my desire for baby photos. *It will be better if I go with her. Can you handle the trolls by yourself?* He glanced toward the house. *You have many allies present.*

Yeah, don't worry about it. Make sure she's happy. I waved for him to leave, not pointing out that none of my *allies,* including Zav, had been successful at finding where the trolls were hanging out.

I could handle this. And if I didn't, no sweat. Only my wedding and the fate of the two most powerful dragon clans in the Cosmic Realms hung in the balance.

Once she is settled, I will return to assist you.

Thanks. I thought about going over and kissing him, but the queen was watching, her eyes cold and reptilian in her dragon form. Technically, in both forms.

Zav managed to shift into a dragon without taking out any mailboxes, cars, or lawn ornaments. He and his kin sprang into the air and headed off toward the northeast. It occurred to me that I hadn't even seen these ceremony grounds yet, not since Zav and Willard had embarked on their improvements. Hopefully, they were handling everything, and it would be fine.

I smiled bleakly.

What were the odds?

CHAPTER 29

I WAS FINISHING MY BREAKFAST WHEN Amber arrived, riding in Nin's car. Surprised that they were hanging out now, I jogged down to greet them. Maybe they had carpooled from Thad's house for the sake of convenience. The night before, I'd texted Nin and asked her to prepare some grenades and ammo for me, just in case I couldn't resolve things today and needed them during the wedding.

With the dragon trio gone, more elves had returned to the house, filling the living room to watch the gamers. Even Eireth was in there, watching as the combatants waged virtual battle on the television. If Dimitri had been the one to introduce video games to the elves, we would have a chat later. Not just about man caves.

I opened the door to Nin and Amber walking up to the house holding a dress bag—my wedding dress and shoes, I realized.

Ugh, I'd meant to pick them up the day before. About the time I'd been battling a giant and a spider.

"Hey, guys." I waved. "Thanks for getting that."

"I knew I couldn't trust *you* to do it," Amber said.

"We are pleased to be of assistance during this very busy week for you." Nin smiled, so much more pleasant and easy to get along with than my teenage daughter. No wonder Thad had decided he needed Nin in his life.

"*Thank* you," I told them both, though I nodded specifically to Nin.

"I also brought makeup." Amber foisted the dress bag into my arms and lifted a zippered pouch in fuzzy leopard print. "The last time I was in your bathroom, you didn't have any. *Any*. That's so weird, Val. You have thin blonde lashes. You need mascara."

"Don't you think the trolls and assassins I fight would be less intimidated if I showed up with long, luscious lashes?"

"Who cares? You're going to kick their asses anyway, right?"

"That's always the goal."

"I also brought something for your wedding." The camouflage bag that Nin held up oozed magic. Grenades and ammo for Fezzik. Perfect. "Though I hope you will not need them there." Concern flashed in her eyes. "Will you? I heard that you were able to find young Reb."

"Young Reb, yes, but his older grumpier troll captors, not yet." I stepped back to make room for them to come in the house, though between the banging coming from the basement—how was Zoltan sleeping with a dwarven blacksmith hammering away on the anvil ten feet from his coffin?—and the roar of Mario Kart on our big living-room speakers, it wasn't the best place for a chitchat. "Let's go upstairs."

Maybe it would be quieter in my room.

Amber paused to gape at the elves crowded around the TV and the beanbag chair. "This place is weirder every time I come over."

"Judging by the new ease of parking, the neighbors agree." I led them up the stairs.

"It was surprising that I so easily found a spot," Nin said. "It used to be more difficult to park near your house."

"I know."

"Some of the neighbors have parked their cars in their yards to avoid the street near your house."

"We're bringing down the home values of the entire neighborhood," I said, "one dragon topiary at a time."

"It's probably all that banging that's bringing down the value." Amber grimaced as we stepped into my room. "What *is* that? Dimitri's not starting a band in your basement, is he?"

"A dwarf blacksmith from another planet is using a magical anvil."

"So glad it isn't something weird." Amber pointed at the bathroom. "Do you want to do a trial run of your makeup now? We should work on your look before the big day." She eyed my jeans, combat boots, and duster. "We should work on your look a *lot*."

"Ha ha. I was about to leave to hunt trolls."

She frowned. "You don't have a minute?"

Did she truly believe my lashes were in horrendous shape and in dire need of a touch up, or did she want to talk about something personal? The drive to get my problems resolved today almost made me ask if it could wait, but I didn't want to bail if she'd come all the way down to talk about something.

"Sure." I waved to the bathroom.

"I will check on Dimitri and see if he needs assistance with the shop repairs today," Nin said.

"Freysha redid the goblin engineering team's blueprints," I said. "The last I heard, they'd finished the repairs but were adding... amenities."

"Not the pool, I trust."

"We all vetoed that. But the second floor is going forward with the gaming lounge."

"We do not own this building, Val." Nin frowned. "I talked to the landlord, and he was delighted to have us handle the repairs, so he wouldn't have to get his insurance involved, but this..."

"Should improve the value of the property," I said, even though I'd brought up the same concern with Dimitri. "What's to complain about?"

"You are a dubious business partner at times."

"You only say that because of her substandard lashes," Amber said, pulling me into the bathroom.

Nin headed back to the stairs with her concerned expression firmly affixed.

Amber wore a similar expression, but it was directed at my bathroom.

"What's wrong? We remodeled." I waved to the big clawfoot soaking tub. "It's great."

"I can't believe you don't have a makeup vanity with a mirror and a stool."

"As you pointed out, I don't have makeup."

"Don't you like to sit when you do your hair?"

"My braid isn't time-intensive. Is there anything you want to talk about besides my lashes?"

"No." Amber directed me to sit on the toilet seat—the closest I had to a makeup stool—and opened her bag. "I just want to make sure you're presentable at your own wedding."

Despite the talk of lashes and mascara, she pulled out blush, foundation, and brushes of various sizes.

"That's thoughtful of you. Thanks."

"I'm coming," she said. "I don't want to be embarrassed."

"So this is a selfless act."

"Of course. Dad's bringing Nin. I guess they're pretty serious now."

"Are you okay with that?"

Maybe this was what she wanted to talk about. I didn't believe her earlier *no*.

"I guess. She's not nearly as annoying as the last girlfriend. And she bought *him* something expensive, so she's definitely not a gold digger."

"Oh? Fine man jewelry?" I smiled, certain Nin hadn't purchased anything so silly.

"A garish custom table for role-playing games. All the positions have slide-outs for people's dice and notes and stuff, and there are cup holders big enough to hold ale steins or—way more likely for his besties—a Super Big Gulp. There's a dragon attacking a castle carved in the top." Amber paused in brushing powder on my face to show me some photos of the table on her phone. "It came yesterday while I was at school. Dad texted me *twenty* pictures of it from all angles. He invited a bunch of geeks over last night to play with it, and I think he slept on it afterward."

"Huh." It did look like something Thad and his *besties* would adore. "He better keep Nin. She either gets him or is willing to humor him completely."

"The second thing, I think. But last night, she let him teach her how to play Munchkin."

"That's a card game, right?"

"Yeah, a gateway drug into all things uber geek."

Amber lowered her phone, but not before I saw a picture of a tall, gangly teenager with shaggy brown hair. He was standing in their backyard, grinning and holding her short sword aloft, more like a baseball bat than a weapon.

"That's not one of Thad's buddies, is it?" I'd met the gaming group. They consisted more of pot-bellied baldies than gangly shaggies.

"No."

"Is it by chance the decoy boyfriend?"

Amber rolled her eyes as she switched brushes. "I'm not doing that."

"Oh? I remember a few weeks ago when Thad called, complaining because he couldn't get a boy out of your house one night."

"OMG, Val." Amber lowered her brush. "Are you the one who told Dad to come after him with one of his toy cannons?"

"I advised him to enforce his rules firmly. He came up with the cannon on his own."

"That was *so* embarrassing."

"Uh huh. Who's the guy? Is he coming to the wedding with you tomorrow?"

"Teenage boys don't go to weddings unless someone makes them."

"So he declined your invitation? Did you tell him there would be dragons racing each other, hunting things, and possibly lighting the forest on fire?"

Amber appeared more scandalized than intrigued. "Those things aren't *really* happening at your wedding, are they?"

"Probably before it. Or after. The normal people can go to the reception while the dragons—and anyone interested in watching the dragons—do their thing."

"Jace might actually be interested in that."

Jace, huh? I tried not to smile, but with Amber standing right in front of me looking at my face, she must have noticed my lips quirking.

"Knock it off," she said. "Or I'll poke you in the eye with a mascara brush."

"You wouldn't find it embarrassing if your mom walked down the aisle with a black eye?"

"Don't you heal quickly?"

"Somewhat. How are things going at school?"

She hadn't updated me for a while. That could mean things had gotten worse or improved, or she'd gotten used to the status quo.

"All right. I'm mostly hanging out with Jace now. We're in debate together, but he's on the basketball team, too, and nobody picks on him for being smart."

"A jock *and* a brain? Sounds like a keeper. What does he think of Thad's table?"

"He likes it. He's a geek too." Amber rolled her eyes again. "And he's not really a jock. He's just tall so the hoop is closer for him, and he can run fast because his legs are long."

"Taller than you?"

"Six-seven."

"*Giant.*"

She snorted. "Just right. We're hanging out. That's all. It's no big thing. But he agreed to punch anyone that bothered me, so that he'd get in trouble instead of me."

"He wants to get in trouble?"

"No, but he knows he won't. His mom is the principal, and all his teachers like him. He's kind of a suck-up, but that's okay."

"It's good that you've made a list of his flaws and decided you can accept them," I said dryly.

"Nobody's perfect. I've seen your dragon with barbecue sauce all over his robe."

"Sometimes, if he doesn't incinerate it fast enough, it drips."

Amber must have finished beautifying my face, for she stepped back and returned her tools to the makeup bag. "Anyway, I kind of started talking more to Jace because of your dumb idea, so… you know." She shrugged.

"It wasn't so dumb?"

"Oh, it was dumb, but it made me think of a better idea, so I guess it incubated things or something."

"Does that mean you're eternally grateful to me?"

"So grateful I didn't stab you in the eye with a mascara brush."

"I do appreciate that."

Dimitri walked up the hall and knocked on the open bathroom door without looking in. "Val?"

"Nobody's naked. You can come in."

"Uh, right." Maybe that hadn't been his reason for staying in the hall. "I just wanted to know if I could bring a guy to your wedding."

"Corporal Clarke?" I hadn't seen sitgns that Dimitri was dating anyone, but he occasionally had Clarke and some other guys over for gaming afternoons. On the rare days he wasn't working at the shop or on his art projects.

"No."

"Someone tall, dashing, and handsome?"

"Lord Chasmmoor," Dimitri said.

"Uh, he's the opposite of all those things."

"I'm not *dating* him. I'm learning from him." Dimitri shrugged. "But he's not bad looking."

"How can you tell? His beard covers most of his face."

"The beard isn't bad looking either."

Amber wrinkled her nose—actually, she wrinkled her entire face. Probably not surprising that she wasn't into huge beards. It wasn't as if dwarves and elves ever hooked up in fantasy novels.

"I was planning to invite him anyway," I said. "He's my mentor this week."

"Mine too. He's showing me how to use the anvil." Dimitri finally stuck his head into the doorway. "I'm going to be able to make some *amazing* yard art. Just give me a few months to practice. I'm going to be in super high demand, and not just for dragon door knockers."

"I believe you."

Dimitri blinked. Maybe he'd expected a sarcastic response.

"Oh, good. Thanks. I'll tell him he's invited." He started to leave but paused. "The shop will officially reopen on Monday by the way. Thanks for the money for the drywall and lumber and roofing. I got a bunch of materials for the goblins too. I was afraid they'd build the new second floor out of tires and mattress springs if they didn't have lumber."

"I was afraid you'd approve of it if they did."

"Please, Val. I have standards."

Being the noble and mature person I was, I didn't point out that his standards included thinking Chasmmoor's big bushy beard was *not bad looking*.

Amber looked at a text. "I've got to go. Dad's taking me shopping for the wedding."

She grabbed her makeup kit and spun a pirouette, almost taking out the shampoo bottles in the tub rack.

"Aren't you supposed to be in school today?" Maybe it should have occurred to me to ask that an hour ago.

"All my finals were earlier in the week, so Dad said I could take the day off to get ready for the wedding. And go shopping."

"Has he grown more lenient of late?"

"He's in a good mood because of his table. I gotta go."

So did I. I didn't dare take the day off to get ready for the wedding.

The face that peered back at me in the mirror, now wearing blush, mascara, lipstick, and who knew what else, appeared strangely soft and girlie. The urge to grab a towel and wipe off the makeup came over me, but I resisted. I would humor Amber for today and tomorrow, but this was not going to become my new look.

Heavy footsteps clomped on the stairs, and I sensed Chasmmoor coming up.

"Is it finished?" Dimitri asked, still in the hallway.

"Yes," Chasmmoor said. "We need only to test it."

"I think Val's looking for some enemies."

"Yes, I am. What have you got that could help?" I stepped out to find my dwarf houseguest carrying a metal box with a funnel attached to the front and something that looked like a multimeter gauge above it.

"A magic de-amplifier," Chasmmoor said as if it were a household item that everyone should know. "Dimitri and I made it with the anvil. It can be used to defend your home and is also portable, so perhaps you will want to bring it to your wedding in case there is trouble."

Maybe portable for a dwarf with the burly arms of a powerlifter.

"It does something to make magical attacks weaker?" I asked.

"Yes. You point the wave-generator cone—" Chasmmoor poked the funnel, "—at your magic-using enemies, press this button, and turn it on. As long as you stand next to the device, any spells they cast at you will be weakened. I've tested it with my own magic, and we also recruited one of the elf mages, but trying it on a true enemy who's trying to kill you would be ideal."

"I have plenty of those."

"Where may we find them?" Chasmmoor asked politely, as if there was nothing strange about my statement.

"I wish I knew. I don't suppose you two want to look for some troll tunnels with me?" With Zav off showing his mom around, I didn't have my usual backup, aside from Sindari. Maybe Chasmmoor, as a full-blooded magical being with strong senses, would have an easier time than I'd had locating the grenade-thieving trolls.

Dimitri had been making an I'm-not-interested-in-that face, but Chasmmoor said, "I will go," and Dimitri said, "Me too."

They headed off together, speaking of the amplification and de-amplification of magic, and I wondered if maybe Dimitri truly *had* found a date for the wedding.

CHAPTER 30

"LET ME KNOW IF YOU guys sense anything." I stretched out my own senses as I navigated my Jeep through the side streets around Lake Union.

Dimitri sat beside me. The back seat was usually down for Sindari, but I'd put it up for Chasmmoor. He sat on one side, and Sindari sat on the other, slumping so that his head wasn't mashed against the ceiling. His window was down, and he sniffed at the buildings and houses we passed. Chasmmoor's anti-magic doohickey rode in the back, along with his big axe and armor. It seemed that sitting with plate mail on was uncomfortable.

Were not the tunnels destroyed when we ousted the dark elves? Sindari asked.

There's been some rebuilding, I replied. *Or at least clearing of them. Zav thinks the trolls are down there.*

"I do sense some artifacts underneath the streets of this area." Chasmmoor stroked his beard thoughtfully. "But magic is obscuring the area, deliberately misleading my senses. I cannot tell if it is of troll origins. It reminds me more of dark elves."

"Dark elves *used* to live there." As I drove by Gasworks Park for the second time, I wondered if that underwater access point was still in the lake. We'd already passed the spot where the huge sinkhole had been. The city had repaired that almost instantly and probably filled in the tunnels and religious chamber underneath it. What the workers had thought of the giant bone statue, I could only guess. "We booted them out last summer. The trolls would have moved in recently, though I suppose all manner of magical beings could be hiding out down there."

"Hm."

"I don't suppose you can sense any entry points into the tunnels?" I asked.

"Nothing as specific as that. Only a vague feeling of magic in use under the ground."

I'd been afraid of that.

"How'd you get in before?" Dimitri asked. "Through the lake, wasn't it?"

I pointed down at the water. "I held my breath and dove."

"You're not willing to do that again?"

"I don't think that entrance is still viable. Between Zav's magic and my explosives, we caused a lot of damage to the tunnels." Unless the trolls had repaired it and were using the lake entrance. It might be worth checking, though it would be a chilly day for a swim.

"The barrier you can create with *Thrallendakh yen Hyrek de Horak* may be able to keep out water, and I am capable enough to use telekinesis to propel a bubble forward."

"I thought magical barriers weren't airtight," I said as Dimitri mouthed the sword's name. I hadn't given him the whole thing before, mostly because I still had to check my Notes app on my phone to remember it.

"Not airtight, no," Chasmmoor said, "but water molecules are larger than air molecules."

"Would you be able to keep a big bubble underwater?" Dimitri asked skeptically.

"That would be a challenge, but I know some tricks for displacing water. Technically, for displacing molten ore, but it should work in the lake."

"Oh? Will you show me?"

"Of course."

With no better ideas, I parked as close as I could to the houseboats where I'd descended before. It was broad daylight this time but raining, so hopefully nobody would be out on the deck in a hot tub watching us. We would be a funny-looking trio diving into the lake in a bubble.

I assume you want to go back to your realm and be summoned after we've found a dry place down there? I asked Sindari silently.

You presume correctly. Summon me before the battle and after you've ensured a river won't gush in and drown us.

What if the battle takes place in a river?

Have a warm towel and a sunbeam ready for me.

How about a blow dryer and a fur fluff?

Are you mocking me?

I would never.

"Will your majestic Del'nothian tiger accompany us?" Chasmmoor asked, getting out of the Jeep and grabbing his gear from the back.

"Not into the water, not when it's chilly. He's not a fan of swimming on cold days. Or of rain, snow, or hail. Or overly vigorous waterfalls splashing droplets onto a nearby shore."

Now I'm positive you're mocking me, Sindari said.

Chasmmoor called you majestic. You should be in a good mood.

He is appropriately respectful to my kind.

He works with the dwarven king. He's probably an expert at sucking up.

It's not unwise to suck up to powerful predators with more than two-thousand-pounds per square inch of jaw-crunching force.

I'll keep that in mind.

Do.

I patted Sindari on the back and dismissed him from our world, then joined Chasmmoor and Dimitri on one of the docks where the houseboats were moored. We opted for a spot with nobody around—or peering out a nearby window. Dimitri held the bulky magical device while Chasmmoor, now wearing his armor, slapped the haft of his battle-axe across his palm in preparation for a battle. I hoped we found it. With Zav's mom now on Earth, and bringing that Silverclaw dragon to the wedding, I had a strong desire to lock up every troll, ogre, and orc who'd ever menaced me, if only for one day so I could have a nice, peaceful, and inoffensive wedding.

"I'm prepared." Chasmmoor stepped close to me and nodded for Dimitri to do the same. "We must stay near Val and the blade."

As I drew Storm and said the command term, I wondered how well this would work. Could we even maneuver off the dock without tripping? An image of a half-elf, a human, and a dwarf in a three-legged—no make that four-legged—race came to mind.

The barrier formed around us, and Chasmmoor closed his eyes and dropped his chin to his chest. His red beard reached to his belt buckle when he did that.

He mumbled under his breath, and a surge of power tickled my senses. Our feet lifted off the dock as if an invisible elevator platform was carrying us into the air.

We floated out over the lake and dropped into the water with a plop. There we bobbed on the surface, our bubble meeting resistance.

"Uhm," Dimitri said.

Another swell of power came from Chasmmoor, and a channel of water opened below us. Our bubble descended as if through a tube and veered under a houseboat. We bounced off a chain anchoring it, then flowed deeper, following the bottom of the lake toward the hatch I'd last seen in the rearview mirror of that submarine. I assumed that little watercraft was long gone. Hopefully, the kraken was too.

"I can use my lock-picking charm to open that hatch," I offered. "If I can find a way to touch it without—"

It opened of its own accord, courtesy of Chasmmoor's magic.

"Never mind."

We floated toward the empty airlock inside, but the bubble bumped against the sides of the entrance, too large to fit.

"Can I modulate its size around me?" I hadn't had much luck with that in the troll pub, but I'd been distracted at the time.

"You must," Chasmmoor murmured. "I cannot do anything to affect the blade's magic."

Since there was no command term for manipulating the barrier, I squeezed Storm's hilt and willed it to shrink our bubble. Surprisingly, the sword responded almost instantly. I'd managed to manipulate it and convey ideas to it before, but this past week, it had grown even easier to do so. Thanks to the training, I supposed.

My lungs tightened slightly, and I frowned. Once we were inside, I would have to use my inhaler.

We squeezed through the hatchway, forced shoulder to shoulder inside the bubble. The chunky dwarven artifact ended up rammed against my back. Later, I would suggest to Chasmmoor and Dimitri that a trinket-sized artifact that could fit on a leather thong around the neck had far more appeal.

As expected, the submarine was gone, but the airlock itself, including the inner hatch, was still sound. After closing the outer hatch and letting the water drain out, Chasmmoor opened the inner one without opening his eyes.

"He's versatile," Dimitri whispered to me.

"Definitely a keeper," I said.

Dimitri snorted. "We're not dating."

"Too bad. I bet he's handy around the house."

"You already have a dragon for that."

"He may be busy working on the *man cave* you told him about but didn't describe in detail."

"I didn't know such things required descriptions."

"He's envisioning a *real* cave and clearing one of the neighbor's houses off the lot to make room to build it."

"Maybe you could offer him the attic."

"It's not big enough to put a cave in."

"I was envisioning dark, manly paint on the walls, a big-screen TV, gaming station, mini fridge, and foosball table."

"This is a man cave for Zav, not you."

"Oh, right."

Once we were in the tunnel, Chasmmoor used his magic to close the hatch behind us. I ordered Storm to flare a bright blue, and its light played on a pile of rubble that blocked the tunnel.

"So much for that idea," I said.

"I can clear that." Chasmmoor stepped forward and raised his arms, fingers splayed toward the rocks. They shifted and scraped, lining up along the sides of the tunnel as they cleared a gap for us.

"Handy," I mouthed to Dimitri.

He nodded and smiled fondly at the dwarf.

Chasmmoor murmured something, and a yellow globe of light appeared and floated into the tunnel ahead as the last of the rubble blocking the passage shifted to the sides. He sniffed.

"I smell evidence of trolls. And also... others."

I summoned Sindari again, careful to stand well away from the puddles that had formed from water dripping from my barrier. I wouldn't want His Regalness to get his foot wet.

I will lead the way, he announced as soon as he arrived.

"I'll go last. Just tell me when and where to point this thing." Dimitri nudged the device in his arms with his chin.

"Not at any of us." I went after Sindari, tempted to tell the others to wait back here. This was my problem.

But we encountered two more rockfalls blocking the way, so it was good that I kept Chasmmoor with me. One time, he glanced back at Dimitri and pressed a hand to the rubble. Instead of simply moving the rocks aside, he somehow re-formed them into an archway that the ancient Romans would have admired.

"Cool," Dimitri said with more reverence than most things got from him.

Here and there, water drained in through cracks in the ceiling. We weren't under the lake, so it could only be rainwater, but Sindari held his paw up and gave me a flat look when the puddles were too large to avoid. Maybe I needed to let *him* spend time in my mother's sauna.

Traffic rumbled above us, making it difficult to hear much in the tunnels. It was a while before I picked up voices somewhere ahead. Troll voices? I couldn't make out the language.

Chasmmoor held up a finger. He'd heard them too.

You know who's up there, Sindari? I asked silently.

I smell ogres, but the scents of trolls also linger.

Hm. I didn't have any interest in ogres, but maybe they knew where the trolls were.

As we crept closer, I tapped my translation charm, but the voices had fallen silent. Had their owners detected us? I didn't know if Chasmmoor had activated his camouflaging charm, but regardless, Dimitri didn't have one.

We hadn't yet reached the stairs I remembered from my first visit, but we'd started passing freshly dug-out side rooms. We'd checked each one, but so far, they'd all been unoccupied.

For the first time since hearing the voices, distinct words reached my ears. "Someone's coming!"

"Brace yourselves," I whispered, dropping into a crouch.

Sindari bounded ahead, charged into a room, and disappeared.

"Guess we're not bothering with stealth." I ran after him, my longer legs letting me outpace Chasmmoor, and created Storm's barrier again. Dimitri lumbered after us with the device.

Sindari roared, someone shouted—that wasn't the trollish language, damn it—and a magical blast of power rattled my senses. Hell, I wasn't even inside yet.

Beware, Sindari warned. *There is an artifact that—*

He didn't finish.

That what? I tried to run into the room, only to bounce back as my barrier struck the walls. It was like trying to run around in a bubble.

Growling, I willed it to shrink. Chasmmoor crowded behind me, trying to get into the room as well.

"They activated the defender!" someone cried in the ogre language.

As soon as my barrier shrank enough, I strode into the dark room. Two ogres faced me, standing in front of a sleeping area, each lifting a club and glowering at me.

Sindari was rising from where it looked like he'd been thrown against a wall. He shook his head woozily.

One ogre took a menacing step toward me but paused. "It's the Ruin Bringer!"

I raised Storm but didn't spring right for them. A spiky ball-shaped object on the floor in the corner was throbbing with red light and malevolent power. It must have been responsible for throwing Sindari, not the ogres.

"Where are the trolls?" I asked. "Are you allied with them?"

"No. They left! We have claimed this—"

Chasmmoor finally squeezed in around me. But in doing so, he slipped into the artifact's area of defense. Crimson light burst from the spiky ball, and raw energy hurled him in the same direction as Sindari. It also caught me, knocking my barrier out, as if a circuit breaker had tripped. A buzz of electricity ran down my arm, and I almost dropped Storm.

The ogres squinted at me, exchanged glances with each other, and charged forward. Maybe they'd sensed my barrier before and hadn't thought they had a chance against me. But with it down…

Chasmmoor recovered and, with a roar almost as ferocious as one of Sindari's, charged the closest ogre.

I tried to explain that the ogres weren't our enemies, and probably hadn't even put that artifact there, but there was no time. Chasmmoor ducked a club the size of a log that whistled toward his helmet, then lunged in, swinging his great battle-axe at a kneecap.

It slammed in with an audible crunch. The ogre screamed as he jerked his leg away. That didn't keep him from countering. Again, he hefted his club and tried to pound Chasmmoor into the floor.

The other ogre stomped toward me. There was no time to reactivate my shield, so I backed away to stand in front of the doorway, half so they wouldn't get out into the tunnel and attack Dimitri and half so I would stay out of the spiky ball's radius.

"Val," Dimitri blurted. "You're in the way of my funnel."

The ogre swung his club at my head, so I didn't answer. I ducked, and it whistled past, smashing into the wall beside me. Before the ogre could recover, I sprang up and sliced into his meaty arm with Storm. The blade drew blood, but he only snarled and backed up, lifting his club for another attack.

"Look, if this is your room, we'll move on." I dodged another swing, this one trying to hammer me into the floor. Again, faster than he could recover, I sprang in and swept Storm toward his ribs.

The blade cut in, and the ogre dropped his club as he lumbered to the side. His route took him nearer the artifact, and it pulsed crimson light again. The light caught the ogre, but it didn't hurl him anywhere. He froze, hands up, a scream of pain echoing from the walls.

I drew back, startled. He hadn't cried out like that even when I'd cut him. The ogre tried to lurch out of the field, but it must have held him.

By now, Sindari had recovered, and he was fighting alongside Chasmmoor, keeping the other ogre busy. The trapped ogre met my eyes, his face contorted with pain, his own eyes pleading.

Ugh, I didn't have a grudge against these guys. How did I release him from this?

I pointed Storm at the artifact and scoured through the command terms in my mind, wishing I had one for a fireball.

"Wait, Dimitri. Come use your thing." I scooted away from the doorway, so he could get in. "Point the funnel at that doohickey."

Dimitri stomped in, carrying the awkward magic de-amplifier, and did as I'd asked. He flicked a switch, and I sensed power building up inside of it, but nothing happened.

"Uh oh," Dimitri said, flicking the switch several more times. "I think maybe it got wet."

"We do it the hard way then." I sheathed Storm and dug into my pack as I checked on Chasmmoor and Sindari.

They'd managed to press their big foe back and disarm him, but they hadn't yet defeated him. Though bleeding from deep gashes, the ogre kicked and punched, throwing all his weight behind the blows. One connected with Chasmmoor's breastplate, and the crack of bone belonged to the ogre.

I pulled out a grenade. "Everybody get out of the room."

The trapped ogre's eyes bulged.

"It's either this or die from that thing," I told him, pointing at the spiky ball.

Tears seeped from his eyes. I had no idea what it was doing to him, but the magic battered at my senses, and I wasn't even caught in it. *Troll* magic. This had to be some artifact they'd left behind. Maybe it had even been meant for me.

Chasmmoor and Sindari saw my grenade and abandoned their battle to run into the tunnel, dragging Dimitri with them. Their battered opponent glanced at the spiky ball—and at me and my grenade—and limped out after them.

I unpinned the grenade and lobbed it at the spiky ball. Common sense told me to run into the tunnel, but I was hesitant to abandon the ogre. I waded into the crimson light—pain pummeled me from all sides, but with Storm glowing a fierce blue, the magic didn't manage to trap me—and when I was close enough, commanded my sword to raise the barrier again.

The grenade exploded, white light flashing and the shockwave slamming into my defenses. Storm protected me, and other than the light blasting my eyes, I wasn't affected. The ogre was also safe inside my barrier. The magic of the artifact disappeared from my senses, and the crimson light and power around us also disappeared.

Only shattered pieces remained of the magical artifact. I lowered Storm's barrier, aware of the tightness in my lungs.

"Thanks, Ruin Bringer," the ogre blurted, then sprinted away.

You wish us to let them escape? Sindari asked from the tunnel, even as he roared at the ogre.

Yeah. They're not who we came for.

A whisper of magic came from the shards on the floor, and I jerked Storm out again. An apparition formed in the air above the destroyed artifact. A short-haired troll in robes and bone necklaces with his arms raised. It wasn't the shaman I'd faced by Willard's apartment, but it looked a lot like him.

"The Ruin Bringer has slain two of my brothers," it intoned. "She shall perish before the next full moon."

"Oh, wonderful," I muttered as the apparition vanished.

"That was invigorating," Chasmmoor announced when I joined the others in the tunnel.

Dimitri was busy frowning at his malfunctioning device.

"It would have been more invigorating if we'd been fighting against the right guys." I slumped against the stone wall, wheezing.

All we'd learned was that the trolls had left the area. Were they already lurking in the woods up north, waiting to ambush my wedding?

"Your breathing is labored." Chasmmoor frowned at me.

"I noticed."

"Were you injured?"

"No. It's a chronic thing. My lungs suck." I dug into my pocket for my inhaler before I could consider that there might be ramifications. Even though I'd passed all of his tests so far—at least I thought I had—Chasmmoor could decide that a health issue disqualified me from carrying a precious dwarven blade. I used the inhaler, then jammed it back in my pocket and glared defiantly at him. If he tried to take Storm, I would show him exactly how capable I was with it.

"You have always had this issue?" Chasmmoor didn't appear concerned by my threatening glower, probably because he wore full armor and carried a battle-axe larger than my head.

"No. I developed it in the last year or so." My lungs slowly loosened under the influence of the medication, though I worried about the day when that stuff wouldn't help. "Getting older is a delight."

"You are not that old for a half-elf." His gaze shifted toward Storm. "How long have you had the sword?"

"Ten years."

"Hm. Strange that it would have taken that long to develop. But perhaps not if you were not drawing upon its powers earlier."

"Wait, are you saying my *sword* could have something to do with my asthma?" I waved at my chest.

"I am not familiar with that word, but even the most powerful blades will draw upon the energy of the wielder. Sometimes even more so than lesser magical weapons, because they have a hint of sentience and can do what you wish. What a wielder wishes is not always wise."

"Tell me about it. Uh, actually tell me about how the sword using my energy could be affecting me. Could it give me a chronic health problem?" I stared intently at him, riveted. It had never occurred to me that the sword might somehow be affecting my health. Was it possible that calling upon its magic, whether consciously or subconsciously, was putting stress on my body—increasing inflammation markers, as my doctor had said—and that it had something to do with my lungs overreacting to *everything*? "Because it's been worse lately. Especially *this week*."

"That is not surprising since we have been training each night. You are presumably using the sword and calling upon its magic more than typical."

"Definitely. I usually *sleep* at night."

"I do not recall it being mentioned in the scrolls dedicated to the dragon blades," Chasmmoor said, "but the most powerful dwarven blades have a command that tells them to assist you with meditation, to place your body in a regenerative state to recover more quickly from the stresses of battle and using so much power."

"Meditation?" I slumped deeper against the wall. "I've tried meditation. I suck at it. Just ask my therapist."

"You have tried using the command and meditating with your sword?"

"Well, no."

"You should do this. The ancient dwarven term for meditation is *zom*."

"That's it?" If so, this would be the first ancient dwarven word I could pronounce without twisting my tongue in somersaults.

"Yes."

"You're sure it's not *ohm?*"

"It is *zom*. Try it when you return home. Only do it in a safe place, as you will not sense anyone approaching when you are deep in the regenerative state."

I was about to say that sounded dangerous but realized it might be exactly like sleep. "I'll try it."

"Do it for an hour each evening or morning. It may take several weeks to have a profound effect."

That sounded suspiciously like regular meditation, but if the sword actually helped me to put my mind into some zen state instead of making mental to-do lists and checking the time constantly, maybe it would work. Dare I hope? If it *did* work, I would ask Dimitri or Zav to record me meditating, so I could send proof to Mary. She would be so pleased.

Zav and Zondia came within range of my senses. I waited warily to see if their mother would too, but they were alone. Maybe some urgent matter had called the queen back to her world and she would have to meet the Silverclaw dragon on another planet.

You are in the tunnels? Zav's telepathic voice was oddly muffled, almost garbled. Due to the magic making this place difficult to detect?

Yes. We fought some ogres only to learn that the trolls had moved out.

Unfortunate. Zondia'qareshi and I will seek a way down to join you.

I attempted to share an image of the underground entrance with him, but after a few minutes, thunderous snaps came from the ceiling in the room where we'd battled the ogres. Swearing, Dimitri and I scurried farther from the doorway, with Sindari and Chasmmoor right behind. Stone tumbled down from the ceiling in that room, and a few ominous snaps came from the tunnel around us as well. Chasmmoor raised his hands, prepared to use some magic. I activated Storm's barrier again.

The snaps stopped, and two thuds sounded. Zav and Zondia jumping down? I crept back to the doorway and peered inside. Zav was indeed inside shaking out his elven robe. Zondia stood beside him in black leather pants and jacket, everything from her lilac hair to her nose rings to her boots dulled by rock dust.

"We located an unused basement and deemed it a suitable entrance place," Zav said.

Two steel kegs of beer and a bag of flour tumbled down to land beside them.

"Unused?" I asked.

"Unused except for storage." Zav strode forward with his arms raised.

For a hug? I dropped the magical barrier.

Zav smiled and gripped my shoulders. "The queen is pleased with the hunting options, and she said that she herself might compete in the races. She has deemed the eyries and platforms that the goblins and I built *adequate*."

"High praise."

"From her it is," Zondia said. "She returned to our world to share the word, and she's coming back tonight with all of our relatives. The Starsinger dragons have started to appear here too."

"Unfortunately." Zav sniffed and lowered his arms.

"They aren't as annoying as you make them out to be," Zondia said. "They don't plot against our family like certain other clans of dragons."

"That's because they are apolitical hippies who don't plot or plan *anything*. They exist only to feast and sate their sexual urges."

"Isn't that what you do with your mate?" Zondia pointed at me.

Zav's eyes closed to slits. "We also capture criminals, and you *know* I'm active on the council."

"Please don't start talking about politics. You'll put your mate to sleep."

"Val finds listening to me speak scintillating."

"That can't be true." Zondia looked at me.

"He's actually not a bad conversationalist," I said. "And he makes me laugh."

"I assumed he only wished to mate with you because your body is appealing to him when he's in human form, but now I understand the truth. If you *like* listening to his lectures on dragon politics, everything makes sense now."

"He's also hot in the nest."

Dimitri made a choking sound.

"Gross." Zondia looked back at the hole in the ceiling, perhaps contemplating fleeing.

Zav, looking rather pleased with himself, slung an arm around my shoulders. "We should relax and feast and enjoy the evening so that we are well rested for the events tomorrow."

"The ceremony?" I asked. "Yes."

"The events. I will compete in the races, the hunt, and the duels to prove my prowess as a mate."

"That's not necessary. And did you say duels?" I hadn't heard him mention that before.

"Yes. I hope to challenge Xilnethgarish, but he will decline, because he is inferior and knows it. Perhaps the Silverclaw dragon will wish to battle me. I do hope that tomorrow is most exciting so that the dragon visitors enjoy themselves and leave harboring no ill will toward this world and our relationship."

"I hope so too."

Duels, hell. As if the troll threat wasn't bad enough.

CHAPTER 31

LATE MORNING FOUND ME SOARING on Zav's back as we flew toward the goblin sanctuary, a glorious sun beaming down upon us. It wasn't a *warm* sun, but given that it was winter, I was delighted that it wasn't raining.

Freysha, Eireth, and two of the king's bodyguards rode behind me, making Zav's back far more crowded than usual. Without magic, we wouldn't have all fit, nor would he have been able to take off with so much extra weight. But his aura crackled with vigorous energy this morning, and I basked in my mate's power and stroked his scales often as we flew. The night before, he'd been considerate enough to wait for me to meditate—and watch over me while I did it—before suggesting we take advantage of how *hot he was in the nest*. He'd managed to use that phrase no fewer than ten times since I'd said it to Zondia.

Zav banked and flew away from the suburbs and over farms and rivers toward the forested foothills where the sanctuary lay. Still worried about the troll threat, I carried my weapons and wore my typical gear. Dimitri was driving up in his camper with my wedding dress and shoes, Chasmmoor, and the rest of the elves who were staying at our house. Mom had promised to enlist the help of Liam and his truck to bring up the rest of my pointed-eared kin. Thad was bringing Amber and Jace, and Nin had mentioned coming early with Willard.

I'd invited Inga and Reb, but they'd opted to work at the coffee shop today instead, since Dimitri, Nin, Tam, and I would all be here. Inga had muttered something about it being safer there than at my wedding.

I hadn't known how to argue against that statement, since I worried it would prove true, but I had a vain hope that all would go well.

I'd also invited Mary, though I didn't know if a forest wedding was quite her thing. I looked forward to telling her about my new meditation practice soon. Maybe after I'd done it more than once, it could legitimately be considered a *practice*. With the sword's help, I had sunk into a deep and restful state for the first time in my life. It had been like a blanket falling over my senses, with the stillness of a deep and quiet lake in a remote cavern forming over my mind. Whether it was going to cure me or not was up in the air, but it had been noticeably rejuvenating.

Willard had texted at dawn, already up at the sanctuary with a team overseeing everything. She'd shoehorned Walker into setting up chairs. I reminded myself to get her a gift. It was pretty awesome that she was handling everything for me. Her and Zav. And however many dozen goblins they'd wrangled into working with them.

What kind of gift one got for one's boss, I didn't know. A book? She'd already read everything. Maybe she needed some sexy lingerie in case things progressed beyond dinner and a battle with Walker.

Distant platforms came into view, hovering well above the treetops. A magnificent blue dragon perched atop one, surveying the sunlit forest as we approached. A green dragon that I recognized from the battle at Weber's house—one of the Starsingers—flew up to land on another platform. Were those considered eyries?

They took off as one, flapping rapidly toward the mountains.

The hunts have begun, Zav announced in my mind. *This is good. The more prey our guests catch, the less human food they will consume during the feast.*

I'm sure Willard and the other guests will be pleased if all the catered food isn't inhaled in the first three minutes. I envisioned my human guests arriving to platters of bread crumbs. Make that incinerated bread crumbs, since the dragons would consume the meat while getting rid of the nonessentials.

As Zav descended toward the road winding through the trees, the place where our guests who were driving cars would park, Eireth rested a hand on my shoulder.

"Your mother," he said, "has requested that I stand beside the human priest and also say the words of the elven marriage ceremony to make it official in both ways. Is that acceptable to you?"

"Yes. I'd be honored."

"Excellent."

All species in all of the Cosmic Realms will know that we are officially married. Zav sounded like he approved. *The goblin work leader has also agreed to speak at the ceremony and make it known to all of their kind that we are a work party of two.*

Uh, does that mean we'll be married in the goblin way?

It does. I have not asked any of the orcs or ogres that are coming to mate us, as I do not know if any of them are religious or ceremonial leaders among their people.

I think if we get elves, humans, dragons, and goblins covered, that's sufficient. We have the rings too. Whenever we meet new people, my fingers will ooze gardening and cooking magic—and the fact that we're mated.

Indeed. This is excellent. Perhaps enemies will sense this and wish you to cook for them instead of battling them.

Was that dragon humor? *I only cook for my mate. I would rather fight enemies.*

This is acceptable.

I'm glad you approve. I peered over his side as we flew past the goblin sanctuary, but the magic that had protected it from outside notice for so many decades remained in place. Even though I could find it from the ground, I couldn't detect anything but forest below us from above.

Numerous cars were already parked alongside the road, a big sign painted green with white lettering announcing that the Wedding Extravaganza was here, with an arrow pointing into the woods, and that tickets were available for ten dollars.

"So that's how goblins make money to pay for coffee." As soon as we landed, I slid off Zav's back and trotted to the sign, wishing I had a pen or paintbrush. Or maybe an entire bucket and a paint roller. The lettering was *huge*.

So far, the cars parked alongside the road were mostly familiar—there was Mom's Subaru, Willard's Honda, Thad's BMW, Liam's truck, Dimitri's van, a huge RV with ogres painted on the side, and Walker's now-repaired toaster—but what if people who didn't know me and hadn't been invited stopped? They wouldn't be able to find the sanctuary without someone leading them, and they would end up wandering around in the woods, either getting lost or being eaten by the imported animals. True, those animals might be busy fleeing from dragons, but why take chances?

"Does anybody have a pen?" I looked at Freysha, Eireth, and Zav as he shifted into human form. "Or some magic that could wipe this out?" I waved at the bit about tickets. "Or cover it up?"

Freysha opened her mouth, but Zav reacted first. His eyes flared violet, and the bottom of the sign burst into flame. I sprang back, bumping against Mom's SUV.

Zav controlled the fire, and only the part about tickets burned, leaving *Wedding Extravaganza* and the arrow intact. I almost asked him to char the word extravaganza—what was wrong with simply calling it a wedding?—but that would have only left a corner of the sign, and it might have fallen off the stick holding it upright.

"Thank you, Zav." I patted his shoulder. "As always, you're a handy dragon."

Amber rolled down the window of the BMW. "Are his nostrils supposed to be smoking?"

She and Thad were sitting in their parked car, maybe waiting for me before committing to wandering into the forest. And was that Jace sitting behind them?

"It's a dragon thing." As I waved for them to get out, I sensed Nin, Willard, and Walker heading this way from the woods.

Thad and Amber were already in their formal clothing, the elegant blue bridesmaid dress for Amber and a tux for Thad. He eyed the faint dirt path winding into the woods, then eyed his leather dress shoes. Maybe I should have told them to come in hiking clothes and plan to change at the wedding grounds. But I hadn't known what there might be in the way of changing facilities. I'd seen the goblin village, made from recycled bits and bobs, but I hadn't known if they would open up a building for us. And since goblins didn't use indoor plumbing, I expected minimal practical amenities inside their dwellings.

"I was envisioning you in something more dress-like." Thad waved to my jeans and duster. "Amber mentioned fittings."

"It's in Dimitri's van, I think. I was afraid it would get wrinkled in Zav's interdimensional closet."

Jace, as tall and gangly as in the photo, wandered up in time to hear that. Or maybe he didn't. Giant headphones were affixed to his ears, and his pockets bristled with electronics. Judging by the Nintendo Switch sticking out of one, he didn't expect the Wedding Extravaganza to be that entertaining, though he was looking at Zav with wide eyes. Zav must not have bothered to hide his dragonness from mundane humans as he was flying in.

Willard walked up with Nin and Walker, eyeing people's dress clothing. Like me, Willard had come in practical clothes and planned to change. Nin also wasn't dressed up yet, and she wore a pair of grass-stained work gloves. Had she been pressed into helping?

"Maybe Lord Zavryd would deign to fly your most special guests to the clearing," Willard said, "so they don't have to walk through the mud."

I almost pointed out that it was a beautiful sunny day, but it had rained the three previous days, so the mud would be there. Mom and Liam had probably tramped back there, his magical werewolf senses letting him find the place, without batting an eye at the mud. Was Mom even wearing shoes for this shindig? I hadn't asked about her fashion plans.

"Ride a *dragon*?" Jace asked with wonder.

"Ride a *dragon*?" Thad asked with horror.

"Are you willing to be a taxi?" I asked Zav, whose lip had curled at this suggestion.

"For my mate and her elven kin, always. For human vermin..." He rubbed the side of his leg, as if he were worried about catching something.

Thad folded his arms over his chest. A second ago, he hadn't wanted a ride, but now he appeared indignant at this rejection.

Willard rolled her eyes. "Is there a less uppity dragon who could be pressed into Uber service?"

Zav squinted at her, and I thought he might protest that adjective, but a new dragon flew within range of my senses. Zav huffed. Xilneth.

Hey, buddy, I spoke telepathically to him. *Can you give some of my guests a ride to the sanctuary?*

I didn't know if Xilneth would be game, but nobody could accuse him of being uppity.

Are any of them sexy and appealing to those in human form? Xilneth asked.

Uh. Yes, but you're not hitting on my daughter. She's too young for you. And she has a boyfriend.

But there are others?

I looked at the people who needed rides. *I think Freysha may be too young for you, too, but I'll ask her to flirt with you if it gets them all rides.*

As I poked into Dimitri's van for my dress, wrinkling my nose at the evidence that he may have been introducing my elven guests to weed on the way up, Xilneth landed in the middle of the road. He held the pose, wings outstretched as much as possible with trees to either side, like a gymnast waiting for the judges to acknowledge that he'd stuck the landing. Then his head turned on his long neck, and he surveyed the guests.

Jace's earphones drooped down the back of his head as he gaped up at Xilneth, his mouth dangling open. Amber reached over with a finger to push it closed.

After scanning the group, Xilneth lowered his big head to gaze into Freysha's eyes. *Greetings, beautiful elf maiden.*

Eireth's brows flew up, and he stepped protectively in front of her. "This is *Princess* Freysha."

Aren't you supposed to turn into an elf before you start flirting with two-legged people? I asked Xilneth.

I will do that later, he told me, then boomed to everyone: *All who wish to fly to the starting point for the hunts and the races and duels may climb onto my back.*

"We will walk," Eireth said, clasping Freysha's arm, though she hadn't taken a step toward Xilneth.

"So will we." Thad reached for Amber, but Jace was already racing to Xilneth and climbing up via his tail.

Amber dodged Thad's grip to walk after him.

"Perhaps we should walk together, Thad." Nin took his hand. "And leave the youths to more vigorous forms of travel."

"Vigorous forms of travel where they could fall off and splat to their *deaths*?" Thad still looked like he wanted to chase Amber down.

"They'll be fine," I assured him. "I ride with Zav all the time. Splat-free."

Your kin may come with us. Zav shifted back into dragon form, nearly knocking Xilneth off the road as he expanded. *I offer a superior flight.*

Oh? I asked. *Do you have reclining seats and an inflight beverage service?*

I offer the supreme honor of being allowed to not only touch my scales but ride upon my broad back.

So, no cocktails, huh?

Zav squinted at me. *You are fortunate that you are my mate, and it is customary on this world for mates to tease each other.*

Will someone get this haughty dragon's large scaled backside out of the way? Xilneth asked, backing up, his talons clacking on the pavement.

Zav *had* planted his butt right in front of Xilneth. I rubbed the back of my neck, wondering if these two would end up in a fight—or a duel—by the end of the day.

With my dress bag in hand, I headed for Zav, and he levitated me onto his back again. Freysha, Eireth, Willard, Walker, Nin, and Thad opted for the trail, following the goblin guide back into the woods. Maybe Xilneth felt rejected, for he watched them go for a moment before huffing a puff of smoke out of his nostrils.

As Zav launched into the air, I spotted three trucks and another RV rolling up the road toward the parked cars, all with ogres, orcs, trolls, shifters, and other beings I recognized from the coffee shop hanging out the windows or riding in the beds. I squinted at the trolls, but they all had the familiar auras of customers, and when I sifted through the magical auras present, I didn't notice any grenades among them.

Maybe the trolls who were out to get me hadn't learned about the location change and wouldn't show up here, and maybe the wedding would go off without a hitch.

"I'm not delusional, right, Zav?"

You have acknowledged that I am a magnificent dragon, sublimely handy, and a superior mate.

"Was that a yes or a no?"

One who recognizes the gloriousness of a dragon cannot possibly be delusional.

"I guess not." I smiled, leaned forward, and rested my cheek on his scales. "You are pretty glorious."

Yes. And you are far superior to any human, elf, or half-elf I have met. We will soon be mated in the human way, and all shall know, and then we will hunt and fly into battles together for all our future days.

I tried to swallow the lump in my throat. A girl wasn't supposed to get weepy until *after* the "I do." Even so, I may have dribbled a tear or two onto Zav's sleek scales. *I look forward to it.*

CHAPTER 32

THE SANCTUARY HAD CHANGED A lot since last I'd been here. Oh, the kludgy goblin village with its walls made from corrugated metal, pilfered street signs, and old box springs hadn't changed, but a field of at least five acres had been cleared of everything except tidily trimmed grass. Folding chairs had been set up amid stumps, creating rows on either side of what might be called an aisle. Several massive log benches in the back had a shot at supporting ogre butts without breaking.

Buffet tables lined one side of the field, with large signs denoting that the food being kept magically warm in covered trays was for humans, dwarves, goblins, and elves. Tarps had been laid out next to the tables with steaming piles of slightly cooked haunches, racks of ribs, and other portions of meat still clinging to the bones. A sign above those proclaimed they were for trolls, orcs, ogres, and dragons. Would my guests obey the instructions? Maybe. In addition to the trays, the tables held a lot of huge bowls of greens that might keep the carnivores away, though the sheet cakes next to them had already been sampled. Even as I watched, two goblin kids sneaked up to the back of the table and swiped pieces. I trusted Willard had stashed the official wedding cake somewhere safe.

On the other side of the field, a number of log-and-vine structures with greenery growing up the sides had been erected. Some were labeled restrooms and changing areas, others storage, and an open-sided log pavilion showed our harpist tuning her harp.

I'd expected a couple of tents, but these structures had foundations and looked sturdier and more permanent than the goblin dwellings. They even managed to be elegant, some rising two stories with artful stairs winding up the outside, leaves and flowers growing from the branches that made up the railings. I suspected Freysha's hand at work.

An elegant gazebo with a wooden floor held a mound of wedding presents that rose nearly ten feet tall. Some were wrapped in what I would consider a normal style with decorative paper and ribbons. Others were enrobed by animal hides and twine. Several were hidden inside repurposed and slightly dented and chewed cardboard boxes. The entire effect was daunting and made me wonder where in the house we would put everything. Or how I would fit all the dubious items that we didn't want to keep into my Jeep for a trip to Goodwill.

Dragons streaked across the sky above us, sun gleaming on their scales. Had the races begun? Blurs of blue, black, silver, gold, and occasionally Zondia's lilac shot past. There weren't starting pistols or announcements, so I assumed the dragons were communicating everything telepathically.

Just as I was thinking that the hunting and racing were relatively far removed from the wedding area and wouldn't likely be a problem, a silver female dragon flew into view over the trees, the mangled corpse of some freshly killed animal gripped in her talons. She flew low enough to drop the carcass—it was easily the size of two steers—from ten feet in the air. It landed with a loud thud and crunch, flattening a couple of chairs in a back row. Without a word, she flew around the clearing a couple of times—were we supposed to admire her magnificence and ability to bring in meat?—before soaring off.

All I could do was stare in horror at the massive bloody carcass and flattened chairs.

"Hell." I rubbed my face. "That's going to wreak havoc on Willard's seating chart."

Or maybe not. A dozen goblins in chef's hats carrying cleavers and coolers rushed out of the trees and set to butchering the carcass. They were fast. Maybe I would get lucky and evidence of the kill would be gone before Willard noticed. And maybe nobody would notice the smashed chairs or garish blood-stained grass.

"That was my cousin Ekirazenia," Zav said, now standing in human form next to me. "She is a superior hunter and wishes all to know it." He sniffed. "A bit of a showoff."

"A dragon who thinks highly of herself?" I asked. "Strange."

"*Very* highly," Zav said as Xilneth dropped off Amber and Jace nearby.

They snagged pieces of cake and wandered our direction. Eireth, Freysha, and the other walkers arrived, also joining us. Eireth pointed around and spoke to Freysha in elven. She nodded and smiled.

I raised my eyebrows, wondering if I should activate my translation charm or leave them their privacy.

"I was telling Freysha that I never thought I would see this place again," Eireth said. "It's changed much, but the smells of the foliage and native growth have given me nostalgia nose."

"Nostalgia what?" I asked.

"It is an elven term," Freysha explained. "When the scents of something remind you of a place in the past that you have feelings of nostalgia about."

"I experience that with the Cinnabon store," Amber said.

Freysha and Eireth looked blankly at her.

"Haven't you taken your houseguests sightseeing, Val?" Amber asked.

"We went to the Space Needle, Pike Place Market, and Discovery Park earlier in the week. I didn't realize Cinnabon was a Seattle sight that had to be seen."

"Duh."

Eireth caught my eye and nodded off to the side. Hoping he wasn't going to say that Amber had offended him somehow, I walked a few steps with him.

"My people and I will need to leave tomorrow," he said, "but I wish to tell you that I'm pleased you have found happiness with Lord Zavryd'nokquetal. When I first saw you together, I thought, as odd and unlikely as it seems, that you were a good match. You tease each other, but it is gentle and filled with love."

"Yeah." There was that lump welling in my throat again. Would the whole day be like this?

"I wouldn't have believed a dragon could experience love in the sense of humans and elves. Extraordinary."

"He is."

A blue dragon flew past and dropped off another carcass. It had a gray hide and reminded me of a hippo.

I sighed. "The *rest* of his people leave something to be desired."

Eireth smiled. "Perhaps true. That one did not crush chairs at least."

When another goblin butchering team appeared—the other team had almost finished packing away pieces from the first deposit—I'd never felt so relieved to have the little green guys present. After this, we would have to give them free coffee at the shop for the rest of the month.

"As I recall," Eireth continued, "when first we met, I also had reservations about what kind of person you would be. Your reputation as an assassin of magical beings preceded you."

"I remember."

"I have no reservations now." He gave me the elven version of a bow. "And I am pleased to have gotten a chance to know you."

"Thank you," I managed, though my voice was raspy, and that lump was even bigger. "I'm glad I got to know you too."

"You are welcome to visit our world anytime. I will *ensure* that my people do not object."

"Thanks. Do elves hug?" I'd never been a touchy-feely person, but it seemed like the appropriate time.

"We do." He hugged me and patted me on the back.

As I returned the gesture, I let myself admit that it wasn't bad having a father. Even if I'd grown up never knowing him, I could see how he'd influenced Mom, who had certainly influenced me tremendously.

We parted, and his gaze drifted past me to where a couple of my elven half-cousins were stroking the living railing on the staircase winding up the outside of the two-story structure. They murmured appreciatively to each other.

"Perhaps my people also would not object to an elven engineer who mingles human and goblin technologies into her works," Eireth said.

"I hope that's true."

Mom and Liam stepped out of the bottom of the structure, eyed the elves curiously, then headed toward us. He wore a gray suit—the perfect color for a wolf—and Mom wore a long kaftan in busy browns and tans. It was the closest I'd seen to a dress on her, though it looked like something a hippie would have worn to Woodstock. Amber might have some fashion suggestions for her.

Colors flashed at Mom's feet as she walked through the grass. I nearly fell over. She wasn't barefoot; she was wearing Crocs. Crocs with holes in them and splashes of rainbow colors that made it look like a paint-mixing machine had exploded as she walked past.

I gripped Eireth's arm for support. "Where did she get *those*?"

Amber would *definitely* have words on fashion for her.

"Greetings, mother of my mate," Zav said. "I am pleased that you have chosen to wear the shoes I acquired for you."

Zav had gotten those for her? When had he had time to go shopping? And how had he known where to find Crocs? His pair had been a gift—a *gag* gift—from Thad.

"They're surprisingly comfortable," Mom said.

Horrified, I shook my head and mentally revoked my admission that Mom had influenced me in any way.

"I originally objected when Val suggested I wear shoes to her wedding," she added, "but these have breathing holes that let the grass through to tickle my feet."

Zav lifted his feet to show off his own fluorescent yellow Crocs.

"He's *supposed* to wear his elven slippers today," I groaned. "He was wearing them *earlier*."

"I am certain he will change his footwear for the ceremony," Eireth assured me. "An elven mage robe and slippers are customary for the groom in an elven wedding."

Zav looked at Liam's feet. He wore boots with his suit.

"They didn't fit," Liam said when Zav raised his eyebrows.

I groaned again. Had Zav gotten *him* Crocs too? They barely knew each other. Unless they'd bonded while Zav had been perched on his rooftop, crushing his stovepipe.

"Mine also did not fit," Eireth said neutrally. "It is possible they will fit some of the elven children in my city."

I rocked back. "He got them for *everybody*?"

"You are certain?" Zav asked Liam. "I magically measured your feet and manipulated the footwear to ensure proper sizing."

"I'll check again when I get home." Liam glanced at Mom's shoes, then shot me a pained expression—no doubt, as a painter, he had a keen sense of aesthetics. And the ability to lie when given gifts that did not measure up to his aesthetics.

I spotted Mary entering the clearing, a bemused—or was that bewildered?—expression on her face as a goblin guide led her into the area. I waved at her, but she was too busy gaping around to notice. The ramshackle buildings of the goblin village drew her eye, or maybe it was the two ogres walking past with clubs on their shoulders. Though glad she'd come, I wondered if *she* would need therapy later.

"Yes," Zav said to Liam. "Do so. They are superior foot coverings."

Mom patted Liam on the arm and continued over to us. She smiled at Eireth, who smiled back. Their smiles were both awkward to my eyes, but they probably always would be.

Maybe Freysha thought so, too, for she cleared her throat diffidently. "With the goblins' help, I repaired the damage done by a dragon to the original treehouses. Would you two like to see them?" She extended a hand in invitation to Liam. "You three?"

"I will come." Liam wasn't bristling at the smile that Eireth and Mom shared, but he also didn't look like he wanted to let her out of his sight.

Although, as another carcass was dropped off via a dragon flyby, I decided his feelings might have more to do with protective instincts than jealous instincts.

"I would be curious to see the area, yes." Mom nodded at Freysha.

Willard, Thad, Nin, and Walker came up as Mom, Freysha, and Eireth, along with most of my other elven houseguests, joined in. Led by Freysha, the group headed off toward the wooded back of the sanctuary. Hopefully, that creature we'd encountered on our first trip was gone or in a cage somewhere. Of course, it had been an elven protector, so maybe it would bound up to Eireth to get its head scritched.

"Smells like a good barbie in progress," Walker said, sniffing the air. "I'm not quite familiar with the type of meat though."

"Nobody is," I said. "I'm crossing my fingers that the goblins slather it with a lot of barbecue sauce."

Did goblins have barbecue sauce? I hoped they had *something*.

"Perhaps I should have brought my special suea rong-hai sauce," Nin said.

I wished she had.

"We've walked the perimeter of the sanctuary to look for trolls." Willard waved at Walker, maybe to indicate that he'd gone lion and used his magical senses. Currently, he wore a suit, waistcoat, and cravat, with a sophisticated gold watch on his wrist, and looked like a model for *GQ*, so it was hard to imagine him snuffling through the ferns on four legs. "We didn't detect anything out of the ordinary. Until we got to the clearing here." She looked over at the goblin butchers descending on the most recent catch.

"Magical sanctuaries are rarely ordinary." I noted the smells of unfamiliar roasting meat wafting out of the goblin village and decided it was unlikely that animals from other planets tasted like chicken. "Thanks for looking."

"You're welcome." Willard looked at her watch, a waterproof digital Casio that probably made Walker cringe. "We'll be starting in less than an hour. Feel free to change any time."

"You think the dragons will be done with their races and hunting that soon?" I was in no hurry to put on my dress and fancy shoes, but guests were starting to congregate by the buffet tables and finding seating. The hulking ogres opted for the benches in the back, and the log frames creaked under their weight but didn't give way.

"I don't know. Is it necessary for them to be here for the actual ceremony?" Willard lifted her eyebrows. "I've gotten the impression that they came for the races and the rides. Have you *seen* the rides? They're set up about ten miles that way." She pointed east. "They're some kind of mixture of bungee jumping, trampolines, and an aerial gauntlet."

"A gauntlet?" I imagined the hand piece from a set of dwarven armor.

"The kind you run through while people beat you with sticks. As the dragons plummet to the ground, branches batter them from all sides. I saw Zav do a practice run with his sister yesterday. They had to make sure it was set up perfectly for their mother." Willard shook her head.

"And the dragons like that?"

"Apparently, it feels good. Like deep-tissue massage. Or maybe the kind of massage where people walk on your back." Willard shrugged.

I scratched my jaw. "That may be evidence to support a theory I've been putting together about dragons landing on lawn ornaments and deck chairs. I think it feels good when things poke them in their scales."

"If that's true, the goblins should have made a more vigorous wedding present."

I glanced toward the pile of presents, though from the dimensions Zav had asked me about earlier, it couldn't be there.

"It's not with those gifts." Willard smirked as she spoke, amusement glinting in her dark eyes. "Didn't you go into the village?"

"No. I've seen the village before. I didn't think I needed to go in."

"There's a massive gift in an even more massive homemade crate sitting in the center of it next to a big garage or barn or whatever they call their storage structure."

"Have you seen inside the crate?" I asked Willard.

"No, but Gondo confided the details to me."

"Will I like it?"

"*Zav* will like it."

"Well, that's what's important." I smiled over at Zav, but his gaze was toward the sky, off in the direction I'd last seen dragons flying.

"Xilnethgarish has challenged me to a race. I cannot fail to appear, or he will tell others I feared to face him." Zav's eyes narrowed. "I would rather duel him and pummel him into the ground than fly beside him. Perhaps afterward, he will deign to engage in a fight."

"Who doesn't want to get pummeled at a wedding?" Willard murmured.

"All dragons should always be eager to join in battle." Zav looked at me. "Do you need anything of me currently?"

"Less than an hour until the ceremony." Willard tapped her watch.

"Go have fun." I shooed him off to join his buddies. With luck, most of them would stay out in the forest and forget to come to the ceremony. "Show your mother a good time."

"*Yes*." Zav lifted his chin. "She has already caught one of the fleet and dangerous yorak. She enjoyed that."

"Good."

He shifted into dragon form but looked to the far end of the clearing before taking off. Xilneth had landed there and was looking toward our group.

"We're going to go for another ride, Val." Amber waved, and she and Jace jogged off toward Xilneth.

Had he *invited* them? Vague images of the aerial gauntlet that Willard had described leaped to mind, as well as thoughts of my kid being pummeled by it.

Xilneth, that is my offspring, I spoke telepathically to him while glancing at Thad.

A goblin had brought up a large drumstick to him, so he hadn't yet noticed our daughter trotting off.

You're not going to engage in anything dangerous, are you? I added. *Like races with Zav?*

I am going to race your haughty mate! The young ones wish to watch. This is natural, since I am entertaining. I watch our queen's hatchling, you know. She finds me fascinating.

I bet. I tugged at my braid, not reassured.

I will remove them from my back and leave them where they have a good view. Riders would slow me down. I must be victorious! It will be glorious and an honor for mere humans to witness.

I'm sure. I envisioned Jace and Amber being deposited at the top of a great pine tree and having to hang on to slender branches to keep from falling. That wasn't much better than the gauntlet imagery.

I didn't want to forbid them to go, especially since Amber might disobey me if I tried, but this might be a bad idea. *Zav? Will you keep an eye on them, please?*

Yes.

"Where are they going?" Thad pointed the drumstick after Jace and Amber as they climbed on Xilneth's back.

"To watch the races." I was about to point out that Amber would listen to *him* if he forbade her to leave, but the aura of another dragon flew within my range, distracting me. This one came not from the races but from the west. A recent arrival from a portal?

It wasn't a dragon I was familiar with, so I thought about ignoring him and going to change—while sneaking a peek at the goblin gift-in-a-crate—but a dragon I recognized was flying with the new arrival. Ston'tareknor, Zav's uncle. Good. I liked him. Other than Zav, Ston and Xilneth were the only dragons that were vaguely enjoyable to be around. Was he escorting the newcomer?

They flew into view, the new dragon a powerful silver with yellow eyes. He flew ahead of Ston, his cool gaze scouring the wedding grounds. That gaze latched on to me, and a chill ran through me. It was full of icy hatred.

Zav and Xilneth had disappeared off in the other direction, so I couldn't ask them if this was the Silverclaw that the queen had invited, but it had to be. Who else would glower at me with such hatred except a dragon who knew I'd been at least partially responsible for slaying some of his kin?

Greetings, mate of my nephew, Ston spoke into my mind. *Has Zavryd'nokquetal abandoned you in favor of hunting and racing?*

Yeah, but that's okay. Human spouses do that all the time—here, it's in favor of football games—so he's blending right in to the culture.

I trust he will finish in time for the mating ceremony. We are not late? I had to personally pick up the queen's... guest. Ston glanced toward the Silverclaw, who'd stopped glaring at me and was looking off toward the mountains now.

You're not late, no. Uh, was inviting that dragon her idea or his *idea?*

If the Silverclaw had been the one to suggest it, I would worry that this was a part of some plot against the Stormforge Clan that would be enacted while they were all out here together.

They have been debating a treaty for some time, Ston said as the two dragons flew out of view at the other end of the clearing. *They mutually agreed that a neutral world that is not dragon territory for either clan would be ideal.*

So you don't know whose idea this was?

That is correct. Their talks should not interfere with your mating ceremony.

I hope you're right.

"Val, Willard," Walker barked from near the buffet tables.

He stood rigid, looking out into the forest. Then he transformed into his lion form and raced toward the trees.

"Oh, hell." I sensed trolls out there. A *lot* of them.

CHAPTER 33

AS WALKER ROARED AND DISAPPEARED into the woods, a grenade flew out of the trees, whistling toward me. Glad I hadn't changed yet, I yanked out Fezzik and took aim. The familiar projectile radiated magic; it was one of Nin's.

I fired as soon as the sights lined up. Fezzik's magical bullet zipped into the sky and struck.

"Look out!" I shouted as the grenade exploded with a thunderous boom.

Even though I'd hit it well above the ground, it blew up with enough force to rock the structures, knock over the ogre benches, and knock me and everyone around me to the ground.

I sprang to my feet, drawing Storm. I almost ordered my sword to raise a barrier, but if more grenades flew out, I would have to be able to fire at them again. Maybe I could get to the trolls first.

"What's going on?" Eyes wide, Thad rose from his hands and knees, reminding me that I had people to protect.

"Just a hiccup. Go get in one of the buildings." I hoisted him up and pointed him to one of the sturdy log structures.

He ran over toward Nin instead, helping her to her feet. As they headed toward cover, I looked around to see who else needed help.

Amber, Jace, Mom, Liam, Freysha, and Eireth weren't in the area, but there were Mary, Tam, and a couple of bewildered shifter women from the coffee shop.

"Over there, you guys!" I yelled, pointing off after Thad.

The goblin butchers and other guests had already scattered. Good.

Another grenade flew out of the trees as the snarls and roars of a battle emanated from the same direction. This time, I was ready and fired while it was higher in the air. The explosion wasn't any less powerful, but everyone left outside managed to stay on their feet.

I tapped Sindari's charm to summon him. "Need some help, buddy."

Before he'd formed fully, I ran around the buffet tables and meat piles and toward the fighting. Willard had produced a handgun—thank goodness my guests knew better than to come to my wedding unarmed—and was advancing into the trees after Walker.

Why did you wait so long to summon me? Sindari charged after me. *The trouble just started.*

You should have assumed that your wedding would be full of it and come prepared with a powerful Del'nothian tiger at your side. He caught up with me and passed, bounding into the trees after Willard and Walker.

You're not wrong.

The clash of a weapon screeching against claw and fang sounded, followed by more gunshots. I grimaced. They weren't all from Willard's gun.

I raised Storm's barrier in anticipation of someone in the trees taking shots at me. But the attack came from the side, not up ahead. A blast of shamanic power burrowed into my shield, giving me an instant headache as it shattered Storm's spell. Sensing the barrier dissolving, I dove to the side. A rush of yellow energy crackled through the air, singeing my scalp as it passed above me.

A troll with short white hair sticking out in all directions stepped out from behind a tree, holding a mace with a star-shaped head that glowed with yellow light. It emanated almost as much power as the troll did. I'd found the other shaman brother.

He swore at me in his own language.

I swung Fezzik up and fired as he pointed the mace at me. As my rounds zipped toward his chest, he flicked a finger, and a square shield appeared in the air in front of him. It deflected the bullets into the trees, then disappeared in time for his mace to shoot another burst of yellow power at me.

This time, when I dove to the side, I angled toward him instead of away. If I could close the distance between us and attack him with my sword, I had a shot.

SECRETS OF THE SWORD III

Once again, the yellow blast flew over me without touching me, but its power sizzled across my skin, and pain erupted in my nerves. I swore. What the heck was that mace?

"You will not evade me, Ruin Bringer," the shaman rasped in throaty English. "You've killed my brothers, and I will have my revenge. You will not live to lure innocent trolls to your cafe, only to poison them or otherwise trick them to their deaths."

"That's not the plan. It's bad for business." Unfortunately, I couldn't say I'd had nothing to do with the brothers' deaths.

A roar sounded as I jumped to my feet, not a lion or tiger this time. It sounded like a dwarf. Chasmmoor. I hadn't even *seen* him and Dimitri yet. Hopefully, Dimitri would stay out of the trouble.

The thought had barely crossed my mind when the *thwump* of the magic de-amplifier they'd built echoed through the trees. A whoop came from Dimitri, wherever he was. Probably because he'd gotten the thing working, but did that mean there was yet another shaman? I hoped not.

Willard also shouted, firing again as Sindari sprang at a troll with a dagger that was trying to flank her. At least I had allies out here. Unfortunately, they were all deeper in the forest. I was on my own with this shaman.

"*Darayknar zerek*," I barked again to reactivate Storm's defenses.

Just in time. A second blast from the mace would have struck me square in the face. It flared when it hit my shield, blinding me with its intensity before it dissipated. I blinked away the stars dancing in my vision only to find that the shaman had disappeared. Not only from my view but from my senses.

Sindari? I spun a slow circle, certain the shaman was still nearby, certain he wanted to kill me. *I could use some help finding—*

A blast of power drilled through my barrier from behind. I whirled, spotted the shaman among the ferns, and willed energy of my own to shoot from Storm's tip. If only it had the power to do that. Almost immediately, I opened my mouth to give a real command, one of the ones from the scrolls, but the sword shocked me by blasting a fireball at the troll.

It didn't shock the shaman nearly as much as it did me. He saw it coming and deflected it with the rectangular energy shield that poofed into existence again. But when the fireball burst against it, he staggered back a step.

Sindari roared, trying to get to me, but two trolls with swords were in the way. Deliberately keeping him from interfering with my face-off with the shaman.

"Again, Storm," I whispered, willing another fireball to shoot from my sword's tip.

It did, just as large as before. Again, the shaman deflected it with his shield, but again he staggered back. He even dropped to one knee.

The fireballs were taking their toll on him. But they also took their toll on me. A familiar tightness spread through my chest. If I kept using Storm to hurl such powerful magic, I would end up on the ground, wheezing.

A new idea came to mind, and I used Freysha's teachings to coax roots up from below the shaman. His shield wasn't protecting him from below. He regained his feet, but before he could take more than a step, my roots wrapped around his ankles and anchored him to the ground.

He swore and swung his mace at them. The blunt weapon crushed the roots, the odor of damaged plant matter seeping into the air, but it didn't cut them. I willed them to grow stronger and farther up his legs as I advanced with Storm raised.

A boom came from the clearing, and the ground shook. Another grenade landing?

I snarled and charged at the shaman while he was distracted. This had to end before people were hurt.

He tried and failed to yank his feet free, then spread his hand toward the ground. Flames flared from his fingers and incinerated the roots. By then, I'd reached him. I swung, willing Storm to slice through any defenses he had up.

His shield flared to life, and my blade clanged off it as if it were made from steel. But a burst of light came from the contact point, and I sensed more than saw the shield disintegrating. I swung again, and this time, Storm whispered through the air unimpeded.

The shaman recognized the threat and whipped his mace up in time. His weapon stopped Storm inches from his eyes. I tried to push through, but his muscles strained, and the mace didn't budge.

"Ruin Bringer, you will fool nobody." He spat at me as we strained, trying to push me back as I tried to push his weapon to the side.

"I'm not *trying* to fool anybody." I leaped back, determined to take another swing rather than testing my muscles against his. "We're just making money and selling coffee, you stupid ass."

"A facade! You would slay our kind in the end, but I will end your life first." He leveled the mace at me.

I leaped in and knocked it aside an instant before his blast went off. The yellow burst of energy slammed into a tree, cleaving it in half. We both scrambled out of the way as it pitched over, branches breaking other branches and pine and fir needles showering us.

Our pause only lasted a second. We sprang at each other again, blade striking mace.

If I could get that weapon out of his hands, maybe I could end this. I didn't want to kill the bastard, especially if he thought he was protecting his people, but this was my wedding day, damn it.

Another grenade slammed down in the clearing.

With the trees in the way, and a mace whistling toward my head, I couldn't see if chairs and maybe buffet tables and Freysha's structures were being blown to bits, but I had no trouble envisioning it. Anger and frustration fueled me, and I whispered, "*Arunnat mak,*" willing Storm to aid me, to guide my movements and make them faster. Its replenishing magic swept through me, and for a few seconds, my lungs loosened, and air flowed freely into them.

With Storm's help, I drove the shaman back. Sweat streamed from his face as he struggled to sweep his mace high and low, defending in time against my attacks. His heel caught, and he almost went down. I urged roots to grow up again, ensnaring his legs. They pulled him to his knees.

"Give up," I ordered him. "I'm not the enemy you think I am."

Shouts and battle cries sounded from the trees all around me. Trolls were fighting trolls. At first, I was confused and couldn't understand why they were turning on each other, but then a troll lady I recognized—she frequented the shop—ran past with an improvised club. She smashed it into one of the big males that had been blocking Sindari.

My guests had come to help. They were fighting their own kind to save my wedding. To help *me*.

"You killed my brothers!" the shaman roared, drawing my focus back to him.

"Because they tried to kill *me*. I'm not your enemy. Surrender." I swung hard at the mace, trying to knock it out of his hands. His fingers loosened, and it tipped into the ferns.

"I will *die* first!" He grabbed for something inside his tunic.

Expecting a gun, I jumped back, raising Storm in case I needed the sword's power to knock aside a bullet. From so close, it would be hard, but the sword's magic still flowed through me, still ready to guide my arms.

But the shaman didn't throw anything. He glared at me with wild bloodshot eyes and gripped whatever it was close to his chest. Triumph lit in his eyes, confusing me until I realized what he held.

"Grenade!" I shouted a warning for anyone nearby as I scrambled backward.

But fear and the uneven ground thwarted me in a way the shaman hadn't been able to. My heel caught, and I tumbled backward before I could recover. Shit, I wasn't going to get far enough away before that thing blew up. I blurted the command to Storm to raise a shield around me but feared it was too late.

Then a huge black tail swung in from above and pounded the shaman into the ground like a pile driver. The grenade exploded as the troll's chest hit the ground, but magical power dropped around the area, muffling the explosion. Though I was less than ten feet away, I barely felt it.

The tail lifted—Zav's tail—covered in bits of troll, all that remained of the shaman.

"Gross," I muttered, though I was relieved that I wasn't also covered in bloody bits. Feeling battered and wheezy, I let Storm drop the shield. No more calling on its powers today, I hoped. "And thank you, Zav."

Why did you not alert me immediately to the trouble? Zav shook off his tail, then rubbed it in the ferns, and I almost laughed.

Everything happened too fast. And you were off at your races, out of my range.

I can hear your telepathic calls when you can't sense me. Zav shifted into his human form.

Sorry, I'll bellow into your mind next time.

Do. He came forward and hugged me fiercely. *Especially if you anticipate tripping at a crucial moment.*

You saw that, huh? I slumped against him, embarrassed. Elves, even half-elves, weren't supposed to trip.

I also saw you defeat a powerful shaman singlehandedly. You did not even have your tiger ally with you. A great many trolls are out here. Until the other trolls—and ogres and goblins and orcs—turned on them, and my kin arrived, it was doubtful your friends would win the day.

Your kin?

The gunshots and roars of tigers had stopped, and I looked around, hoping nobody had been seriously hurt—or worse—in the fighting. That was when I grew aware of the auras of dragons—*all* the dragons—in the area. My troll wedding guests weren't the only ones who had come to help.

The dragons were swooping through the trees, occasionally knocking *over* trees, as they chased after the invaders. Gouts of fire spewed from their throats, torching trolls, or at least incinerating their clothes as they sprinted off toward the road. One had the gumption—or suicidal tendencies—to spin and hurl a grenade at two dragons pursuing him. Was that the queen? And... the Silverclaw dragon? Flying after that poor troll together?

The grenade bounced off one of the dragon's shields and exploded in the treetops. They flew out of sight as they weaved through the trees, the troll screeching as he fled. *All* of the trolls were fleeing. I would, too, if a legion of dragons was after me.

"I believe they waited until my kind were all far away from the area before attacking," Zav said, stroking my hair, or maybe just picking fern fronds and pine needles out of it. "The trolls knew they could not win against dragons, so they sought to be sneaky. Cowards."

"I just hope they're done attacking me, my friends, and our coffee shop." I turned toward the clearing, though I couldn't tell from there how much damage had been done. "Can you tell if everyone is okay? Was anyone hurt?"

Willard, with Walker in lion form on one side of her and Sindari on the other, trod through the woods toward me. She gripped her sidearm with one hand and rested a hand on Walker's broad furry back with the other. Was she limping—or trying to hide a limp—and using him for support?

Pain tightened her face, but she greeted me with a complaint instead of commenting on her injury. "Your dragons drove them all away, Thorvald. Me and the kitties were just getting the upper hand."

Kitties? Sindari looked up at her with slitted eyes.

Walker shifted back into his human form, his expensive suit not even rumpled. "*Kitties*? I object highly, Willard. Kitties do not roar."

That is correct, Sindari said, though his telepathic words were probably only for me. *Next time, I shall fight at your side, Val, since you recognize me as the great and majestic predator that I am.*

"So sensitive," Willard murmured to Walker.

A great, majestic, and regal predator, I told Sindari.

Yes. Sindari came to my side and sat, tail swishing in agitation at Willard's slight.

"You know what I *don't* object to?" Walker asked.

"What's that?" Willard eyed him warily.

"Your hand on my ass." He grinned at her.

"It was on your *back*."

"Yes, but then I turned into a man again, and somehow, there it was. Caressing my lower cheeks." He glanced over his shoulder. "And it's still there."

She smirked and swatted him on the butt. Goodness, was that flirting from Willard?

The lady troll strode up with her club—was that the leg of one of the benches?—on her shoulder and two of the butcher goblins ambling alongside while swinging their meat cleavers and pantomiming battle moves.

"All have lived?" The troll lady looked around, blue fingers flexing on her club. "Good. The owners of the Coffee Dragon must be kept alive. This is the new place for our kind."

"The *Ruin Bringer* must be kept alive," one of the goblins said. "She is the mate of a dragon." He pointed at Zav without lifting his gaze from Zav's shoes—the Crocs had survived the battle and whatever duels and races he'd been engaged in. Alas. "Dragons must be kept pleased," the goblin added. "It is our honor to serve dragons!"

Did I not tell you this many times? Zav asked me telepathically.

You did.

Dragons do not lie.

"It is also our honor to drink the special goblin fuel blend at the Coffee Dragon," the other goblin said. "This wonderful aromatic substance will continue to flow there?"

"Yes," I said. "The remodeling is almost done. Come on by on Monday."

Overhead, visible through the smoke and tree branches, Xilneth soared past. Jace and Amber were on his back again, leaning over his side to peer down at us. Jace was gaping, his earphones half-falling off his head. How much of the battle had they seen? Amber gave me a thumbs-up. Relieved she was all right, I returned the gesture.

As Xilneth circled the area, he performed some aerial acrobatics, using his magic to keep his riders from falling off. My heart only climbed *halfway* up into my throat as Amber and Jace hung upside down on his back.

Zav, watching with eyes narrowed, sniffed disdainfully. Xilneth's display looked like the dragon equivalent of a victory dance. Maybe he'd flambéed a couple of trolls while he'd been flying around with Jace and Amber. I supposed that was better than having them down on the ground and in danger from grenades.

Your kin approach, Zav told me.

Eireth, Freysha, my half-cousins, and the bodyguards were jogging toward us from the direction of the old elven village. The battle had ended so quickly that they hadn't had a chance to participate. The bodyguards were probably happy about that.

Bits of frosting and cake stuck to one elf's cheek, and was that blood or ketchup in Freysha's hair? Maybe they'd participated after all. Or they'd been running through the field—and past the buffet—when that last grenade went off.

"Trolls?" Eireth peered through the trees toward the crumpled bodies of those who hadn't fled in time. "Why would they dare attack you when half of your guests are *dragons*?"

"I believe they thought the dragons were out of the picture." I waved in the direction they'd been hunting before they'd learned of the sport right here.

"Actually," the troll lady said, "I heard them cursing at each other. They didn't know dragons would *be* at the wedding. The invitation failed to mention it."

"Because," I said, "I didn't think anyone would show up if they knew fire-breathing beings capable of crushing a person to death with a single careless landing would be here."

"I do not land carelessly," Zav said.

"A chimney, a stovepipe, a mailbox, twenty-seven deck chairs, six reindeer, and a Santa suggest otherwise," I said.

"You are teasing me."

"Yes, I am."

"I will allow this," he murmured, "since I plan to tease you later."

"Hopefully not during the ceremony."

"In the nest." His eyes glinted. "With the feather."

"I look forward to it."

"Good."

"The shaman coerced them into attacking," the troll lady said, ignoring the steamy looks Zav and I were giving each other, "against their better judgment. It is good he is gone. He and his brothers were buzzkills."

I blinked at the term.

"I am learning human slang," she said. "From the goblins at the Coffee Dragon."

"They are the ultimate resource in all things human," I said.

"Is there more food?" The troll slapped her club against her palm and strode toward the field. "I have worked up an appetite." The goblins trotted after her while calling toward their village in their own tongue. Maybe putting in orders for roasted haunches.

"There goes the rest of the food." I batted at smoke wafting toward us from fires that had started either from the grenades or from the dragons breathing flames through the trees. "How about we get this place cleaned up, get everyone healed up, and have a wedding?"

"I am amenable to this," Zav said. "The troll female has reminded me that it is time to feast."

"Is it hard work flattening trolls with your tail?"

"It is. Also, I had to exert myself in the races and the duels."

"Did you beat Xilneth?" I asked.

"I defeated three opponents in duels and excelled in the races."

"You didn't answer my question."

"Correct."

"Because you lost to him?" I smirked, now understanding the aerial victory dance I'd witnessed.

"Since he is a coward and a hippie, he is accustomed to fleeing from fights frequently. Since I face my battles, I am less practiced at racing off at top speed."

"You lost to him by a *lot*."

"I did not. It was a very close race."

"Will he tease you about it later?" I couldn't stop smirking at him.

"If he does, I will smash him."

"With your tail?"

"Yes." Zav wrapped his arm around my shoulders. "Come, my mate. We must feast and wed."

CHAPTER 34

SEEING WILLARD IN A DRESS was the strangest part of my wedding. Battling trolls, feeding ogres, and dodging dragons dropping carcasses paled in comparison. She was, however, impressively elegant as she walked down the aisle in a flowing blue A-line dress with a V-neck—terms I only knew thanks to Amber. She'd picked out the bridesmaid ensembles, proclaiming that I couldn't be trusted not to get something horrendous with poofy sleeves.

Amber, Nin, and Freysha walked ahead of Willard in matching dresses with silver-and-blue headdresses of leaves in their hair—Freysha's contribution. The height disparity between Amber and Nin was prominent, but all four women managed to walk in step, as if they'd practiced this numerous times.

As far as I knew, nobody had practiced, including myself—it had been a busy week. And ever since the guests had assembled, standing and sitting in the chairs and benches that had escaped annihilation, I'd been glancing at Willard for cues. After all, she had watched her niece's wedding footage enough times to memorize it.

Eireth, who stood at my side, ready to *give me away*—I'd known enough to explain that part of the ceremony to him—kept glancing at *me* for cues. Maybe humans were inherently supposed to know how weddings went.

Mom was on my other side. After I'd teased her about her paint-splattered Crocs, she'd removed them and now stood barefoot in her kaftan, wriggling her toes in the grass. No biggie. We weren't a formal and proper family. And none of the ogres, trolls, orcs, shifters, or goblins seemed to mind. Half of *them* weren't wearing shoes either as they sat or stood on the grassy areas in between the craters the grenades had left.

Behind them, the dragons had taken up positions between the end of the clearing and the start of the goblin village. A *lot* of dragons. I'd stopped counting at twenty. Everyone was giving them a wide berth as they traveled to and from the village, though they were much more sedate than I'd envisioned. Most, tired after the hunt and sated after gorging on food, were lying down, some openly sleeping in the sun. *Xilneth* was snoring. Who would have thought a dragon could snore? None of his kin were. Maybe he had a nostril obstruction.

The Silverclaw dragon glared at him whenever a high-pitched nose whistle mingled with the snores. I caught Xilneth opening an eye to check on him once. Maybe he was deliberately irritating the old gray dragon.

Zondia and the queen sat upright, watching the goings on, though the queen kept clacking her jaws, possibly in disapproval. Earlier, she'd wanted to know why Zav couldn't marry me in his true form. I'd explained the requirement of the kiss and how odd that would be if he were a dragon, and she'd curled her lip—inasmuch as dragons had lips—and said she trusted we would not engage in a human mating ritual in front of her. Zav had promised we would wait until we were in the nest to do that, which hadn't done much to fix her lip curl.

Zav's three brothers, whom he'd introduced me to briefly, were also alert, though they were more focused on the Silverclaw dragon than our ceremony, maybe making sure he didn't cause trouble. To my surprise, he hadn't started anything—he'd even flown into battle with the queen and helped drive off several trolls. The last I'd heard, he'd enjoyed himself here, and the talks he and the queen were having might actually lead to the formation of a peace treaty between the two powerful clans.

That didn't keep him from glaring balefully at me from time to time, but he could hate me all he wanted as long as he didn't act on those feelings. Besides, Zav hadn't shown any concern for the Silverclaw, at least while I'd been watching.

He stood in his spot, waiting patiently with his hands clasped behind his back, looking handsome and tidy in his elven robe. No sign of the troll bits that had stuck to his tail were visible on his clothing. He was alternating between smiling over at me with his lustful bedroom eyes and sending equally lustful looks toward the buffet. The food Willard had ordered from the caterer had all been devoured, despite the shockwave from a grenade knocking over a tray-laden table and flinging canapés everywhere. Fortunately, our goblin hosts had been assiduous in bringing out freshly roasted meat from the dragons' kills. My non-human guests were enjoying that. I'd caught Willard slipping a protein bar out of her purse and lamenting that she hadn't sampled the catered food earlier.

Dimitri, Zav's sole groomsman, was decked out in a tuxedo that Amber had chosen for him, likely the most expensive and dressy thing he'd ever worn. He'd balked at the price until I'd pointed out that he could wear it again when *he* got married. He'd started to scoff, but then his eyes had narrowed in speculation, and he'd said okay.

He stood off to the side with Chasmmoor, glancing over at their magic de-amplifier, which rested in the grass. Dimitri was proud that he'd used it to remove the magic from a troll warrior's weapon and knock a minor shaman on his butt—earlier, he'd lugged it up from his van *just in case*. But during the battle, he'd pulled a back muscle and now kept touching the spot gingerly. The injury hadn't come from fighting a troll but from carrying the heavy device through the mud. I suspected a more compact version would be in the works soon.

Chasmmoor hadn't changed clothes for the wedding. He wore his usual attire of dusty brown trousers and tunic, but his plate armor gleamed under the afternoon sun, and nobody suggested he was anything but handsome. Given that he'd rushed into battle with his big axe and chopped the heads off three trolls—literally—I doubted anyone would insult him. Ever.

Sindari sat with them, alternately getting his ears scratched by Dimitri and Chasmmoor. Either all dwarves had good hands, or all smiths, artisans, and enchanters did. The latter seemed likely.

The harpist, who'd survived the attack unscathed, and even played *O Fortuna* as the dragons swept in to drive off the trolls, was poised to start the *Wedding March*, as Willard had ordered. I'd slipped the harpist a twenty and asked for it to segue into something more appropriate to my tastes.

Up in the second story of one of Freysha's structures, Tam had taken the job of recording the wedding and was set up with Zoltan's equipment.

I hadn't realized it earlier, but she'd been recording since before I arrived and had gotten footage of the dragon races, food gorging, and of course the battle. I wondered how much of that would go up on YouTube and envisioned advertisers pulling their ads and blocking them from playing on Zoltan's channel ever again.

"Are you ready, Val?" Mom asked quietly, nodding toward the clear aisle and the human priest and goblin shaman waiting to marry us in both languages. After giving me away, Eireth would join them for the elven version.

I stretched out with my senses and scanned the blue sky for trouble, though trouble would be suicidal to attack with more than twenty dragons lounging nearby. "Yes."

"Is it concerning that those ogres are watching everything while avidly ripping the flesh off drumsticks?" Mom was eyeing our audience.

"No, that's normal," I said as my ring bearer and flower girl—two young goblins who'd volunteered for the duties—headed down the aisle.

The flower girl decided it was more fun to pelt the people in the seats with the petals instead of scattering them on the ground. Mary ended up with a flower sticking out of her ear, making me wish I'd chosen a safer seat for her, something farther from the aisle.

The ring bearer poked the flower girl in the side, trying to get her to stop. That earned him a flower up the nose. Maybe I should have taken Mom up on her offer to train Rocket to carry the rings. An orc, who did not appreciate the flower petals that ended up dusting his drumstick, stood up and roared at the kids. The girl shrieked, threw the basket in the air, and scurried to safety behind the goblin shaman. The disgruntled orc sat back down and picked petals off his meal.

"You have an eclectic assortment of guests," Mom said blandly.

"Zav wanted a lot of presents."

"You accomplished that." Mom glanced toward the gazebo holding the towering pile of gifts, then looked toward the crate in the village, the top visible over a one-story dwelling. "Do you think there's anything useful in there? Like an espresso machine?"

"That would be on *your* wedding registry, not mine."

"If you got one, you wouldn't use it, and you would give it to me."

"True, but I think most of the things in there are for Zav." I'd walked close enough to the gazebo to catch whiffs of beef jerky, pepperoni sticks, and salami logs. "Our guests were more concerned about pleasing him than me."

"Aren't you the Ruin Bringer?" Mom asked as we started walking, Eireth listening to the conversation but not chiming in. He might not know what an espresso machine was. After all, he'd only recently learned about frozen yogurt.

"Only to enemies. And obtuse trolls."

Aware of Tam's camera running, I smiled and attempted to look radiant as we walked slowly up the aisle. Zav shifted his focus from the buffet to me as I approached. It was good to know I ranked at least as important as food in his eyes.

The *Wedding March* played, per Willard's request, then shifted into something else familiar, though it took me a moment to identify it. The Han and Leia theme from the original trilogy. I grinned over at the harpist as Willard shot her a suspicious and scathing look.

After my parents moved to the side, Mom joining Liam, and Eireth joining Freysha, Zav came forward, hugged me, and kissed me—ardently.

We're supposed to say our vows before we get to that part. I kissed him back but only briefly before using my arm to rotate him to face the priest and shaman.

I had a haunch of yorak before this began.

Feeling extra amorous, huh?

Indeed. He beamed a smile into my eyes and ignored the priest until the poor fellow cleared his throat.

A short, wispy-haired man with gnomish blood, he didn't appear fazed by anything going on today, including the shaman chanting a goblin blessing at his side. I had no idea if Willard had known about the priest's magical heritage when she'd chosen him, but it now made sense why *quirky* weddings didn't bother him.

The priest raised his arms toward the sky. "Dearly beloved, we are gathered here today to join this man and this woman in holy matrimony."

The goblin shaman raised his arms to the sky, shook a hollow stick full of beads, and said his bit. "Workers, today we join this dragon and half-elf as a work party of two before the great and wise eyes of the gods of labor, fecundity, and pleasure."

I'd activated my translation charm earlier, figuring it would be wise to know what everyone was promising to the gods on our behalf. That Zav and I would be happy, fecund, and good workers, apparently.

Eireth pressed his hands together in front of his chest and said, "Esteemed family and colleagues, it is the will of the earth and the sky and all of the nature that thrives in the Cosmic Realms that these honorary citizens of the elven world be wed in the elven way."

The priest waited until he was sure they'd said their parts, then asked us, "You have your own vows, I'm told?"

"Yes." I clasped Zav's hands and faced him. "Lord Zavryd'nokquetal Stormforge."

His brows rose. *You said my whole name,* he spoke telepathically. *You've overcome your tongue impediment.*

I've been able to say it for a while. I winked at him. *I was waiting for a special occasion.*

Hm.

"I, Valmeyjar Thorvald—" I expected someone to snicker at my full name but only caught an amused smirk from Amber, "—promise to ride into battle on your back, to remain faithful to you in the nest, and to use the power of my ring to prepare finely smoked meat for you on a regular basis for as long as we both live. I love you and will kick the ass of anyone who tries to keep us apart."

Zav radiated satisfaction at me—especially at the part about smoked meat.

"Are you allowed to say *ass* in a wedding?" Amber whispered to Thad and Jace.

"I, Lord Zavryd'nokquetal Stormforge," Zav said, ignoring her, "promise to let you ride on my back whenever you wish, protect you in battle, please you in the nest, and use my power to kick the ass of anyone who tries to keep us apart."

He gave a pointed look to the Silverclaw dragon, but the big silver had plopped down next to the queen and appeared to be sleeping, his tail touching the tip of hers. In a moment of startling and unasked for clarity, I realized those two might be dating. Well, Zav's father had been gone for a while, so why not?

"I also love you and will mate with no other," Zav finished, squeezing my hands.

"That's so romantic." One of the female goblins in the audience dabbed a greasy rag to the corner of her eye.

"If that's all," the priest said, "I now pronounce you man and wife. You may kiss the bride—again."

Zav did, and I melted against his chest, relieved that we'd survived the day, and excited to officially be married to one sexy dragon who thought I was pretty amazing too.

I was too busy enjoying the moment and returning his amorous kiss to hear what Eireth and the shaman said for their concluding words. Claps, shouts, and whoops came from the audience—and that roar either belonged to Sindari or Walker. They subsided before our kiss did, and our guests beelined for the buffet area. This was the hungriest group of wedding-goers I'd ever seen.

My family and close friends—those who weren't that interested in haunches of yorak—came up to congratulate us with hugs and kisses and thumps on the back.

Work Leader Nogna squeezed through the crowd of taller people and tugged on our sleeves. "It is time to open the wedding gifts."

"Uhm, humans don't usually open gifts at the wedding," I said. "Or if they do, it's after cake and—"

"*Goblins* open gifts immediately," she interrupted, her eyes gleaming. "So that all may appreciate the fine craftsmanship of the goblin gift givers." She looked toward the massive crate with pride in her eyes.

"Ah." I pointed toward the village. "Shall we, Zav?"

Since the goblins had lent us their sanctuary and offered so much help with the wedding, I didn't want to offend them. As we headed toward the village, I practiced my version of a delighted smile. And wondered how many semi-trucks and forklifts it would take to transport their gift to our house. Maybe it would be *impossible* to transport, and we would be forced to use it only when we visited the goblins. A maximum of once a year. This was an appealing idea.

My son, the queen spoke telepathically as we walked past the dragons.

Yes? Zav asked warily, stopping and facing her.

I clasped his hand in case she was about to lecture him and he needed support.

This festivity was not displeasing. The troll hunt at the end was most enjoyable.

Zav's jaw dangled open in surprise for a few seconds before he closed it, lifted his chin, and nodded firmly. *I am pleased you found it acceptable.*

We will return to our world shortly. Do not remain too long at a time in that meager form, and do not forget to build a suitable dragon cave for when you must stay on this world with your mate.

I will heed your advice. With his chin still up, Zav headed toward the village.

Mate of my son, Zynesshara spoke telepathically, singling me out.

I released Zav's hand and faced her, feeling just as wary as he'd been. *Yes?*

She stared into my eyes and sent telepathic images into my mind. I braced myself, expecting her to show me something awful, such as what might happen to me if I failed to be a good mate to her son, but she was sharing images—no, *memories*—with me. Of Zav. Young Zav hatching out of his egg, then learning to walk, learning to fly, learning to breathe fire—oops, that tree hadn't made it—and stalking his first prey—something that looked like a fat squirrel. He wasn't goofy or snaggletoothed, but he *was* cute.

Remembering that she denied dragons were ever cute, I kept that thought to myself. But I couldn't keep from grinning.

You are satisfied, mate of my son? she asked as the images faded.

Yes. Thank you.

Zav came back, clasped my hand, gave his mother a suspicious look, and led me toward the village. I kissed him on the cheek as we walked.

He turned the suspicious look on me and muttered, "Females."

Dozens of goblins and other guests trailed us to the towering crate in the center of the village. Dimitri, Chasmmoor, and Freysha were already in the area, letting a goblin guide them around and show off various enchanted objects, such as a silver hitching post with a bridle hanging from it. Since there weren't any horses in the area, I could only guess what was out here that the goblins wanted to domesticate. Maybe that elven guardian?

I stepped far enough away from the crate that it wouldn't crush us if the sides fell down. Zav stood at my side, not relinquishing my hand.

Do you know what's inside? I asked.

His suspicious look faded, and he smiled slyly at me. *Yes.*

Will I like it?

You will enjoy using it with me.

That was vague. *Will there be room for it at the house?*

We will make *room.*

Ah.

The goblin shaman appeared with his stick full of beads and chanted a few things as he strode around the crate, tapping each side and saying what sounded like a blessing. Finally, he lifted his arms and with a trickle of magic, one of the sides creaked open from the top. It tipped outward, landing with a thud on the packed-dirt road and revealing…

I tilted my head to either side, regarding it from several angles. "Is it… a sauna? And… something else?"

There were *two* doors to two corrugated-metal and plywood-paneled cabins attached to each other with metal bars supporting a hot tub in the middle. It was like some bizarre giant dumbbell. The hot tub was familiar, and I realized it was the one the goblins had made for us before, but it had been upgraded and was now powered by a magical heater—my senses told me it was magical, not the fact that it looked like twenty rolls of aluminum foil crinkled together into a ball. There were *three* magical heaters, the others hidden in the cabins.

"A hot box—" Zav pointed to one of the doors—a red one made from recycled stop signs—with a flourish, "a water box—" he waved to the hot tub, "—and a *steam* box." He walked up and rested a loving hand on the last cabin.

I'd never seen anyone lovingly caress rusted corrugated metal before. The idea of this thing in the yard behind my beautifully remodeled Victorian house was appalling.

"A hot box?" Amber asked from behind me. "Really, Val. I didn't know you were into that."

"It's a sauna," I said over my shoulder.

"Sure it is."

When I noticed Dimitri gripping his chin and gazing thoughtfully at it, I made a note to put a *no smoking* sign on the door. Assuming this went back to the house. I didn't see how it could. Everything was attached.

All of the goblins were looking at me. They seemed to assume Zav loved it, but maybe they wanted to know what I thought.

"It's a fabulous gift. Thank you. But it looks too large to transport back to our house in Green Lake." I attempted to put a sad note in my voice. "Zav and I will happily come visit you to use it here."

Zav lowered his hand. "Too large to transport? We will use *magic* to transport it."

"Isn't that asking a lot of even dragon magic? It's huge."

"You married a dragon, and you do not even realize how powerful dragon magic is?" Zav touched his chest.

"Surely, you can't put it in an interdimensional pocket."

"There is no need." Zav stepped back and lifted a hand, his fingers splayed.

With a great swelling of power, his magic wrapped around the entire structure, eased it out of the crate and then, without even spilling a drop of hot-tub water, lifted it into the air.

The goblins whooped and cheered. I watched, not sure whether to be impressed by his power or horrified that this thing was on its way to my house.

Led by Xilneth, several dragons in the clearing sprang into the air and flew up to surround the structure. Was there any chance they would think it was a heinous threat to all of dragon kind and torch it? Alas, no. They were *escorting* it.

"You might want to try to beat them home," Nin murmured, stepping up beside me. "So they don't put it in the *front* yard."

"Uh, yeah." I patted Zav's shoulder. "We need to go now."

He hadn't heard Nin's comment, so he smiled broadly. "You are eager to try out our gift? And then mate? I understand that mating is important to do promptly after the wedding. It is a human cultural imperative."

"As is making sure the huge box trio gets appropriately placed."

"Excellent. I will take you home now."

As he shifted into dragon form, I caught Willard's eye. She'd watched in horror until the huge contraption disappeared over the trees.

"Do you need us for anything? Or can we go?" I tilted a thumb in the direction our gift was going.

"Oh, you better go quickly." She nodded after it. "I'll handle the cleanup."

"You're a good woman."

"I'm a saint. You owe me big time."

"Three jobs on the house?"

"That'll do." Willard waved as Zav levitated me onto his back and added, "Godspeed!"

As we sprang into the air, the goblins, and maybe a few others, cheered and waved.

A fine wedding, my mate, Zav spoke into my mind as we flew up over the trees.

Yeah, it was. And you're a fine dragon.

Yes, I am.

I patted his back. *Now fly faster, so we get home before that thing.*

EPILOGUE

ZAV AND I ARRIVED EARLY Monday morning for the grand reopening of the Coffee Dragon. Dimitri had surprised me by accepting that we needed to rename it—maybe he'd also heard numerous patrons referring to it that way—and he'd used his artistic skills to revise the sign. There was still a huge black dragon on the front—a fair likeness of Zav—but now the dragon had a taloned foot wrapped around a mug of coffee as steam wafted out of his nostrils. It was supposed to be a result of the beverage rather than any incipient incineration, but that was open for interpretation.

The previously damaged wall had been repaired—in fact, all of the old yellow siding had been replaced by something extremely sturdy and flame retardant. Since I'd seen Freysha's blueprints, I wasn't that surprised by the new second-floor addition. Its *size* was a little startling.

"I didn't know you could build a second floor that has a larger footprint than the first floor," I said.

Zav sniffed. "How long will we stay here? I am eager to return to our domicile to start working on my man cave."

"I already told you that you can't tear down the house next door."

"Dimitri has informed me that it would be appropriate to turn the attic into a man cave. I am contemplating how this might be done with magic. A cave needs rocks, dirt, and pools filled by water dripping from stalactites."

Oh, wouldn't it be lovely to have those things in the attic?

"We got a new sauna, a steam room, and a hot tub. Why don't you spend your free time out there?" I'd hoped the three-in-one contraption would fall to the ground during its journey to the city, but no such luck. Dragon magic had prevailed, and the structure now occupied an enormous portion of our backyard. Freysha was concerned that it was blocking morning light to the conservatory and was now making plans to add a second floor to *that*.

Being a homeowner wasn't bad, and I liked the location of the old Victorian, but a couple times this past week, I'd caught myself wondering if we needed to move out to the country—or maybe the woods near Mom—so we could have more room. Maybe we could find a house on acreage with a cave already on the property. Would Dimitri and Zoltan follow us to a new home? Would I mind if they *didn't*? If Zav and I had our own place, we wouldn't have to worry about being too noisy in the nest—not that *he* ever worried about that.

At least my elven houseguests had gone back to their world after the wedding. I understood Liam was pleased about that and had resumed morning coffee dates with my mother. Now that he was showing up with elk steaks for Rocket, there had been fewer golden retriever barking sessions.

Freysha and Chasmmoor were still staying at our house, Freysha because she was finishing her year of study on Earth and Chasmmoor because I needed more training with my sword. Or so he said. He spent a couple of hours with me each night and the rest of his time chumming around with Dimitri.

When Zav and I had left this morning, they'd been in the basement, building a device for deterring birds—the flicker's pecking was interfering with Zoltan's beauty rest, so he'd commissioned it. He'd said that as long as Dimitri and Chasmmoor were in his basement using the anvil so often, they could craft him something. Zoltan had also suggested that they might enjoy using anvils on the dwarven home world even *more* than the one in his lab, and wouldn't Chasmmoor like to take Dimitri for a visit? Chasmmoor had agreed that it would be educational for Dimitri to visit the homeland of his ancestors, so they were planning that trip with even more fervor than Zav and I were planning our honeymoon.

"I *do* look forward to using the sauna frequently," Zav said. "Each morning while you are meditating. Perhaps each night. And for mid-afternoon naps. When did you say winter ends on this world?"

"In another month and a half." I didn't have the heart to tell him that Seattle springs tended to be as rainy as the winters and not much warmer.

"Until this time, I may need *multiple* naps in the sauna."

"I can have your ribs served to you there if you wish."

"That would be magnificent. You may join me, and we will eat together and bask in the luxurious dry heat." Zav shivered and eyed the cloudy sky, no doubt fantasizing about it right now.

His gaze shifted toward a handsome man in a brown leather jacket strolling along the sidewalk toward us. Our eyes met, and he started to give me a flirtatious smile, but then glanced at Zav. He wasn't close enough to hear the growl in Zav's throat, but *I* heard it. The man glanced at my hand—or maybe my new wedding ring—then looked toward the sidewalk and hurried past without further eye contact.

"Excellent," Zav said. "The ring works. Now all males, even verminous humans with no ability to sense magic, know that we are mated and you are unavailable."

"Even without the ring, I think he would have figured that out when you loomed at my shoulder and growled at him."

"An intimidating growl reinforces proper behavior."

"Is that a dragon saying?"

"It is a Lord Zavryd'nokquetal saying."

"I'll make a note of it in case I ever pen your memoir."

"You are an attentive mate. This pleases me."

Nin must have noticed us outside, for she jogged out and clasped my hand. "Come inside, Val and Lord Zavryd. I will give you a tour of the new upstairs and the new bathroom."t"We got a bathroom remodel?" I asked. "I thought we were just replacing the toilet. And the wall it flew through."

"The goblins, after someone mentioned that heated seats and bidets were popular in some countries, crafted a few upgrades."

"Do they work?"

"Mostly."

"Remind me to go before leaving the house whenever I come to visit," I muttered to Zav.

I clasped his hand and led him inside, though from his glassy-eyed expression, he was fantasizing about his new sauna/steam room/hot tub. Or maybe eating ribs in his new sauna/steam room/hot tub.

"We replaced the little kiosk with a full-sized coffee counter." Nin gestured toward the permanent fixture that had replaced the portable one. "This will make things easier on our barista and prevent ogres from bumping the kiosk and sending it skidding across the floor."

"Practical."

I noticed Willard and Walker sitting at a small table in the back and didn't pay much attention to the rest of the tour of the first floor, which included some improvements to the display cases and more seating nooks. Were they on a date? Or was this a work meeting? Willard had a messenger bag, and Walker had his medical kit, but they were also drinking coffee.

"Yes. This way." Nin headed toward the hallway in the back. It had been widened, and a staircase now climbed up over the storage closet to the new second floor.

"Hi, guys." I couldn't keep from pausing at Willard's table. I had to know. "Is this a date?"

"Dr. Walker brought me an invoice." Willard sipped from an extremely dark cup of coffee. Was that the special goblin blend?

"For services rendered at the wedding?"

He *had* pulled out his medical kit there and bandaged a few people, though Zondia and Zav had healed those who'd been seriously injured.

"I wouldn't charge for those," Walker drawled with a smile. "I got all I needed in return for my work there."

"The satisfaction of seeing me married? Or Willard squeezing your butt?"

"Yes." His smile widened.

"There wasn't any *squeezing*," Willard said. "And he only got a touch because he *tricked* me by shifting forms while I had my hand on his back."

"You did pat his butt afterward," I noted.

"She doesn't admit to that," Walker said. "Says I imagined it."

"I saw it," I said.

"You're not helping," Willard told me.

"Given all the wicked glints you got in your eyes when Zav first claimed me, I think it's my turn to not help."

Willard rolled her eyes.

I gave Walker a thumbs-up. He was wearing her down. I could tell.

"Have you and Zav planned your honeymoon yet?" Willard asked.

"We've started to. He's intrigued by pigs roasted in pits in Hawaii."

"If it can wait a week, I've got a new gig for you. Trouble at a lavender farm over on the Olympic Peninsula."

"I hear lavender attracts bad guys like honey attracts bears."

"I'll text you the details. Nin is waving for you from the hallway."

"Right." I remembered that I'd promised to do three jobs for free for Willard, so I didn't bother asking about pay.

As I walked to join Nin, I almost tripped over Reb. He was dancing around the shop with the wooden practice sword I'd given him. He thwacked a display case, a coat rack, a chair, and challenged a potted rubber-tree plant to a duel. I'd started teaching him a few moves. It was encouraging to see him practicing.

"Hey, Val." When the tree declined the challenge, Reb waved his sword in my direction. "You said my new sparring partner is coming here today?"

"Yes." I glanced at the time on my phone. "She'll be here in a few minutes, and we'll go to the park."

"She?" Reb wrinkled his nose. "I thought it would be someone tough. A *guy*."

"She's tough. Trust me." I hoped Amber didn't show up in her pink and purple athletic wear. I'd told her she would meet a new sparring partner today, but I hadn't mentioned that it was a nine-year-old troll boy. If I had, she might not have agreed to come.

"Okay, I guess." Reb thumped off down the hallway, practicing the lunges I'd taught him during our first lesson.

According to Inga, he'd been lunging and thrusting all around their apartment and had left three holes in the walls. Impressive considering it was a blunt wooden sword.

With the way clear, Nin and I headed for the wide wooden stairs, but she paused before starting up.

"I should inform you, Val, that I have decided to close the magical-weapons-crafting portion of my business."

"Completely? You're not making bullets or grenades anymore?"

Nin hesitated. "I will keep my tools and craft ammunition for you, because you are a good friend."

"I appreciate that."

"But I will no longer make weapons for strangers who may use them to harm others."

"If you're closing down the more lucrative half of your business, does that mean you've saved up enough money to buy a house and bring your family to America?"

"I believe that if I purchase a house for them in the suburbs instead of in Seattle, I have enough for a sizable down payment."

"The suburbs out near Edmonds perhaps?" I nudged her, aware that she'd gone home from the wedding with Thad.

"Edmonds is an expensive suburb. I am looking in Mountlake Terrace."

"So five minutes from Edmonds."

"Yes." Nin smiled. "The median home price there is more than one-hundred-and-fifty-thousand dollars less."

"That's because there aren't any views of Puget Sound. Just trees."

"Trees are lovely. After living in a small apartment in the city, my family will enjoy them."

"And will you live *with* your family or in the adjacent suburb?" I arched my eyebrows. "In a house with a huge table dedicated to role-playing games?"

"You can also dine at it. It is very versatile."

"I heard about the cup holders."

"It is possible that I will one day live there, but there is no hurry."

There might be once her huge family was sharing a house with her. She only had *three* roommates at her current place. When she was back up to eight or nine, things might feel a touch crowded. Not that I would know about excessive roommates.

"I will show you our new upstairs now." Nin nodded toward the stairs.

"I look forward to it." My senses told me that Zav was already up there. He must have been indifferent to whether or not Walker and Willard were on a date.

As we turned the corner at the halfway point on the stairs, a twenty-sided die clacked off the wall above our heads. Nin picked it up without comment, carried it to the loft-like upstairs, and plopped it down on a table surrounded by goblins and supporting no fewer than twenty coffee mugs, most empty.

"Is that a catapult?" I pointed to the dice launcher in the center of the table. "On a lazy Susan?"

I'd never seen a catapult that rotated before.

"On a what?" Gondo gave the contraption a bewildered look. Maybe goblins had another term for those spinning disks.

"Never mind."

Once we were certain our heads weren't in the way of the next dice launch, Nin showed me around the high-ceilinged open space. Vining plants wound up the walls and across the beamed ceiling. Freysha's touch, no doubt. The lines were also softer than typical in a modern loft space, and one wall held an engraving of a tree that radiated faint magic.

More of Zoltan's and Dimitri's wares were behind display cases against walls, but most of the space was dedicated to couches, coffee tables, reading chairs, beanbag chairs, and a video-game area with three large-screen TVs on the wall. Goblins and werewolves were competing at a shooting game where the avatars battled giant dinosaurs in the jungle. Zav stood behind the couch with his hands clasped behind his back and his eyes narrowed as he watched. Hopefully, he realized those were dinosaurs and not dragons, and wouldn't take offense. Those TVs were brand new—and doubtless expensive. Dimitri would object to them being incinerated.

"Did we come into some extra money?" I whispered to Nin. "I didn't give Dimitri enough to buy TVs and furniture." I pointed to one of the brown couches. "Is that leather? That looks like leather. *Nice* leather."

"I believe it is," Nin said. "Many of the furnishings and all three TVs were wedding gifts addressed to you. They came in one large shipment. Someone ordered them online and had them delivered."

"*Who*? Mom and Liam brought all the gifts over from the wedding, and we weren't missing any from anyone." After seeing the giant goblin gift installed, we'd opened the huge stack of presents and confirmed that most of them were meat snacks for Zav, though there had also been a tasteful selection of chocolates from Sarrlevi, along with a note in elvish wishing us good fortune. Mom, who'd stuck around for the unwrapping, had been disappointed by the lack of an espresso maker that she could hijack.

"An unknown benefactor. But this also came at the same time, so it might contain the answer. I did not presume to open it." Nin held up a finger, went to a cabinet, and withdrew a rectangle wrapped in brown paper. *Val Thorvald* was written on the front but nothing else.

I opened it and found a silver plaque with a triangular play button on the front. "Presented to The Alchemist for passing one-hundred-thousand subscribers. YouTube." I grunted. "*Zoltan?* All this stuff is from Zoltan? He bought me wedding presents that are for a business he's an owner in? A larger owner than I am?"

"Vampires are perhaps not the most tactful gift givers."

"No kidding. At least the ogres gave us meat. Meat that was for Zav, not them."

A small card slipped out and fell to the floor. I opened it and read it aloud.

"Greetings, dear robber. I have made you a special alchemical formula that will enhance your bedroom activities—ahem, your *nest* activities—with your strapping dragon mate, and I left it on the table in your hallway, but I am most grateful for the role your wedding footage played in helping me blow past one-hundred-thousand subscribers. I am now well on my way to one million, at which point I will receive a new and larger plaque. The ad revenue has more than doubled already for the month. Who knew so many people wanted to see dragons torching trolls into charred pieces? And, of course, the wedding itself was most popular. People are watching the entire four hours of footage. Amazing. I dedicate this plaque to you, and I've had a few baubles delivered to the shop so there is more seating and our customers will stay longer. No need to thank me. Ta ta."

"What kind of formula enhances bedroom activities?" Nin wondered.

"I don't know, but I'm not rubbing anything Zoltan made on my lady bits."

Nin touched a finger to her lip. "Maybe it goes on Zavryd's lord bits."

I wrinkled a lip, as that notion deserved.

Two people clomped up the stairs, one banging something against the wall. Amber came into view with her gym bag slung over her shoulder, the tips of her wooden swords sticking out. Jace was right behind her, large wireless earphones affixed to his head with hip-hop beats leaking out. When Zav looked over at him, Jace nodded in appreciation and gave him a sign-of-the-horns hand gesture. It might have meant Zav rocked or it might have been a reference to the actual horns he had in his dragon form.

What does that gesture mean? Zav asked me telepathically. *Does he insult me?*

No, I replied. *I think he's into you. You let everyone see your majestic dragon form during the wedding, even the mere mundane humans.*

Yes. I gave them this honor on our day of public joining, so all would know that you are mated to a dragon.

Well, now you've got admirers.

Hm.

Jace ambled across the room, plopped down in a giant chair, and bobbed his head to his tunes. Zav eyed him, then sat on the couch next to the goblin gamers and cocked his ankle up on his opposite knee. As usual, the hem of his elven robe hiked up into scandalous territory, but he was too far away for me to adjust his position. Since everyone over there was male, maybe it didn't matter.

Jace propped his own ankle up on his knee, an innocuous gesture since his ripped jeans covered him suitably. Zav looked smugly over at me as if to say he'd *known* this was how human males were supposed to sit. I had a feeling Jace would emulate him even if he sat with his ankles behind his head and spun like a top.

"This place is *huge* now." Amber had stopped next to me and was gaping around. "That tree is wicked good art. Who made it?" She pointed to the wall.

"Freysha, I believe. Your aunt." I'd told Amber that Freysha was my half-sister, but I hadn't ever pointed out the relationship that gave them.

"The blonde elf girl? She gets to be my aunt *and* a princess?"

"Two equal honors, I'm sure."

"*I* think so. Uh, what is the goblin doing?" She pointed toward Zav's couch. All except one brave goblin had cleared off, and that one was showing him how to use a game controller. A car-racing track had replaced the dinosaur-hunter game on the main TV, and Zav was leaning left and right as he steered his virtual vehicle left and right.

I sighed. "Humanizing my dragon."

"Geekizing, you mean."

"Possibly."

"When do I meet my new sparring partner?" Amber wasn't wearing pink and purple, but she *was* wearing a girlie pale-blue hoodie decorated with sequins. Would Reb crinkle his nose at an opponent in sequins? "Is it someone really dope? Another high-school kid?"

"Not exactly. But it'll be a good learning experience for you." I patted her on the shoulder and nodded toward the stairs, trusting Jace would stay and hang out with his new idol.

"That means I'll hate it, doesn't it?"

A thwack floated up from the floor below, followed by a challenge—in the troll language—to the coatrack.

"It'll be good for you," I repeated.

Amber halted at the top of the stairs. "It's not that troll kid, is it? He almost pronged me with a stick when I walked back here."

"It's a practice sword, not a stick."

"*Mom.* I helped you get an amazing dress and did your makeup for you for the wedding, and you're hooking me up with a ten-year-old troll?"

"He's nine and big for his age, and did you just call me *Mom*?" I grinned at her.

She rolled her eyes. "Yeah, but don't be weird about it. *Weirder.*" She stomped down the stairs.

I grinned back at Zav, though I didn't expect him to be paying attention. But he'd stopped the game and was looking back at me. He smiled and duplicated the thumbs-up gesture I'd given Walker.

THE END

THE CHRISTMAS GIFT

A Death Before Dragons short story

AUTHOR'S NOTE

This short story originally appeared on my website, so you may have already read it there. If not, I hope you enjoy this bonus tale (it was actually supposed to be a bonus *scene*, but it expanded). I've had it edited and included it here so you can have a permanent copy.

"The Christmas Gift" takes place between Books 8 and 9, so if you just finished 9, you're jumping back in time a couple of months for Val and Zav and the gang. As always, thanks for reading!

~

"Who goes skiing for Christmas?" I paced around the living room, eyeing the photo Amber had sent of herself and a friend on a gleaming white mountain slope. "Christmas means spending obligatory time with your loved ones, opening sweaters knitted by grandma, and cringing over how lame your family is."

Dimitri paused hanging Star Wars ornaments on the tree to peer at the photo. "I thought she was up there with your ex and that they went every year."

"She is, and they do. But that's only *half* of her family." I placed a hand on my chest, then spread it toward the room. "Look how cool our decorations are. And normal, not *weird*."

When I'd suggested that Amber and Thad come by for Christmas Eve and wait to start their ski trip until later in the week, Amber had rolled her eyes and said my place was too weird for Christmas. Not true. Star Wars ornaments aside, the robust eight-foot noble fir, the star threatening to scrape the textured paint off the ceiling, was completely normal. And so were the five stockings dangling from the fireplace mantle. Never mind that one of the stockings was for a dragon, one was for a vampire, and if my mother had her way, we would soon add one for her dog.

"If anyone had invited me skiing," Dimitri said, "*I* would have gone."

"You hate skiing. Didn't you say that's why you left Bend?"

"I left because Seattle has more work and a better club scene, but we're enjoying a wet Christmas instead of a white one, so I can see the appeal of going up to Whistler." Dimitri thumped me on the arm. "You should be happy she sent you a photo. That means she's thinking of you."

"It's in a group message to twenty people. I think she's just bragging to everyone that she got to go someplace fun."

"Are you going to be grumpy all night?"

"No." I sent Amber a photo of our tree and stuffed the phone in my pocket. "I'm just voicing some disgruntlement."

Maybe it had been selfish to want Amber to come over for Christmas when I'd avoided having any contact with her or Thad for ten years, during which I'd missed all of *their* Christmases. Just because I'd reached out to Amber and managed to establish a relationship with her this year didn't mean I should expect them to change their tradition.

"That's what being grumpy is." Dimitri hung another X-wing between a Roswell alien and a Jupiter ornament. Other people got pretty sparkling balls. We got the blown-glass solar-system set.

"These decorations are even geekier than the ones Thad usually puts up," I said. "Where did you get them all?"

"The internet is a shopping sanctuary for those with eclectic tastes."

"I kind of miss the good old days when all you could get was what Hallmark offered."

Dimitri held up a finger, opened a box, and pulled out a chunky metal four-legged robot.

"Is that an AT-AT?" I asked.

"From Hallmark." He showed me the emblem on the back of the box.

"Huh. The meek are inheriting the Earth."

"The *geek* maybe."

SECRETS OF THE SWORD III

Magic flared above the house, pinging at my senses. Someone had opened a portal.

I was expecting Zav—he'd gone home to help his mother with a few dragon concerns at their Justice Court but had promised to return for our holiday—but took a couple of steps toward my weapons. After all, our house was a popular target for vengeful members of the magical community.

Zav flew out of the portal and boomed, *Greetings, my mate!* into my mind. *I smell meat.*

I smiled, relieved that he'd made it. If I couldn't see my daughter for Christmas, my fiancé would do.

I knew you'd be back so I put some hams in the smoker. I would have cooked a Christmas ham, regardless of whether he was coming, but since dragons could down slabs of meat faster than a tiger shark, I'd crammed the smoker full.

You are a most excellent mate. Dealing with the politics of the court, as well as the quibbling of my own kin, was stressful. I wasn't even permitted to duel with anyone. I look forward to relaxing with you. We will dine and then mate vigorously.

I'm open to that but not until later. My mom and Nin are coming over, and Dimitri and Zoltan are going to hang out with us too. It's customary to spend time with one's family and friends on Christmas Eve. I wasn't sure I considered the vampire alchemist who lived in the basement a *friend* exactly, but it had seemed appropriate to invite him.

They would object to us mating?

While they're here, yeah. Our bedroom is above the living room, you know. Though I'd heard from my half-sister and occasional roommate Freysha that certain activities were audible even in other parts of the house, at least to her keen elven ears. I'd given up on feeling embarrassed about that. Mostly. Too bad she wasn't here for Christmas, but the elves were having the Grooming of the Trees Festival on their own world, something that sounded more like odious volunteer work than a time of fun and relaxation. I'd declined her invitation to join in.

They will not object to us eating, *will they?* Zav beamed disapproval into my mind.

No. They'll want to eat too.

I will allow them to share some of our meat.

The ham with a brown-sugar glaze is for the humans. I know how you feel about sweets.

They're loathsome. Why would you poison your meat so?

Humans have vices. It's what gives us character.

My phone buzzed as Zav landed in the front yard, shifting into his human form.

"Hey, Willard," I answered. "Is everything okay?" I was glad she'd called. Earlier, she'd texted to say her plans had changed and she wouldn't need me to cat-sit. "Oh, and Merry Christmas."

"Merry Christmas? You do know I've been stuck in the office all day, managing six agents and gathering the intel necessary for the police to apprehend the Teriyaki Torcher, right?"

"Did you finally find your arsonist?"

"Yeah, it was an orc stealing food, then lighting the restaurants on fire, so people would be thrown off his trail. I should have put you on the case. Then maybe I would have made my flight back home this morning."

Ah, that was why she no longer needed cat-sitting.

"Why didn't you?" I asked.

"It's the end of the year, and we're out of funding. I have to use agents already on the staff."

"I would have helped for free." Thanks to the ridiculously lucrative gig Nin's grandfather had given me, I was no longer scraping to make rent each month. Or to buy shopping carts full of hams to keep Zav fed.

"You would have asked for a *favor*," Willard growled. "I'm still working on your last favor."

"Planning the wedding of a dragon is an honor, not an obligation."

She grunted. "You sound like him."

"I might have been quoting him." I pulled back the curtains to see what was holding up Zav. It had been a few minutes since he'd arrived. He was out front with his fists on his hips as he considered the dragon topiaries he'd magically grown and shaped—and given powers to—at the corners of our property. Maybe I shouldn't have let Dimitri string Christmas lights around them.

"I just called to let you know I got quotes from the caterer and the harpist. I'll go over them with you after the holiday."

"Thanks, Willard. Hey, if you're stuck here, why don't you join us this evening? We're having a small family-and-friends Christmas Eve dinner."

"I have plans."

"Staying at home, petting your cat, and reading a book doesn't count as plans."

"You only feel that way because you're not an introvert."

"Why don't you come over? You can sit in the corner and read if we get too rowdy for you."

"Too rowdy? This isn't a party, is it?" She said it as if that would be the most distasteful way to spend an evening. An introvert, indeed. "Who all is coming?"

"My mom and possibly Rocket. Zav, Dimitri, and Zoltan. Oh, and Nin may come by for a few. That's it. Just a small family gathering."

"You're only related to one of those people."

"Family isn't just about blood. Sometimes it's about staying rent-free in the basement and overcharging your roommates for your services."

"I hope you put coal in Zoltan's stocking."

"As an alchemist, he might find a use for that. Are you coming? We have plenty of ham." I was positive Zav wouldn't touch the glazed one. I peeked out the window again—what was taking so long? Uh oh. The Christmas lights were out. No… I squinted. They weren't out. He'd incinerated them and was now nodding with satisfaction.

"Can I bring Maggie?"

"You want to bring your cat to my house?"

"You don't leave family home alone at Christmas."

"Is she a big celebrator of the holiday?"

"She likes ornaments and wrapping paper."

I eyed Dimitri's ornament collection and imagined Maggie batting the X-wings off the tree. At least they looked pretty indestructible. The gifts under the tree would be in more danger from Rocket, especially since I'd wrapped some expensive filet mignon beef jerky for Zav.

"I guess it'll be fine." I'd thought about summoning Sindari to hang out with us for a bit, but I could keep that to a minimum since Maggie didn't get along with him. "She won't do that meow-screech the whole time, right?"

"Not as long as she's fed and happy."

"Okay." Maybe I would wait until they left to summon Sindari. "Uhm, how does Maggie feel about dragons? Has she met Zav?"

"I don't think so, but as long as he's not scent-marking the furniture and calling her an inferior predator, he can't be as bad as your pet tiger."

"We try to keep the scent-marking to a minimum around here."

Dimitri's eyebrows rose. He was still in the room hanging ornaments.

"It's my boss," I told him.

"That's the kind of work you discuss?" he asked.

"Our work requires conversations on wide and varied topics."

"I'm on my way," Willard said. "Do you want me to bring anything?"

"We've got all the dinner fixings. If you want something to drink besides beer, hard cider, or sparkling water, you might want to bring it."

Zav opened the door, the wind gusting and stirring the hem of his black elven robe, which drew my eye to his yellow hole-filled Crocs. I couldn't believe he hadn't gotten tired of those yet. I missed the elven slippers that matched the robe.

"Someone attempted to strangle the topiaries with cords," he announced, "but I rescued them from this vandalism."

"Cords?" Dimitri peered out the window. "What happened to the Christmas lights?"

"Don't ask." I patted him on the shoulder and guided him back to the tree. "I'll get you a couple more sets for next year."

Zav's nose was in the air as he appreciated the aromas of ham wafting out of the kitchen, but he noticed the new addition to the living room and tilted his head in puzzlement.

"Why is there a dead tree in our abode?" Zav asked.

"It's a Christmas tradition," I said.

"That is the holiday you are celebrating this week? Is its purpose to venerate dead trees?"

"No, it's to celebrate the birth of Jesus. He was kind of a big deal on Earth."

"When we celebrated your birthday, we did not erect trees."

"That's true."

"We exchanged gifts and mated vigorously." Zav came forward and hugged and kissed me.

"Ew." Dimitri hid himself behind the Christmas tree. Or hid *us* from his view, was perhaps more accurate. "I'm still in the room."

Later, I told Zav telepathically, patting him on the chest and breaking the kiss. I sensed Nin driving up, and judging by the barking out front, Mom had also arrived with Rocket.

So far, I do not like this holiday as much as your birthday.

We'll exchange gifts later. You'll like that part.

Zav stepped back, a frown creasing his brow. "Does celebrating the birth of your dead religious leader mean that I should have gotten you a gift?"

"That's not necessary." I hadn't told him about holiday gift giving, because I hadn't wanted him to feel compelled to go on another quest to get me something. The engagement and wedding rings were great, but challenging other dragons to battle to take items from their hoards was a touch more involved and dangerous than ordering meat sticks from the sausage catalog.

"But it *is* the custom." He watched my face.

"You brought the gift of yourself. That's all I require." I hugged him again.

"I'm still here," Dimitri said.

"We're not kissing," I said.

"Yeah, but you're being mushy."

"You're as bad as Amber."

"Is your offspring giving you a gift?" Zav asked, still hung up on presents.

"She's not here. She's skiing in Whistler, Canada." I thought I managed to say that without sounding chagrined or resentful, but Zav squinted thoughtfully at me.

"You wish she were here."

"It would have been nice, but I get why she'd rather be skiing. And having eggnog in some rented condo instead of our fabulous house."

"Eggnog is disgusting," Dimitri said. "It's wrong to *drink* eggs."

"You hang out with someone who drinks blood."

"That's because he's a vampire. We're not egg-pires. We shouldn't drink eggs."

"More for me then." Sensing Nin's approach, I opened the door.

Rocket was the first one to bound into the house, then around the living room, onto the couch, and finally to the tree for enthusiastic sniffing.

"Make sure your dog doesn't scent-mark our tree, please," I said as Mom walked in next, handing me a present wrapped in paper with golden retrievers all over it.

"He knows not to do that indoors," she said.

"You don't think having some of the outdoors indoors might confuse him?"

"No. He's smart."

Rocket finished sniffing the tree and presents and flung himself onto Dimitri's overstuffed beanbag chair, then rolled onto his back with all four paws in the air.

"A veritable genius," I said.

"Hey," Dimitri protested. "That's my favorite chair."

"It looks like an extra-large dog bed," Mom said.

"It puts you in the ergonomically correct position for gaming," Dimitri said.

"Which also happens to be the ergonomically correct position for a dog to scratch his back." I waved Mom to a seat.

Nin stepped in, handing me a present in a tasteful gift bag. It emanated familiar magic, and I had a feeling she'd made me a fresh batch of grenades.

"Many people have arrived," Zav said. "Will there be enough meat for our meal?"

"I got five hams," I said.

He gave me a blank look.

"Four are for you."

"I will check on them. If they are insufficient, I may have to go acquire more meat." Zav strode toward the kitchen.

"They're sufficient," I called after him, but he disappeared into the kitchen. "Dragons," I muttered.

"How many pounds are the hams?" Nin asked curiously. "Perhaps I should have brought extra suea rong-hai."

"They're fifteen pounds each. He'll be fine. Have a seat." I waved to the couch. "Do you want anything to drink or eat?"

Rocket sat up, woofed, and wagged his tail.

"I wasn't talking to you," I told him.

"He likes ham," Mom said.

"I bet."

Zav strode back out. "The meat supply is insufficient."

"It's fine," I told him. "If your stomach has emergency gauntness, I can thaw some hamburgers from the extra freezer."

"Insufficient. I will obtain more meat." He strode out, ignoring my protests, and sprang off the porch, shifting into a dragon and flapping off before he hit the ground.

"That was weird," I said.

"You sound puzzled," Mom said. "Isn't he always weird?"

I almost said *not for a dragon*, but he wasn't much like other dragons, either, from what I'd seen. Which was why I loved him. Most dragons were dicks.

Before I could go to fetch drinks, Willard arrived—with her cat carrier. I didn't need my sense for magic to know she was coming up the walkway. Maggie's half-Siamese meow-wails announced their approach.

I opened the door for them, and Rocket woofed again. He looked at the cat carrier and wagged his tail hard enough to endanger a nearby lamp. Mom leaned over and rested a hand on the base so it wouldn't go flying.

"Welcome, Willard," I said. "And Maggie."

The cat meowed uncertainly.

"Your tiger isn't here, is he?" Willard handed me a canister of something. It wasn't wrapped. Was it a gift?

"No." I read the label: *Golden Mellow Turmeric Drink Powder. Reduce stress, anxiety, and inflammation naturally.* Well, I had told her to bring whatever she liked to drink... "Sindari is only interested in coming here to do battle. When I summon him to hang out, he's less than enthusiastic. He also doesn't appreciate Rocket's exuberance."

Rocket demonstrated his exuberance by jumping off the beanbag chair, running around the living room, and dropping down to his forelegs in front of Willard's cat carrier.

"What is he doing?" Willard asked.

"That's a play bow," Mom said. "Rocket has met Maggie before. They're buddies."

Maggie hissed through the grate in the cat carrier.

"Close buddies," I said. "Didn't Maggie once throw books out of your loft and try to hit Rocket as he ran around below?"

"Yes. Rocket enjoyed having someone to play with him."

"Play," I mouthed to Willard.

Mom patted her thigh. "Over here, buddy. I'm sure Maggie will throw something at you later."

Rocket bounded to her side, and they sat on the couch together.

"Why do I get the feeling that Rocket would enjoy being targeted by paintballers on a range so long as he was getting attention?" I asked.

Willard walked around the room, eyed our Christmas decorations, and prodded Dimitri's Gamersac. "I see you've purchased new upscale furnishings since you came into all that gnome money."

"It was gnome *gold*, and I don't think someone who uses a weight bench for an ottoman should talk."

"It's an upscale adjustable weight bench by Precor."

"Colonels do make the big money."

"Not as big as freelance assassins."

"Hey, don't envy me my glamorous job. It's not my fault you didn't get proper career counseling in your youth."

"Uh huh. Can I let Maggie out?" Willard pointed at the cat carrier. "She'll be happier if she can find a nice high bookcase to watch the goings-on from."

"And so will Rocket."

"Apparently."

I waved for her to open the cat carrier and headed to the door to make sure it was firmly closed, but I sensed someone else coming up the walkway. Gondo.

"I'm positive I didn't invite him," I murmured. "Willard, did you ask your shortest agent to bring you information tonight?"

"My shortest agent is Corporal Nash."

"Think shorter. And greener."

"Gondo is an *informant*, not an agent," she said.

"What's the difference?"

"I pay him in sodas from the vending machine instead of direct deposits to the bank."

"It's a wonder goblins always have money to spend at our coffee shop."

The doorbell rang. Rocket woofed. Maggie meow-screeched from atop a bookcase. She'd beelined up there quickly.

"I'm surprised they don't try to pay you in recycled cans," Willard said.

"They need those for their projects." I opened the door and smiled down at our green-skinned, white-haired, overalls-and-tool-belt-wearing visitor. "Hey, Gondo."

"Greetings, Ruin Bringer. I have brought a gift on behalf of my caffeine-enjoying people." He held up what looked like a miniature goblin holding a wrench aloft. It appeared to be made from… yes, those were recycled soda cans. How had Willard known?

"That's thoughtful of you. What is it?"

"A Christmas tree ornament. It gyrates "

"It what?"

Gondo spun the goblin's head around several times. The ornament clicked like a wind-up toy. He released the head, holding it by a thin chain loop attached to the top, and the goblin lifted the wrench up and down and wiggled its hips. Actually, those were more like hip thrusts.

"Gondo, is that goblin dancing or… something more suggestive?"

SECRETS OF THE SWORD III

He grinned wickedly, answering the question.

"I see. Ah, Dimitri, is there a place left on the tree for this?"

Nin's mouth formed an O as she caught a glimpse of it. Maybe it was just as well that Amber hadn't come. Thad wouldn't approve of our daughter seeing pornographic Christmas ornaments.

"In the back, I think." Dimitri picked it up gingerly by the chain.

Make it the way back, I told him telepathically.

Oh, I will. It might accidentally fall under the heat register.

Gondo's nostrils twitched as he inhaled ham scents. "Do you have room for more at your dinner table?"

How could I say no to someone who'd brought a gift?

"Yeah. Come on in." I waved, intending to shut the door behind him, but Gondo leaned back outside and pumped his arm vigorously.

"She said we could join them."

Whoops came from the sidewalk. I hadn't noticed the auras of seven more goblins out there, maybe because they were standing near one of the dragon topiaries, its magic overshadowing them. One of the goblins was slapping a smoking hat on the side of his pants. The nearby topiary's eyes glowed as smoke wafted from its verdant nostrils.

"Will you deactivate your security system, Ruin Bringer?" Gondo asked politely.

Should we let them in? I asked Dimitri telepathically, worried that so many goblins were bound to make *improvements* to the house if they were inside for more than an hour.

I think we have to, he replied. *It's Christmas. Also, they're paying customers at the coffee shop.*

All right. I touched one of the magical remotes on the built-in shelves near the door. Outside, the orange glow to the topiaries' eyes dulled. "They can come in."

"I thought this wasn't going to be a party," Willard said as the goblins trotted inside, eliciting protesting noises from Maggie. Rocket, who adored all people, no matter what their height, skin color, or engineering persuasion, ran up and knocked over a few goblins with his love—and powerful tail whacks.

"I didn't plan for it to be one." I closed the door firmly and headed toward the fireplace to light some festive cheer. "They'll probably scatter when Zav comes back," I whispered to Willard on the way past.

"Where did he go?"

"To get more meat, he said. I'm not sure if that involves hunting or mugging people in the Costco parking lot."

"He *mugs* people?" Willard's eyebrows rose. "Am I going to have to hire you to hunt down your own fiancé?"

"Technically, he doesn't touch them. He just lands in front of shoppers as they're pushing their carts full of food out to their cars. He doesn't use his magic to camouflage himself; if anything, he *enhances* his dragonness. They have a tendency to flee and abandon their carts. He doesn't take everything, just a frozen turkey or box of hamburgers or five."

Willard rubbed her face. "Thorvald, that's *not* acceptable."

"As I told him. He hasn't done it recently."

Whistling came from the back door, and I sensed Zoltan coming into the house. I'd wondered if he would join us this evening. Parties, which this had undoubtedly become, weren't his thing. It was quite possible he was coming up to complain about the noise.

When Zoltan entered the living room, wearing red-tinted goggles to protect his sensitive eyes from our blazing table lamps, he carried several small metal canisters.

"Merry Christmas, dear robber and associates. I have brought—" Zoltan lurched back as Rocket ran past with a goblin riding his back, "—gifts." Zoltan curled a lip and plucked a golden strand of fur off his black lab coat. "Gifts for the ladies. I have already given Dimitri his gift."

"Yes, my chin is still tingling." Dimitri rubbed his jaw—was it redder than usual?

"Some kind of alchemical beard-removal potion?" I guessed.

"*Potion?*" Zoltan's eyes flared with indignation behind his lenses. "As I have informed you on numerous occasions, I am not a witch stirring a cauldron. I am an alchemist, and I create formulas, tinctures, lotions, and occasionally essences."

"It was an essence that exfoliated my face," Dimitri informed me. "With the gentleness of sandpaper."

"Real men do not want gentle skin-care products," Zoltan said. "They want effective ones. Your pores are radiant now."

"Thanks."

I eyed Zoltan's canisters, having no wish to be exfoliated by sandpaper. Nobody would. Or so I thought.

Gondo stepped up to Zoltan. "How much for the radiant skin-pore essence?"

"Twenty dollars," Zoltan said without missing a beat and pulled out a small vial. Nothing was written on the label yet. Maybe it had been meant as a sample for people to try.

Gondo dug into six different pockets, withdrawing rumpled dollars and coins from each. He placed it all on the floor, counted carefully, then dumped the appropriate amount into Zoltan's hands and took the vial. He skipped over to my side.

"Are pores problematic for goblins?" I asked him.

He smiled and pulled a pen out of his pocket. "One of the goblins out at the elven sanctuary has been teasing me mercilessly lately for becoming a city goblin, even though *he's* the one who's adopted strange human habits. Such as rubbing deodorant under his armpits."

"That is strange."

"Very." Gondo wrote *deodorant* on the label and slipped it into his pocket. "I look forward to visiting him on his upcoming birthday and delivering this gift."

Zoltan walked around the room, giving his small canisters to all of the women present. Nin and Willard accepted theirs with murmurs of *thank you* but with skeptical expressions. Zoltan also handed them pencils and little squares of paper.

"This is an anti-wrinkle cream," he said, "which I know all ladies appreciate, at least those who are not undead and, therefore, freed from the unpleasant rigors of aging. Please write down any experiences you have while using this product and return your notes to me."

"What kind of *experiences* are we likely to have?" I asked. "Besides the smoothing of wrinkles?"

"That's the ideal outcome, but if there are any side effects, I would like to know."

"This isn't, by chance, your first batch ever, is it?"

"The first that's turned out well enough to share," Zoltan said. "It's a challenging formula."

"It's a formula, not an essence?"

"Correct."

"Is your alchemist turning us into test subjects?" Willard asked me.

"It's probably hard to find lab rats and monkeys in Seattle," I said.

"Actually, it's not," Zoltan said. "But their fur makes it difficult to test skin products on them without extensive shaving. I am not interested in keeping bald rats in my lab."

"But furry rats would be okay?" Dimitri asked.

"Neither is ideal. Animals must be fed and their cages cleaned. It's all rather tedious. Besides, I *have* test subjects." He smiled and spread his hand toward us. "Oh, and be careful about where you store my product. It should be kept at room temperature, not next to candles or other heating elements, such as dragons."

"Zoltan…" I frowned at him. "Is your formula explosive?"

"One of the ingredients is flammable, but it only makes up a tiny percentage of the formula. Spontaneous combustion is unlikely."

Unlikely but not impossible. Great.

"I'd chuck this gift into the fireplace," Willard murmured, "but I wouldn't want to blow up your house on Christmas Eve."

"My house appreciates that." I set the canister down well away from the fireplace as I knelt to put kindling in.

Meanwhile, Dimitri turned on the TV and fired up one of his video games. Let the festivities begin.

Nin came over to help me with the fire. "I am not certain that Zoltan understands the concept of gifts."

"You know scientists." I stuffed rumpled newspaper into my stack of kindling and grabbed the fire starter. "We're all just test subjects to them."

"At first, I felt bad that I had not thought to bring him a gift."

"But you're over that now?"

"Yes."

I looked over at Nin. "How come you didn't go up to Whistler with Thad?" I assumed he had invited her now that they were dating and spending nights together regularly. "Did he ask you to? And were you too much of a workaholic to take four days off from your food truck?"

"He did, and I am, but I also did not wish to interfere with their family tradition."

"You were worried Amber would be grouchy the whole time if you came?" I hoped Amber hadn't said anything surly to Nin. They'd been getting along fairly well since our adventure in the fae realm.

"A little, but I also do not know how to ski. I did not want to intrude on their time together. Thad did give me a gift before they left." She smiled shyly over at me.

SECRETS OF THE SWORD III

"Another rice maker?"

"No, I did not need a second one. The RiceMaster 57155 fulfills my needs."

"That's good. What'd he get you then? Not jewelry, I trust."

"No." She lowered her voice and leaned close. "Sexy lingerie."

"Oh, good. Er, it doesn't have dragons or castles or anything geeky on it, does it?"

"No, it is lacy and purple like my hair." Nin lifted her eyebrows. "Did he once get *you* castle underwear?"

"No, not Thad. But recently, Zav got me *dragon* underwear. He found boxers with a black dragon on it, and he altered it to have violet eyes."

Nin looked far more concerned than intrigued. My initial reaction to the gift had been similar.

"Are they... sexy?"

"*He* thinks they are, but they're not even women's underwear. He doesn't know the difference. Why would he? He doesn't wear any himself."

"Maybe you should get *him* sexy underwear."

"I'm afraid it's a gift that would never be used." I made my voice deeper and haughtier in an imitation of his. "One does not wear *underwear* with an elven mage robe."

Nin giggled.

As we finished with the fire, I sensed Zav flying back to the house.

I stood, about to ask him how the meat acquisition had gone, when my phone buzzed. Surprised someone was texting on Christmas Eve—especially when almost everyone I knew was here—I pulled it out.

I'd call the police if I thought they could arrest a dragon, Thad messaged.

Uh, what?

I want Amber back by eleven. Midnight at the latest. Teenagers need their beauty rest.

It was only when Zav landed in the front yard and I sensed a second familiar aura next to his that the meaning of Thad's words clicked.

He picked her up? I texted, heading to the curtains to peer out.

He kidnapped her. I did not give my permission, and I would have kicked his ass if he hadn't said it was because he needed a dead-religious-leader present for you.

You've never kicked anyone's ass in your life, Thad. A dragon would be a bad person to start with.

So he told me. Merry Christmas, Val.

Thanks.

Zav and Amber were in the yard, and he'd returned to his human form. She shot indecipherable looks over her shoulder at him as she headed up the steps to the door.

I grimaced, worried she would be irked at having been kidnapped and dragged—flown—here. What if they'd been playing games or something *fun* and she thought coming here would be the opposite of fun? I opened the door, intending to apologize. As much as I appreciated Zav wanting to get me a gift—and I couldn't think of one I'd rather have—he had the diplomatic skills of an axe murderer.

Rocket woofed as Amber walked in, then ran over, tail wagging. There was still a goblin riding on his back. Ugh, Amber was right. Our Christmas *was* weird.

"Hey, Mom. Your flying Uber is lit."

"I… Is that Zav?"

Amber rolled her eyes. "You're not at your swiftest tonight. Have you been drinking?"

"Unfortunately not. Though I do have an anti-inflammatory turmeric-powder tea to try."

"Weird." Amber handed me a box. "This is from me and Dad."

I blinked, more startled that she didn't seem annoyed to have been brought down than that she'd brought me a gift.

"It's a cheesy snow globe from the gift shop at Whistler. We were going to give it to you *next* week, but I guess this works." Amber shrugged and eyed the goblin riding Rocket around the living room, then my eclectic assortment of guests, including Zoltan in his tinted goggles and Maggie meowing from atop the bookcase. "So weird." Amber pointed at the TV. "Is that the new Legend of Zelda?"

"I think so. You'll have to wrest the controller away from your grandmother if you want to play."

"I'm a sword fighter now. I can take on Grandma."

"Is that so?" Mom asked.

"You know she packs heat, right?" I asked.

"At Christmas dinner?"

"It's a dangerous neighborhood."

"Especially the part that's in your house."

I looked over at the anti-wrinkle formula. "That's possibly true."

Amber shooed a goblin out of the way and plopped down on the couch with Mom.

Zav strode in and slung an arm around my shoulder. *Your gift, my mate. I endured the words of your mouthy, sarcastic offspring to fly her here to be with you. Also, your inferior former mate threatened to prong me with a long narrow stick.*

A ski pole, I'm guessing. I leaned into Zav, touched that he'd flown all the way up to Whistler and back. *I'm surprised Amber was willing to come with you. You didn't have to magically compel her, did you?*

Certainly not. I am a dragon lord and the son of a queen. I am skilled in diplomacy.

Your idea of diplomacy is challenging people who disagree with you to duels.

That is not the only tool in my tool cave. He considered me. *Did I get that human saying correct?*

More or less. How did you convince her to come?

She expects you to give her a gift of two hundred dollars.

You bribed my daughter to come spend Christmas Eve with me?

I did. I have seen you employ this tactic on her.

That's... technically true. Teenagers require a special kind of diplomacy. One that demands human currency.

Yeah. Thank you. You're an excellent mate.

I know this.

I smiled and kissed him.

"Ew," Amber said. "That's going to cost you an extra hundred."

"Hundred?" Willard had coaxed her cat off the bookcase and was sitting and stroking her.

"Amber objects to displays of passion," I said, deciding not to explain the bribe.

"Wait until she sees the goblin sex ornament," Dimitri muttered.

"I thought you hid that under the heat register," I muttered back.

"It wouldn't fit."

"Ornament?" Amber asked.

"Never mind," all the adults in the room said together.

THE END

Made in United States
Orlando, FL
30 November 2023